The Sweetest Poison

The Sweetest Poison

Jane Renshaw

Cover design by The Cover Collection.

ISBN: 978-1-5272-4117-6

When she was eight

1

Helen looked up at the tree. There were plenty of pods hanging down from it, like peapods only skinnier.

How many would she need?

Yesterday when she was helping Daddy with the bales she had asked him, 'How many laburnum seeds would someone have to eat before they died?' and he'd shaken his head and said, 'Hel'nie. You mustn't *ever* take seeds from that tree,' and she'd said, 'I won't. But how many *would* someone have to eat?' and he'd shaken his head and said, 'I don't know, and I'm not just awful keen to find out.'

Helen wriggled her schoolbag off her back and dropped it down on the grass.

No one would see. The byre was between the tree and the kitchen window, and Daddy had gone up the fields to look at the calfies.

To reach the pods she would have to climb up on the fence, but Suzanne had shown her how to climb on barbed wire. She put one hand on the fence post under the tree, and one hand on the top wire, and climbed with her bum sticking out to keep her legs away from the jags. The wires were wobbly but she didn't fall off. When she was high enough she let go the hand on the fence post and reached up and grabbed one of the pods.

It was as if the branch didn't want to let go.

When they were little, Suzanne used to say peas were the pea plant's children, and the peapod was a coat it had made for them, and when you ate peas you were eating the children. Even when she was little Helen hadn't actually believed that, but now she couldn't help thinking that the seeds were the tree's children.

It had plenty though.

She leant out away from the fence so she could pull better, and the branch stretched and stretched but then it suddenly let go and flapped back. Helen grabbed the post.

She didn't fall.

She could see the bumps of the seeds inside the pod. There were six.

Would that be enough?

She put the pod in the pocket of her pinafore dress and reached up for another. When she had five pods she jumped down off the fence and snatched up her schoolbag. She got into the straps and ran past the end of the byre and onto the track. If Mummy was at the kitchen window she might think, *What was Helen doing round behind the byre?* but if she asked after school Helen would say, 'Playing with Baudrins.'

Her foot kicked a stone and it bounced down the track towards the bridge. She ran and jumped over the stone. The burn was gurgling under the bridge but she didn't stop to look, she kept running until she got to the pine trees. Then in case of nettles she pulled her socks up and kicked her legs through the long grass at the side of the track until she was under the trees. Here the grass was short, with dead pine needles on it, and humps of moss. Through the trees she could see the wall of the steading at Mains of Clova, the big farm where Uncle Jim and Auntie Ina and Suzanne lived, but she couldn't see the house. That was up past the steading.

She squatted down, took the laburnum pods out of her pocket and put them on the grass. Then she got the plastic box out of her bag and opened it, and took the top slice off one of the sandwiches. She picked up a pod and pressed its sides till it came apart. Inside was fluffy with the little black seeds snuggled down. The seed at the end was just little, like he was the baby.

She picked them all out and put them under the biggest juiciest slice of tomato. Except for the baby one. She made a hole in the earth and put him in it so he could grow into a tree. So he wouldn't have to go inside Robin Beattie.

If someone stole a poisonous sandwich and ate it, that wasn't murder.

That was their own fault.

Helen didn't want to be a murderer, even if you didn't get hung from the neck until you were dead any more. You still had to go to prison for about sixty-five years. What if Robin died before he'd finished the sandwich, and people found the bit he'd left and said, 'Helen, why did you have poisonous laburnum in your sandwich?'

She would say, 'I didn't. I saw Robin put those seeds in that sandwich.'

She ran past the steading and up across the yard towards the house. Auntie Ina didn't have any flowerbeds, just hard ground and concrete at the front. At the back there was the Bleach Green, but that was just grass where she hung out her washing. Mummy said Auntie Ina liked it all bare because she thought it was neat and tidy, and nature and gardens were orra and in the way of things that had to be done on the farm.

The back door was open.

She could see Auntie Ina standing inside the scullery, and Suzanne's feet kicking against the side of the kist where she always sat.

The scullery and the kitchen were in the bit of the house that stuck out at the back, and up above was the playroom. That used to be Jeannie Bell's room. Jeannie Bell had been Grannie's maid, before Daddy and Uncle Jim were born – sort of like a servant, but not like rich people had. Not like at the House. Grannie had needed someone to help her because there were six men working at the Mains then. They had all needed to be fed and have their clothes washed and everything. So Jeannie Bell had helped her.

Suzanne said Jeannie's ghost haunted the playroom, and when she was little Helen had believed that, and once Suzanne had said, 'What's that noise like footsteps?' and they had both screamed, and Helen had fallen right down the stairs from Jeannie's room to the kitchen, and bumped her head, and Auntie Ina had taken her on her knee and put a cold cloth on the sore place. And she'd said it must be a queer kind of ghost to be stumping round the Mains with Jeannie alive and well and living in a scheme in Aboyne. Suzanne wasn't to frighten poor Hel'nie like that. But Auntie Ina hadn't really been angry at Suzanne. She had smiled and smoothed Suzanne's hair at the back where it stuck up.

Helen ran across the yard to the door and two hens ran in front of her and she nearly tripped over them. Silly craiters.

'Well, Hel'nie,' said Auntie Ina.

'You're late,' said Suzanne. 'Have you peed your pants?'

'No.'

'Have you got a sore stomach?'

Sometimes Helen told Mummy she had a sore stomach. Then Mummy would say, 'Go as far as the Mains and see how you feel when you get there, and tell Auntie Ina if it's still bad,' but when she did Auntie Ina would just say, 'I'm not as green as I'm cabbage-looking,' and Helen still had to go to school.

She said, 'No.'

Auntie Ina said, 'Saving that for tomorrow?'

Helen shook her head, and Suzanne took her hand, and they ran across the yard.

This time tomorrow, Robin Beattie would probably be as dead as a doornail and she hoped he would be.

Helen was Malfolio and Suzanne was Wonder Woman, and they were racing up the brae. The road sparkled where the shiny bits of stone were, like slices of diamond roadrollered in. Malfolio's feet had thick brown fur all over them, and claws at the end that scratched on the pink and grey sparkly stones. He was a fast runner, and at the top of Worm Hill he had to stop by the Big Stone and wait for Wonder Woman. It was nice, with the wind, and the clouds all racing up in the sky and over back the way they had come. He couldn't see home because of the woodie, but he could see the Lang Park up by the plantation and the calfies. He couldn't see Daddy.

Helen wished she could run and run, back down the brae and down the track and past the Mains and home.

But that was stupid. She had to go to school, or else how could Robin eat the seeds? And there was still most of the way to go. She had plenty time left of being Malfolio.

Malfolio jumped up onto the Big Stone and looked up at where the moon would be and howled. It was bloodcurdling, and all the people in the houses grabbed their children and told them they couldn't go out playing tonight because it just wasn't safe.

Wonder Woman had stopped running, pretending she hadn't been racing at all. She was picking flowers from the side of the road – campion because that was her favourite, and water aven because that was Malfolio's. She said, 'Okay, now *you're* Wonder

Woman, or you could still be Malfolio, and I'm a beautiful wedding bride. I'm called Demerara. This is my bouquet... and for the bridesmaids.'

'And I'm your intended husband Malfolio, only *you don't know* I'm a werewolf.'

'We're going to the kirk to get married.'

From the top of Worm Hill you could see down into Kirkton and the school playground, and the manse where Robin Beattie lived, and the kirkyard next to it.

Helen said, 'All the people are waiting in the kirk.'

They started to run again, this time with Suzanne in front. Helen watched her thin legs in the white socks running and her purple coat flapping out behind her like her wedding dress. She should smooth her hair at the back before they got to the kirk. Mummy said it stuck up at the back because Auntie Ina cut it too short. But Malfolio didn't care about things like that. Malfolio loved Demerara with all his heart and he didn't care if her hair stuck up. He only bit nasty people. He'd been just a little boy when he'd become a werewolf and his parents had said, 'Eeeuch we don't want a werewolf in *our* house,' and he'd lived in an orphanage.

Whoever she started out as, she always ended up being Malfolio.

Demerara wasn't a very fast runner, and if Malfolio had wanted he could have caught her. Suzanne was just little, even though she was five months older than Helen, because she had been born before she was ready. She'd been a special baby because Auntie Ina had thought she couldn't have any. But she'd had Suzanne.

When Robin Beattie was dead, he wouldn't be able to tell Suzanne what to do. Helen put her hand round behind to her schoolbag and felt it jiggling. She would have to make sure the seeds hadn't jiggled out of the bread.

At the kirkyard gate Demerara took Malfolio's arm. 'Now we've got confetti all on us... We're going away on our honeymoon. *Oh, Malfolio...*' She put her other hand up in the air and moved it about.

'What're you doing?'

'Waving to the people. And now I'm going to run away and jilt you because *I've found out you're a werewolf.*' She pushed Helen's arm away and ran.

'And *I'm going to bite you and werewolf you.*'

Suzanne screamed, and ran away past the manse and over the

bridge and along by the playground wall. Helen didn't run after her though. She just walked. She always wanted the time before school to last forever because she didn't want *this* time to come, when she almost had to go into the playground. When she was at home she always thought, *There's the whole of breakfast and brushing teeth and the walk to go*, and when she was on Worm Hill she always thought, *There's the whole road to the crossroads and past the kirkyard to go*, and when she was at the kirk she always thought, *There's past the manse and over the bridge and along the wall to go*, but here was where there was hardly any road left to go at all and she had to keep walking and make the road between get less and less until there was none and she was *there*.

But maybe *he* wouldn't be there. Maybe he'd be off.

But then he couldn't eat the seeds.

He was at the gates. He was wearing grey shorts and a navy blue jersey. When she was little, Helen had thought he was called Robin because he looked like one. His head was big and round and his legs were thin. His hair looked like it would be soft if you touched it, like feathers. When he was angry his face went red. But robins were sweet, and she was glad the reason he was called Robin wasn't really because he was like one. He was called Robin just because it was a boy's name like John.

He was standing at the gates with Suzanne. She was whispering and he was doing his cough. Cough-cough *cough*. Helen tried to walk past but he stood in front of her. She looked past him to see if she could see Hector, but she couldn't. Hector was always late.

She reached behind to touch her schoolbag.

He stepped forwards.

She stepped back.

She tried to go to the side to get past but he went to the side too. She went to the other side, right against one of the big stone pillars, but so did he, and she had to squeeze back against the hard stone, all cold through her cardigan and her pinafore dress. He had a little bit of yellow crust in the edge of one of his eyes. He smelt of toast.

People were staring.

Helen looked down at the ground.

Robin grabbed her arm and his nails dug in through the sleeve of her cardigan. 'Did you have a nice time at the shops on Saturday? Did you have a nice time when you *peed your pants* in Crawford's?'

'I didn't pee my pants.'

'You did so,' said Suzanne.

'Did they have to throw away all the bread and cakes cos Smellie Nellie had been and peed on them?' He dug his nails in harder.

Helen's lip and the bit of her chin under it had gone funny but she didn't cry.

'No.'

'They did,' said Suzanne. 'They had to put up a sign saying "Closed Cos of Pee".'

Suzanne had to say those things. If she didn't Robin might hurt her, and she was just little. Sometimes she got wheezy. If Suzanne was wearing a cardigan, Auntie Ina said Helen had to always check that the buttons were done right up to the top so her chestie didn't get cold.

Robin let go Helen's arm. 'See this fist?' He held it in front of her, white and knobbly with a jaggedy thumb nail. 'If you tell a lie again, this fist is going to hit you right in the nose.'

If that fist *did* hit her in the nose, what would happen? Would it bleed? Norrie's nose had bled yesterday when he'd fallen over, and there had been blood dripping out of it and he'd cried.

'Did you pee your pants in Crawford's, Smellie?'

Helen looked at the fist.

'Yes,' she said.

But she hadn't.

Cough-cough *cough*. 'Did you pee your pants just now?'

She didn't say anything. She hadn't peed her pants.

'Did you?'

'Yes,' she said.

'Eeeeeuuch!' shouted Robin.

Suzanne ran away across the playground and Robin ran after her.

'Helen Clack peed her *paaaa-aants!*' he shouted. 'She *stiiiiiinks!*'

Robin and Suzanne ran right round the edge of the playground and past the sycamore tree where Norrie and his brother were hitting each other with bits of branch.

'Helen peed her pants!' Suzanne shouted at them.

They stopped hitting each other and turned to look.

Robin and Suzanne came running back to the pillar where Helen was standing. Suzanne jumped up and down and Robin shouted, 'Pee danger zone!' He ran up to Katie Walker and Shona Morrison and shouted, 'Get back, get back, pee danger zone!' and pushed Katie hard so she nearly fell over.

Everyone was looking at Helen.

Jennifer Gordon shouted: '*Smellie Nellie!*'

'Bubbly baby!' shouted Robin.

Helen wanted to run away back out of the gates so no one could see her crying, but she couldn't. She had to stay or she would get in trouble, and Mummy and Daddy would say she mustn't *ever* go off on her own like that, and why had she? And she wouldn't be able to tell them why, because Robin said if she ever told, he was going to get his dad to ask God to kill her mum and dad.

She looked down at the ground and sniffed up the wet.

She wished Hector would come.

'Bubbly bubbly *baaaaby*,' said Jennifer.

The bell went.

Helen wiped her hands over her eyes and her nose. She had forgotten her hanky. She sniffed and sniffed and Norrie came and said, 'Are you all right Helen?' and she said, 'Yes,' and when he ran away to the door she wiped her hands on her pinafore dress.

Robin was running with Suzanne to the door, where everyone was getting into two lines, one on each side – the Big Class and the Infant Class. Robin put his hands on Suzanne's shoulders as if they were a train and choo-chooed her to the front of the Infant Class line. His head stuck up higher than everyone else's because he was ten, but he couldn't be in the Big Class because he couldn't do their work.

Helen walked to the back of the line. Her arm was sore and she could see in her cardigan where his nails had been. Her face was all wet and horrible.

Then the door opened and Miss Fraser was standing there in a long dress with big flowers on it holding Lorna's hand.

Miss Fraser had told them that today would be a Lorna day, but Helen had forgotten. Lorna had on a blue dress with a sweet little duck on the front, and matching blue shoes and white socks with lacy patterns up the sides. Her hair was light brown and shiny like a Cindy's. All the girls always wanted to play with Lorna at playtime and lunchtime and keep her with them, and pretend she was their little girl. She was only four. She came to school sometimes so she could get used to it for next year. Then she'd be here all the time.

She was probably the nicest and most beautiful little girl in the world – but she was *Robin Beattie's little sister.*

At the front, Suzanne said, 'Hello Lorna!'

Lorna smiled. Her eyes were big and round and she held on to Miss Fraser's hand. Helen would have liked to have been Lorna, but then she wouldn't have Mummy and Daddy and Suzanne and Uncle Jim and Auntie Ina and Baudrins. And she wouldn't know how to be Malfolio. And she would have Robin Beattie as her brother.

Across at the gates someone was running. Hector. His socks were down at his ankles and he was swinging his schoolbag by its strap. Sometimes it bounced on the ground. He skidded up to the end of the Big Class line and Miss Fraser said, 'Good *afternoon* Hector,' and Hector smiled and everyone laughed because Hector was always late.

2

The bell would go for lunchtime when the clock was at half-past twelve. When it was at twenty past, Miss Fraser said, 'Little Ones and Robin, have you finished copying this down?' and when they said, 'Yes,' she started wiping their work off the board. They just had easy words like bat and cat, but that was still too hard for Robin, because if dominoes were brains he'd be chapping. That was what Auntie Ina said. He couldn't even do a 'd' and a 'b' the right way round.

When Miss Fraser was picking someone to read the Little Ones' words off the board, Helen always thought, *Please pick Robin*, and quite often she did. And Suzanne wasn't allowed to whisper the answers. Sometimes Robin started kicking the legs of his desk and wouldn't look at the board, and Miss Fraser said, 'Well you'll never be able to do it if you don't try, will you, Robin?'

He once threw his pencil at Miss Fraser. It hit her arm. She grabbed him and his face went all red and so did Miss Fraser's, and she had to pull him out of the door.

Miss Fraser put the blackboard duster down on the shelf under the board and said, 'I'm going next door for five minutes.' She wiped her hands, all chalky, on her dress, and the chalk puffed up round her. 'Get your pictures out of your desks and carry on with them until I get back. And I don't want to hear a *sound*.'

Helen wanted to run after her as she walked across the long bit of sun on the floor and opened the door into the other classroom. Helen's desk was at the front, so when the door opened she could see through to the Big Class. She could see the back of Hector's hair and his jersey. His hair was dark brown and Helen's was light, but he was wearing a grey jersey that matched her pinafore dress. And their names matched: *He*ctor and *He*len. At playtime she'd pulled her pinafore dress out next to him and said, 'Look, matching,' and he'd said, 'Um, yes.'

She'd given him her apple. That was okay, because it hadn't been in the box with the poisonous sandwiches, it had been on its own in her schoolbag because it was her playpiece. Hector never had a playpiece.

He'd said, 'Are you sure you don't want it?' and Helen had said, 'Yes,' and he'd said, 'Thanks very much, Helen.'

Miss Fraser went through into the Big Class and closed the door.

Helen didn't look round behind. She carried on doing the sky with the lovely dark blue felt-tip. She was doing a purple dinosaur with green spikes and a sky that came right down. She'd started just doing a blue strip at the top of the paper like she always did, but Miss Fraser had said, 'Look outside, the blue of the sky comes right down to the trees, doesn't it – maybe you'd like to try doing the sky right the way down.' So she had, and that was why it was taking so long, carefully filling in round his spikes and his face. If she squinted her eyes she could sort of see him moving as if he was real.

Someone was standing in front of her desk.

She quickly looked up, but it was just Lorna.

Lorna took her finger out of her mouth and whispered, 'Are you doing a dinosaur?'

'Yes. Do you like dinosaurs?'

Lorna put her finger back in her mouth and nodded.

'You can have him when he's finished, if you want.'

Lorna smiled round the finger.

'I'll help you finish it.' Robin Beattie grabbed her felt-tip case. 'If that's a dinosaur, where's its ears? I'm good at ears.'

He shoved his big face right into hers and went cough-cough *cough*. His hand opened the flap of Helen's felt-tip case and his fingers took out the black one and popped its top onto the floor. He drew huge big ears on the dinosaur. Helen grabbed at the pen but he jabbed at her hand with it. Lorna had gone back to Miss Fraser's desk.

Helen looked at Robin's face. She said in her mind, *You're going to be in a dirty cold coffin under the ground where there's no air to breathe, and things crawling all over you.*

She watched him scribble on the sky, and the trees, and the dinosaur's smile. She couldn't do anything to save the dinosaur so she picked up the blue felt-tip and started scribbling too, harder and harder over the dinosaur's head until the paper ripped.

Suzanne skipped past to where Lorna was standing at Miss Fraser's desk. Lorna was drawing with a brown crayon.

Suzanne said, 'Is that Scamp?'

Lorna nodded.

'You're a really good drawer.'

Robin snatched up Helen's picture. 'Do you still want this, Lorna?' He went to Miss Fraser's desk and slapped down the picture. 'Because if you do, you'll be Smellie Nellie's friend and not ours.'

Lorna looked down at the dinosaur. She took her finger out of her mouth and touched the paper.

Robin said in a squeaky voice, 'Eeeeuch, don't touch where she touched – it stinks. Do you know how come she stinks? Her mumindad are such spastics they don't know how to make babies, so her mum knitted her from slurry.'

Jennifer and some other people laughed.

'So do you want to be Smellie Nellie's friend, or ours?'

Lorna whispered, 'Yours.'

'Good choice,' said Suzanne. She picked up the dinosaur picture and came and put it back on Helen's desk. She didn't look at Helen.

Robin came too and jabbed at Helen's head with the black felt-tip.

'Leave her alone, Zombie,' said Norrie.

Robin grabbed Helen's ruler. Norrie ran behind the nature table and Robin ran after him. Helen felt all hot and horrible for being glad he was going to hurt Norrie and not her.

'Robin Beattie and Suzanne Clack! Get back to your desks! And you, Norrie Hewitt! I can't leave you for five minutes, can I?' Miss Fraser stood at the door with her angry face.

As soon as the bell went and Miss Fraser said they could go, Helen took her lunch box out of her schoolbag and fast-walked to the door and through into the Big Class in front of everyone. Fiona Kerr was at the blackboard, writing under one of the sums. Hector and everyone else were still at their desks.

Mrs Mackay said, 'Quietly please, Infant Class.'

Helen walked down the side of the classroom. She could hear feet fast-walking behind and Suzanne giggling. As soon as she got to the corridor she ran, outside to the sun and across the playground and into the sort of passage without a roof that led to the toilets. But

Robin was a fast runner and he was right behind her, she could hear him breathing and he grabbed her cardigan but she pulled away and in through the doorway to the girls' toilets.

Safe.

She ran into one of the cubicles. She slammed the door and locked it.

The toilet was dirty and the floor was cold stone and smelt of wee-wee and cleaning stuff. She didn't sit down on the toilet, she stood holding her box against her.

Bang bang!

The door of the cubicle shook.

'I'm *hungry*. Can I have some food *pleeeease* Smellie?'

Robin Beattie had come inside the girls' toilets!

But boys weren't allowed!

She moved back until her legs were touching the dirty toilet. She didn't want to be a murderer. She just wanted Robin Beattie to be dead.

A hand with white fingers came under the door.

She wished some of the other girls would come. She could hear a skipping rope on the ground outside and the skipper's feet jumping between. 'Where's Lorna?' someone shouted.

The hand waved. 'Do you want me to die of hunger?' Cough-cough *cough*.

She opened the box and looked at the orange, the Club biscuit and the sandwiches. She knelt down and put the Club biscuit into the hand. It disappeared and then came back. She put the orange in it.

'Not *fruit*.' The hand threw the orange away and it rolled into the next cubicle.

Poor little orange, getting all dirty. She knelt down and tried to reach it, but the hand grabbed her arm. She dropped the box, and the sandwich on top fell out next to the toilet. The two bits of bread flopped apart. Some of the tomato came out.

The hand was damp and sore on her skin, pulling her arm under the door so she had to stay kneeling on the horrible wee-wee floor.

She needed to go to the toilet.

'I want *proper* food,' said Robin's voice.

She reached out with her other hand to put the tomato back on the bread. The cheese hadn't fallen off because it was stuck to the butter, and so were the seeds. She covered them with the tomato and pressed the other slice of bread on top.

The hand was digging in to her arm.

She needed to go to the toilet. 'Let me *go*!'

The hand loosened on her skin and she tried to pull away but then it suddenly dug in even more. She pulled and pulled, and hot wetness spurted on the inside of her legs. It ran down to her knees and onto the floor. She bunched up all her muscles and whacked the hand on the bottom of the door.

It let go.

There was a grunt like an animal, and it disappeared.

'Right Smellie, you're dead for that.'

She carefully lifted up the sandwich and held it out under the door.

The hand snatched it. 'What kind is it? Better not be tuna.'

'Cheese and tomato.'

Helen stood and hugged her hands under her arms and listened. She heard his feet scuffing on the stone floor, away from the cubicle. Going outside.

Hector's voice said, 'What were you doing in the girls' toilets?'

Cough-cough *cough*. 'Lorna needed me to help her.'

'One of the girls could've done that. Is she still in there?'

'No.'

Hector shouted, 'Is anyone in there?'

Helen stood still. Hector couldn't know she was here because then he might think, *Robin probably took that sandwich from Helen*, and even if Helen said she wanted Robin to have it, Hector would make him give it back.

Fish's voice said, 'British Bulldogs or British-and-Jerries?' and Hector's said, 'Football. Where's the ball?'

'James burst it.'

'Okay, British Bulldogs then.' And he shouted: 'Who wants to play?'

When their voices had gone away, Helen took the other sandwich out of the box. It didn't have any seeds, but she couldn't eat it in case some of the seeds' poison had got on it.

She dropped it into the toilet and pulled the plug. Water whooshed down. Then she opened the door of the cubicle and went to one of the sinks. She took her knickers off, and her shoes, and her socks, and put in the plug. Robin was probably eating the sandwich now. The seeds would be going inside him. She hoped there would be enough.

'Have you had an acc'ent?' someone whispered.

Helen jumped round.

Lorna was standing inside one of the other cubicles. How had she got there? Maybe she had come in while the toilet was flushing, and that was why Helen hadn't heard her.

Helen scrunched up her knickers and socks in her hand. 'No.'

Lorna carried on looking at her.

The orange was squashed on the floor.

Helen said, 'Do you need a wee-wee?'

'No.'

She pulled her stinking knickers back on, all cold, and her socks and shoes. Then she went back into the cubicle and stepped over the pee. She picked up the empty lunch box and its lid.

Lorna squatted beside her. She was holding something between her thumb and her finger.

It was one of the seeds.

'*Don't!*' Helen grabbed Lorna's hand. 'Give me it. It's *poisonous*.' She took the seed away from her and dropped it into the toilet and pulled the plug. 'It's dirty.'

Lorna started to put her finger in her mouth, but Helen grabbed her hand and spat on it and rubbed it on her pinafore dress. Just in case.

The seed must have fallen out of the sandwich. Helen looked at the floor in case there were more. She couldn't see any, but she held onto Lorna's hand and said, 'You mustn't *ever* pick things up off the floor of the toilet. It's *dirty*. Okay?'

Lorna nodded.

There were footsteps coming. Helen stood up, and so did Lorna. Helen kept hold of her hand.

It was Katie and Shona and Jennifer.

Shona said, 'What are you doing with her, Helen?'

'Nothing.' She let go of Lorna.

'Have you peed your pants again? Eeeugh, is that wee *on the floor*?'

'The toilet's *right there*,' said Jennifer. 'Why couldn't you do it *in the toilet*?'

Helen held her lunch box tight. *Because of Robin*, she wanted to shout. She pushed past Shona and Katie and Jennifer and ran out into the playground. Her feet squelched. They left wee-wee footprints on the ground.

She looked but she couldn't see Robin.

On TV, when the lady in Victorian times had drunk the poisoned drink, her eyes had gone funny and then she'd lain down on her bed and held her stomach and gone, 'Oh... Oh...'. And then she was dead. Robin was probably needing to lie down. Maybe he'd gone inside and said to Miss Fraser, 'My stomach hurts,' and she'd let him lie on the green sofa in the teachers' room.

'*Helen Clack's peed her pants!*' shouted Jennifer.

Helen ran away round the corner. The Big Boys were playing British Bulldogs on the football pitch marked out with white lines on the playground. Hector wasn't wearing his grey jersey, he just had a shirt, and he was running towards the big wall between the playground and the river. Fiona Kerr and the other boys were running after him.

Hector crashed into the wall. Fiona Kerr did too, and sort of slid down it. They were both laughing. Fiona put her hand out and Hector took it and pulled her up, and Fiona's ponytail bounced and she shouted, '*We* are the champions, *we* are the champions!'

Now Helen could see Robin. He wasn't lying down. He was standing at the side of the shed with Suzanne.

3

She walked across.

Robin said, 'I'm still hungry, Smellie.' He threw a stone at the wall of the shed, and it bounced off and nearly hit Suzanne. 'Give me your other sandwich.'

'I haven't got another one.'

He grabbed at her lunch box but Helen kept hold of it and looked at his face. Soon his eyes would go funny and his stomach would hurt and he'd have to lie down.

Robin said, 'Give me it.'

But then Hector was there. He shoved Robin away.

'What's going on?' His shirt was pulled outside his shorts on one side and his shoes were all scuffed. He had a scrape down his arm with dust on it.

Fiona came running up. 'Is Robin bullying her?'

'She's peed her pants,' said Suzanne. 'She needs to take them off.'

Everyone was crowding round. Helen could feel her face going red.

'She *has* wet herself,' said Fiona. 'Look.'

Helen put her head down so she couldn't see Hector looking.

Norrie said, 'Aye, because of Robin, probably. He's been calling her Smellie Nellie. And scribbling on her picture. And jagging her with a pen.'

There was a scuffling noise and Robin shouted out. Helen looked up. Robin was trying to get away from Hector, and Hector was holding on to his jersey and his arm. Fish was staring with his mouth hanging open.

Hector kicked Robin in the bottom so he fell down on the hard playground. 'Just because you're a zombie doesn't mean you have to go round proving it, bullying girls. Everyone already knows you're brain-dead.'

'Ha ha *Robin Beattie*!' screamed Shona. '*Zombie*!'

Robin didn't move or say anything, he just lay there looking at Hector with his teeth shut together. James Christie kicked him on the leg.

'He can't even write his name,' said Fiona.

Suzanne scowled. 'He can so.'

'If this was a big school, he'd be in a special class. That's what our mum says.'

Fish nodded. 'She says he's retarded.'

'Your mum's as glaikit as you,' said Suzanne, 'with your big glaikit mouth. She doesn't know anything. He isn't retarded. He's a slow reader.'

'He's a *zommmmmbieeeee*.' James Christie kicked him again. 'Listen to him making that noise.' Robin was doing his cough.

Hector pulled James back and said, 'Okay,' and then he bent down and said something to Robin, and Robin got up and ran off round the side of the school. Suzanne grabbed Lorna from Shona and they ran after him.

Fiona said, 'Are you okay, Helen?'

'She's okay.' Hector put a hand on her shoulder. 'Come on. Let's go.'

She walked with Hector across the playground. She didn't look at him. She didn't want him to look at her.

'You can wash in the river.'

'We aren't allowed.'

'No one will see.'

He took her out of the gates, and onto the road, and along past the manse to the kirkyard. Behind the old gravestones there was long grass, and the river. There was a nice sandy bit like a beach. If you looked in the water you could see little fish.

Helen sat down on the sand.

Hector said, 'You can wash while I go back for my lunch.'

When he'd gone, Helen went to the edge of the river and pushed her feet down into the sand, so that the water came right up over the red straps and sides of her shoes. Right over her socks. It was shivery but it smelt nice, like hay when it was cut, only wetter. The only thing she didn't like was that there were flies and midgies.

Malfolio was exploring up the Amazon. He had blood all on him from werewolfing, and he needed to wash himself. He didn't take off his pants, he just waded out into the water. Shivery on his legs. He bunched up his pinafore – his explorer's cloak – to keep it dry. The water tugged at him as it went past. Some of the big stones had weeds growing from them like hair pulled back by the river, spongy under his feet, but some were slimy, and if he stood on them he could slip off and fall and get eaten by piranhas.

Helen squatted down so the water went over her pants, then she stood and struggled her legs back to the beach.

By the time Hector came running through the gravestones she was cold.

'Here, these'll be a bit big but they're dry at least.' He dropped some black rubbery gym shoes in the grass next to her.

They didn't go back to the playground, they sat on one of the flat table graves in the sun. It wasn't very comfy because of the knobbly carvings of skulls and angels and things but the stone was warm on her bottom. She lifted up her pinafore so her pants could dry, and her shoes and socks steamed on the stone next to her. She had put her socks on an angel's wings.

Hector took a squashed tinfoil shape out of his pocket and unwrapped it on the gravestone. There were two soggy sandwiches inside. Mrs MacIver made his lunch, and she wasn't very good at it. Hector didn't have a mummy because Mr Beattie had asked God to kill her, and God had.

'Looks and smells and probably tastes like something a cat's vomited up, but I'm hoping it's meat paste,' Hector said. 'What've you got?'

'I've eaten mine already.'

She pushed her empty box away to the other side of the angel. How long would the seeds take to kill Robin Beattie? She hoped by the end of lunchtime.

His grave would be over where all the new ones were, next to the road. It wasn't so nice there. There was just short grass and the wall and the railing.

Hector said, 'Like one of these?'

'No thank you.' But she was hungry.

He didn't say anything more until he'd finished the first sandwich. Then he said, 'When Robin Beattie bullies you, why don't you come and tell me?'

Helen didn't say anything. She couldn't tell Hector because God would kill him if she did. When Robin Beattie was dead, he wouldn't be able to get God to kill people any more.

'I've told him he'd better not bully you again. If he does, you've got to tell me. Okay?'

'Okay.'

She watched him eating the other sandwich. You never knew how long Hector would stay with you for. He didn't like just sitting. He liked playing football and other boys' games like British Bulldogs and Thief and fighting, and when he wasn't doing that he liked exploring. Mummy said he shouldn't be allowed. Helen and Suzanne weren't allowed past the track end unless they were with each other, and even then mostly only to go to school or the shoppie, but Hector went everywhere. He'd been right up Ben Aven on his own. He killed rabbits with Mr Cranston's ferrets.

Helen let the gym shoes slide down her feet into the grass. On the long stalks there were those spit-gobs made by little insects. The insect was inside, and spat and spat to make a big gob all round itself. A fly was climbing towards one of the gobs. Its legs were long and so thin they looked as if they would snap off if you touched them.

'Have you seen how Fish runs?' Hector got up and pretended to be Fish running, with his feet sticking out. 'It's possible he really is a fish.'

Helen laughed.

Hector sat down and put the last bit of sandwich in his mouth. 'You're a better runner than most of them. If they really had been British Bulldogs, they'd have been mown down by submachine-gun fire in about two seconds.' Hector was going to be a real soldier in the Army when he grew up, and so was Malfolio. Hector and Malfolio were best friends.

'Someone who could run fast would be all right though, wouldn't they, in a real war?'

'If there is another World War, we'll all just get fried by nuclear bombs.' He picked some green stuff off the letters on the grave.

'In wars, people kill other people but they're not murderers.'

'Of course not. Unless it's a war crime. In a battle you can kill as many people as you like.'

'Murderers go to hell, don't they?'

He smiled at her. 'There's no such thing as heaven and hell. They're just made up. God's just made up. You didn't think God was real, did you? It's just stories, all that guff in the Bible.'

She stared at him.

'My father says the idea of heaven and hell is to make people be nice to each other. To make them scared of what might happen if they don't behave themselves.' Hector didn't speak like everyone else. He spoke like an English boy, but he wasn't. His daddy was the Laird and so Hector was posh. That was why he was going away to a school in England after the summer holidays.

Helen didn't want Hector to go away. Thinking about it made her feel funny. How could there be school without Hector?

She looked down at the angel. Hector scraped green stuff off it. 'That's meant to be the soul going up to heaven. That's what the wings are for. See, it's rising up from the skull.'

'I thought he was an angel.'

'And that's a coffin.' His fingers moved across the stone. 'And an hourglass. And a scythe. They're called emblems of mortality. To make people think about what happens when they die – to make them behave themselves, and go to church.'

'People who believe in God, though – they still go to hell if they're bad, don't they?'

He smiled, and crumpled the foil and put it in his pocket. 'Just because you believe something doesn't make it true.' He stood up on top of the table grave. He took a few steps back and then ran and jumped, through the air, and landed on top of the next table grave. Then he jumped to the skyscraper one with the cross on top. Helen put on her socks and her shoes, which were still a bit wet but not too bad, and slid down to the ground. She picked up her box and the gym shoes.

'We'd better go back,' Hector said.

Helen looked up past the trees and over the wall to the manse. Mr and Mrs Beattie were probably in there having their lunch. Maybe Mrs Beattie was saying, 'I've made some nice biscuits for when Robin and Lorna get home from school.' She wouldn't know that Robin was probably dead now.

Hector scrabbled down the skyscraper, his grey socks at his ankles, and half-ran and half-leapt along the path to the steps and down to the gate. Helen ran after him, and Hector held open the gate for her and she jumped through.

The bell went, so they started running. At the gates of the manse Helen looked up the drive. Maybe Mr Beattie would be saying, 'What are we going to do about Robin? He's so horrible,' and Mrs Beattie would be saying, 'I know. If we just had Lorna and Scamp it would be better, but we have to keep Robin or God would be angry.'

Someone was running out from the school gates. Suzanne and Lorna. They were holding hands, and Lorna was crying. Robin came after them – but walking, not running.

Hector put out his hand to make Suzanne stop. He looked down at Lorna. 'What's he been doing to her?'

'Nothing.'

Lorna's head was bent over and her hair was hanging down. Hector pushed back her hair, and then they could see her face was all red with crying, and all wet. Her mouth was open and a dribble was coming out. Her eyes were scrunched up.

'What's wrong with her?'

What if Lorna didn't get that seed off the toilet floor? The seeds had been stuck to the butter, so it would be hard for one of them to fall out. What if Lorna got it *from the sandwich*? What if Robin gave her a bit of the sandwich, and Lorna ate it all up except for one seed?

She asked Lorna, 'Have you got a sore tummy?'

Lorna carried on crying and pulled her hand away from Suzanne.

'There's nothing wrong with her,' said Suzanne. 'Robin cowked and some got on her shoes.' She pointed.

Lorna's blue shoes had splatters of sick on them, and up her socks.

Suzanne grabbed back Lorna's hand, and Lorna's crying got louder. She stomped her feet up and down really fast, as if she was trying to get them away from the splatters. She pulled at Suzanne's hand.

Robin walked up behind them and said, 'Stop – being – *such a baby*, Lorna.'

He had his arms across his stomach and he was walking in a funny way. He didn't say anything else. He just walked past.

'We're taking her to her mum,' said Suzanne. 'Can you tell Miss Fraser? I might be late, and Robin might have to stay off.'

Helen nodded.

Lorna was tugging at Suzanne's hand, leaning forward so her hair hung down even more. Suzanne said, 'Come on, then,' and they started running again, past Robin and in at the gates to the manse.

'Have you shat yourself, Zombie?' said Hector.

'No,' said Robin. He didn't turn round.

'Yes you have. I can smell it. When your mum's finished cleaning up Lorna, you'd better get her to wipe your arse.'

Robin kept on walking until he got to the manse gates. Then he stopped, and Helen waited to see if he was going to lie down on the ground. But he didn't. He looked round, and Helen looked back, and said in her mind, *You're going to die now.*

He went in at the gates.

Hector said, 'We'd better hurry up or we'll be late,' and she ran after him along the road by the playground, and stretched out her hand to brush the tiny, pale, brand-new ivy leaves hanging like waterfalls of green stars from the top of the wall.

When she was eighteen

4

She climbed the gate, jumped off it and ran up the cowpat-dotted slope of the Lang Park towards the plantation. The binoculars bumped against her hip bone but she didn't care. She needed to run, to let out the energy that'd been building up inside her all day with nowhere to go, making her feet tap and her brain somersault when it should be checking invoices, or deciding what she should wear tomorrow, or putting sensible words in her mouth when Mum asked if she was all right.

'Yaaa!' she shouted at the stirks.

They didn't move. They were standing in a row by the dyke, watching her, bored-looking, but she knew that really their little stirkie brains were somersaulting too. This was their mad time, the long still summer gloaming, the time when Dad used to say the devil got into the coorse buggers. But Helen liked to think it wasn't the devil, it was just the wild part of them, the part that remembered being free.

When it happened, the weirdest thing was that there'd be no bellowing or snorting or pounding of hooves. If you'd turned away you might not even realise they'd moved, until something made you look round and you'd see the silent pack of beasts rushing down the field at you, all shoulders and haunches and hooves, big doe eyes rolling with bloodlust.

They'd never actually trample a person. They always veered off at the last second, whether you shouted and waved your arms about like she did, or just stood there with your hands on your hips like Dad.

'Yaaaa!' she encouraged them.

They didn't move. They just watched her, all the way to the top gate and over it into the resin-smelling plantation. Here the old drove road curved away round the hill, but she only ran a short distance along its grassy ruts, past the pet cemetery with its little wooden crosses, before taking the path that went vertically up through the trees.

The binoculars were bugging her now.

She took the strap off her shoulder and let their weight swing from her hand.

Mum's face, when Helen had asked where they were! But nothing had been said. Mum had just reached in to the cupboard under the stairs and pulled out the case, and run her hands over it to rub off two years' worth of dust.

She always used to have plenty to say about Helen's 'obsession'. That it was an old man's hobby, sitting on your own up a hill staring at a lot of flechy animals for hours on end. That she should be off having fun with Suzanne and her friends. That she spent too much time on her own as it was.

What she'd meant was *It's not normal*. And Helen used to hug to herself the thought that what she was really doing up the hill was about a million times less *normal* than watching badgers. And a million times better.

And then, two years ago, it had all stopped. Mum and Dad had eventually noticed that it'd been a good while since Helen had been up to the sett, and she'd told them she'd been put off after getting a tick on her bum.

She'd been a miserable little cow for months. Mooning around, leafing through her diaries, reading and rereading the best bits. She was going to have to burn those diaries. What if Hector found them? It would hardly take an Enigma Machine to work out who 'H' was – and that the last entry coincided with his last visit home two years ago. She could just imagine him looking at her, and raising his eyebrows, and saying, 'Should I be flattered, or checking the rabbit hutch?' but deep down thinking, *Oh-oh*.

She could never tell him about 'badgers'.

Oh God oh God oh *God*. Tomorrow was almost here, and she still hadn't a clue what she was going to say to him.

And she'd been getting in a right state, trying on the cream dress, and then every alternative she could think of, even ridiculous things like an old school skirt, and she'd got all sweaty and had to have a shower. In the end she'd put all the other stuff back in the wardrobe, and hung the cream dress up on the back of the door, and run downstairs.

When she'd asked Mum where the binoculars were, she'd expected her to sigh and shake her head. To say she'd hoped Helen had outgrown all that. But all she'd said was, 'Don't stay out too long. Make sure you start back before the light goes.'

And the light never really went, not at this time of year. 'Simmer Dim' they called it in the Northern Isles, this weird not-day-not-night of midsummer, when the air lay still over the fields, and hung in the sweet-smelling, midgie-ridden shadows under the trees.

The trees swayed and a branch creaked as a breeze got up out of nowhere. She didn't like the plantation. It was a dead place. Looking to either side of the path was like looking into a Grimm's fairytale forest, dark and spooky, the ground covered in decades of brown needles and not much else. But right by the path there was grass and ferns and wood sorrel, and wood anemone, and sweet mini-trees where the lucky cones had fallen.

She slowed to a walk, pulling at her top so the air could get to her skin, her feet finding a new rhythm as the path left the plantation behind for the open spaces of the native forest. Here the pine trees were wonky, and all different sizes, from tiny little asterisks to huge big giants. But Helen's favourites were the birks, the birch trees, slim and delicate. When the wind blew, their leaves flipped up to show their pale undersides. In the evening light everything was muted, but in bright sun the wind through the birks was a shimmer of silver. That was the Ghillie Dhu, Dad used to say, reeshling his siller for a penny to pay the tinker.

The path was springy from the peat, and soft from all the layers of pine needles and dead leaves on top. It wound its way among mossy stumps and heather and blaeberry bushes. If she really had been wanting to watch badgers, here was where she'd leave the path and make for the ridge above the sett, and find a comfy place to sit and wait.

She carried on up the hill until she was out of the trees, and the path petered out in the short heather and the scree. Here rocks came poking out of the ground, little ones, and big rounded lumps, and flat ones like pavement slabs.

She stopped at the heathery ledge, with its wall of rock behind to lean back against, where she'd sat so often and for so long that she wouldn't be surprised to find a shadowy figure lingering, the ghost of that skinny girl with the spotty face and the hair that stuck out at the sides like something on a cartoon character.

She wished she could reach through time and grab that little ghost and say: *Look! Look at this!* And pull from her pocket the last letter from Hector. The little ghost's eyes would open wide, and she'd take the letter in her hands like it was a holy relic; but then she'd probably shake her head, and bite her lip, and say Suzanne was right. What made her think he didn't have a string of drippy idiots carrying his letters about in their pockets? What made her think it wasn't all going to end in tears?

The little ghost had misery down to a fine art. Her fantasies about Hector hadn't been the kind where he took her in his arms and told her he loved her, and kissed her, and made wild passionate love to her – oh no. In her daydreams she'd be attending his wedding to Fiona, and Hector would smile at her as he walked down the aisle, arm in arm with his beautiful bride, and Helen would smile back while inside her heart was breaking. And then she'd get leukaemia, and as she lay dying suddenly Hector would be there, and she'd finally confess that she loved him, and he'd weep bitter tears as she died in his arms, knowing too late that he loved her too.

She laughed out loud, and batted the heather in case of late-to-bed bees before lowering her bum and leaning back against the rock, and letting her breathing slow and her eyes wander, down the hill and across the fields and treetops to the grey bulk of the House of Pitfourie. By road it was nearly three miles away, because you had to go round by the junction at Kirkton. But as the crow flew – or the eye looked – it was less than two.

She didn't lift the binoculars straight away. She held them in her hands, running her fingers over the snakeskin-effect plastic. They had a magnification of ×25. When she was thirteen she'd saved up for a year to buy them, but she'd known it had been worth it the first time she'd sat here and focused them on the first floor windows. Often they didn't draw the curtains, and if the windows were lit up you could see the people inside. Tiny people, so small it was difficult to tell the Laird and Hector apart.

But you could actually see them.

If they came near enough to a window. And *if* they were in a room on this side of the house, obviously, and on the first floor or above. You couldn't see any of the ground floor because, even though there were just the gardens and fields directly in front of the house, the woods between it and the road were on higher ground, so the tops of the trees hid a lot.

But the library, where they tended to sit in the evenings, was on the first floor.

And so was Hector's room.

Every sighting of him had been carefully noted down in her diary, like she was a scientist observing the habits of some rare and wonderful creature. She'd document the time; what she thought he might have been wearing, although that was pretty much guesswork at this distance; which window or windows she'd seen him at; what he'd been doing; and who else she thought might have been with him. FK, usually. Fiona Kerr. Twice she'd watched their two figures pressing together – kissing, presumably, and touching each other.

Of course he'd only been home during his school holidays, and then his holidays from Sandhurst. And then, after the Laird married Irina, he hadn't been home at all. No more 'badgers'. He'd spent his Army leave jetting off to exotic places with his dubious friends, as Irina called them, instead of coming to Pitfourie.

He hadn't even come back when Stinker was born.

That had been in December, just after Dad had died. Everyone had been sure Hector would be home for Christmas to see his new little brother. It had been the one thing she'd been able to hang on to: *Hector will be here, Hector will be here.*

Only he hadn't been.

And then into her misery had come the letter.

The first letter he'd ever written her, with her name, 'Helen Clack', and her address in his neat sloping writing. Inside, a single sheet of writing paper. And his words, telling her how sorry he was about Dad, how much he'd liked him, that he wished he could have been at the funeral. That he hoped she was all right. That it was something, that Dad hadn't had to suffer through a long illness, that his death had been so sudden, at home at the Parks rather than in an anonymous hospital ward.

And then the words that she'd never forget as long as she lived: *I've been thinking a lot about you –*'

Well, *you and your mother.* But still.

She'd carried the letter around for days. Suzanne had found her staring at it, and snatched it away and read it, and then perched on the kitchen table and said, 'So. Have you replied?'

And when Helen had said she hadn't, Suzanne had offered to help.

'They don't think like us. They don't spend – how many days have you been mooning over this? – *six days* analysing and pulling apart and putting back together every little thing we say. You have to treat them like they're simpler forms of life. Stimulus–response.'

'Hector's not a "simpler form of life". That's the whole problem.'

'I'm not saying it's a *bad* thing. God, I'd hate it if Rob suddenly went all New Man on me, trying to work out what I was thinking, and greeting at films. Yuch. Might as well be a lesbian and have done with it.'

'So what should I say?'

'Keep it light. Ask him questions, so he has to write back: what's the Army food like, do they have a TV, is it cold? Does he have any funny stories to cheer you up? No harm in playing the dead parent card. But whatever you do, don't ask when he's coming home.'

'Could you help me write it?'

That had taken another week. Somewhere in the process, Helen had managed to lose Hector's letter – tragedy! – but, as Suzanne had said, so what? They both knew its contents off by heart. In the end, Suzanne had taken their latest effort, shoved it in an envelope, slapped on a stamp and posted it to the address for his regiment that she'd found in the Laird's desk, a PO box number in Aberdeen.

They'd plotted together like a couple of witches to reel him in. But all the other letters had been her own work. And she hadn't let Suzanne see any more of his, and had sworn her to secrecy about the whole thing. Hector didn't want anyone knowing they were writing to each other because his father would go ballistic if he found out. Nothing personal – but he was a hide-bound old Tory who felt the peasants should know their place.

She hadn't thought the Laird was like that, but it turned out that Hector had never really got on with him, and had been champing at the bit to get away for years.

She reached into her pocket and unfolded the warm sheets of paper, and scanned down to the sentence that had been putting a feelie's smile on her face all day:

Not much looking forward to seeing the old goat or the slut, and very little desire to spend time with an infant with the soubriquet of Stinker - but there must be some reason why I'm counting down the hours to the prodigal's return... Hope maybe you are too...?

She put the letter back in her pocket and lifted the binoculars.

The windows on the first floor were big Georgian and Victorian ones, a row of sixteen. The Laird and Irina's bedroom was all lit up, and so were the library's three windows, but she couldn't make out if that was a person sitting on the sofa with their head sticking up, or if it was just a vase or something on the windowsill.

Hector's room was at the end of the house on the right-hand side. There was no light on, but that didn't mean anything. Suzanne said the Laird was fascist about people switching lights off behind them.

She panned back along to the library window. The shape that could have been a vase wasn't there any more. And now there was movement, in the next window along, the middle one of the three. Two people were standing at the window looking straight at her.

One of them had to be the Laird, and one of them had to be Hector. The one on the right – yes –

The binoculars dipped in her hands.

The one on the right was Hector.

Standing talking to his father and looking out at something in the garden, maybe, or the horses in the field, and little did he know that she was up here on Craig Dearg looking down at him. Or, all the time he was talking about what he'd been doing, and what had been happening at Pitfourie, and about Stinker and the christening, was some sixth sense telling him she was out here?

'Hector,' she said out loud, to the air.

She really was going to see him, and speak to him...

She lifted the binoculars again, but instead of turning them immediately to the library window she panned up to the second floor.

Suzanne's room faced the other way, over the courtyard at the back. It had eaves sloping in and a little iron fireplace where she was allowed to light fires. She did light them, even when it was really hot, because then she could say the smell of cigarettes was the fire if anyone accused her. She wasn't meant to smoke near the baby.

'Stinker's getting a thirty-a-day habit,' she'd say. 'When he starts speaking he'll be –' And she'd make her voice deep and growly '– *You lookin' at me?*'

Helen counted along to the dark window of the nursery bathroom that was across the corridor from Suzanne's room. If both doors were open, maybe she'd be able to see into her room. But there was just the darkened window. Would Rob be with her? He wasn't allowed to stay the night – he wasn't really allowed in her room at all – but that didn't mean he wouldn't be there.

She panned back to the library windows, but Hector had gone. She lowered the binoculars, retrieved the letter from her pocket and turned to the second page.

You should be getting your invite soon, thanks to yours truly. Relevant part of phonecall went something like this:

H: So, which of the tenants have you invited?

OG: The Taylors, the Duncans... Jim and Ina Clack...

H: What about Helen Clack? Doesn't she help Suzanne with Damian?

OG: We can't ask everyone. We're up to over a hundred already.

H: But how many of them have wiped vomit off his romper suit, and shit off his arse?

Tom and I (Do you know Tom Strachan? Bit of a prat to be honest) have organised an unofficial shindig up on the Knock for afterwards, at the stone circle (Bring Your Own Druid), so warm clothes required. Needless to say, the 'adults' don't have to know about it. Tell your mother you're staying over with Suzanne. Could be an all-nighter.

Better play it cool at the official do – make out we're just two old schoolmates catching up. I don't want to be looking over my shoulder the whole time. Let's wait till we're up on the Knock, under the starry heavens – ugh, I'm starting to sound like Mr Beattie. But seriously, we don't want the old goat ruining it. Plenty time to tackle him later.

Re christening present: I'm swithering between a reversed pentagram and a skull ring. What is the well-dressed young Antichrist wearing this season?

See you on Sunday.

Love

Hector

She touched his name on the paper. No kisses, no flowery words, no telling her how wonderful she was and how he couldn't wait to hold her in his arms at last. The word 'Love' looked as if it had scratched itself out of his pen against his will. Even 'starry heavens' was something to apologise for. He was a lot more comfortable making jokes about his baby brother being the Antichrist.

It was as if, to Hector, love was something you had to edge around and about and not look in the eye, like a wild creature you'd come across in the woods, muscles bunched, head lifted into the wind, ready in an instant to kick out its legs and run.

Probably it was because of his childhood. His mother had died when he was six, and it didn't sound like his father had ever really given him any love. When he was eleven he'd been packed off to boarding school to live with strangers who whacked him with a cane if he put a foot wrong. It was tantamount to child cruelty, Mum said, the way the upper classes brought up their children, and it was no wonder they turned out the way they did.

She folded the sheets of paper together and pushed them against her mouth.

5

At first she wasn't sure what it was that made her stop, just at the point where the path passed near to the badgers' sett, and stand and listen. And then she heard it: a noise in the undergrowth, a snapping and crashing – something moving in there. Something big.

A deer or a badger.

She couldn't see what it was. There were too many trees in the way.

She started moving again, down the path, trying not to make too much noise so she could listen.

The noises were moving too – level with her.

She stopped.

The noises stopped.

The trees were still blocking her view through to whatever it was. It was probably a deer.

She moved again, more slowly, and immediately the noises were back, but not as loud now, as if whatever it was was mocking her, imitating her stealthy steps.

She made herself stop and call, in a normal voice:

'Hello?'

She made herself move to the left, so she could see round the trunks of two birks.

And now she could see that it wasn't a deer, it was a person, moving amongst the trees. Moving towards her.

It was Rob Beattie.

And right at the back of her head a little girl screamed:

Run!

But she stood where she was, and smiled, and said, 'Oft, *Rob*! I thought you were a mad axeman or something!'

'Hey, not with my coordination. Probably end up chopping my own head off. Sorry – didn't mean to scare you.' He came panting up, lurching to a halt in front of her and steadying himself by grabbing her arm.

Hally-wrackit, Auntie Ina called him. He was always bumping into the furniture and breaking things, hytering about as if he hadn't got used to the length of his legs and arms yet.

He wasn't all that tall, but he was lanky, and the wide head made him look even lankier. A neep on a stick, Norrie called him. But his face wasn't fat like it had been when he was a kid, and the jutting brows and chin sort of balanced the width of it and made him, actually, almost handsome – although if you had to cast him in a film, you'd make him the goofy side-kick rather than the hero.

Unless you were Suzanne of course.

She took a step backwards. 'What're you doing up here?'

She could smell the sweat on him. His hair was dark with it; almost the same colour as Hector's.

'Your mum sent me to fetch you back.'

'Why?'

Since Dad died, every unexpected summons, every *Helen, can I speak to you a min'tie?* from a teacher, every trill of the phone had her stomach lurching.

'Getting a bit late.' He opened his eyes wide. 'Getting *daaaaark*... But I'm here to protect you from any mad axemen that might really be lurking in the undergrowth.'

'Well thanks. I think.' She smiled at him, and started to walk down the path.

He fell into step beside her. Cough-cough *cough*. 'It's spooky enough at the best of times, isn't it, up here?'

'Not really. You're a lot safer here than you would be on a street in Aberdeen. Or even Aboyne.'

'True.' He was walking too close to her side, their arms touching now and then. Like he didn't quite know where his body ended and the rest of the world began.

'What were you doing at the Parks?' She took advantage of a narrowing of the path to walk ahead.

'Suzanne sent me with those – things – for your hair. For tomor-row.'

'The hairclips! Oh, God, I completely forgot! Thanks, Rob.'

'Vitally important, apparently.'

'Oh, vitally.'

'And she told me – can you stop a second?'

Helen stopped; turned. He smiled at her, and lifted both hands to her head.

She pulled back. 'What're you doing?'

'For a proper demonstration I really need the clips, and I left them at your house, but... Suzanne gave me strict instructions about where you should put them – and I was to show you. Stand still.'

Big white fingers pushed into her mop of hair. 'Here – and here.'

'Right. Okay.' She made herself not flinch. She made herself wait until he took his hands away before turning back round; setting off again down the path.

Just when she thought she was okay with him, something like this would happen.

'Hey Helen, you're good at puzzles. Here's a riddle for you. One of the old folks at The Pines told me it last week and it's been tormenting me ever since. Help me out?'

She smiled at him over her shoulder. 'If I can.'

He had stopped walking, so she had to stop too.

He started in a sing-song voice: 'I am a garden of delights... I am a wasteland *frozen*.'

On *frozen*, he thrust his chin out.

She stepped back.

He took one step forward. 'I am the dagger in the night...' He opened his eyes wide, and brought his face right up to hers, as if he was about to kiss her. 'I am the sweetest *poison*,' he whispered, so close she could feel the warmth of his breath on her cheek. 'What am I?'

She couldn't even move away from him. She couldn't move at all. Oh God.

He knew.

He must know.

She had thought at the time that he must, when he'd come back to school after his 'tummy upset', raised from the dead like Lazarus in Mrs Beattie's Sunday School story. He'd come running in at the gates and danced about, as if he was saying, *Ha ha ha, I'm not dead.* And into Helen's sick little eight-year-old head had come the picture of Lazarus, jumping up from his grave, white shroud trailing.

She'd run, past Katie and Jennifer, and Katie had shouted: 'Smellie Smellie Nellie, pees in her wellies!'

Robin had run after her, but instead of grabbing her he'd grabbed Katie by the hair, and said into her face: 'Don't call her that.' And he'd come and put his arm round Helen. 'We're friends now.' His white hand had flopped on the top of her arm, and Suzanne had come and put her arm round Helen on the other side, and they'd walked round the playground like that until the bell went.

She'd said *Thank you* to God, and 'Thank you for making Robin be nice to me' when she saw Hector, because she wasn't sure which of them had done it. She knew Hector had told Robin to stop bullying her, but the rising from the dead aspect suggested divine intervention. Maybe God had said, *Well, okay Jesus, raise Robin Beattie from the dead if you want, but then we have to make him be Helen's friend.*

But Helen didn't want him to be her friend. She wanted him to be dead.

She'd known that sometimes God did things to test you. Like telling Abraham to kill his little boy Isaac, and then, when Abraham had the knife ready, saying, 'Only joking.' Maybe God had made Robin her friend as a test: *Okay, now he's your friend – do you STILL want him dead?*

Yes please.

But God helped those who helped themselves, so she'd asked Mr Cowie in the library van if he had any books about laburnum, and a few weeks later he'd produced a book on trees. She'd said it was for school, and got Mum to help her read the relevant section. There'd been a bit about the seeds being poisonous, but then it had said that they usually only made people a little bit ill. So getting more seeds would probably be a waste of time.

But whenever there was something on the News about a young boy or girl dying, she'd tried to pay attention and find out what had happened. Usually, though, Mum or Dad switched the TV to a different channel before she could hear. Once in the shoppie Mrs Smart had been talking to Mum about a little girl in Aberdeen who'd drowned in a pond, and how sad it was, and the poor parents, although they had only themselves to blame really. But that little girl had been only five and couldn't swim. Robin was a good swimmer because the river was right by his house.

In the end she'd just asked God each night: *Please kill Robin Beattie.*

But he hadn't.

And Rob must know what she'd done.

'Helen?'

'Sorry. Um...' She smiled at him desperately. 'Some sort of drug?'

He stepped past her, continuing on down the path.

She made her legs move. She made herself follow him.

'This is Mrs Robertson we're talking about. In her world, heroin is the nice young lady in a Mills and Boon.' He grinned back at her.

'Sugar?'

'Hmm. How is sugar a "dagger in the night"?'

'Maybe someone on a sugar rush...'

He chuckled. 'The well-known donut defence. Right enough, there have been times I'd have killed for one.'

He *didn't* know. He couldn't. If he'd known, he'd have found a way to punish her all those years ago, no matter what Hector had threatened.

'So what's the answer?' she said.

'I don't know and it's driving me nuts.'

'I'll have a think.'

He stopped again. 'Sorry Helen, where are my manners, eh? After you.'

So she had to go ahead of him. She lengthened her stride as the path dipped into the plantation, the ranks of closely packed Sitkas cutting out the light.

'Reckon Hector will show up for the christening?' His voice came from right behind her.

'Isn't he here already?'

'No idea.'

'But haven't you just been at the House?' How else would he have got the hairgrips from Suzanne?

'Yes, but remember, Helen – I'm confined to below-stairs. No "hobnobbing with the gentry" for yours truly.'

'But you'd have heard if Hector had arrived, wouldn't you?' She turned to look at him.

He shrugged. 'The hypothetical Hector.'

So maybe that hadn't been Hector at all, the figure at the window? But surely it had been? Rob was looking at her with an odd expression. Sometimes she thought Suzanne must have told him about her and Hector, even though she swore she hadn't.

'It's your mum I feel bad for.'

'Eh?'

'Bit of a slap in the face, isn't it, you and Suzanne and Jim and Ina all being invited, but not her? I always feel it must be hard – I mean, I know she always jokes about not being "accepted into the tribe", but it can't be much fun, being treated like she's some kind of alien just because she's from Edinburgh.'

'The Laird probably hasn't asked her because he knows she doesn't like going to things without Dad. And he can't invite everyone. There wouldn't be room in the kirk.'

'Not once he's asked all his nob friends, no. But being passed over for her daughter? That's got to hurt.'

It was the talk of the parish: who had and had not been invited to the christening. Rumours, and rumours about rumours, chasing from door to door. Margaret Begg had told crabby old Willie Simpson that she'd heard he'd been asked but wasn't well enough to go; this had stirred Willie into a fury, because he hadn't been invited at all – who'd told Margaret that he had been? Jennifer Gordon. Willie had then gone whinging to Annie Gordon, who'd told Jennifer's mother Cathy, who'd marched straight round to Willie's to announce that Margaret Begg was blethering – Jennifer hadn't told her any such thing – how could she, when she hadn't even seen Margaret to speak to for a fortnight?

It made you want to scream.

'I'm only invited because I'm there a lot, helping Suzanne with Stinker.'

And because Hector had pointed that fact out to the Laird. She hadn't merited a proper written invite like Jim and Ina's. Hers had come, two weeks late, through her cousin.

Suzanne hadn't been exactly subtle about it.

She'd come breezing into the kitchen and pinched a chip off Helen's plate, and plomped herself down on the chair opposite, legs tucked under her. 'You can come to Stinker's christening, can't you? Irina really wants you there.'

Mum had looked round from the sink. 'Well it's –'

'Oops!' Suzanne had made a face, blowing on the chip. 'Sorry Auntie Viv, I just meant Helen. *The adohhhrable cousin.*' She waved the chip about in an Irina-ish way. 'I've already said "Yes" for you. You can come, can't you?' She opened her mouth and flipped the whole chip inside.

Helen nodded.

And then she heard 'Cough-cough *cough*,' and saw that Rob had come in at the door, and was smiling at her. 'Thank goodness for that,' he said. 'At least that means there'll be someone there I can talk to.'

'Ahem?' said Suzanne.

'You'll be busy with Stinker. I had visions of having to make polite conversation with the furniture. And I'm not even sure how well that would go. The table in the hall looks like it could be very "sneistie".' He always said Scots words – and the phrases he picked up from the people in the old folks' home – like they had inverted commas round them.

He went and got a dish towel from the rail at the front of the Aga, and a wet plate from the draining board.

Mum smiled. 'Now Rob, you don't need to do that.'

'And you, Mrs C, don't *need* to let me eat you out of house and home whenever I'm here, but somehow it always seems to happen. Least I can do is earn my keep.'

Suzanne started on a long story about how Rob hadn't been invited, 'Until I told Irina, "If Rob's not coming, neither am I." It's my day off and she can't make me. I'm only doing it as a favour, that's what I said, and Irina knows fine that Mrs MacIver will be too busy with the food to see to Stinker, so if I wasn't there she'd have to change him and everything herself, so she's all, "Oh *Suzanne*, well of *course*, if it means that *much* to you…".'

'Charming,' said Mum.

'I don't imagine the Laird's too happy about having to let me loose amongst the valuables,' said Rob. 'But if it's a choice between that and having to actually look after their own kid for a few hours…'

'It's ridiculous that you should be confined to the servants' quarters in the first place.'

'There's no such thing as *servants* any more, Mrs C.' Rob opened a cupboard. 'It's *staff*. If I remember correctly, his exact words were that I was to confine myself to "downstairs" when I came to see Suzanne.'

'Pffh!'

'To be fair, I was half way up the library steps at the time, grub-by little paw reaching for the first edition Dickens. I suppose you can see it from his point of view. Hector's probably told him all sorts of stories about my exploits at school – and let's face it, I was a right little monster.' He glanced at Helen. 'Just the kind of kid you'd expect to grow up to have criminal tendencies.'

'All little boys are monsters,' said Mum. 'Hector Forbes was hardly an angel himself. *Is* hardly an angel, if half of what we hear is true.'

'Hector's –' Helen blurted, and stopped.

'Hector's a good guy,' Rob nodded. 'A good guy who probably still hates my guts, but a good guy nonetheless.' He took another plate from the draining board. 'I used to think he was some sort of cross between James Bond and Superman. I'd have given anything to be his friend. But I was just Zombie. Why should he bother with me, other than to give me a good battering when he'd nothing better to do?' Cough-cough *cough*. 'Not that I didn't deserve it.'

'No one *deserves* to be hurt,' said Mum.

'He was only keeping me in line. And deep down I think I knew that.'

Suzanne snorted. '*Keeping you in line*? Beating the crap out of you; calling you "Zombie"?'

'But at that time I hadn't been diagnosed. Even the teachers just thought I was stupid. *I* thought I was stupid. Why shouldn't Hector?'

Mum shook her head. 'All the more reason for him not to be so cruel.'

'Kids – they don't think, do they? About the effect they might be having on someone?' He was wiping the plate round and round. 'We see it all the time with the younger ones in the Youth Fellowship. They can't seem to see beyond the so-called joke to the misery of the person on the receiving end. They have to have it pointed out to them – and no one did that for Hector.' A rueful smile. 'But every cloud has a silver lining. After I was diagnosed, I was determined to prove to everyone that I *wasn't* a zombie. If I get the Higher grades I need, maybe I should send Hector a "Thank You" card.'

'Well,' Mum had said. 'If there's any justice you'll get straight As. You've worked so hard.'

He'd been getting extra tuition at home, and now he had a condi-tional offer to study for a Bachelor of Divinity at Aberdeen Uni.

Mum said he was going to make a super minister – after his struggles with dyslexia, he'd be all the more sensitive to his parishioners' problems.

Oh yes, very sensitive.

Touching Helen's arm at Dad's funeral; smiling with anxious sympathy, like he'd been practising in a mirror; leaning in to whisper: 'He's gone to a better place. I'm sure he has. I know he didn't go to church regularly. I know he was – well...' Pausing; frowning; smiling brightly. 'But he was a very good man in other ways, wasn't he.' Widening his smile; squeezing her arm.

They were out of the plantation at last. They could either carry on down the drove road and go the long way round, or take the short cut through the field. But Rob wasn't good with beasts.

As they passed the pet cemetery he stopped to look down at the wooden crosses. 'Aw. Your "catties".'

She didn't say anything. When she was nine, she'd been convinced that he'd asked God to kill them: Baudrins and Susie and Fergus.

'It was weird, wasn't it? I mean, some mad tractor driver, going round squishing cats' heads? Or maybe it was just the tractor... like *Christine*. You know, the Stephen King film *Christine*?'

She'd noticed this same phenomenon with very religious people before. It was as if animals didn't matter because they didn't have souls.

'I think it was a book before it was a film.' Cheap shot. 'You don't mind going through the field?'

Most of the stirks were strung out in a loose group between them and the lower gate. As Helen ran towards them some of them began to shift and one did a little jump back.

'Yaaa!' she shouted.

But the stirks just trotted out of their way, and then turned to stare as they climbed the bottom gate.

6

Mum wiped her floury hands on a cloth. 'Oh, don't you look gorgeous? But unless that bag's a tardis, you might want to think again about what you need to take. Have you got a nightie?'

Helen moved into the morning light shafting in through the end window and put the bag down on the kitchen table. It was the one she'd bought in the Dorothy Perkins sale last year, a cherry-red rectangle of flimsy plastic with a zip along the top and two straps to go over your shoulder. She'd stuffed a pair of jeans and a jumper and trainers into it.

'If I've forgotten anything, I can always borrow from Suzanne.'

'A nightie of Suzanne's would barely cover your modesty.'

'*Mum.*'

'She's a lot smaller than you are.'

'Suzanne's nighties have adapted to conditions at the House. Ankle-length winceyette.'

'Surely not at this time of year.'

'I've got a nightie, anyway.'

'Well why didn't you just say?'

Helen sighed.

'Are you taking your camera?'

'No.'

'It'd be nice to send some photos to Sheila, wouldn't it?'

'Lots of people will have cameras. I can get prints to send her.'

And it was mad, but into Helen's head popped an image of Sheila, slumped in her wheelchair, lopsided mouth twisted in a smile as she contemplated a photo of Helen and Hector together at the christening.

At first Sheila had just been a girl Helen had met years ago at guide camp who'd suddenly started up a correspondence. Then Mum had said Helen could phone Sheila any time she wanted –

47

money wasn't so tight that Helen couldn't do that. So Helen had had to make Sheila deaf. Then Mum had seen the Aberdeen postmark on one of the letters – for security reasons, everyone in the regiment had their letters home parcelled up and sent to headquarters in Aberdeen, from where they were then posted out, so that the postmarks wouldn't give away where they were deployed. Mum had said she thought Sheila lived in Oban… Yes, she used to, but now she lived in Aberdeen. Oh – well, Helen must ask her out to the Parks. So Sheila had acquired cerebral palsy, a wheelchair and overprotective parents.

Hector thought it was all a great joke. He'd started making the writing on the envelopes a bit wonky. But Helen had, ridiculously, begun to feel bad for Sheila – that it was wrong of Hector to laugh at her. *It's your fault she's in a wheelchair*, she'd felt like scribbling back.

But it wasn't Hector's fault she had to lie to Mum. If it was only up to Hector, he'd be telling everyone they were 'involved'. That was the word he'd used: *involved*. Like their lives were tangled up together.

An engine rumbled outside, getting closer.

'You've got the present, and the card?'

She nodded.

'You really look lovely, Helen.'

'Thanks.'

Did she look okay? The cream dress was only polyester, but it had a very cinched-in waist which made it look like she at least went out a bit at the breasts and hips. And she was wearing a padded bra to help things along.

Her skin was about ten times better than it had been last time Hector had seen her, although there was a spot starting on her chin. Typical. She'd covered it with concealer, and put foundation and powder all over her face. And some lipstick, and eye liner and mascara and eye shadow. And the tortoiseshell-effect hair slides were perfect. They held her mop of hair off her face, but not in a severe way like a ponytail. She didn't have the bone structure for severe.

Well, so what? Hector already knew she wasn't exactly Cindy Crawford.

Mum had the back door open and Helen could see past her to the car that had stopped in the yard, and Fiona Kerr's long shiny hair caught by the breeze as she ducked her head to get out from the passenger side.

She'd asked Fiona if she could have a lift, because Uncle Jim and Auntie Ina had offered to take the Smarts so there was no room in their car.

And now Fiona was at the door, saying she was sorry they were late, it was Steve's fault, he hadn't thought to check whether his suit needed ironed until about five minutes ago. She was wearing a long flowery skirt and strappy top and Jesus sandals.

Helen grabbed her bag up off the table and nodded and smiled as Mum said, 'Have a great time.'

The cobbled bit of the yard was difficult to walk on in her new shoes. She kept wobbling about. The spurgies up on the gutter of the steading were going *cheek-a-cheek-a-cheek.*

'Love the dress,' said Fiona. 'It really suits you.'

'Thanks.'

'As you can see, I've made a big effort as usual.' She swished her hippie skirt. 'Got this at the Scout jumble sale.'

'You look lovely.'

And she did, and she knew it, with her perfect skin and hair and cheekbones, and her big round breasts pushing out against the cotton top. It was obvious she wasn't wearing a bra. *Oh look at me, I'm a refugee from the seventies, I wear stuff from jumble sales because I'm so radical but I still look great.*

'I'm hoping people will just think I've gone for the natural look.' She wasn't wearing any make-up either. Apart from something transparent and shiny on her lips. Probably just lip balm. *Oh look at me, I don't wear make-up because I'm so beautiful I don't need to.*

Well, if she didn't, that wasn't her fault, was it? Any more than it was her fault that Hector had once kissed those shiny lips, and put his hand –

She concentrated on Steve, sitting in the driver's seat watching them crossing the yard. He gave her a *hello* lift of his eyebrows.

Fiona, bouncing along in her Jesus sandals, was singing under her breath. She interrupted herself to say, 'Is Norrie going to be there?'

'I think so.'

'This'll be his chance to make a move.'

Helen pursed her lips to stop the huge grin that wanted to split her face. 'It's not like that.'

'You're just friends?'

What was everyone going to say, when they knew she was Hector's girlfriend? How great would it be, to go into the shoppie holding Hector's hand, and maybe Jennifer and Shona would be there –

'You've got to tug at that door.' Fiona reached past Helen to pull the rear door open, then bounced round to the passenger side.

Helen got into the car. The seat sagged under her bum and she could feel something hard pressing up against her right thigh. There was a funny fooshty smell. But it wasn't dirty inside, and there were no wrappers or crisp bags or anything on the floor like in Rob's car.

As they started slowly down the track, Fiona said: 'He'd like to be more than friends, wouldn't he?'

'I don't think so.'

Steve flicked Helen a smile in the mirror. 'Who's for skiving off down the pub?'

'Stop it!' said Fiona.

'Well I'm sorry, but standing around in a suit listening to a load of Hoorays gooing and gahing over another inbred offspring isn't my idea of a fun day out.'

Helen stopped herself from snapping that there were plenty of people who'd have liked fine to be going but hadn't been asked. No point. Steve didn't even drink Coke because it was 'culturally imperialist'.

'So why are you going?'

'Mine not to reason why –'

Fiona snorted a laugh. Typical Fiona though, dragging her new boyfriend to the christening of her ex-boyfriend's little brother, just so she could swan around being the girl everyone fancied.

Helen unzipped her bag to check she'd got the card and present. There was the envelope, and – yes, there was the present, wrapped in shiny blue paper with silver stars on it. She pulled it out.

She'd wanted to get him something good. Just about everything in the House was antique, and even in the nursery all the toys were wooden. Irina wouldn't have anything plastic near Stinker because she'd read something about babies that chewed plastic getting harmful chemicals off it. But almost all the money Helen made at her holiday job in the office at Davidson AgriTech went to help pay the bills and the overdraft. In the end she'd just gone for a soft animal. Stinker's favourite thing was a soft elephant, so Helen had bought a little rhino – sort of like an elephant, but different.

She hoped he'd like it. When she'd told Suzanne what she'd gone for, Suzanne had said, 'He only likes the elephant because he can chew its ears.' The rhino's ears were tiny. Probably not chewable.

They'd come to the track end. As Steve eased onto the public road, Fiona twisted round in her seat. 'Oh God, is that what I think it is?'

'It's a present. For –' She caught herself in time. 'Damian.'

Fiona clutched at Steve's arm. 'A present! We should have brought a present! We're not normal! We're not fit to be let loose on patients!' Fiona always managed to work into the conversation something about her being a medical student. Just in case anyone had forgotten. 'I'm sure that's your fault. Somehow.'

'Well of course it is. Somehow.'

'And can't this jalopy go at more than ten miles an hour? We're late already.'

Steve was edging the car round the narrow bend at the foot of Worm Hill. 'When you've passed your test, maybe I'll start listening to your advice on negotiating blind corners on single-track roads.'

'Hector used to do this thing, where he wasn't allowed to use the brakes on the way down, and he'd see what speed he could get up to. I used to scream my head off. *Mental.*'

'Playing Russian roulette with your girlfriend's life, and the life of anyone in a vehicle coming the other way. Yep, "mental" is the word. Inbreeding depression in action.'

Helen breathed. 'Hector's a good driver. He passed that advanced test thing –'

'Institute of Advanced Motorists,' said Fiona. 'Although I don't imagine he was pulling stunts like that at the time. Talking of which...' She twisted round in her seat again. 'I mean, presumably Hector's actually turned up this time?'

'I think so.'

And then they were at the junction with the road through Kirkton, and in two more minutes they were turning in at the gates of the

House of Pitfourie, into the cool green tunnel of trees. The car surfed the potholes outside the East Lodge and Helen's bottom bounced onto the hard bit in the seat.

There was another car in front of them: a sleek Jaguar.

On the left side of the drive a big mossy bank rose up, and on the right, through Helen's window, there was a drop down to the Glass. She couldn't see the river from here but when she wound her window down a bit she could hear it hissing and smell its peatiness. She wound the window right down and stuck out her head and looked up; up and up into the leafy branches of the big sycamore where the remains of The Swinger hung – a grey, rotten old bit of rope.

And she was ten years old again, muddy-kneed and fed up, kicking at the shallow hole she and Norrie and his brothers had dug in a hummock in a field, spades discarded on the grass. Looking for buried treasure hadn't turned out to be much fun after all.

Then: 'That's not a burial cairn,' Hector had said, appearing out of nowhere. 'It's just a heap of stuff from the house that used to be here.' He'd been at the talk in the church hall too; a talk by a local historian about Pictish hoards and kings and Bronze Age burial customs. 'I've fixed The Swinger,' he'd told Norrie, and the four boys had gone running off across the field and along the road and down the drive to the House of Pitfourie.

Helen had run after them.

One end of The Swinger had a big knot to sit on, and the other end was tied to a high branch that only Hector was brave enough to climb up to, so if the rope started to work loose, or you were worried it was fraying, you had to throw the knot up into the branches so people couldn't get on it, and ask Hector to fix it.

When she got to the tree they were all up on the wide, low branch that was the jumping-off place, smooth and slippy from years of feet and bums.

'You can go first, Helen,' Norrie offered, holding out The Swinger.

Helen climbed up onto the branch. She had to, or Hector would think she was scared. But then Hector took the rope from Norrie and said, 'Hasn't been test driven yet,' and jumped off the branch, swinging out across the water and right up into the treetops on the other side, and then back again, laughing and shouting, 'Someone else jump on' as he swooped up to the branch, and before she had time to change her mind Helen had leapt into thin air, and Hector had caught her, and she was sitting on top of his legs, her chest pressed against his shirt, his arm holding her safe, her stomach somewhere miles below and the rest of her swooping across the weedy-smelling river with Hector and up and up, across the hard ground on the other side – too far below – and then slower and slower until they were suspended amongst the branches, not going up and not going down, like two birds that had landed there.

Hector had reached out and grabbed one of the leaves, and Helen had too, before they'd started to plunge back down. Hector had thrown his leaf onto the water but she'd pushed hers into the pocket of her shorts.

She still had the brittle crumbs of it in an envelope in her chest of drawers.

I'm never going to be this happy again, she'd thought as she'd grabbed that leaf.

They were out in the sun again, in fields dotted with big trees. Oaks, and chestnuts. Horses twitching their tails and lifting their heads to watch the cars.

Helen put her tongue round her gums and sucked out some spit from her cheeks. Her heart was bumping.

Now they could see the House. A long plain slab with odd gothic bits at the far end.

'It's a bloody castle,' said Steve. 'Turrets and all.'

'That bit's Victorian.' Fiona's tone was patient, like a teacher's. 'Scottish baronial. The original part's the bit in the middle – but the Georgian frontage hides it.'

Before Suzanne had started working at the House, Helen had only been inside three times. Once had been when they'd done a school project on it. The Laird had let the whole class come and look round, and he'd told them about its history, and there'd been juice and Jaffa cakes. She'd been all excited because she'd thought maybe she'd see Hector, but of course he'd been away at his boarding school. But she'd been able to see where he ate his tea and where he must walk down the stairs and things like that. She'd been able to touch door knobs he must touch all the time.

And she'd listened hard to everything the Laird said, even the horrible bits about the feuds between the Forbeses and the Gordons, and the Jacobite rebellion, and people getting their heads cut off and stuck up on spikes. In the library the Laird had shown them a little dark painting of a man, just the top half of him. He was wearing a funny high collar of white lace, and his arms were in black sleeves that disappeared into the background. But on his body he had smooth shiny armour, and you could just see the top of his sword in one of his hands. He looked out at you with evil eyes. The Laird said no one knew for certain who he was, but he was maybe Black John Forbes, who'd lived at the House in the 16th Century.

'He's a bit scary,' Norrie had said.

The Laird had agreed, and said that Black John hadn't been a very nice person. He'd burnt down a castle at Ballochtowie with everyone inside, even little children. And he'd been one of the worst for chopping people's heads off and putting them on spikes.

Suzanne had said, 'Were some of the heads still alive when they got put on the spikes?' and everyone had gone, 'Euuugh *Suzanne*,' and Robin had put his hands round her neck and she'd made her eyes cross.

'Robin and Suzanne,' Mrs Mackay had said. 'Don't be so silly. Robin, stop that *now*. Has anyone got a *sensible* question?'

In the oldest bit of the house, Mrs Mackay had got them to find out how thick the walls were by measuring at the windows. At the little window in the scullery they were nearly four feet thick. Up on the back stairs there were some really narrow windows that had been arrow-slits, and the boys had pretended to be Black John, shooting out arrows.

All of that had been pretty much what she'd expected. But what she hadn't expected was that a lot of things were scruffy. There were chairs that had holes in them and stuffing poking out, and curtains that were all faded and ripped, and the kitchen and scullery and pantry and game larder were cold and dingy and smelt fooshty. When the Laird was talking to some of the others, Norrie had whispered to her to look up at the walls, and she'd seen there were disgusting mushroom things up near the ceiling.

And the gardens had been all overgrown.

They still were. Worse now, even.

Suzanne said there just wasn't the money.

The 'formal' gardens in front of the house consisted of straggly lines of yew hedges and lichen-covered bits of stone and urns, and a little rose garden and some flowerbeds, all with weeds growing up higher than the flowers. At the far end of the house was a terrace and then a big lawn, and behind that a tennis court which was all slimy and mossy. Irina was too embarrassed to ask anyone to come and play there. Past the tennis court was a walled garden with old rotten fruit trees and more weeds, and greenhouses with broken panes.

Irina's family were very rich, but Suzanne said the Laird wouldn't let her ask them for money. They argued about it all the time, and Irina sulked about the place and told Suzanne she was thinking of going into a decline, like Victorian ladies used to. And then he'd be sorry.

Gravel popped under the tyres, and Steve nudged the car into a space between the Jaguar and a Range Rover.

7

The big double doors were standing open, and so was the vestibule door with its etched glass panels, and there were a whole load of people in the hall, talking and laughing. Steve put a hand on Fiona's back and a hand on Helen's, and they stepped across the black and white tiles in the chilly little vestibule and through into the hall.

And then Fiona was telling Irina that Fish was sorry he couldn't make it for the christening, or for lunch, but he was hoping to roll up at some point in the afternoon. And now Irina was grabbing Helen.

'Thank goodness you're here. You're our *saviour*.'

She was *what*?

Irina had been a model when she was Helen's age – at the same time as she was doing Classics at the Sorbonne. She was blonde and leggy and beautiful and brilliant, but Helen couldn't hate her because she was like this, grabbing you and telling you she'd been *just waiting* for *you* to arrive; oh, but a *present*? Oh no, that was so kind of Helen. And then she was taking the present and squeezing it and opening her lovely blue eyes wide.

'It's just a soft animal.'

'Oh but he *loves* soft animals *more than anything*. You *are* a darling.' And Irina's thin arm was round her, pulling her through the people standing around in the hall – Helen looking left and right, but no Hector – and then down the back stairs to the kitchen.

He wasn't here either. Just Mrs MacIver and Lorna and Suzanne. And Stinker. Red-faced and wailing in his big fancy push-chair.

Irina said over the noise: 'He's being a little bastard as usual.'

Suzanne was standing shoving the push-chair back and forwards across the flagstones. 'Had me up all night.'

Mrs MacIver pursed her lips. She was over at the worktop, shovelling something brown into vol au vent cases. Lorna was slicing carrots by the sinks. She was wearing a black dress that was too big at the shoulders and hitched up at the waist. With her neat bob, she looked like a little girl playing at being a grown-up.

She looked round at Helen, eyes cool as they swept her from head to toe and back. Then she smiled. 'Your hair's nice like that.'

Helen realised she'd been holding her breath. Lorna might be different from Rob in every other way, but one thing she had in common with her brother – she noticed everything. And if she'd found something to criticise, she wouldn't have held back.

Irina swooped on the push-chair. 'The one day of the year when it would be good if he could behave himself for a few hours... but no, not going to cooperate, are you, my little stinky one?' She lifted Stinker out and held him against her, jiggling him gently. 'Oh, oh, oh, why the big drama? Lorna, could you show Helen where to go?'

Stinker's noise had stopped. He was staring at Irina, one little hand in her hair. They had the exact same colour of hair, although Irina had a lot more of it.

Lorna wiped her hands on a towel. 'Come on then.'

She followed Lorna along the passage. There was a fresh clump of mushrooms above the door to the pantry: smooth, wet-looking grey hummocks. Every so often the Laird got up on a stepladder and cut them away and fichered about with some chemical stuff you painted on. But they always came back again.

Lorna opened the door into Mrs McIver's sitting room. The damp was kept at bay here by the fire, which Mrs McIver always had blazing away in the evenings. She had a TV and some comfy chairs, and lots of pictures of cottages and fat children. Helen had been expecting to see piles of coats and bags and things, but there was just one dress laid out on the back of a chair. A black dress like Lorna was wearing.

'It probably won't fit you either.'

Helen could feel her face turning bright red.

'Haven't you got some flatties? Those'll be a killer, up and down the stairs about two thousand times.'

She looked down at her new shoes. 'I've got trainers. They're a bit grotty though.'

'You think they care how we look?' Lorna tugged at the material bagging round her waist. 'And we're only getting twenty pounds each for the whole day. Not exactly break-an-ankle-on-the-stairs money, is it?'

The door opened and Suzanne said, 'Mrs MacIver's binding on about the carrots. She says you've to do twice as many again.'

When Lorna had gone, Helen could ask at last: 'Is he here?'

'Didn't you see the fatted calf out the back? He got here yesterday.'

'Where is he?'

Suzanne shrugged. She was looking at the black dress lying over the chair.

Helen chucked down her bag and snatched up the dress, hysteria rising. 'I'm really going to knock his socks off in this, aren't I? What exactly did Irina say to you, about me coming today?'

'She said – I was to ask if you could be here – oh.'

'Yes, *oh.*'

'Oh God. She meant – as a skivvy?' Suzanne was trying not to grin. 'But I thought Hector had got them to invite you?'

'They must have misunderstood. Looks like everyone's had their wires crossed, doesn't it?'

'Oh God. It's like Cinderella in reverse!'

'Yes, it's hilarious.' Helen held the black dress against herself. And then they were both giggling manically, and Helen was twirling, posing – kicking off her shoes and rummaging in her bag for the grotty trainers, slipping them on to complete the ensemble, making a daft Cinderella face.

'Belle of the ball,' snorted Suzanne. 'Stand still and I'll undo you.'

The cream dress slipped down her hips and puddled on the carpet at her feet.

'How long is he staying for? Do you know?'

'Straight off again tomorrow. He –' Suzanne broke off as a voice called:

'*Suzanne!*' Irina.

Suzanne shouted back: 'Coming!' But at the door she stopped, her pixie face suddenly serious. 'You're not Cinderella, and he definitely isn't Prince Charming.'

'Right. Thanks for that insight.' And as Suzanne turned to go: 'He doesn't want his family knowing about us yet. So don't say anything to Irina or anyone.'

'Oh God.'

'He's going to tell them. After we've had a chance to talk. He's organised a party for afterwards, up on the Knock, and we're going to talk properly then.'

'You're going to *talk*.'

'Why do you always have to think the worst of him?'

Suzanne opened her mouth to speak; shut it again; absently turned the silver ring on her finger, a hideous thing in the shape of a snake eating its own tail. In the end, she said only: 'Just be careful.'

When she'd gone, Helen bunched the black dress up in her hands and lifted it over her head. Burrowing with her arms, for a moment she was trapped in its stiff folds, rough against her skin, in the choking claustrophobia of old wardrobes and forty years of other girls, other farmers' daughters with arms and hands made for swinging a pail over a trough, not tilting a bottle of champagne. Or whatever she was supposed to be doing.

Then her head was out again, and she was smiling.

Just be careful.

The new sensible Suzanne.

No more Suzanne Clack the bizzum, the limmer, the girl people shook their heads over and joked about being another of Rob Beattie's good causes. Who'd been thrown out of the Youth Fellowship for slapping Katie Walker's fat face. Suspended from school God knew how many times. Caught nicking Wagon Wheels from the shoppie.

And Suzanne didn't even *like* Wagon Wheels.

She'd probably have ended up in a youth detention centre or something if her social worker hadn't wangled her a place on a childcare course in Glasgow, and she'd surprised everyone by coming top of the class, and getting rave reports from the instructors; and if the Laird hadn't offered her a job as Stinker's nanny.

It's been the making of her, Auntie Ina said.

And Helen supposed it had. But these last few days she'd really wished she could have the old Suzanne back: the Suzanne who used to laugh off Hector's 'reputation' and say bad boys were more fun, who'd got a kick out of the lies and subterfuge and egged Helen on rather than channelling the voice of doom.

A couple of days ago it'd all come to a head. They'd been bathing Stinker. Helen had been wrestling with him for the sponge, which he'd been sucking the water out of as usual, when Suzanne had said:

'Don't you think it's a bit suss, that it has to be this big secret?'

'What?' Although Helen knew fine.

'You and Hector writing to each other.' Suzanne reached past her to yank the sponge away from Stinker. 'Yes,' she told him. 'It's your brother we're talking about.'

Stinker beamed at her, and held out his hands for the sponge.

'It's because of the Laird,' said Helen.

'Na!' said Stinker.

Suzanne picked up the wooden turtle from the side of the bath and started to wind it up. Stinker bounced in anticipation. But when Suzanne put the turtle in the water and let go, he didn't shriek and splash, he just stared as it churned through the water towards him, flippers whirring. Only when it got within grabbing distance did he react, but he didn't grab – he put his hand down into the water and let the turtle butt up against it. Then he took his hand away and the turtle moved forward again and nosed up against his fat little tummy. He laughed as the turtle butted and butted him.

Until it ran down and stopped. Then he looked up at Suzanne.

She lifted the turtle back out. 'But why doesn't he ever call you, or let you call him?'

'They're not allowed to give out their phone numbers for the same reason they can't give out addresses, and have to use a PO box – it would give away where they are.'

'Even James Bond gets to use a telephone.' She started to wind the turtle.

'*He* can't phone *me* in case Mum answers.'

'So what if she did?'

'Because then Mum might tell people, and the Laird might hear about it.'

'*It*. What's *it* anyway? You're penpals. He's never even kissed you.'

'I can't explain it to you.'

'Because a little slapper like me wouldn't understand true love?'

'Because you don't understand about *Hector*. About the kind of person he is.'

'Like you do?'

'Na na na,' said Stinker.

'Yes, I do.' She could feel her face going red. 'I love him. I've always loved him. Even when I thought there was no way he'd ever be interested in me... I didn't want anyone else. I never will want anyone else.'

'Oh God, Helen.'

'That sounds really soppy. I'm not explaining it properly.'

'I do know what it's like to be in love with someone. But – Hector – You think he's some kind of saint, but he's not.'

'I know he's not.'

'You don't know anything! You don't know anything about him.'

'It's not like Rob's a saint either, however much he tries to make out he is.'

'Awow wow wow,' said Stinker.

'God!' And Suzanne was suddenly fierce, telling Stinker to '*Just shut up*' and rounding on her: 'You're such a bairnie, Helen. A lamb to the slaughter.'

'No I'm not.'

Stinker splashed both hands down on the water.

Suzanne stood. 'Right, that's it, you're coming out.'

Stinker had started to girn as Suzanne grabbed him under the arms, and Helen had got the towel, a big soft white one, and wrapped it round Stinker's slippery, writhing little body. Hector's own little brother. She'd hugged him close, and looked over his head at Suzanne, and said, 'Why can't you be pleased for me?'

Suzanne had given her a queer little twisted smile, like one of Mum's when she was trying not to cry, but in Suzanne's case Helen was pretty sure it wasn't tears she was holding back. Then she'd reached into the bath and pulled out the plug, and as the water gurgled away she'd muttered, 'I don't want you getting hurt.'

As if Hector would ever hurt her.

She fastened the belt on the black dress.

What was he thinking, right now? Had someone told him she'd arrived? Was he scanning the room, adjusting his tie, rehearsing what he'd say to her?

In the kitchen, Suzanne had Stinker on her knee and was putting mush in his mouth. Lorna was chopping carrots. Irina was fussing with the vol au vents and going on about her parents. Helen wanted to run past them all and up the stairs and run through all the rooms of the house until she found him.

She walked to the table and smiled at Stinker.

'They're Russian Orthodox,' Irina was saying. 'That means they're practically Catholics. They think it's outrageous to wait over six months between the birth and the christening.'

Mrs MacIver said, without looking at Irina, 'Forbes babies are aye baptised on the closest Sunday to Midsummer's Day. But a year like this, with Midsummer's Day falling on the Sunday itself – that's special.'

'Oh?'

'It means the childie will be blessed. That no evil will come to him.'

Irina hooted. 'Wait till my mother hears *that*. She's convinced there's some dark Celtic ritual at the bottom of it all.'

Mrs MacIver pursed her lips.

'Bacchanalian orgies. Naked dancing round bonfires. *I wish...* Oh God, no I don't. What am I saying? *Joseph Begg and Billy Duncan naked*? Just shoot me now!'

Mrs MacIver's lips tightened so much they disappeared.

'Is this part of the country endemic for some sort of revolting medical condition that makes old men's arses *balloon* sideways to fill those *huge* trousers they all wear? Like elephantiasis, but just their arses?'

'Elephant-arse-is,' spluttered Suzanne.

Mrs MacIver grabbed the platter of vol au vents from under Irina's nose and pushed it at Helen. 'Take these up.'

Irina grinned at Helen, took the platter from her, and put it back down on the worktop. 'First things first. You have to give Stinker his present.'

It was lying on the table. Helen picked it up and made a funny face at Stinker and held it out to him.

He looked back at her with those blue eyes of his, like he couldn't look at her enough, like it was a matter of life and death to him to drink in every detail of her. And then he smiled, and held out his hands, fingers opening and closing on air, and Helen put the present between them and felt her whole face smiling back.

'He can't take the paper off himself,' said Suzanne. 'Can he? Can't do anything for himself.'

Both his little fists were closed on the paper now, and he was focusing all his attention on it, his head bent over, breathing hard. When Suzanne tried to prise his hands off he just held on all the tighter.

'Give it me.'

He held on. 'Ba ba ba ba.'

'Oh for God's sake.' Suzanne snatched at the paper, ripping it, exposing the toy underneath. She pulled it free and dumped it down on the table. 'Something else for you to dribble over.'

'A rhino!' Irina squealed, snatching it up and making it dance in the air towards Stinker, who opened his mouth in delight, and bounced on Suzanne's knee, waving his hands towards the toy. As he grabbed it Irina grinned at Helen and said, 'I told you he'd love it.' Stinker beamed, and held the rhino out to Irina, but she was off, clicking away up the stairs, and Stinker was looking after her with the rhino pressed against his mouth.

'These have to go upstairs,' said Mrs MacIver.

'Oh. Yes. Sorry.' Helen picked up the platter of vol au vents.

The stairs were steep and narrow and dark. At the top there was a long passage with a row of cupboards and then a window, and then the back stairs twisting up to the floor above, and beyond the stairs the green baize door that led out into the hall.

When Helen was half way along the passage, the door opened and the Laird came through.

'Ah. Helen.'

Oh God.

She never knew what to say to him. Even when he'd been so nice after Dad died, all she could think of to say was 'Thank you.' It was no wonder Hector was terrified of him.

He was the same age as Uncle Jim but he looked a lot younger. He wasn't fat. He didn't have a big beer belly. His face was weather-tanned, like Dad's had been. He looked like she imagined Hector might in thirty years' time, only his eyes weren't brown – they were dark blue-grey, the colour of slate.

'Good of you to help out. What's this?' He looked down at the platter.

She didn't even know.

'Mrs MacIver's work?'

'Yes. I'm not sure...'

'We'd need a forensic scientist, I suspect, for a precise identification.' But he took one and put it in his mouth and raised his eyebrows, and went on past her and down the stairs.

She breathed out.

Dad would never hear a bad word about the Laird. He used to say Alec Forbes had been a thran-headed sort of a loon and he was a thran-headed sort of a man, but you wouldn't find a better landlord in all of Aberdeenshire.

And maybe that was true.

After the funeral he'd come back to the house with everyone else, in his beautiful black suit, complete with waistcoat, which had made all the other men's suits look like they didn't fit properly. Mum had asked to speak to him and they'd gone out into the garden, and Helen had listened at the door. Mum had started crying. She'd said she and Helen were moving to Edinburgh to live with Auntie Anne (the first Helen knew), but she wanted to wait until the summer, when Helen would have finished school, but then the rent –

The Laird had said of course he didn't want any rent for the Parks this half-year or the next. That went without saying. And Mum had said no, she would pay, but it might be a bit late. And then he'd said, 'Geordie did so much for the Estate, without any thought of recompense. A few months' rent on the Parks is little enough in exchange.'

Tears prickled at the back of her nose.

Someone was coming up the stairs from the kitchen. Very slowly.

Lorna. With a tray of drinks in tall glasses. The tip of her tongue was visible between her lips, and her legs were bent at the knees, as if the closer she was to the floor the shorter distance the glasses would have to fall.

'Put them down here a minutie,' Helen suggested.

Lorna slid the tray onto the windowsill. 'We should pour them out up here, shouldn't we? We should bring up the bottles and the cartons and the glasses, and pour them out here.'

'That would make more sense. What's in them?'

'That's champagne... and that's orange juice... and that's a mixture of the two in the same glass. Want a taste?'

They finished one between them, leaving the empty glass on the windowsill. Then Lorna bent her knees and picked up the tray, and Helen, balancing the platter on her arm, pulled open the baize door.

Noise, suddenly. People talking and laughing. Jennifer Gordon, in too much eye make-up, looking at her and saying something to her mum out of the side of her mouth and laughing. Kids chasing each other. The double doors into the dining room on one side of the hall and the big drawing room on the other were opened up, so they had a running track three rooms long.

A girl came rocketing out of the dining room and banged into Helen and the platter went flying. Vol au vents filled the air. The platter tumbled and bounced once, on its end, on the Persian carpet and then flopped over.

An ironic cheer went up, and Jennifer shrieked on a laugh: 'Oh my *God!*'

Helen scanned the faces turned towards her.

None of them was Hector's.

'Nice one, Iona!' said Lorna.

Iona Penney put her hand over her mouth and looked at Helen and said, 'Sorry!' through the hand, but Helen could tell from her eyes that she was grinning like mad.

'Right, you can help me pick them up.'

'Can't. We're going. My Grandpa's dead and Mum's crying.'

She ran off. Helen gaped at Lorna.

'Willie Duff. Not *here*; the food's not *that* bad. Ten days ago. Lung cancer. Funeral's tomorrow.'

Lorna always knew who had died, and where, and how, because of her dad being the minister. She was looking down now at the vol au vent casualties. 'I'll come back and help you when I've got rid of these.'

Helen got down on her knees and started putting the vol au vents back on the platter. Through the doors to the drawing room she could see Auntie Ina's bright green back.

Where was he?

As she was reaching for a vol au vent, a graceful foot in a yellow pump came down on top of it and moved on, followed by a feminine leather loafer and a Sloaney voice saying, 'I *know*, I *know!*'

Steve squatted down next to her. 'What's the story?'

She scraped at the mess on the carpet with a fingernail. 'I – made a mistake.' She turned away to deposit the remains on the platter. 'They meant for me to come as a helper. Not a guest.'

'And here's me thinking slavery was abolished in the 19th Century.'

'We're getting paid.'

He picked up the platter and, before Helen could stop him, stood and tipped its contents into the big urn on the table. 'Which is more than can be said for the "guests" who've been summoned to kowtow. Look at those poor sods.' He meant Charlie Duncan and his elderly father, standing together by the foot of the main staircase, holding their glasses of champagne as if they weren't quite sure what to do with them.

'Charlie Duncan was at school with the Laird. And Dad and Uncle Jim.'

When he was nine years old, Charlie Duncan had set the Laird's breeks on fire. They'd been striking matches and trying to fart on them.

'Primary school, I mean.'

'I didn't think you meant Eton.'

People from towns and cities – they didn't get it, what living in a place like Pitfourie actually meant. In biology, when Mrs Keith had explained about how plants had to adapt especially well to their environment because they were rooted in the soil and couldn't move about, Helen had thought of Pitfourie. *We're like plants. We've had to adapt ourselves to our environment, to each other, because we're rooted here, whether we like it or not.*

There'd been Duncans at Boghead for two hundred years.

She took the empty platter from Steve. And, through the door to the dining room, she saw him.

8

He was standing by the table with Fiona. He was wearing a grey suit, a white shirt, and a blue tie.

He looked different. His shoulders were bigger. His face looked tougher, like the bones in it had got stronger. He looked the way a soldier should. And so handsome.

But he could be the ugliest person in the world and it wouldn't matter.

'Hail the conquering hero,' said Steve. 'Although I doubt he's conquered much more than the parade ground at Aldershot.'

'He's been in Bosnia.'

Every time anything about Bosnia came on the News her heart started thumping. Once when the newsreader said, 'A British soldier has been killed in peace-keeping operations in Bosnia,' everything had gone splotchy and grey, and she'd had to put her head over her knees. 'Helen? What's wrong?' Mum had rubbed her back. 'What if it's Hector?' And Mum had smiled. 'If it was Hector we'd know by now – there's no way the BBC's going to beat Ina to *that* sort of news.' And that was true, but Helen had felt shaky and strange and sick all the rest of the day. At night she'd taken the radio to bed to listen to the World Service. And she'd prayed and prayed, *Please God, let it not be Hector*, until they'd announced the soldier's name.

And she'd cried and cried and cried.

Why would anyone want to be a soldier?

She wanted to run at him, to hug him so tight, to never let him go back there again. To keep him safe with her forever. Instead she walked away, through the people – Norrie smiled at her, but she didn't stop – to the back of the hall. She pushed open the baize door and then she was in the cool of the long passage and she was alone.

For about two seconds.

'Helen.' Irina's voice, from the stairs to the first floor; Irina's sleek blonde head catching the light as she came down into the passage, a white bundle balanced on her hip: Stinker in his christening robe, his face fat and blotchy and sulky, like a little grumpy old man's.

'I don't suppose you know where Suzanne's got to?'

'No.'

'In that case, can you be a darling and take him to meet his public? I have to get ready for church.'

Her hair was perfect. Her face was perfect. The single row of pearls, the turquoise silk sheath, the long tanned legs, the strappy heels – everything about her was perfect. What was there to *get ready*? Maybe she meant she had to go to the loo.

'And when you find Suzanne, can you tell her we're leaving in ten minutes?'

Helen nodded.

'Where are those lovely smart shoes you had on?'

'I thought these would be more practical. But I'll change back again for church.'

'Oh sweetie, I'm sorry, but you'll need to stay and help with lunch and everything. The christening's going to be *utter tedium* anyway... But *yes please* to the lovely shoes!'

'I'll go and get –'

'But not *right now*. Can you take him?'

The long robe trailed as Irina lifted Stinker towards her. Helen took him against her left side and he immediately clutched on to her collar, legs clamping round her waist, the robe bumfling up a bit between him and Helen's hip.

'He's in a *foul* mood still.' Irina bent over him, but then quickly straightened as he belched and some sick came out onto his chin. 'Eee. Do you have a tissue?' And she swept back up the stairs.

Helen didn't have a tissue. She used a trailing bit of christening robe.

Stinker looked like he was about to start crying.

'In a foul mood, are you? Hmm?' And she whispered: 'My little cushie-doo,' and kissed him.

Back in the hall, people crowded round her, bobbing their faces at Stinker and saying, 'Oh, the craiter.' One of the Sloane girls said, 'He's going to be a proper little heartbreaker. Aren't you, Mr *Gorgeous*?'

Stinker turned his blotchy face against Helen's neck. She edged down the hall.

'Helen! I was wondering where you'd got to.' Rob stepped in front of her. 'Where've you been hiding?'

'Nowhere. In the kitchen.'

'No rest for the wicked, eh? Hey hey, little man.' He bent over Stinker. 'Ready for your big day? Ready to scream the church down when the nasty man pours water on your head? Yup, I reckon so.'

Get away from him!

She forced a smile. 'He's only crabby because he's teething.'

'Tell me about it. I don't think Suzanne's had more than four hours' sleep a night for about three weeks.' He fingered the big square buckle on his belt, and leant in close. 'Although that's not just down to Stinker.'

She went to move past him, but someone else was blocking her way.

Someone in a grey suit.

She looked up.

Hector smiled at her, and put a brown hand on Stinker's head. 'Hello.'

'Hello.'

His smile got wider. Her heart was hammering at a hundred miles an hour. She felt a bit odd. What if she fainted? What if she dropped Stinker, right in front of him?

Rob was grinning. 'Well, I think this –'

'Piss off, Rob.' Hector didn't even look at him.

'Well, and it's nice to see you too Hector.'

When Rob had moved away, Hector said, 'I've been looking for you. You've been helping out downstairs?'

'Yes.'

Stinker was slipping off her hip. She hitched him back up. He started to girn, and suddenly reached out his hands to Hector.

'Come here then, you little brat.' Hector lifted him off Helen and swung him up above his head. The christening robe streamed out behind him like he was some sort of superhero baby, and he choked and spluttered and girned all the more.

A man with a fruity voice said, 'That's the way, Hector – if in doubt, apply a bit of centrifugal force.'

'Hasn't he just been fed?' said a woman.

'We'll send you the dry cleaning bills.'

Irina's mother was laughing. 'What's he doing to you, Shoo-Shoo?'

Hector was laughing too. 'Oh God, take him.'

'Come to your old granny.'

Zenaida wasn't like any granny Helen had ever seen. She looked like one of those women in black and white films, slender and elegant and beautiful, grey hair swept up into a plain gold clasp with a diamond at the end of it.

'It worked before,' Hector muttered at Helen. 'The flying baby thing. Looks like I've lost my touch.'

She loved the way he spoke. When she was little she had thought of his accent as 'English' and 'posh', but as she'd got older she'd picked up the nuances in it, like how he pronounced 'r' in words where English people wouldn't, and realised that someone like Prince Charles would probably think Hector and the Laird had broad Scottish accents.

All she could do was smile. Stinker was still whimpering, and Zenaida was jiggling him and walking him about, and people were crowding round her.

Hector said, 'I'm so sorry about your father.'

Helen nodded.

'I'm sorry not to have been here, for the funeral and so on –'

'I didn't expect you to –'

'Did you get my letter?'

'Yes.' Silly, to feel shy of him, when he knew more of her innermost thoughts than anyone else here. She smiled. 'I've brought warm clothes.'

He lifted his eyebrows just like the Laird had.

But then Rob was back, flicking a look at Hector and saying, 'You know Helen and Vivienne are leaving the Parks?'

'Yes. I had heard.' He still didn't look at Rob.

'In August.'

'We're going to Edinburgh,' said Helen. Like he didn't know the address and phone number and the name of Auntie Anne's dog. 'I've got a place at University there. To do archaeology.'

'Aha. Archaeology? Pictish kings the length and breadth of Scotland will be trembling in their barrows. Skeletal hands closing convulsively on crumbling treasure chests.'

She laughed, too loudly.

Hector cupped his hand under her elbow. 'If you've a couple of minutes to spare – I wonder if you could help me with something?'

From the place he was touching her, little shivers were going up her arm and down her body. Her throat had closed up. She couldn't breathe properly. She managed to nod and smile.

He guided her down a corridor and opened a door and took his hand away, standing back for her to go into the room first.

It was the Laird's study. Ancient leather chairs with patched arms; the smell of wood ash and tobacco; dark red walls covered in Victorian and Edwardian photos of estate workers, mainly, posed in rows in front of the house. Somewhere in one of them was her Great-Great-Uncle Willie.

Hector closed the door and all the noises from the hall were muffled and she heard the tick... tick of the clock on the wall.

This room probably hadn't changed since those photos were taken, since Willie was walking past outside with a hoe on his shoulder, and the sound of his whistling was coming in through the open window.

Hector went past her to the table under the other window, sunlight streaming hot across its shiny dark wood.

'Take a look at this.'

This was a book, its paper thick and yellowy and rough at the edges. On the right-hand page there was an engraving of a bonfire, with a man standing beside it holding a flaming branch, and, in the dark behind, shadowy figures and faces.

He lifted the front cover so she could see the title:

Customs of the North-East

'Midsummer's Eve rituals. Mr Cranston says that even in the 1940s there were still some farmers who kept a midsummer vigil – staying up all night by the fire, making sure it kept burning through the shortest night. Have you heard of that?'

Why was he talking about this stuff? Was he worried about his father – that maybe he'd come in and find them together – or was he as nervous as she was?

He smiled at her. The clock ticked. He was standing very close. She breathed in the scent of him, clean warm skin and the very faint trace of something sharp – not aftershave, but maybe shaving cream? Or soap?

And at last she could speak. 'I can't believe you're actually here.'

'The ghost at the feast?' His mouth quirked. 'No, well, it's –'

And then the door opened and Suzanne was puffing, 'Where's Stinker?'

'Stinker?' said Hector.

'Okay: Damian.'

'You call him Stinker?' Hector frowned at the same moment as Helen said, 'Zenaida's got him.'

'*Irina* calls him Stinker,' said Suzanne. 'Surprised he's not being christened it. God, can you imagine Mr Beattie? "I baptise this child *Stinker*"!' She came over to the table. 'What's that?'

Well, Helen had wished for the old Suzanne back, and here she was: eyes bright, face shining, voice higher and louder than usual. Helen risked a glance at Hector, but he was looking down at the book, speaking about midsummer rituals again.

Helen tilted her head towards the door, hoping Suzanne would get the message.

'I'm planning a midsummer vigil of our own,' Hector was saying, 'up on the Knock. A bonfire in the stone circle… Bit of a party, basically.'

'Brill!' said Suzanne.

'And I'm going to need a script.' He picked up a sheet of paper from the table with a couple of paragraphs on it in his neat, sloping writing. Neater and smaller than in his letters – less uneven. When she wrote to him, she often had to go back with Tippex where her hand had gone wobbly with emotion. It had never even occurred to her that he might have the same problem. She could feel her face burning.

He was going on: 'I've got the basic superstition side covered – the vigil, the souls of the dead, etc. – but it's not exactly shivers-up-the-spine stuff. What I need are some "real-life" stories about people who've seen ghosts while keeping a vigil, or gone suddenly psycho, or who've been found mysteriously dead in the morning…'

Helen smiled. 'Or disappeared, never to be seen again.'

'Yep, I knew you were the girl for the job.'

'But – I don't know of anything like that that's actually happened.'

'Of course you don't. It's all nonsense. But you can come up with something convincing, can't you? Something suitably grue-some?'

'Well. There was Sandie Milne, at Greenmires. He shot himself.'

'Or did he?' leered Suzanne.

'Aha.' Hector was writing on the paper. 'When was this?'

'In the sixties, I think,' said Helen. 'You could say it happened on Midsummer's Eve. No one's going to know if it did or not. You could say there was always some doubt about it being suicide because the shotgun was found a bit away from the body... and the fire was out.'

'He always kept the vigil, but on this night he let the fire go out...'

Helen grinned. 'And the evil spirits got him.'

The door opened. The Laird came only half into the room before immediately turning back out again. 'Hector, we need to get off to the church.'

'Okay, with you in a sec. Just, um, giving Helen the numbers of some people I know in Edinburgh.'

'People?'

'You don't know them.'

'Mmm. And I don't imagine Helen will want to either.' He shut the door.

Suzanne looked at Hector with owl eyes. 'So your dad doesn't know about this party?'

'Best not, I think, for the sake of his blood pressure – and mine, for that matter.'

'Are we invited? And Rob?'

'You and Helen, of course.' He folded the piece of paper and tucked it inside his suit jacket. 'On the one condition that you *don't* bring Rob.'

Before Suzanne could say anything to that, the door came open again. Irina this time. 'Suzanne. Helen. Where is he?'

'Stinker?' said Suzanne.

Quickly, before Suzanne could add something like *God knows*, Helen said, 'Your mother took him.'

'Okay.' Irina was studying Suzanne too closely. 'And what about his things? Come on girls, let's move. Hector, can you take my parents in your car?'

'Yes, of course.' As he moved towards the door he looked back at Helen with a smile that seemed casual, careless – until she met his eyes, and felt her face flush all over again.

The hall was emptying. Car engines were turning over outside, and through the open door Helen could see a convoy heading off up the drive.

'Hey, you know what we should do?' said Suzanne. 'Get an eye pencil and write "666" on Stinker. What do you reckon Mr Beattie would do, if he went to pour on the holy water and there was "666" on the kid's head?'

Helen pushed open the baize door, her own hysteria rising. 'The sooner we get some water into you the better.'

9

It was a queer feeling, to be with all these people, all the noise they were making, and sit with her back to the fire and look down the steepness of the hill over the tops of the pines and the birks to where the last of the light was streaked across the sky. The dark outlines of the hills stood out against it: Ben Aven and Tom na Creiche, and behind them Monadh Caoin and Morven and Lochnagar.

This must have been what it was like in the Bronze Age, sitting by the fire with your tribe and looking out at the Simmer Dim. There must have been a clearing here then, too, to put the stone circle in. It was a good place for it – a wide expanse of flat ground above a drop, so the trees down the hill didn't block your view and you could see straight over their tops to the hills and the sky.

The air was still and soft and smelt of pine, and the midgies were out, so everyone was clustered round the fire in the middle of the stones. It wouldn't get properly dark, not tonight, not even at midnight – except under the trees, where the shadows were blackening. There was something eerie about the quality of the light. Eerier than moonlight. The sky wasn't black but a faded china blue, and the hills, the trees, the grass of the clearing weren't shades of grey but shadowed versions of their daytime colours. And there was something weird about the way things in the distance had blurred and darkened, but she could see, starkly, the individual blades of grass at her feet; the words on the piece of paper in her hand.

She turned back to the fire, to the brightness that made everything beyond it recede into black, into how the night should be.

She'd changed into her jeans and jumper, but she wished she'd known Hector was going to bring some of his own clothes for people to put on. One of the Sloanes was wearing his Aran jersey, Jennifer Gordon had a blue and white Norwegian one, and Fiona had grabbed a waxed jacket.

They'd left the cars and the Land Rovers on the track and carted all the stuff up the stalkers' path – the rugs and the bottles and the boxes of food left over from the official party, and the bag of potatoes to roast in the fire. And a can of paraffin, which Norrie had been going on about.

'The ground's gey dry. If we use that we'll set the whole place up.'

'Go for it,' said Suzanne.

Norrie had given her a quick, wary look, as if he really did think Suzanne was capable of deliberately setting the hillside ablaze.

She was kneeling now at the fire, arguing with Lorna about the best way to cook the potatoes. Foil, or no foil. Lorna was saying they burnt away to nothing unless you wrapped them in foil, and Suzanne was insisting they tasted better without, naked as God intended.

Helen closed her fingers on the paper. She'd left her glass in a dip in the ground while she went round the circle looking at the stones, and when she got back she'd found this piece of paper tucked under it, and two lines of Hector's sloping writing:

Meet me at the Land Rover – the one I was driving – at the stroke of midnight!

It would be midnight in an hour.

When they were alone together, what would happen? Would they just talk, and maybe kiss, or would he want to do it? In the Land Rover?

She knew she wanted him to touch her. When he'd touched her elbow it'd been like her skin had little wires in it sending the feeling of his hand tingling through her whole body, and she'd wanted him to keep touching her, to move his hand on her skin – But actually having sex... Would he expect her to know what to do?

Well, she *did* know what to do. You couldn't grow up on a farm and not know which bits went where.

She looked out at the dark hills, out in the direction of the Parks, and thought of her little bed under the eaves. The next time she got under those covers, would she be different? How would it feel, to have done it?

Everything was changing. Soon some intruder family would be

living at the Parks, running water into the kitchen sink, shutting the back door and walking across the yard. And they would probably take out the old doors in the byre that Dad had patched and put new ones in, and paper over all the gouges and cracks in the plaster above her bed – the mark that looked like a dog on his hind legs, and the witch's face.

When she came back to visit at the Mains she'd have to see them living there, the intruders, when she should be able to run up the track and into the yard and see Dad leaning on a graip and smiling at her and saying, 'Well, Hel'nie.'

She turned back to the fire, and Norrie said, 'Do you want some of this?'

He was holding a bottle over her empty glass. She must have drunk all the cider that was in it. She nodded.

'No Rob,' said Norrie.

Someone said, 'Shame.'

Fiona laughed. 'What do you reckon the Church of Scotland line is on midnight shenanigans in stone circles? On a Sunday? I'm guessing *burn in hell*?'

'Not exactly a ticket to heaven, certainly,' said Steve.

It was just as well Suzanne had gone round to the other side of the fire and couldn't hear this. But Helen kept her voice low. 'Hector told him not to come.'

Steve poked at the fire. 'Why, what's wrong with the guy?'

'Oh, nothing really,' said Fiona. 'He can just be a bit... If you're in a group and Rob's there, you subtly try not to get landed next to him.'

Steve chucked a stick into the blaze. 'Or not so subtly? How do you go about telling someone they're not welcome at a party because their social skills aren't up to scratch? What exactly did Hector say to him?'

' "Piss off you little shit"?' said Norrie.

Fiona yelped, and Helen and Norrie grinned at each other.

Everyone looked like they were in an Old Master painting, the firelight flaring on Helen's glass, Tom Strachan's hands taking something from one of the boxes, a beautiful girl's face, Fiona's face as she leant forward over the fire.

'Midsummer's Eve,' said a menacing voice, and someone screamed.

Hector was standing between the two tallest stones in the circle.

'I hope you all realise what we're doing. What it means to light a vigil fire in a stone circle on the summer solstice...'

He stopped, and the wind came shivering through the trees. Someone snorted out a laugh, but Hector's voice, pitched low, cut through it:

'Midsummer's Eve. When the veil between the worlds of the living and the dead weakens and thins... When the dead can visit the living... When hallowfires must be lit and lanterns set in windows to ward off evil spirits, and call home the souls of the dead.' He stepped back, outside the circle, and began to move round it, appearing and disappearing as he passed behind the stones.

'For God's sake Hector,' said Fiona.

'I suppose,' said Steve, 'you're going to tell us this is where the evil spirits hang out? In stone circles?'

'Where else? You have to take care where you light your hallowfire. In your own grate – fine. There it acts as protection. But light one in a stone circle and you can call up the Sith, the fairy-daemons, from their hidden barrows and cairns. The Sith, who lead travellers from the road; who steal babies from their cradles and substitute changelings; who murder men as they sleep.'

One of the girls giggled.

'The Sith are no laughing matter, Perdita. They come upon you without any warning – other than, sometimes, the faint sound of the bells hanging from the harnesses of their phantom horses.'

Fiona grinned at Helen across the fire, and snuggled against Steve.

'Oh, it's all nonsense, of course... But as recently as the turn of the century, orra loons were sent round the farm boundaries with flaming torches to ward off evil. On this night, at Mains of Clova, at Unthank, at every farm in the parish there would have been torches moving through the dark.'

Norrie said in her ear: 'What a load of crap.'

'No – it's true,' Helen whispered back.

Hector's voice became brisk. 'But that's all just superstitious nonsense. No one believes it any more.'

Another long silence.

'Or do they? As recently as the 1960s, Sandie Milne still kept a vigil at Greenmires. Every Midsummer's Eve, when the work of the farm was done, he'd set a fire in the grate in the little sitting room off the kitchen, and switch on the wireless, and make the first of many cups of coffee to keep himself awake through the night.

'When his wife Betty was alive she'd sit up with him and they'd chat and keep each other awake – but since she'd died he'd kept the vigil alone. He'd set a candle in the window, though he laughed about it and called himself a silly old bugger. But still he hoped... Maybe this year she'd come back to him. The dead soul of his Betty.

'No one knows exactly what happened on Midsummer's Eve 1964. But on the morning of June 22nd, farm workers John Dunbar and Willie Duff found the old man lying dead on the hearth, a carving knife in his throat. A bottle of whisky and a glass sat on a sidetable by his chair.

'And the ashes were cold in the grate. The fire had been out for hours.

'The official verdict was suicide. There were no signs of a break-in. All the windows were snibbed, and the doors locked from the inside. The two farm workers had to break a window to get into the house after looking through the sitting room window and seeing Sandie motionless on the floor.

'So no foul play was suspected.

'But if you read the Procurator Fiscal's report, you'll see that there were some odd anomalies. There were no tentative "test" wounds on the old man's neck, as are usually found when someone stabs themselves. Even more oddly, there were no fingerprints on the handle of the knife, only a strange powdery deposit. John Dunbar and Willie Duff were questioned about this – had either of them, in the first moments of shock, tried to remove the knife from the old man's neck? Perhaps with a dirty rag, such as farm workers often carry in their pockets? That would explain how the old man's fingerprints were wiped from the handle of the knife.

'Both denied having done any such thing. But the report surmises that 'interference' with the scene before the police arrived must have been to blame for the lack of fingerprints on the handle of the knife.

'Two more odd things were *not* mentioned in the report. One, which spread like wildfire through the parish, was that, when the two men turned the body over, they found a look of terror frozen on Sandie Milne's face. And the other... that night, in the small hours,

Sandie's nearest neighbour, Jenny McKenzie at Newbigging, had heard the sound, faint but clear, of bells, moving through the woods behind her house.'

He stopped, and there was no sound but the crackling of the fire and the wind sifting the pines behind him. No one spoke. No one moved.

Then Fiona laughed, and reached forward with a stick to flick her potato from the fire and inspect it. 'And if you believe that you'll believe anything.'

Hector laughed too, coming out of the shadows and grabbing a can from the cool box. 'Makes a good story though, doesn't it?'

'Brilliant!' giggled Jennifer.

'Hanging on every word,' said Steve.

As he passed round behind Helen, Hector leant over her and whispered: 'I felt the Sith would be more likely to use a knife than a shotgun.'

She cricked her neck to smile up at him. 'Oh, definitely.'

Hector took a seat on the Sloane girls' rug, and one of them asked, 'But what do Sith actually look like?'

'Like ordinary people. From a distance, at least. No one who's seen them up close has lived to tell the tale.'

'Ooh.' Sloane Girl wriggled closer to him.

'Oh come on,' said Lorna.

'No way did Willie Duff ever do anything as interesting as finding a guy with a knife in his neck,' said Suzanne. 'You just put him in the story because folk have been talking about him. Because it's his funeral tomorrow.'

'And you think that's a coincidence?' said Hector. 'That he's died *at midsummer*?'

Suzanne snorted.

Lorna shook her head. 'He died over a week ago.'

'What's a week, to an evil spirit condemned to wander the Earth for all eternity?'

Fiona laughed, and pushed her potato back into the fire. 'Fish once saw a ghost in our garage. He was ten years old and had just sucked all the centres out of a box of liqueur chocolates, but he swears he saw it, a "shape" moving through the wall.'

Suzanne snorted again. 'Where is Fish, anyway?'

Hector was lighting a cigarette. 'He phoned earlier to make his apologies. Apparently he'd rather sit in a pub making small talk with lawyers.' He leant back, exhaling.

Fish had a job in a lawyer's office over the summer.

Lorna came and plomped herself down next to Helen, and whispered: 'That's dope they're smoking. Suzanne and those airheads, and Hector.'

'Are you sure?'

'You can smell it from here. Hector's been handing it out like sweeties. And that Tom and Perdita are snorting something. I've had enough of this. Do you think Norrie would drive me home?'

'He can't. He's been drinking.'

'Great. So we have to stay up here all night until someone's sobered up enough to get behind the wheel?'

'That seems to be the general idea. I think –'

'Shh!' One of the Sloane girls had jumped to her feet. 'Everyone be quiet!'

Suzanne was the last to shut up. As she stopped talking, a metallic jangling sound drifted, very faintly, down through the trees.

'Oh my *God*,' whispered Sloane Girl.

Someone laughed, and was quickly shooshed.

The sound was louder now. The high, cheerful sound of little bells.

Hector stood, and called out: 'Okay, very funny, Norrie.'

'*Norrie's here*,' Helen hissed.

Hector turned to look at them. The firelight picked out the line of his jaw, his nose, the brightness of his eyes.

'Well who's missing? Tom?'

'I'm here.'

Everyone looked around at each other. 'There's no one missing.'

'Shit.'

'Oh God, *what's that?*'

Jennifer screamed, shot to her feet, tripped over something, fell over, scrambled round the fire. Two others followed her.

In the space behind where they'd been sitting, between the stone circle and the trees, something was moving. A figure. Helen grabbed at Lorna, and Lorna grabbed at Helen, and Hector shouted, 'Get back behind the fire!' and he was snatching something up and jabbing its end in the blaze.

Flames shot out. Helen smelt paraffin, and saw that Hector was holding up a branch with rags tied round it at the top, and they were covered in flames. But the sudden flaring light only made it harder to see beyond it.

The figure was still moving.

'Who's that?' said Hector.

The figure stopped.

Then:

'Death,' came groaning through the dark, and suddenly the figure was flapping, and leaping into the stone circle, and coming round the fire at them, and it had no face, and it held up something that glinted, a knife, and everyone was screaming, Helen's throat was raw with it, and then it stopped and flung back the hood of its cloak and tore a black oval from its face, and it was screaming with laughter, and it was Fish.

And then everyone was shouting at once.

'You bastard!' said Fiona, and ran at him.

'Ow ow ow,' said Fish as she thumped him.

Hector had dropped the flaming branch. He was laughing so much he was bent over, gasping, and Steve was saying, 'Arse.'

'How is that *funny*?' yelled Suzanne, but then she was laughing too.

Norrie had the black oval in his hands. 'Painted cardboard.'

Typical Norrie – everyone else was going mental, and he wanted to know what the mask was made of.

After that Helen remembered everyone getting more drinks and the girls giggling and giggling and she found her glass of cider, and before she knew it she had drunk it all and Norrie had got her some more, and she was smiling all over her silly face, lying on the rug and looking up at the eerie pale-blue sky.

Then: 'I feel like *shit*,' Suzanne was growling, like it was Helen's fault, collapsing beside her on the rug and rolling slowly onto her front.

Helen started to laugh, and Suzanne grabbed her and said into her face: 'Helen. You *stupid cow*.'

On the other side of the fire they'd lit more torches. Tom had one, and Fish, and Hector. They were weaving in and out of the standing stones, acrid smokiness trailing behind them, people getting up to join on the end of the line.

When Helen looked back at Suzanne she saw that her T-shirt had ridden up, exposing the white skin of her narrow back, luminous in the light of the fire – and the dark marks that leapt across it.

'What are those?' Helen grabbed at the T-shirt but Suzanne, drunk as she was, got there first, pulling it back down over the bare skin.

'Bruises. Fell against the edge of the table in the nursery.'

Helen frowned. 'Not while you were holding Stinker?'

'Course not.' And, defiantly: 'Okay, so I'd had a bit to drink, I'm a stupid cow, but *so are you*.'

Helen sighed. 'What time is it?'

Suzanne's forehead had dipped to rest on the rug, the mussy halo of hair hiding her face. 'Dunno.'

Helen moved her watch's face, angling it to the light from the fire. Ten to twelve. She stood, and looked across the fire, not expecting to see Hector this time.

But there he was, striking off across the clearing like the Pied Piper with everyone following behind. Fish was still in his stupid cloak. When they were in the woods, Hector would give someone the torch and sneak back, she supposed, and down to the Land Rover.

'I have to go,' she told the back of Suzanne's head.

Suzanne didn't look round, or say anything, or give any sign that she'd heard.

She found the stalkers' path, and then lost it. After that it was hazy. She remembered being in the darkness of the trees, stumbling, ducking unseen branches that snagged in her hair, and the relief at finding the path again further down the slope. The path being too steep; tripping, slipping, bumping; finding her feet again. A hand on her arm, pulling her off the path, and another hand over her mouth, and she couldn't breathe.

And that was all she remembered.

10

Helen didn't want to open her eyes. She wanted to go back down into that warm, blurry place where nothing made sense but it didn't matter, where everything happened a long way away and was nothing to do with her.

But there were voices, very close.

A woman: 'Don't you *dare* tell me what I need to do!'

There was a smell of sweat, and hot disinfectant, and soap. A hand suddenly clamped round Helen's right arm and squeezed it, hard.

'Mrs Clack!' said a man.

'Ina, *stop it*!' Mum?

The hand squeezed again, even harder, and then let go.

'Mrs Clack, I'm going to have to ask you to leave.'

'I'm not going anywhere!'

'It's all right. Please. Let her stay.' Yes, it *was* Mum. It was Mum. 'Ina, sit down and let's –' And then much closer, much softer: 'Oh dearie, dearie…' A hand again, very gentle this time, closing round Helen's. 'It's all right, you're all right… Can someone get a doctor?'

Helen opened her eyes. One of her eyes. The lid of the other wouldn't move – something was pressing it down tight. It was hot and stinging and itchy. She was lying down, and Mum's face, thin and pale, was leaning over her, and next to it Auntie Ina's, big and red and shiny. There was a white ceiling above them, dazzling.

'Shh,' said Mum. 'You're all right. You're safe now.'

But she hadn't been?

Something crashing into her, the scream knocked out of her, an arm rough round her neck, an animal grunt, a hand pressed over her mouth and her nose –

That had really happened?

'My eye's funny.' She put up a hand to feel it, and her fingers touched skin too soon – a big tight swollen mass from her eyebrow to her cheek, like her eye had inflated to fill the whole socket. 'What's wrong with it?'

'Your eye's fine – the flesh round about's just a bit swollen. And you've got some bruises, and maybe a cracked rib – and you've had a knock on the head that's made you very sleepy and woozy. But the doctor says there's nothing to worry about.'

'What happened to me?'

And suddenly Auntie Ina's face was huge, and she had her hands on either side of Helen's face and Helen could feel her wedding ring digging into her cheek, and her eyes were staring, the skin round them puffed up and red.

'*Where is she*? You tell us *right now* Helen! *What have you done*?'

There was movement and voices, behind Ina, and the ring dug in all the more and then the hands were gone, and Auntie Ina's face was gone, and instead Mum was smiling at her, stroking her hair, telling her to never mind Ina, she was worried about Suzanne and she didn't know what she was doing or saying.

'Suzanne?'

'*Where is she?*' Helen couldn't see Auntie Ina now but she could still hear her. 'Oh please *where is she?*'

11

There was a bald man in a white coat, asking her questions, his fingers cool, his eyes kind. She remembered him, vaguely, from before – so that had been real too. His voice was very calm. Mum asked him if Helen could have a drink of water, and he said, 'Of course.' The water in the blue-tinted glass was lovely and cool, but Helen's teeth chinked on the edge of it and she couldn't get her mouth to work properly. Some of the water spilt on the sheet.

She sank back down on the pillow. Her head felt massive. Heavy.

Mum wiped Helen's chin and patted her lips and whispered, 'Okay?'

Helen tried to smile.

Another man's voice, a loud voice, not the doctor's: 'And don't let anyone else in until I tell you otherwise. Other than medical staff, obviously.'

She turned her head. A man had come in and was sitting down on a chair next to the bed. Quite young. His legs were big, not fat but big like a rugby player, and the suit trousers were pulled tight across his thighs. In one hand he had a little black notebook, the kind with a padded cover. He smiled at her. 'Well, Helen. Hello.'

'Hello.'

'This is DS Stewart.' It was Mum's tight, polite voice, the one she used for people she didn't like. 'He's a policeman. He needs to ask you some questions, dearie. It's very important.'

Above Mum's pale face there was a strip light, too bright. There were black dots along the inside of the light casing where insects must have crawled in and not been able to get out again and died.

Her right arm and side ached.

She had a question to ask too. An important one.

'How are you feeling?' said DS Stewart.

'A bit weird. Thank you.'

'Would you like another drink of water?' Mum was still holding the glass. There was a yellow plastic jug with one of those flip-up lids on the table by the bed.

Yes, another drink of water.

But she had to ask her question first.

'Has something happened to Suzanne?'

DS Stewart opened the notebook. The pages were lined in green. 'We were hoping you could tell us that.'

'But I can't. I don't know. How –'

'All right,' Mum shushed her, stroking her hair.

'How did I get here?'

'You were found lying unconscious,' said Mum. 'And Hector and Fiona and Steve brought you here to the hospital.'

The man called DS Stewart was staring at her. 'Do you know where Suzanne might be, Helen?'

'No.'

'Did you have an argument? A fight?'

'No!'

Mum squeezed her hand. 'No one's going to be angry. We all know what Suzanne can be like.'

Helen touched the swollen flesh at her eye.

'Helen?' DS Stewart's voice was suddenly loud in her ears, but she didn't think he'd raised it – it was like the volume on the TV had been turned up. 'If Suzanne's been hurt too, we need to find her. As soon as possible. There's a search going on, but we need to know what happened so we know where to look.'

'For Suzanne?'

'Yes,' said Mum. 'The police, and the men from the Estate, and Uncle Jim and everyone – they're all out looking for her. What happened, dearie? You need to tell us. Who did this to you?'

'Someone – someone grabbed me. It wasn't Hector. He grabbed me, and put his hand over my mouth. I couldn't breathe. I couldn't get away. And then – I don't know. Then I was here.'

'Oh Helen,' said Mum. 'Oh dearie.'

She lifted her head off the pillow. 'Is Hector all right?'

'*Hector's* fine,' said Mum, gently pushing Helen back down.

'I don't remember anything else.'

'Never mind.' Mum stroked her hair. 'You're safe now.'

It was like trying to remember a dream. It was there, and she could nearly reach it, but when she tried it only slipped further away.

DS Stewart said, 'Was Suzanne with you?'

'No.'

'Helen.' He leant forward. 'Can you tell us who it was who attacked you?'

'No. I don't know. He was behind me.'

'But it was a "he"?'

'Yes. But it wasn't Hector.' She looked at DS Stewart. At Mum. 'Where was I, when they found me?'

DS Stewart consulted the notebook in his hand. 'Malcolm Kerr and Tom Strachan found you in the trees just off the path. The stalkers' path, on the Knock. About half way down it.' He looked at her suddenly. 'Okay, Helen. Can you tell me about the last time you saw Suzanne?'

The last time? The *last* time?

No. Nothing bad had happened to Suzanne. She was just lying drunk somewhere, the bizzum – there must be about a million units of alcohol swilling around in her system.

'We were lying by the fire. She'd had a lot to drink. She fell asleep. I told her I was going but I don't think she heard me. I left her. I left her there. By the fire. Hector and Tom had torches, and everyone was following them into the trees. Maybe Suzanne did too.'

'None of the group with the torches remembers her being with them. The last time they saw her, they say, she was with you by the fire.'

'Maybe she got lost in the trees. It was dark in the trees. Maybe she fell –'

'If that happened,' said Mum, 'they'll find her. Shh.'

Helen closed her one working eye.

The policeman said, 'You said that it wasn't Hector who grabbed you. Why *would* it have been Hector?'

She opened her eye. 'I was – he said to meet him. At one of the Land Rovers.'

DS Stewart wrote in the notebook. 'And when did you have this conversation?'

'He left a note, under my glass... I put it in my pocket. My jeans pocket.'

'Why did he want you to meet him?'

She didn't know what to say. In the end: 'Just to talk, I think.'

'Okay. So you were going to meet Hector, and someone grabbed you.'

Mum said, 'If it was Hector Forbes who attacked her –'

Helen yelped as she tried to sit up and pain shot up her right side. 'He didn't!'

'All right, dearie.'

DS Stewart turned to Mum. 'Hector Forbes is under arrest for a number of offences – which we'll be charging him with imminently, once we've finished speaking to everyone involved. If on the weight of evidence it looks like he's responsible for the attack on Helen too, he'll be charged with that in due course... Don't worry – he's not going anywhere.'

Mum said, 'What "offences"?'

'Supplying cannabis and cocaine. Driving under the influence of both, plus a hefty dose of alcohol.'

'He didn't attack me,' Helen said. She was so tired. 'It wasn't Hector.'

'Okay.' DS Stewart made another mark in his notebook. 'Okay... Helen, I know you don't want to talk about this, or even think about it. It sounds as if you've been through a terrifying ordeal, and the last thing you want to do is relive it. But I'm afraid I'm going to have to ask you to do just that. You want us to find Suzanne, don't you?'

She could feel tears at the back of her nose. 'I'll tell you everything I can remember but I can't help you find her because the last time I saw her she was just lying on her own by the fire, and I don't know what happened to her after that or where she went or anything, I don't know anything about where she is!'

'You might know something that can help us, even though you don't realise it.' He looked at her. 'Whoever it was who grabbed you – did he say anything?'

'No. He just sort of – grunted.'

Mum squeezed her hand.

'I couldn't scream. I couldn't breathe. I'm sorry, but that really is the last thing I remember. It *really is*. I must have blacked out then because I couldn't breathe?'

'We know you must have been conscious for at least some of the attack. There are – what we call defensive injuries on your forearms. Bruises. Where you must have put up your arms to ward your attacker off.'

Your attacker. As if he belonged to Helen, as if she was somehow responsible for him, like a weird sort of pet. Like a lion or a snake, the kind of pet stupid people insisted on keeping. Instead of going to prison he would live in a cage in her room, and she would have to change his wood shavings and fill his water bottle every day. 'What is it?' people would ask, peering through the bars. 'Oh, that's my attacker.'

Hysterical laughter wasn't far away.

She lifted the arm whose hand Mum wasn't holding, and pushed up the sleeve of the hospital gown. There were purple and brown marks on her skin.

'Try to think, Helen. Try to remember… He has his hand over your mouth… Does he pull you to the ground?'

'I don't know. I suppose so.'

'You're putting up your arms to protect yourself – Can you see his face?'

'No.' She let out a breath. 'I can't remember putting up my arms, I can't remember if I saw his face or not, I can't remember *anything* after his hand on my mouth. I'm sorry! I can't –'

Mum was rubbing her arm. 'That's all right, dearie.'

'Did he – rape me?'

There was a silence in the room and then Mum's hand was squeezing hers tighter than ever.

'No, Helen. No.'

'But… the button was torn off your jeans,' said DS Stewart. 'And when the boys found you – your jeans had been pulled down your thighs… Which suggests… There may have been a sexual motive.' His face had flushed.

A sexual motive. Hands in the dark, hands pushing under her jeans.

'Do you remember *anything* more about what happened?'

She turned her head so she couldn't see the policeman's blushing face. 'No.'

There was only a sheet and a thin blanket over her. He would be able to see the shape of her body underneath.

The quiet, calm voice of the doctor – she hadn't realised he was still in the room – said, 'Shock can have a powerful amnesiac effect. That's why people in car crashes often can't remember them. And we're not dealing only with shock – there are the added complications of concussion, and the effects of alcohol and hallucinogens.'

'I didn't take any drugs,' Helen said, and looked back at the policeman.

He frowned, and looked like he was about to say something, but then there was the click of the door opening and a tall woman in a police uniform came just inside the room. DS Stewart went over to speak to her. After what seemed like a long time she left, and he sat back down, tapping his pencil on the notebook.

'What's happened?' Mum said. And, her voice rising: 'Have they found her?'

12

'Is she dead?' Helen whispered it, as if saying it out loud would make it true.

'No. No no,' said DS Stewart. 'In fact, there's been a very positive development.'

'*Positive*?' Mum's voice sounded strange.

'It seems your niece's boyfriend, Robin Beattie, is also missing – he didn't come home last night. His sister – Lorna? – says she saw his car parked, further down the track than the others, at the Knock. She was heading off on foot, intending to walk to the phone box on the Tillybrake road and call her dad to come and get her. But when she saw her brother's car, she went back up the hill to find him and cadge a lift home. She got back to the fire just after the torchlight procession had left. She followed the torches, assuming Rob was with the group. She never did find him, but she swears his car was there, although no one else saw it. If she's right, though, and he *was* there, that puts a completely different complexion on things.'

'Rob,' said Helen.

The doctor put his hand on her arm. She felt suddenly dizzy.

'So – what?' said Mum. 'You think Rob and Suzanne have gone off somewhere? But Rob's a responsible lad. He wouldn't just take off like that, worrying his family. Suzanne's another matter, of course.'

Suzanne. There was something Helen had to tell them about Suzanne.

'A good proportion of our time is spent dealing with the fall-out from parties like this. When you get a bunch of youngsters together and add drugs and alcohol to the mix, you'd be amazed at the situations they can get themselves into. This pair's intention may not have been to stay out all night. Maybe they went off in his car... zonked out and left the headlights on, ran down the battery... Or he could have put the car off the road. Who knows. But I'll lay odds that she's with him, and they're either sleeping it off or trekking back to civilization as we speak.'

'But if they've had an accident –'

'The search is being widened with that possibility in mind. In any event, it's looking like the attack on Helen probably has nothing to do with Suzanne going missing. Could be that the only connection is that they were all out of their heads on a range of intoxicating and hallucinogenic substances.'

Mum said something, and Helen shut her eyes.

The next time she woke, Mum was sitting in the chair DS Stewart had been in, and standing by the window was the tall policewoman, saying, 'He's admitted everything, he's been fully cooperative – that'll be taken into account – but I can't see them handing down anything other than a custodial sentence.'

Helen pushed herself up. 'Have they found her?'

'Not yet,' said Mum. 'But they will.' She took hold of Helen's shoulders. 'Lie back down.'

'I need the loo. I'm okay.' She pushed back the sheet and blanket and swung her legs over the side of the bed. When she sat up everything went swimmy. She concentrated on the opposite wall, on a plastic shape above the little metal sink – a soap dispenser? Mum held onto her as she stood, and Helen asked her: 'Who are you talking about? Who's "admitted everything"? Admitted what?'

Mum looked over at the policewomen, who said, 'Hector Forbes has admitted the drugs and driving offences.'

'Custodial sentence? You mean he's going to *prison*?' She sat back down on the bed. 'But none of this is *his* fault!'

'You're not going to tell me you'd have taken cocaine if it hadn't been Hector Forbes handing it out?' Mum said his name like it was a disease.

'I didn't take any cocaine.'

'They found it in your bloodstream… Come on dearie, lie down. There's a bedpan you can use.'

The policewoman left the room while Helen did so, but she was back in a couple of minutes, pulling a chair next to Mum's. 'I should have introduced myself. I'm Pamela. Pamela McBride. Now, Helen... We've shown Hector Forbes the note from your jeans pocket, and he denies writing it.'

'Oh. I must have made a mistake.'

'He's given us a handwriting sample and there are similarities, but we'll need an expert to have a look before we can say for sure one way or the other.'

'I must have made a mistake,' Helen repeated.

Mum looked at her. 'Helen. Why did you assume Hector had written the note?' And before Helen could answer: '*The truth.*'

Helen didn't say anything. Pamela had a notebook on her knee, and a pen poised over it.

'If Hector didn't attack you,' said Mum, 'there's no reason for you not to tell the truth, is there?'

'We've been writing to each other. Sheila – there's no such person as Sheila. The letters were from Hector.'

Mum took in a long breath. 'Right. So you arranged... an assignation.'

'No. It's not like that.'

'Not as far as you're concerned, maybe.'

'He would *never* hurt me.' She put a hand to her face but she couldn't stop the tears, and then her face was wet with them, her nose running, sobs gulping from her throat, and Mum was wiping her face and hugging her carefully, and Helen clung on to the soft wool of her cardigan and buried her face in her shoulder.

'No one's going to hurt you now.'

'Suzanne...'

'They'll find her.'

She'd remembered what she had to tell them: that Suzanne had had bruises on her back. That she'd not wanted Helen to see them.

Rob had been there, at the Knock. Rob Beattie. Whispering poison at Dad's funeral; stalking her through the trees on Craig Dearg; watching her face as he spoke about her cats dying.

Her catties. Baudrins and Susie and Fergus.

She'd found Baudrins, after looking for days, stiff and cold down by the burn, near the bridge, as if someone had thrown him over it. His head wasn't Baudrins' head, it was like something in the butcher's, purple-red mess and sticky fur. She'd carried him home, and Dad had taken him and buried him up the hill, and told Helen he must have been run over on the track – hit so hard he'd been tossed over the bridge.

He wouldn't have felt anything.

They'd got Susie from the Cat and Dog Home. She was stripy, orange and brown and white, and the people at the Home said she'd probably been weaned too soon because she loved sitting on you and kneading you with her paws and purring.

Three weeks later Susie went missing. Mum and Dad found her body, but they didn't tell Helen how she'd died, and Helen hadn't ask.

They didn't have a cat for a long time after that. Then on her ninth birthday she'd come downstairs and there was the sweetest grey kitten in a box by the Aga. And he was Helen's new cattie, and she could call him whatever she liked.

She had called him Fergus.

Robin and Suzanne had come to see him, and after they'd been playing with him for a while in the sitting room Robin had picked him up and given him a bosie. 'Do you want me to bless him?'

Helen didn't, but she said, 'Okay.'

'Blessed are the dead who die in the Lord.'

'He's not dead!'

'I know. But those are the words you have to say, to do a blessing.'

'No they're not. Stop it!'

'I'm commending him to God.'

'Stop it! Give me him!' Helen had run with Fergus into the loo and locked the door.

Three days later he'd gone missing.

Helen and Suzanne had found him on their way to school. He'd been lying in the middle of the track. His head had been squashed like Baudrins', with bits of white and red stuff coming out of it. Suzanne had hugged Helen and told her not to look, and taken her home.

She'd told Mum that it was Robin's fault, that he'd asked God to kill Fergus. Mum hadn't listened. Helen had been allowed to stay off school that day, but no one had believed her about Robin.

No one would believe her now. Not about the cats, and not about the bruises.

'It was Rob who attacked me,' she said.

It must have been.

Mum released her; sat back, and looked into her face. '*Rob?*'

Pamela was leaning forward. 'What makes you think so?'

'I remember now. I remember him hitting me.'

'Okay, Helen. Can you tell us *exactly* what you remember?'

'But Rob –' Mum's face was very pale. 'I can't believe that *Rob* –'

'That's because you don't know what he's like. What he's really like.'

'Was Suzanne there?' Pamela asked.

'I don't know. After he grabbed me off the path, he pushed me down on the ground – that's when I saw it was Rob.'

'There was enough light to see his face?'

'Yes. He told me to keep quiet but – I shouted out, and he started hitting me.'

'What with?'

Could they tell from her bruises what had been used? She took a chance. 'His fists. I think just his fists.'

'Where did he hit you?'

'He was punching my face.' That was a safe guess. 'I tried to stop him.' And there was her rib. 'He kicked me. In my side. Then I think I must have blacked out. I don't remember anything else. I don't remember about Suzanne.'

Mum hugged her. 'Oh Helen.'

She could hear Pamela standing up; saying to Mum, 'I'll be back in a minute'; the door opening and closing.

13

It didn't seem real. Sitting at the kitchen table with a mug in front of her, looking across at DS Stewart and Pamela, and DS Stewart's fleshy lips moving as he kept talking.

'... And given that you had no deep cuts, and the pattern wasn't consistent with a nosebleed, the forensics people always did think it unlikely that the blood was yours.'

They were talking about the blood they'd found on the jersey Helen had been wearing.

It was Suzanne's.

Oh Suzanne Suzanne Suzanne.

Mum was sitting close, a hand on her arm.

'How can you know for sure?' Helen said.

DS Stewart flicked a look at Mum. A look that said, *Maybe she's not ready for this.* But he smiled at her. 'Don't ask me to explain the DNA analysis. All I know is that the DNA sample they got from hair follicles from Suzanne's brush matched the blood on your sweater. They used something called DNA fingerprinting – it involves looking at lots of bits of DNA, each of which is variable among individuals, so if they get a match across the board they can be pretty sure it's DNA from the same person.'

Helen said, 'So now you know Rob killed her.'

DS Stewart flicked another look at Mum.

They'd found Rob's car a week ago, up a forestry track on the Hill of Saughs. And it was all round the parish that Caroline Beattie wasn't speaking to her husband after he'd told the police that Rob's bike was missing from their shed.

Officially the police were still dealing with a double missing persons inquiry, but unofficially it was obvious they were assuming Suzanne was dead and Rob had killed her, although DS Stewart said that, given the state everyone had been in, it may well have been 'unintended'. They were 'keeping an open mind' about what had happened, and urging Rob to come forward.

But it was obvious what had happened.

Rob must have driven up to the Knock, left his car some distance from the other vehicles, and sneaked up the path. He'd watched them all from the trees, waiting his chance.

His chance to get Helen.

Maybe he hadn't meant to kill Suzanne. But he *had* killed her. He'd attacked Helen and killed Suzanne, and carried her down to his car, and put her in the boot. They hadn't found any traces in there, so he must have wrapped her in something – a tarpaulin from one of the Land Rovers, maybe.

He could have taken her anywhere. Maybe he drove up to Fintry Moss, to the end of one of the tracks up there, and carried her to one of the high lochans. Suzanne was just little. He could have carried her for miles. And then opened out the tarpaulin, got some heavy rocks, tied everything together with binder twine and thrown her into the water.

Police divers had been up there and found nothing. But there were hundreds of lochans. And hundreds of square miles of hillside. He could have buried her. Dug a hole in the peaty soil, packed the earth in on top of her.

Once he'd got rid of her he'd driven to Kirkton, got his bike from the shed and put it in the boot, driven up the Hill of Saughs, abandoned the car, cycled off. Disappeared.

There was a police car permanently stationed in the yard outside, in case Rob came 'in about', as Uncle Jim put it, trying to attack Helen again – although DS Stewart had said the chances were he was hundreds of miles away by now. They had no real reason to think he'd come to the Parks, but just in case...

Helen knew she should be scared, but all she could think of was Suzanne. How could *Suzanne* be dead? How was that possible?

Mum, though, was going spare. She was insisting they put forward their plans to leave, to move to Auntie Anne's. Probably a good idea. But Helen couldn't make herself care about that either.

DS Stewart rubbed the big knuckle of his thumb under his chin. 'The other thing we have to tell you – the blood found around the gear stick in Rob Beattie's car is his. Not Suzanne's. Its DNA fingerprint matches hairs obtained from Rob's room.'

'So he was hurt,' said Mum. 'I can imagine how Caroline Beattie's interpreting *that*.'

DS Stewart didn't say anything, but his lips twitched in a grimace.

Mrs Beattie had taken a mad turn, Norrie said, joining in the search each day in Wellingtons and a boiler suit – but making it clear she was looking not for Suzanne's body but for Rob's. She'd done an interview with a reporter from a tabloid, going on about how Suzanne had a police record and was always in trouble, while Rob was a lovely boy, leader of the Youth Fellowship and volunteer at an old people's home; a boy who was 'incapable of violence.' Helen's story of him attacking her must be a mistake. There'd been a photo of Mrs Beattie looking awful, and under it: 'Caroline Beattie: fears for "caring" son.'

Pamela opened the briefcase they'd brought – one of those solid black ones – and began lifting sheets of paper in clear plastic out onto the table.

'There's something else,' Helen said. 'The day before – before it happened, Rob told me this stupid riddle. He said Mrs Robertson at The Pines told him it, but I've been to see her and she didn't.'

DS Stewart raised his eyebrows.

'I've written it down.' She pushed the sheet of paper across the table, and read it again, upside down, as he looked at it:

I am a garden of delights
I am a wasteland frozen.
I am the dagger in the night
I am the sweetest poison.
What am I?

'The answer's obvious,' she said. 'The dagger in the night... It's *him*. The answer's *Rob*. It must be. This shows he was planning it, doesn't it? He was planning to bring a knife and... And attack me.'

'Well. Thank you, Helen. Anything like this you can remember is useful. It all helps us to build up a picture of what might have happened.'

Helen made her voice uncertain. 'And I've been wondering... about Suzanne's bruises.'

Pamela stopped rummaging in the case and pulled her notebook towards her.

'Bruises,' said DS Stewart.

'She had bruises on her back. Maybe Rob made them.'

'When did you see these bruises?'

'That night. The night of the party.' And she told them, too, about the cats.

When she'd finished, the police officers exchanged glances. DS Stewart blew out his cheeks.

And then she was in Mum's arms, and Mum was saying, 'I know, I know,' and Helen was choking: 'Why didn't you listen, when I told you about Fergus?'

'I should have listened.'

'When something like this happens,' said DS Stewart, 'a lot of things, in retrospect, can take on a sinister cast. We've one woman who's convinced Rob Beattie stole a statue of Pan from her garden.'

He meant it kindly. He meant to make them smile.

But Helen pushed away from Mum and glared across the table at him. 'Well maybe he did.'

Mum rubbed her back; pressed a tissue into her hand.

DS Stewart said, 'Would you like to leave the rest of this for another time?'

'No.'

He looked at Pamela, who said, 'We've had the note you thought was written by Hector Forbes analysed by a graphologist, and it seems he was telling the truth, about this at least. It's not his handwriting.' She pushed one of the plastic-covered sheets of paper across the table. The words leapt at her:

Meet me at the Land Rover – the one I was driving – at the stroke of midnight!

'And he claims not to have written any letters to you either, except one – after your father died. The letter you said you lost.'

It was as if all the blood in her body was draining away through the soles of her feet. She couldn't speak.

'And the graphologist confirms it. He didn't write them.' She handed Helen another sheet of paper inside plastic. It was a page from one of Hector's letters, which the police had taken to have analysed:

... Never enough of course, and we have to... The same one as I remember, but... If you're worried about...

Stupidly, she said: 'But they're from Hector.'

'I'm sorry,' Pamela said. 'They aren't. The PO Box number you wrote to – it's nothing to do with the Gordon Highlanders. It's rented in the name of Brian Smith, and was paid for every month in cash by a young man whose description matches –'

'Rob,' said Helen.

She wanted to snatch the letter up, away from everyone.

Stupid.

The 'Hector' who'd written those words, the 'Hector' she'd loved... He hadn't even existed. No – he *had* existed, but he'd been a monster.

He'd been Rob Beattie.

The sweetest poison.

Rob must know that she'd tried to poison him, and all these years he'd been biding his time –

'He wrote them,' she said. 'Rob.'

'No,' said DS Stewart. 'The graphologist thinks it was Suzanne.'

Mum moved in her chair, and made a little sound in her throat.

Helen shook her head.

'There are certain "tells", apparently, that leak out, even when you're copying someone else's writing –'

'He made her, then. He must have made her.'

'It's certainly a possibility. His dyslexia would mean he'd be unable, probably, to copy someone else's writing himself.'

'But how could they?' This couldn't be right. 'There were things in those letters that Rob... Suzanne... couldn't have known... Like the party on the Knock. In his last letter, he talked about the party he'd organised on the Knock, and Suzanne and Rob didn't know about that until days later – until the actual day of the party. So they *couldn't have written that letter!*'

'We understand,' said DS Stewart, 'that Suzanne learnt about the party some days in advance from Malcolm Kerr. Hector Forbes had been in touch with him about the party, and the Kerr boy mentioned it to Suzanne when he bumped into her one day in Kirkton of Glass.'

'But *why* write them?' asked Mum, tightly. 'Was it just a cruel joke, or was Rob planning some sort of – *attack* on Helen all along?' She shook her head. 'Rob. Of all people...'

'Aye, well,' said DS Stewart. 'Lot of teenage boys go through a wild stage – in most cases, of course, it –'

Helen jumped up. Her chair crashed back onto the flagstone floor. 'At the Knock... He got Suzanne to write that note so he could –'

Mum had stood too. She had an arm round Helen. Pamela righted the chair, and they eased her back into it. There were grey splotches over everything. She blinked.

'Suzanne tried to warn me.' She laced her fingers together on the table to stop them shaking, pressing down on them with her thumbs. 'She said I should be careful, with Hector... And all the time she was talking about Rob. Not Hector. *Rob*.'

Suzanne must have come after her down the path. And when Rob... She must have tried to stop him. And that was why she was dead.

She closed her eyes, and opened them again, and stared across the table at DS Stewart. 'Oh God,' she said. 'Oh God – I...'

'What?' said Pamela.

'I remember... I remember Suzanne...'

'*What*?' said DS Stewart.

'Suzanne *was* there – she grabbed Rob, she tried to stop him hitting me, and he punched her – he punched her... and she wasn't moving...'

That was what happened.

It must have been.

14

It was a day like any other. The sun fell across the windowsill like it had yesterday morning, like it would tomorrow. She put her palm flat on the warm ledge and looked out across the yard and down the track to where it kinked across the burn. Then she turned and slowly walked right round the room, trailing her hand on the wall like a blind person, and thinking, stupidly:

Goodbye. Goodbye. Goodbye.

Stupid because it was just walls, a little metal fireplace, a window, an old hook on the back of the door.

'Helen?' Mum called from downstairs.

'Coming.'

In the kitchen Mum was standing in the middle of the room, like a visitor.

'Right, I think that's everything.'

Their steps sounded too loud as they walked across the empty room, and Helen put her hand on the doorknob and opened the door and went through and out into the yard like she'd done all her life.

And now she was looking across the yard at the byre tap, set into the stone, a huge old thing, green where the copper had tarnished. She and Suzanne used to shove their fingers up it to make the water spurt out at each other. But the person doing the spurting always got just as wet as the one being spurted.

And – how daft was this? – she wanted to pull the tap off the pipe and put it in her bag.

'Eh me,' said Uncle Jim, on an indrawn breath.

She wasn't going to cry. She got in to the back of Uncle Jim's car and Mum got in the front.

No Auntie Ina. Someone had phoned up and said they'd seen Suzanne in Newcastle, and Auntie Ina had got the next train down there.

If I could go back, I would, Helen wanted to scream into the air, all the way to Newcastle. If she could go back... if she could have seen that of course Hector Forbes wouldn't write those things to her, of course he wouldn't love her – If she could go back even further than that, if she could stop her eight-year-old self putting laburnum seeds in that sandwich –

Then Suzanne wouldn't have died saving her life.

She shouldn't be leaving. She should be staying, she should be helping. Or trying to. But Dr King, the psychiatrist they'd made her see, had told Mum that the best thing would be for Helen to get away, to go to Edinburgh as planned. And Helen hadn't argued about it.

Because she wanted to go. To be somewhere people didn't know who she was.

To be somewhere Rob couldn't find her. Somewhere there were plenty of people, if he did.

Selfish as she was, she'd started to worry about that. To be scared. She'd started imagining she heard him, at night, sneaking through the garden and in at the front door and up the stairs while the policemen dozed, oblivious, in the car out the back.

She wanted away.

In eight months Hector would be out of prison and then – what could she say to him? What could she say to anyone?

Norrie had told her what had happened at the hospital. While she was being treated, the police had taken Hector away, and Norrie and Steve and Fiona and Fish had been left in a waiting room. Fiona had wanted them to lie about the drugs at the party, and tried to get Steve to say he was driving – he hadn't taken any drugs and hadn't drunk as much as Hector, so the police wouldn't come down on him so hard – and when Steve said he wouldn't, she'd started on Norrie. 'You know what like she is,' Norrie had said, and admitted he was on the point of agreeing when Steve had gone mental, shouting over Fiona, shouting that they all had to tell the police *the truth* about *everything*, because it might help them work out what had happened to Suzanne, and wasn't that a bit more important than whether or not Hector got his just desserts? And Fiona had shouted back that Steve was just a coward, and in his place Hector wouldn't have hesitated to take the rap for *him*.

Now Fiona and Steve had split up, and Steve had gone back to

Paisley.

Jennifer Gordon had sold her story to the *Daily Express*.

Hector had written Helen a letter, but she hadn't read it. She'd thrown it on the fire and watched the black spread over the envelope, over the *Helen* in his neat sloping writing.

Uncle Jim turned the key in the ignition and the car rolled down from the yard onto the track. Helen said, 'Stop! Can you stop a second?' and pushed open her door.

The ditch at the side of the track was a late-summer tangle of long, dry grass and nettles and brambles, the tight fruit starting to form. No campion flowers, not at this time of year, but there was a mauve pom-pom of scabious down amongst the grass. She snapped its stem and took it back with her into the car, setting it on her lap and watching it, during the three-hour drive south, wilt and curl in the sticky heat.

When she was twenty-three

15

It couldn't be him.

Hector.

Could it?

Standing by the bar, dark hair slightly tousled, handsome face slightly flushed. Looking straight at her.

Hector was in South America.

It's just some random person.

The lighting was bad. She couldn't see his face properly. It was just some random person who looked a bit like Hector.

Then someone moved between them and she couldn't see him at all. And Martin leant over the table, his blond curls still damp from the rain, and said, 'Helen? Are you OK?'

She was hemmed in by Gabby on one side and Dave on the other. They were all squished up on the U-shaped bench round the table, fleece- and wool-clad arms pressed companionably against each other, coats and scarves and gloves and bags in a pile on the windowsill over their alcove. Safe from thieving hands. On the darkened panes the rain dripped and ran, distorting the yellow streetlights and the white rectangles of the windows in the building opposite.

It's just some random person.

How many times had that thought looped through her head when she got a glimpse of Suzanne's back in the street ahead of her, Suzanne's hand reaching to a shelf in the supermarket, Suzanne's darting way of moving through a crowd?

But still her heart would leap. Maybe those medieval philosophers were right, and the heart really did have its own consciousness. It was as if her brain knew that Suzanne was dead, but her heart wasn't so sure. Her heart reckoned that if Suzanne was anywhere she'd be in London, maybe with Rob; maybe the two of them had set the whole thing up as a big sick joke. Or maybe he hadn't killed her, maybe he'd kidnapped her and she had escaped and... because of all the trauma she'd lost her memory...?

Her heart wasn't too bright. And it never learned. Each time, her brain would be saying *No* but her heart would be thudding out: *Maybe it is! Maybe! Maybe it is!*

A couple of times it had been Rob she'd thought she'd seen: a wide head on a lanky body; a jutting chin. And her heart and her head had both gone haywire, pounding away, sending adrenaline coursing through her, readying her nerves and her muscles and her heaving lungs to run – until she saw that it wasn't him.

But her heart and her head both knew he'd be back.

Part of her brain was constantly on high alert for him, constantly checking everyone she saw, looking behind her in the street, checking she'd double-locked the door, jumping when someone put a hand on her shoulder. Constantly throwing up false alarms.

But this was the first Hector.

Martin said something else. She turned to Dave: 'Can I get out for a sec?' and edged past his long legs.

The pub seemed to be full of giants, tall young men with wide shoulders and backs. She 'sorry'-ed her way through the crush until she could see him.

Hector.

She swung round; pushed her way back to the alcove.

'Have to go. Sorry.'

Surprised faces. 'What? Why?'

Why? 'Migraine coming on, I think.'

Martin blinked. 'I'll come with you?'

He knew she hated walking anywhere alone.

'No. It's okay. Could you hand me over my bag, and my coat?'

She didn't stop to put the coat on. She hugged it against her as she weaved through the crush of bodies to the door. It opened as she reached it, and as she stepped back to let the people in out of the rain she couldn't resist just glancing over her shoulder at the bar.

He wasn't there any more.

He was right behind her.

He smiled, and put a hand on her arm, and said, 'Over here?' and then she was standing facing him in the free bit of space behind the door, her back against the varnished panelling, and all the voices in the pub were in her ears.

She was shaking. His hand was still holding her arm – warm through her fleece – and he had to stand close to her because of the people behind him, and she couldn't breathe. Her face was too close to him, to the tanned skin at the open neck of his shirt.

He took his hand away and said, 'Sorry, Helen – your flatmate said you might be here – but if you don't want –'

'My flatmate?' She kept her eyes focused on the lights behind the bar. 'Steph?'

'Your uncle gave me your phone number.'

'Oh. Right.' Still she didn't look at him.

But then he said, 'You don't want to talk to me,' and so she had to, she had to look into his eyes and say, 'No – yes. I'm sorry,' at the same time as he said, 'Of course you don't,' and moved back.

She grinned frantically. 'I thought you were in Venezuela.'

'I am. Working there, I mean. Back on holiday.' And then: 'I wanted to say – pointless, I know, but – that I'm sorry. I'm so sorry. About what happened.'

'It wasn't your fault.'

He shook his head, and moved further back, to give her room to get past him. 'But you're well? You look very well.'

'Yes. I don't blame you for any of it. Why should I?'

He shook his head again.

And the words came tumbling: 'It was *my* fault, to ever think that those letters – that they were from *you*, how could they have been, I should have known that they weren't. He made her write them. She kept trying to tell me – she didn't want me to get hurt. And then when – it was because of *me* that he –'

Her mouth wouldn't go round the words.

She pushed past him, pushed to the door and out, dragging on her coat.

She ran.

16

The pavement was streaming, huge puddles, a slimy mush of newspaper, a man with his head down, and then she was at the junction with Fulham Road and she had to wait for a car to sloosh past and he was there, catching her arm again, and saying again, 'Helen – Helen, I'm sorry.'

What was *he* sorry for?

She looked up at him, at his face in the sickly glow of the street lamps.

In five years, she'd almost managed to convince herself that he was nothing special. That there must be plenty of other men like Hector. That she would find another man to match him, another man who would make her glad just to be Helen Clack and alive in the world, in *his* world, another man with whom no words would be needed when the sun suddenly slanted through a line of beech trees and across a yellow field, who would turn to her and know she would be smiling too.

Another man who would claim her, heart and head and body and soul.

Ian? Kenneth? Martin, sitting back in that pub wondering if he should go after her but never quite managing to detach his hand from his pint or his arse from his seat?

Oh God.

Hector.

And suddenly she had to know.

'That night – did you give me cocaine? Did you put it in my drink?'

She felt the muscles in his hand tense. 'No.'

'At the hospital they did blood tests. They found cocaine.'

'Yes. I know.'

She said, 'I don't –' at the same time as he said, 'It wasn't meant for general consumption.' The rain was running down his face.

'Suzanne...' She was shivering, making his hand on her arm shiver too. 'You didn't see Suzanne, did you? After I left her – you and the others were off in the trees, with the torches – you didn't see her?'

'No.'

'What were you doing?'

He let her go; ran a hand over his wet hair. And then both his hands were on her shoulders. 'You saw her again yourself, didn't you? Suzanne was there – you saw Rob hit her, before you blacked out? Does it matter where she was in the interim? Does any of this matter, now?'

She should tell him. She should tell him she lied.

She wrenched herself away and gulped, like a child, 'She – was –'

He said, 'I know,' and the bulk of him was against her, her face against his shirt, his chest, his arms tight so she couldn't pull away; and her hands were clinging to him, and from deep inside her something started to rise up, something that had been pressed down and down and down, and she shut her eyes.

And he held her.

It rose right up, the thing inside her, and she couldn't do anything except open her mouth and let it out, disgusting, dribbles from her nose and down her chin, onto his shirt, and from her throat a mad howling, and she couldn't do anything to stop it.

But when it did stop he eased her away, and she kept her eyes shut and felt his hands on her cheeks, her forehead, her closed eyelids, her mouth, her chin; his open palms gently wiping, smoothing. She stood there and let him do it, turning her face up to him like a dog, pushing her face against his hands.

She opened her eyes.

Rain was soaking his hair, his shirt. Running down his nose.

She reached out and touched his face – ridiculously, the end of his nose, where the rain was dripping. His chin. It was very slightly rough, very slightly stubbly.

She must look awful.

She ducked her head, and he put his hands on her back and when she looked up again he brought his lips down on hers, warm and hard and tasting of beer and cigarettes, shooting sensation through her and –

Oh God.

Hector.

She said his name aloud, onto his lips: 'Hector.'

His hands moved up her back, sending a shock all the way up her spine, all the way down it.

'So,' he said. 'Where exactly is your flat?'

17

In the dark of her room, in her bed, when she started to stutter something he said 'Whatever you like,' and his hands were showing her, and his lips. At some point he said 'You're lovely,' but by then she was beyond caring what he thought. She was beyond all she had ever cared about, as if everything that had tied her to the world had simply come loose and there was only this, her own self, set free.

Her own self, and her own love.

Later, lying against his shoulder, her thoughts already half-drifting into the dream this must surely be, she said, reaching for something, anything, that would anchor her to the world: 'What do you do, in Venezuela?'

'Oh... Grunt work for an oil company. Nothing as remotely high-powered as museum curatorship.'

So he knew what she was doing? Had he asked someone about her, or had someone, Uncle Jim maybe, just randomly told him?

'I'm only an assistant,' she said. 'Grunt work definitely covers what I do too. An oil company – are you involved in the engineering side of it?'

'Oh God no. I'm just in the security division.'

Her heart bumped. 'That sounds – dangerous.'

'Secretaries pilfering paper... Kids nicking hubcaps... The boss getting rat-arsed and somehow managing to lock himself in his office... Yes. It can get pretty hairy.'

But what about the fact that he'd been in prison? Maybe in Venezuela they weren't too bothered about whether people had criminal records? Was that why he'd gone there? But she could hardly ask him that.

'How much longer are you here for?'

'Flight out's on Monday.'

'Oh.'

So she probably wouldn't see him again before he left. Even if he wanted to, he probably wouldn't have time.

'Have you been home? How is everyone? Your family?'

'Yes. They're very well, thanks.'

Was this really happening? Was she really lying here in bed with Hector, *Hector*, talking normally, as if this was a perfectly normal everyday event?

Well, to him, it probably was.

OK. She could do normal.

'Damian must be – almost six?'

'Mm.'

Their little Stinker. But he wouldn't even remember Suzanne. 'Does he still have a nanny?'

'Well, they call her an au pair. Hand-picked by Zenaida, who seems to have scoured the arrondissements for the surliest girl in Paris – and that's saying something. Although to be fair, the surliness may partly be down to having to look after Damian... No, really, he's an au pair's worst nightmare.' She could hear the grin in his voice. 'Obsessed with jumping off walls and out of trees – in fact any structure high enough to have the potential for fatal injury.'

'Oh God!' Suzanne would soon have put a stop to that.

'His other main interest is skulls. Other kids bug you for plastic figures and luridly coloured ice lollies. Damian whinges on if you don't stop the car so he can get out and scrape up maggoty roadkill.'

No way would Suzanne have stood for *that*! 'And someone then has to get the skull out? The au pair?' She giggled. 'Irina?'

'Can you imagine? No. He's got one of the keepers onto that. And – you might be interested in this – he's got all the skulls displayed on tables in one of the outbuildings, complete with indecipherable labels. The Pitfourie Natural History Museum – admission charge 20p. Attractions – forty-odd skulls, mainly rabbits and deer; a desiccated bat; and a hideously deformed fungus, although that's starting to go mouldy.'

'Sounds like he needs to look at his humidity levels. A common issue with organic material.'

'Really? I'm sure he'd be glad of your help with conserving the collection generally. The bat looks like something's been having a good chew on it.' She felt his fingers in her hair. 'Have you been back, since you left? To Pitfourie?'

'No.'

How could she go back? Mum, Uncle Jim, Auntie Anne – they thought it was because she couldn't face being back where it happened. But it wasn't that. What she couldn't face was the corner of the steading at the Mains where the dollies had had their shoppie, the shelf maybe still there where the empty packets of cornflakes and tins of pineapple and condensed milk had sat... The bit of the road to Kirkton where Norrie's brother Craig had caught a forkytail in a jar, and chased them screaming all the way down the hill... A harvest night, leaning out of her bedroom window to smell the dust off the barley and wondering if Suzanne was doing the same, watching the lights of the combine and the tractors in the Back Park, their fathers and Sandie Cowie from Croftgloy, and over them the million stars of the constellations.

'I've kind of lost touch with everyone. I saw Fiona a few times, but – not recently.'

She'd even spent a weekend in Fiona's student flat in Aberdeen – Fiona trying too hard to be cheery, as if she was someone else attempting the role of Fiona and not quite getting it right. There'd been long silences and lots of TV. They'd avoided the subjects of Pitfourie, Steve, Hector – until at the bus station Helen had blurted: 'Is Hector still in prison?' and Fiona had nodded.

Hector moved his shoulder a little under her. 'So you weren't at the wedding?'

'*Wedding*? She's *married*?'

'Doesn't your uncle keep you up to date with the gossip?'

'If it isn't to do with either farming or someone he was at school with, it's not really news as far as Uncle Jim's concerned. But... who has she married?'

'Who do you think?'

'Not Steve?'

'Why not Steve?' He breathed out on a laugh. 'Poor sod.'

He had no regrets about Fiona, then. Suddenly her face was too hot. She shut her eyes, and his fingers moved to her temple, her hairline. So gentle. He was so gentle. But every touch, every little caress sent a thrumming all the way through her.

'So is London where you want to be?' he said.

'No.' She opened her eyes. 'I hate it.'

She felt his chest move as he laughed again. 'Then why stay?'

'Because of my job. And – this will sound daft. But if Suzanne's anywhere, if she's alive, I think she'll be here.'

His fingers stopped moving in her hair.

Oh God. He thought she was off her trolley. He thought she was a right nutter, roaming the streets of London looking for her dead cousin. He was probably thinking *Oh-oh* and *How do I get out of this?*

'I know it's stupid! But I can't help thinking, if there's even just a tiny little chance… I don't go out looking for her or anything, like Ina does.' Well, not any more. Or not often.

'Ina's still in Glasgow?'

'Yes.'

Ina was in Glasgow, because that was where there'd been the most 'sightings' of Suzanne. She'd left Uncle Jim. He'd dropped it in at the end of a conversation with Mum one day, after they'd talked about all the important things, like how beef prices were holding up: the information that Ina had packed her things and gone.

'I don't think Ina will ever stop looking.' And maybe she would find her yet. There was a chance, wasn't there? Maybe Suzanne *was* in Glasgow?

'But she must be dead, Helen. You know she must be.'

'We don't know that for certain.'

'One day, Robin Beattie is going to resurface –'

'I know. I know he's going to come after me.'

He puffed out a sigh. She felt it on the top of her hair. 'No he's not. I didn't mean that. Why on earth would he come after you?'

'Because he's always hated me. He's always wanted to hurt me. I can't tell you why because I don't know.' That was true, of course, only up to a point.

Up to the point she'd tried to kill him.

'He did it because he was a little shit. He'll be getting his sick kicks at someone else's expense now, wherever he is – why should he risk getting caught by showing his face anywhere near you? Rob always was gutless.'

'He killed Suzanne.'

'A girl half his size who made the mistake of trusting him.' A silence. 'I'm sorry.'

She heaved in a breath.

He continued: 'And then he wasted no time making himself

scarce. There's no way he's ever going to risk coming anywhere near you. Please tell me you're not still living in fear of that *fucking* little shit, Helen.'

She shrank, inwardly, from the sudden anger in his voice. 'No. No. Not – on a daily basis or anything.'

'When I said he's going to resurface, all I meant was... whatever stone he's crawled under, one day he's going to crawl back out again. Blow his cover. His luck's going to run out. They'll catch him.'

This was another of her fantasies, of course – that one day she'd turn on the TV and there would be Rob in handcuffs being led to a police van. 'I hope so.'

'And maybe then we'll find out what happened to Suzanne. But in the meantime... You've got your life to live.' He took a long breath. 'Isn't it time to let it go? To let *her* go?' He ran his fingers around the curve of her bare shoulder.

Could it really be so simple? Was it really a choice she could make? Was it a deal that God, fate, the Universe was offering her? *You can have one of the things you want, but only one. Forget about Suzanne, forget about Rob, and you can have him.*

As his lips kissed her neck, the place under her ear, her mouth, she pushed away the thought: *What if I could?*

But later, when he was asleep, and she was lying propped on one elbow looking at him, at the contours of his face, other-worldly in the dim yellow wash of the streetlight, she let herself admit it:

She would do anything if she could have him.

She would forget anything and everything. All the trappings of her mortal existence. Like Janet Duncan from Bridieswells, stolen away by the Ghillie Dhu.

She and Suzanne used to love that story – Daft Janet and the Ghillie Dhu. Janet's mother had told her to be home before the moon rose, but Janet dawdled on the Coynach Road, and the moon rose high in the sky, and into her shadow crept the Ghillie Dhu.

The Dark Man.

He wasn't scary, like the Sith – but that was the whole problem. You didn't want to run away. Once he started singing to you in his fine sweet voice you were powerless to resist, and Daft Janet certainly hadn't. She'd gone dancing off with him into the pinewood of Corrachree and out of mortal ken. When eventually she came back to her family after eight long years, she was 'nae use to naebody', her face forever turning to Corrachree. She was deaf to all mortal sound: her mother's wailing; her father's scolding; the blacksmith's hammer when the minister pushed her ear to the anvil. If it wasn't the song of the Ghillie Dhu, Daft Janet wasn't interested.

It had become one of their games, but the Ghillie Dhu creeping up on Janet had soon palled, and the whole thing had taken on a more domestic quality. Daft Janet and the Ghillie Dhu had a housie in the woods, and various dollies for naughty children and/or visitors, and plastic cups and plates, and an old blue and green rug for the floor. Sometimes the Ghillie Dhu brought home a dollie he'd enchanted, and Janet would huff and puff and tell him to take her right back; she'd enough mouths to feed, thank you very much.

Helen smiled, and with the tips of her fingers touched his hair.

Long ago, she'd picked out their housie. The East Lodge. Gingerbread gables and little bedrooms with sloping eaves. A range fire in the kitchen. The Laird and Irina would give them furniture from the attics, and Helen wouldn't like to refuse, and it would look ridiculous, big grand Georgian stuff squashed into the tiny rooms. And Stinker would sometimes come and stay the night, her little cushie-doo, all sweet and sleepy in his pyjamas. Irina would have a great long list of rules about what to feed him, but Helen would get in a stash of Jelly Tots and Dolly Mixtures and Smarties, and the three of them would gorge themselves silly. On Saturdays Hector would sometimes take her to the Forbes Arms for a bar lunch, and Jennifer Gordon would have to serve them.

She shook her head and, very lightly, put her lips to his cheek.

When she was thirty-four

18

She didn't really need a hair cut but she loved the pampering, especially this bit, relaxing back on the chair at the sink while Karim massaged conditioner into her scalp. Getting your hair washed at the hairdresser's used to be an ordeal, sitting with your head tilted back at such an unnatural angle at the sink that you felt your neck was never going to recover, muscles screaming in pain after about two seconds, the worst of it being that you knew you had to hold the position for the next five minutes, minimum.

But now they had state-of-the-art chairs that were more like beds, and specially designed sinks that let you, somehow, lie flat as gentle fingers moved in your hair.

'This conditioner's jojoba and... I want to say aubergine?' A pause while Karim presumably consulted the bottle. 'Ha ha, no, it's argan. Argan. What's argan? Smells nice though?'

'Mm.' It was sometimes hard to work out when Karim was asking you a question.

His fingers moved on her scalp. 'Hard day at work hmm Helen?'

'Mm,' was all she could say again, already half asleep.

Most hairdressers would have kept talking at this point, but Karim just went on massaging her head with slow, deliberate, soothing circular motions of his fingertips.

Karim maybe wasn't the best hairdresser in the world, and sometimes she ended up having to even up the levels on either side of her face with nail scissors, but he was so nice.

She was only vaguely aware of what was going on around her – girls laughing, the beat of some dance track on the music system, someone walking past and shouting: 'Milk and one sugar, yeah?'

The receptionist saying, 'That's great then, we'll see you Tuesday next week at two-thirty' and a low man's voice saying something in reply.

And then, as the dance track ended, in the sudden quiet she heard it.

A cough.

Or not a cough, exactly. A nervous tic, Fiona Kerr had called it.

In another time, and another world.

Cough-cough cough.

She shot upright in the chair, wet hair slapping the towel on her shoulders, water dripping down her neck inside it. The reception counter wasn't visible from here – there were high mirrors in the way, with people seated in front of them and various hairdressers standing wielding combs and scissors and hairdryers over their heads.

The air was thick with the smells of perfumed product, hot hair and coffee, and she felt suddenly sick, her pulse loud in her ears.

Could it be?

Could it actually be?

'Oh, you okay?' she heard Karim say behind her.

She swung her legs off the chair, seemingly in slow motion, and next thing she found herself standing in the gap in the run of mirrors down the middle of the salon. A man in a suit was walking away from her to the door.

Middle height, with a broad head on a strong neck, and collar-length brown hair.

She had frozen. She couldn't make herself yell out, or go after him, or go back to her bag for her phone. How could she call 999 anyway? What would she say?

There's a man coughing.

He opened the door and stepped out onto the pavement and turned to the right. She couldn't see his face as he turned because of the huge photograph of the sullen model, hair fanned around her head, that took up almost that whole window, and now he was out of sight completely.

Karim had his hand on her arm. 'Helen, you okay?'

As if his touch had woken her from one of those dreams where you can't move, one of those nightmares, she nodded and made for the door. 'I just need to –'

A cold wind whipped at her wet hair. The pavement was busy, mainly with purposeful people striding along in their workwear – which in this part of Edinburgh meant suits for men and sombre tailored outfits for women.

He couldn't do anything to her, could he, with all these people around?

She started to walk, to run, along past the hardware shop and the florist's, all the time scanning around her and behind, expecting any minute that he'd suddenly appear out of nowhere and grab her, pull her into a doorway, into a car –

She would scream if he did that. She'd sit down on the pavement so he couldn't pull her anywhere, and scream until all these suits had no choice but to take notice and stop him. Grab him. Make a citizen's arrest and call the police.

Where was he?

So many suits, but none of these men was him.

He couldn't just have *vanished*.

No.

There he was.

He was standing on the traffic island by the Canonmills clock, standing quite still, and looking right at her.

A wide face. Heavy brows and chin. Deep-set eyes –

Then he turned his head to look across the street, and she saw his profile.

The nose was pointed; aquiline. And the build was wrong too – that thick neck, and muscular shoulders and torso.

It's just some random person.

He turned his head again and she realised he wasn't looking at her at all, he was looking past her up the road, at the cars coming towards him, waiting for a break in the stop-start of the rush hour traffic.

She turned away and walked slowly back up the pavement like an old woman, each step a conscious effort, each breath not deep enough, as if all the oxygen had been sucked out of her body and she couldn't replace it fast enough, she couldn't get it to her brain fast enough for it to be able to function.

Karim was standing in the doorway of *Medusa* in his tight jeans and winkle-pickers. As she approached he shook his head at her as a mother might at a naughty child. 'Helen, Helen, where you off to, eh? Is it not bloody Baltic out here?' He reached out to fuss with the towel around her neck.

'Sorry,' she gulped. It felt so good to have this kind man pat her shoulders and guide her back to the chair at the sink. She slumped back down on it, still gasping air. 'I thought... that was someone... I used to know. But... it wasn't.'

'Let's get you warmed up huh? My God your head is like a block of *ice*, Helen – what were you thinking eh? What were you thinking?'

She laid her head back against the porcelain and as Karim's hands smoothed her hair back from her forehead, and she felt the nozzle of the hose thing press against her scalp and a gush of soft warm water run down over it, her breathing finally slowed. Her heart rate slowed. Her brain clunked back into gear.

Just some random person.

'Old boyfriend huh?'

'No.' She closed her eyes. 'I just thought it was – someone I used to know.'

19

Karim always insisted on using hair straighteners to flatten her bouncy mane, no matter how often she hinted that she didn't think it suited her to have her hair flat and limp against her head. Now she just let him get on with it. Who cared what her hair looked like anyway?

Nevertheless, she told herself she was stopping at the darkened window of the now closed hardware shop to check it out. But rather than examining her own reflection superimposed on the displays of latches and doorknobs, she was watching the people passing behind her. Studying each face.

Stop it.

It was just some random person.

It wasn't Rob Beattie.

Rob Beattie wasn't about to loom up in the window behind her like something from a horror film, grinning maniacally, hands lifted, claw-like, above her ruthlessly straightened hair.

She had her phone tucked into her palm as usual, three nines already tapped in, thumb just touching the call key, ready to press it in an instant. Last time it had been a jogger coming up behind her suddenly at the green man, and the police had traced her through her Vodaphone account and said she was lucky they weren't cautioning her for wasting their time – one false alarm too many, apparently.

She had promised to stop.

But it was getting dark. Once she was on Warriston Road there would be fewer pedestrians, fewer people she could scream at for help if need be. That was the one downside of her new flat. She'd been attracted to it by the fact that it wasn't overlooked, as her previous flat had been, by tenements across the street where anyone could be hiding behind a window watching. Warriston Road was narrow and one-way, snaking along the Water of Leith, with just a wall and the river opposite her flat and, on the other bank, a line of mature willows and sycamores shading gardens which she regularly scanned with binoculars.

She crossed over at the roundabout and stopped at the Warriston Road corner, checking the people in view: a mother with two little girls in matching pale blue coats, two tall thin men in suits, a fat man in a grubby yellow tabard with reflective stripes on it, a group of teenagers in school uniform.

The yellow tabard man was heading down into Warriston Road.

Good.

She always waited for company, as she thought of it, before leaving the bustle of the roundabout for the relative isolation of her road. She followed close behind tabard man – so close that at one point he turned and looked at her. She avoided his eye, pretending to be absorbed in the three nines on the screen of her phone.

The whoosh of the unseen river in spate drowned out the noise from the traffic on Canonmills Bridge. At the door of her building, she checked behind her again before unlocking the door, slipping inside and shoving it shut against the resistance of the self-closing mechanism. She made sure the Yale had snibbed by pulling on the big cold metal handle screwed to this side of the door next to the laminated notice she'd taped there:

Please make sure the door has locked behind you. Thanks!

She didn't go straight up the stone stairs; instead, she made herself brave the dim dustiness of the dark little passage under them. This ended in a solid old door that gave onto the communal garden.

She made sure it was locked, that both the Yale and the mortice were engaged. The big old key for the mortice was kept on a hook on the wall, which wasn't the most secure arrangement, but when she'd suggested an alternative system with a key safe to Mrs Cunningham, the neighbour she'd decided was most likely to go for it, Mrs Cunningham had laughed and said 'What on earth would be the point of that? You young people would always be forgetting the combination and have to come knocking on my door for it.'

She hurried back along the passage and up the stairs. There was a window on the little half-landing that looked over the garden, with its square of lawn and flowerbeds and line of old brick sheds. She stopped and scanned it, the gathering shadows under the flowering currant and the lilac, the grass an odd yellow colour in the city glow, before ascending to the first floor.

Her flat was on the left, its dark blue door the original Victorian one constructed of close-grained old pitch pine more than two inches thick. But before opening it she ran quickly up the final flight to check the top landing.

It was empty and silent, lemon-yellow walls bright and stark in the fluorescent glow of the stair light.

No one lurking.

She ran back down the stairs to her own door, transferring the phone to her left hand and drawing her keys from the compartment inside her bag. There were three locks to open – two deadbolt mortices and the Yale. She always did them in the same order – first the top mortice, then the bottom one, then, obviously, the Yale.

And then she was in, the door shoved shut behind her on the Yale. If someone was coming after you, the Yale was good because you could just slam the door shut and it would lock itself.

She turned the keys in the mortice locks and slid the two chains into place. Lionel thought this was taking things too far. 'What if you were trapped inside and the fire brigade had to force entry?' he'd said, last time he and Mum were up and had to wait 'an age' at the door while she unlocked and unchained it. She had shrugged and said breezily, 'I guess I'd burn to death,' and that had prompted one of Lionel's looks at Mum.

She wondered what Mum had told him.

Had she told him about what had happened at her last flat? It would have sounded so ridiculous. To sell up and move just because someone kept banging on your door. But it had happened five times. Five times, all late at night. By the time she'd got to the door and put her ear against it (she hadn't even had a peephole then!), there had been no one there. Or at least no more sounds of anyone. Someone could have been standing right on the other side of the door, waiting for her to open it.

Probably just kids, the police had said. Or the students upstairs, drunk.

The students had denied it, though, and she'd believed them, because she was pretty sure it was Rob. She couldn't explain how she could be sure, of course – not to the police and certainly not to

Mum. But it hadn't just been kids or students messing around. There had been such violence in that *bang bang bang bang bang* on her door, such anger, such... yes, such *hatred.*

She had known it was him.

She had known he had found her.

But he wouldn't make his move at once – oh no. He'd have fun torturing her first. Banging on her door, shouting at her along a dark street – she was sure that had been him too, back in November, when she'd been walking home from work on a dark evening – she'd had to stay late to help Eilidh with a report – and suddenly someone in the street behind her had shouted:

'Hello! Hello! Hello!'

She hadn't even turned round to look. She'd just run.

Security at her old flat had been laughable. She'd often found the door to the street propped open by the students or tradesmen, and the garden door left unlocked.

Here was much better. The flats were all tiny, so no students. No kids. A Neighbourhood Watch sign on the lamp post outside, and a nosy pensioner in the flat downstairs who seemed to monitor every coming and going.

In the living room, she set her bag down on the countertop that separated off the kitchenette area from the rest of the room and went to the sink.

She was still holding her phone.

She put it down on the counter next to her bag. In the sink were her breakfast cereal bowl and spoon and mug. She tipped the cloudy water out of the cereal bowl and rinsed it under the tap, swishing the water round with the little washing up brush. Then she washed the spoon and the mug, and filled the kettle, and while it boiled she went to the window and opened it and breathed in the cold spring air.

The front of the flat looked over the Water of Leith to the trees at the foot of the gardens opposite, their skeleton outlines now just starting to come into bud. She loved those trees. She liked to sit on the sofa and look at them. Sometimes a squirrel would run along a branch.

No squirrels today. And no one lurking on the pavement across the road. No one on the banks of the river or in the gardens.

The little one-way road was a rat run, and because it was one-way, people felt entitled to speed round the bend – never mind any pedestrians who might be crossing. There was a pavement on the opposite side of the road, but none on this side. The short path from the main door led straight out into the road. Mrs Cunningham in the ground-floor flat was always saying it was an accident waiting to happen, her little eyes bright with anticipation, implying that, now that the problem had been brought to Helen's attention, it would be her fault if someone was run over.

But Helen liked to stand and look down at the cars whizzing by, cutting off access to the building, meaning that anyone wanting to approach had to stand on the opposite pavement, making themselves very visible, before diving across the road. It wasn't possible to sneak up on the building in its shadow because of no pavement and the dangerous bend.

When Mum and Lionel were last up, Mrs Cunningham had way-laid Lionel, and now he was always asking whether Helen had got on to the Council yet about the road safety issues. He didn't see why she and Mrs Cunningham couldn't form a pressure group to lobby for speed bumps. Helen had tried to explain that Mrs Cunningham didn't want speed bumps, she just liked moaning on about the lack of them, but Lionel probably thought she was being facetious.

When the kettle started to bubble, she turned back into the room and allowed herself a glance at the laptop. It sat behind the sofa on the big desk in the corner of the room. She'd bought the desk for £30 from the junk shop up the road. Well, it called itself an antique shop, but it just sold junk like the desk, with its mottled top and shoogly back leg.

In order to maintain some sort of grip on normality she'd had to impose a ban – no switching on the laptop until seven o'clock at the earliest.

And it was only six twenty-eight.

Her work colleagues would be in The Dome by now, letting the good times roll. In a couple of hours Stuart Gourlay would be recounting his ex-wife's latest insanity, and Marc would be laughing like a maniac. And Eilidh and Susan's bitching would have reached the hysterical cackling stage.

She should be with them, having fun normal-person style. Sooking up to Stuart. If Eilidh really was getting promoted, that would be the Section Head position up for grabs, and she should probably make an effort to pretend she enjoyed her colleagues' company. But she just couldn't bring herself. And why should she put herself through it, why should she have to stay out late and come home on her own when there'd probably be no one around and she couldn't trust the taxi driver to wait until she'd got inside and flashed the lights?

And, false modesty aside, it wasn't as if there was any serious competition for Section Head. They were hardly going to give it to Marc: twenty-five, and clueless. Didn't know his arse from his unguentarium.

She smiled, imagining what Suzanne would have had to say about Marc. She'd probably have done something outrageous, like phoning up Stuart pretending to be one of the Directors complaining about Marc's work.

She went to the counter, dropped a teabag into a mug and poured on the water, swirling the teabag around with a spoon and watching the water darken.

Sometimes she felt as if the parallel world in which Suzanne hadn't died was the real one and this – this was just a ghost world, an imaginary 'what if' world in which disaster hadn't, after all, been averted. Back in the real world, surely, the real Helen and the real Suzanne drank tea together and did all the other normal things of normal life – called each other to bind on about men and mothers and the bitches at work; agonised in changing rooms; pored over menus and colour charts; carefully avoided the subject of Rob; laughed till they cried about Helen's schoolgirl crush on Hector Forbes.

But in this other world, the ghost Helen bought clothes without bothering to try them on, and sat in cafés with people she didn't care if she never saw again, and lived in terror of Rob Beattie, and stalked Hector Forbes on the internet. And the ghost Suzanne couldn't do anything except lie under the ground on the Hill of Saughs or Knockbeg or the Muir of Aven, or under the water in Loch Deer, while the rain and the snow fell, and the sun rose and set, and the wind blew by.

She looked across at the laptop.

Oh God. She really was turning into a sad mad old bat like Mrs Cunningham. Next thing, she'd be accosting people on the stairs and complaining that she never heard them coming in and out: 'You young people and your soft-soled shoes.'

If Stuart ever found out how she actually preferred to spend her evenings... Probably not something she'd be adding to the 'Interests' section of her CV: cross-stitch, wildlife, 19th Century novels and internet stalking.

Pathetic.

But harmless, surely? And it was the one thing guaranteed to distract her from obsessing about Suzanne. The one thing that could bring her down off the ceiling when she heard a strange noise in the building and was immediately convinced it was Rob, jimmying open the door.

And it wasn't just Hector she stalked – it was all of them.

Did that make it better or worse?

She loved finding out what they were all up to; imagining what they might be doing at any given moment. Maybe today Fiona and her two older girls – Cat and Ruth – had been out on their bikes after school, along the back road to Logie Coldstone, the spring air sharp and sweet, high voices raised above the whir of the bicycle wheels. And Damian had had the dogs out, Hector cursing him when they came back covered in mud – Irina wouldn't let him have a pet in their own house because of the mess, but Damian was at Pitfourie so much it didn't really matter.

Ridiculous. She knew that Cat and Ruth had bikes because there'd been a photo of them on Fiona's Facebook page. But she didn't know if Hector had any dogs. She didn't know where Irina and Damian were even living.

Yet.

She unlocked the top drawer in the desk, removed a scrapbook at random and took it and the stewed tea to the coffee table. She sat down on the sofa, shrugged out of her jacket and kicked off her shoes.

The first photo was of Norrie and another man, photographed against a misty hillside. In the accompanying article, some freedom-to-roam person was moaning on about Pitfourie Estate putting a deer fence across the hill at Crask. Hector was quoted as saying it was necessary for regeneration of the forest, and he was sorry if anyone was going to be inconvenienced, but the gates in the fence were clearly marked on maps that could be downloaded from the website. Norrie, Pitfourie Estate's 'Forest Regeneration Project Manager', gave facts and figures about how long regeneration had been shown to take with and without exclusion of deer.

Norrie looked like some sort of native creature himself, blending into the hillside in his estate tweeds.

He'd come to see her not long after she'd left Pitfourie, and they'd all sat round the table at Auntie Anne's making polite conversation, and then she and Norrie had gone out to see a film and on the way back he'd gently taken her hand, and she'd gently removed it.

The next photo was of Fish – District Procurator Fiscal, no less – outside a courtroom with some other lawyer types, very smart and actually a bit intimidating-looking, with slicked-back hair and an opaque expression.

And then Hector, handing over a prize to some child who'd won the under-12 girls section of a charity fun run sponsored by Pitfourie Estate. The little girl was rabbit-in-the-headlights. Hector was grinning, very handsome in tweed jacket and tie.

It was worth the subscription to the *Press and Journal* for that photo alone.

Suzanne would have gone absolutely mental.

You sad sad cow! Get over it!

But she didn't want to get over it.

Even in the aftermath of London she hadn't been able to harden her heart against him. She'd tortured herself with 'what if's: what if she hadn't taken him to the Tower of London – the most famous *prison* in the world, for God's sake? What if she hadn't been a silly little idiot, giggling at the carvings of a lion and a bear in the Beaufort Tower and saying how cute they were? What if she'd managed to talk to him in a mature and intelligent way about things he was actually interested in? What if she hadn't kept mentioning Suzanne and Rob? What if she hadn't been so pathetic and clingy and needy and weird?

What if she could have been what he wanted?

She'd written to Irina at Pitfourie, a brief note saying she'd 'met up with' Hector but had lost his contact details – could Irina let her have them?

Three weeks later a note had come back in Irina's flamboyant handwriting, with an email address and a PO box number in San Carlos. Another week and Helen had composed an email message she was happy with. She'd sent it off, and a couple of days later a reply had come into her inbox.

Opening that email had been one of the hardest things she'd ever done in her life.

She had it still, in a folder called 'HF_email'. She still remembered it word for word. She closed her eyes and saw the black typeface.

And in the quiet of the flat she heard it:

A footstep.

She jumped off the sofa, sending her mug flying, tea arcing over the carpet. She stared at the open door into the tiny hallway.

Another footstep.

Footsteps.

Footsteps, but through the wall. Muffled footsteps on stone. On the stone landing outside.

She laughed breathlessly. Oh God. She really was turning into Mrs Cunningham. It was just Linda, who lived in the flat opposite. Or someone coming to see Linda.

She waited for the sound of a key in the door of Linda's flat, or the sound of her doorbell, or knuckles rapping on her door.

But there was nothing.

She slipped into the hall, noiseless in her stocking feet, and put her eye to the peephole. The fish-eye gave her a distorted view of the whole landing, stark in the fluorescent lighting bouncing off the lemon walls and the huge worn old flagstones.

There was no one there.

But she could hear the footsteps again, moving up, above her head...

Someone going up to the top floor.

But wait a minute.

Callum and Jo in the flat above hers were away in Dubai for two months. And the other flat was empty while Mrs Ritchie was in hospital. She knew this because she needed the agreement of every household on the stair before she could get CCTV installed, and when she'd asked Mrs Cunningham why she never got a response from the top floor flats Mrs Cunningham had started moaning on about how irresponsible it was for people to leave flats empty. An invitation to squatters.

Maybe it was Mrs Ritchie's daughter come to collect the mail or something.

She really was channelling Mrs Cunningham.

But there was no way she was going out onto that landing to check. She made sure both chains were securely fastened, and the mortice locks engaged. Then she tiptoed back to the living room and sat back down on the sofa and stared at the wet streak of tea on the carpet as she listened out for any other noise.

She closed her eyes.

Hector's email. She had been thinking about Hector's email.

Helen, for God's sake, it's I who should be apologising. You're quite wrong – I don't think you're a bunny boiler (!) and you have nothing at all for which to reproach yourself. I'm the one who should be doing that. I've behaved appallingly, as usual, and I wouldn't blame you if you hated my guts.

I should have told you from the outset what the situation was. I somehow managed to convince myself that I'd made it clear, but of course I hadn't.

Nothing that you've done or said has made me think badly of you. How could it? You are, and have always been, one of my favourite people in the world, and I'll always remember our weekend together. But I can't have a relationship with you. Not the kind you need and should have. You seem to have developed a very idealised view of me – I don't quite know how! I'm afraid the reality is very different.

I don't think any sort of correspondence is a good idea, and in any case my internet access will be intermittent over the next few months. What I told you, about working for an oil company – that wasn't exactly the truth. My circumstances preclude any sort of regular contact, let alone anything more.

I'm sorry for treating you so badly. It's the last thing you deserve.

Thank you, and yet again, sorry. I always seem to be apologising to you, for what apologies are worth, which of course is very little.

Love,
Hector

He probably thought he'd been pretty convincing. That she'd believe he was just a bad boy who wasn't capable of commitment. That the truth wasn't buried in there, between the words. That it wouldn't hit her like a sledgehammer.

He'd spent those two days with her as an act of charity.

When Hector had been back at Pitfourie, Uncle Jim must have let slip something about how Helen still wasn't coping with Suzanne's death, was still beating herself up about it, had terrible self-esteem issues, was a paranoid mess – not that Uncle Jim would have put it like that. And Hector had sought her out, as he had long ago in the school playground, to dry her tears and kiss it better – only literally, this time, after she'd sobbed at him that she should have known he could never have written those letters. In other words: *I know I could never be good enough for you.*

And so those two days had been his gift to her. A gift to say: *But, you see, you are.*

He couldn't know that it wasn't a question of self-esteem but of love; and that his gift was always going to be too much, and not enough.

She had replied with just nine words:

Thank you. I could never hate you. Love, Helen.

There had been no reply.

She'd started going out with a guy called Pete, who'd turned out to be a card-carrying gold-plated bastard. She hadn't cared. She'd moved on to Richard. And then Jeff. And then someone whose name might have been Rod. And then no one for a while. And then back to Jeff again.

And then something unexpected had happened – in M&S, of all places. Jeff's mission had been to get a treat for dessert while she checked out the clothes, only she'd decided she'd better make sure he didn't get something healthy like a melon, so she'd gone after him. And there he'd been, lifting a chocolate cheesecake from the chiller cabinet, a long-faced man with accountant-channelling-Romantic-poet hair, and it had hit her:

I'm happy.

And not just because of the cheesecake.

For the first time in her life she'd felt like a proper adult in a proper adult relationship: they were 'Helen and Jeff', taking photography classes together and going off to Cornwall to stay with his parents. They'd rented a basement flat in Battersea – a hovel, but they'd splashed out on Farrow & Ball paints – Cooking Apple Green over the dark veneers of the kitchen units – and Jeff had spent a month breaking up the concrete in the 'outdoor space' at the back, and trailing the bits through the flat to the wheelie bin, so she could have grass and flowers and herbs and even, one year, courgettes under a cold frame made out of a window he'd found in a skip.

And she'd convinced herself that Jeff was right, Mum was right, Hector had been right – Rob Beattie wasn't going to come after her. Jeff had even got her to 'face her fear' and go jogging with him, early in the morning or in the evening, when it was dark and anyone could be lurking. A couple of times he'd even persuaded her to go on her own, greeting her on her return with big sloppy kisses all over her sweaty body that had made her scream with half-hysterical laughter.

Even Mum had liked Jeff.

Maybe that had been part of the problem – everyone liked Jeff, and he returned the sentiment. He loved being with people, brunches and lunches and dinners with his huge extended family, conversations going on across and around her. And oh God, the parties – waking up to find Jeff with three new best friends in the kitchen, discussing American foreign policy and feeding them the contents of the fridge.

She remembered, as things had deteriorated, Jeff snapping at her that he was the kind of person who needed company, and snapping back: 'So what am *I* – part of the furniture?'

After the split, it had seemed the right time to get out of London. To accept that she wasn't ever going to find Suzanne sitting at the back of a bus or standing in the queue at the chemist. New job, new city. Back to Edinburgh, and Mum and Auntie Anne.

She opened her eyes and picked up the scrapbook.

The next photo showed Hector as one of a group of 'local landowners' opposing plans for a windfarm near Lochnagar. She liked this one of him best of all. The men – they were all men – had been photographed outside, with a backdrop of the hills, and Hector was looking slightly to one side, as if he'd been distracted at the last minute. The wind had tousled his hair and he looked like a schoolboy at a sober gathering of old men, eager to be off doing something else.

But he was thirty-seven now. The lines of jaw and nose and

cheek more defined; the planes of his face no longer so youth.

She'd done an osteoarchaeology course at uni and had been surprised to discover that the bone structure of people's faces changed not just when they were growing in childhood but through-out adulthood too. A twenty-something man tended to have more gracile, more delicate, less masculine-looking facial bones than his thirty-something older self.

In most people the changes were subtle. If you put a photo of Hector in his twenties next to this one, you'd see some differences but you'd have no problem recognising him. But in other people the changes could be much more marked.

She closed the scrapbook.

Other people.

Rob Beattie's face had changed a lot from when he was a child to when he was a teenager. Was it possible that it had changed just as much in the sixteen years since Helen last saw him? Since anyone last saw him?

Oh God.

Oh *God*.

She flew to the desk and flipped open the laptop.

It didn't take long to find a photograph of Rob on an 'unsolved crimes' website. He smiled goofily from the screen, his face white in the flash. He held a beer bottle in one hand. The photo seemed to have been taken at a party in someone's kitchen, oak-effect country-style wall units behind him.

His nose was a completely different shape from the nose of the man she'd seen today. But there was such a thing as plastic surgery. She put a hand up to the screen to hide the nose –

Was it possible?

Was it?

20

It was one of the hardest things she'd ever done: opening the door of the flat and stepping out onto the cold flagstones of the landing. But Medusa would be closing in five minutes and she couldn't go through a whole night not knowing. She clung on to the door after she'd shut it behind her, the Yale key still in the lock, ready to snap it open and dive back inside at the first sound from the top landing.

But there was nothing.

Heaving in a breath, she locked the top mortice and then the bottom one, yanking the key from the lock and running for the steps, careering down them two at a time.

Good decision to change into joggers and trainers.

Adrenaline was pumping so hard it was almost like flying, her feet skimming the steps as she plummeted down them in near free-fall.

She ran for the outside door, not looking behind her, concentrating on flicking the Yale open and hauling open the door and diving outside, eyes constantly swivelling, checking the tiny front gardens, the pavement opposite...

Then she was across the road and running.

Up to the junction.

Across the roundabout.

Lights were blazing from the windows of Medusa, bouncing off the shiny surfaces of mirrors and glass and glossy black hairdryers neatly lined up on their rack. But it was deserted – a Marie Celeste version of itself.

The sign on the door was turned to Closed.

She was too late.

She rattled the door handle. She slapped at the glass of the door, the breath almost sobbing in her throat.

And from the back of the salon Karim appeared, carrying a cloth and a can of cleaner, swaying slightly to silent music. She windmilled her arms at him, grinning manically, and he pulled out his earbuds.

'Karim,' she gasped when he'd opened the door and she'd half-tumbled over the threshold. 'This is going to sound really weird, but – the man who was in here before... The one I thought I knew... Would you have a record of his name on the database? He's got an appointment for two-thirty on Tuesday. That's what your reception-ist said. Two-thirty.'

'Helen. What is going on with you, huh? Who is this guy?'

What could she say?

'I – I think he's maybe stalking me.'

He reached out a hand and touched her arm. 'Have you gone to the police?'

'I will. But first I have to know if it's him or not. Please. Could you just check the database?'

'Yeah, not really supposed to give out client details?'

'Karim –'

'He might not have used his real name?'

'*Please?*' She let her eyes fill with the tears she'd been fighting.

He grimaced. Leaving the can and the cloth on a glass table, he walked across the shiny tiled floor to the reception counter. Helen followed him. Under the blazing lights she felt exposed, on view, as if they were performers on a stage. Helen's role: sad little stalking victim.

'Can I just – do you mind if I lock the door?' She reached for the key and turned it.

When the computer had booted up, Karim muttered: 'Two-thirty on Tuesday?'

'Yes.'

'Okay... two clients at two-thirty... Elaine Roberts and Moir Sandison.'

'Okay. Thanks. That's not his name, but – as you said, he proba-bly wouldn't have given his real name, would he? If he only came here to –'

'You need to go to the police, Helen, yeah?'

'Is there an address?'

He gave her a long look, then scribbled on a big yellow Post-It, pulled it from the pad and pushed it across the counter.

31 Eglinton Crescent, Flat 1F1

21

Back in the flat, door shut and triple-locked, chains on, she took a packet of crackers with her to the desk and nibbled one as she waited for the laptop to boot up.

Googling on 'Moir Sandison' brought up several pages of hits. There was a Moir Sandison on Facebook, but he lived in America, and most of the top hits seemed to refer to this person, a man in his sixties who was CEO of a graphic design company. When she restricted the search to the UK, she found another Moir Sandison on LinkedIn – an architect. But he lived in Manchester. A Moir Sandison, again from Manchester, had left comments on a rugby forum about the Scotland/Ireland game, and on the website of a company selling antique pens, thanking them for their excellent service.

No Moir Sandison in Edinburgh.

But it was a Scottish name. Could Moir Sandison from Manchester have family in Edinburgh and be here visiting them? There was no photo on the LinkedIn page. She brought up the website of the architecture firm he apparently worked for, but could find no mention of him there.

That was suspicious, wasn't it?

What if Rob had created the whole fake identity of Moir Sandison just for the purpose of coming after Helen? What if Moir Sandison from Manchester only existed on the internet in case anyone decided to Google him? Maybe he was renting 31 Eglinton Crescent and needed a backstory in case the landlord Googled him?

She needed to call the police.

But they wouldn't go round there demanding a DNA sample just because Helen had heard him cough in a particular way, would they?

She needed more.

She needed to go to Eglinton Crescent herself and make sure.

Only problem was that she would never in a million years be able to pluck up the courage to do that. Could she hire someone? Pay someone, a private investigator, to look into Moir Sandison? But how long would that take, to find someone, to set up a meeting…?

She needed to act *now*.

But do what?

She sat back, rubbing her eyes, and almost on automatic pilot she found herself reaching for the laptop and clicking on the Favourites menu.

She would let her subconscious work on the problem while she did a spot of cyberstalking. That was when people came up with their best ideas, wasn't it, when they were relaxing in the bath or whatever? Well, this was her equivalent.

Already she could feel the tension leaving her body.

A smile tugging at the corners of her mouth.

She was scrupulous about not doing this at the museum. She only ever used the internet there for genuinely work-related stuff. Today she'd been downloading photographs of pottery fragments that had been found on an eroding bank of the Orbe River. Oskar Dufour at Berne University was convinced they dated from the late 1st Century BC, but she thought they were earlier, and perhaps Middle Eastern. He'd suggested she take a trip over there to have a look at them and some other finds he'd like her thoughts on. And maybe she would.

What would Suzanne have said about Oskar?

Probably: *He's practically collecting his pension?*

She scrolled down her favourites list to 'Pitfourie Estate' and clicked.

And there it was, the homepage with its panoramic banner photograph – the view from Aucharblet across to Lochnagar, with sheep in the field in the foreground, and on the left a big old sycamore spreading its branches across the screen.

Underneath was 'Pitfourie Estate' in big blue letters, and on the right a photograph of a capercaillie with his tail feathers fanned out. This photo changed regularly. Last month it had been a snowdrop with the sun on its petals. And the month before that there had been a lovely one of what Helen had decided was the field right in front of the house, thick with snow, the branches of the trees outlined in white like lace, the horses' breath steaming around their heads.

She wondered who took these photos. Maybe Hector.

She smiled.

It was like immersing herself in a wonderful fictional world, only a hundred times better because it was real, it existed, and it was *her* world – or at least it had been.

What had she done before she had this?

Just after she'd moved back to Edinburgh from London two years ago, Auntie Anne had been diagnosed with an aggressive brain tumour. She'd been dead in six months. And then Lionel from the theatre group, Mum's 'tower of strength', had married her and whisked her off to a Victorian villa he'd inherited in a picturesque part of Yorkshire.

And then the banging on the door had started, and Helen had had to sell that flat and buy this one.

She'd begun to have serious trouble sleeping. One night she'd given up trying; got up, made a cup of tea and switched on the laptop. She'd typed in, before she could think better of it, 'Hector Forbes Pitfourie'. The first hit had been the Pitfourie Estate website. All the familiar names and places. Photographs of curlews and drifts of bog cotton. Touches of humour, here and there, that clawed at her heart.

She'd felt like a character in a kids' book, waking at midnight and wandering, barefoot and wide-eyed, into a lost world.

On the left of the homepage was the menu:

Home

About Us

News

Woodlands and Forestry

Farms

Sporting and Tynoch Lodge

Holiday Cottages

Conservation Projects

Pitfourie History

NatureDork

Walks

Contact

The text on the homepage never changed much.

Welcome to our website. Pitfourie is a traditional estate encompassing 31 000 acres of native woodland, forestry plantation, farmland and moorland on Upper Deeside in the north-east of Scotland. The landscape here is amongst the most beautiful in Britain (not that we're in any way biased!), from the high summits of Ben Aven and Tom na Creiche, to the ancient pinewood of Badentoul, to the slow pools and spectacular falls of the River Glass.

Our business interests include tenanted farms and houses, forestry, holiday lets and sporting activities.

Conservation is at the core of our management policy. We are currently working in partnership with the Woodland Trust, the Red Squirrel Survival Trust, Scottish Natural Heritage and the local community on a range of projects, foremost of which is the Caledonian Pine Project, which aims to expand the acreage of native woodland at Crask and Aultmore. The Inverdraught Scout Group and the children at Kirkton of Glass Primary School are helping us eradicate invasive bracken in Garble Wood.

We welcome visitors to the Estate. In the Walks section of the website you can download a range of maps and guides with suggested walking routes. Self-catering cottages are available to rent throughout the year, and Tynoch Lodge can accommodate sporting parties of up to twenty-two.

Our sporting team offers traditional pheasant and grouse shoots, salmon and trout runs, and red deer stalking. We can provide vehicle and gun hire and also transport to and from Aberdeen Airport or railway station.

Campers are asked to contact the Estate Office for information on suitable sites. Visitors should ensure that dogs are kept on a leash if crossing a field containing livestock, and note that the area around the House of Pitfourie is strictly private. The house and grounds are not open to the public.

Helen clicked on the 'News' link in the menu. The screen changed to show a photograph of a man with a gun over his arm, and under it the title 'Bill Coull retires', followed by three paragraphs about Bill and his wife Cathy, which finished:

> It only remains for me to thank Bill for all his hard work on the Estate over the years, and to say that his expertise, his energy and his cheerful presence generally will be greatly missed – if not his obsessive and some would say inexplicable enthusiasm for Aberdeen Football Club. I and all at Pitfourie wish him and Cathy many happy years of well-earned retirement.

Hector Forbes

Usually these News items weren't signed, although she thought she could tell the ones Hector had written. She read it again, and a third time, hearing his voice in her head. The bits Hector wrote never had any of the spelling mistakes or grammatical errors that sometimes appeared elsewhere on the website – although those errors usually disappeared within a few days.

She thought she knew what the set-up must be. Someone in the office –probably the person called Gillian Webster who was listed on the Contact page – looked after the website on a day-to-day basis, and Hector only had time to look at it every week or so. That was when he picked up the mistakes.

She'd checked the online marriage records at ScotlandsPeople, and nothing had come up for any 'Hector Forbes' in the last eleven years. That didn't mean he hadn't married in England or abroad, of course. But if he'd had a wife, she would have been mentioned, surely, on the website; shown with him there sometimes, and in the *Press and Journal*? It was likely he had a partner, of course it was, but Hector hadn't splashed his private life all over the internet so she didn't know. He wasn't on Facebook or Instagram or Twitter. Ridiculously, she felt faintly aggrieved about this, a little bit annoyed with him, as if he was deliberately thwarting her.

Damian was surprisingly cagey too. She thought she'd found him on Facebook – it was the only page, anyway, for someone called Damian Forbes in the right part of the country. She took a second to bring up the page in a new window, but there was nothing new on it – still no public information other than 'Lives in Aboyne', which probably wasn't quite right, but people in rural areas often seemed to give the nearest town. The profile picture was still a big black slug, and the cover photo a spectacular one of the Northern Lights – just illuminated sky, green and yellow and blue, with only a sliver of darkened, unidentifiable hillside beneath it.

She closed the window and returned to the Pitfourie Estate website, where she copied the 'News' text and saved it into a fresh Word document. Then she opened the NatureDork page.

There was a new photo of a robin with a mealworm in his beak, and underneath:

Robin Wars Part 2

News from the Western Front: Napoleon has been forced to concede the stretch of territory from the Clearing to Nest Box 1. Attila has taken possession of the tree formally favoured for hanky-panky by Napoleon and Josephine, and can be seen there at intervals throughout the day, calling loudly. It's pretty much total humiliation for Napoleon.

On the Home Front, Napoleon has been spotted at the feeding station making an **** [Ed: censored] of himself in a pitiful attempt to impress Josephine, and offering her the occasional mealworm, but seems more interested in stuffing his own beak than hers, while keeping a constant wary eye out (let's hope not literally) for a fresh offensive from Attila.

The task of building up Josephine's energy reserves in preparation for the breeding season seems to have been delegated by Napoleon to NatureDork, whose expenditure on mealworms from the online RSBP shop threatens to create personal debt of such unmanageable proportions as to finally bring down the UK economy. Not that Napoleon, Josephine or Attila is worried about NatureDork's financial embarrassment. More worrying for them is the possibility that NatureDork's actions, in providing a superabundance of mealworms, have tipped the finely tuned natural balance of their ecosystem into a catastrophic spiral of irresponsibility and aggression.

But that's humans for you.

NatureDork

NatureDork was always anonymous, but she was pretty sure he wasn't Hector – there was just something about the turn of phrase. And Hector would be too busy to sit around birdwatching all day.

Her theory, based on nothing at all, was that NatureDork was Damian.

A little boy fascinated by animals' skulls was likely to go on to have an interest in nature, wasn't he? And his activities at school tended to support this idea. He would presumably be going into his final year (already!) at Glencoil in the autumn. She didn't know for sure because, no doubt in line with some absurd politically correct directive, the school never posted any details about individual pupils on the website. But she knew he was a pupil there – or at least he had been two years ago – from Googling on 'Damian Forbes'. She'd found his name in articles about an interschools chess tournament and a debating competition, and, another three years back, a science workshop run by Aberdeen University. And he'd won a national mathematics competition when he was thirteen. Maths, science, nature – they all went together in the general scheme of dorkdom, didn't they?

She couldn't find a proper photograph of him. There was a photo on someone's blog of all the children who'd attended the science workshop, but there were over a hundred of them and each face was too small to make out features properly. She'd been able to pick out the Glencoil contingent from their uniforms, though, and there was just something about one of the boys, in the middle of the second row – she was sure he was Damian.

His hair was no longer bright blond – it was just ordinary mud colour now, and messy, in an I've-got-better-things-to-do-than-bother-about-my-hair kind of way, rather than in an attempt to ape the latest fashion. His face was chubby and smiling. He looked like he was really happy to be there, and she could imagine him being unselfconsciously enthusiastic about everything in a completely uncool way. But he'd be one of those boys who didn't care about being cool, and was popular in spite – or because – of it.

She'd looked up Glencoil in the *Guide to Fee-Paying Schools in Scotland* and it had come out above average, but not brilliant. Presumably the estate finances didn't run to Eton, what with having to pay inheritance tax when the Laird died – although she'd have thought Irina's parents might have coughed up.

Maybe Irina didn't want him going away to boarding school. But Helen couldn't imagine Irina letting her own feelings get in the way of her son's education. She would want the best for him, surely?

It was so frustrating, knowing so much but not quite enough.

Maybe Irina and Damian lived at the House with Hector, but something made her think not. In a cottage on the estate maybe, although the idea of Irina in a cottage... It was far more likely that she'd remarried and was installed in some other stately home in the area.

There was no second marriage for her in the online records. A Google search on her name had just turned up obituaries for the old Laird.

Surely Irina would have a new partner by now, though? Helen hoped he was good with Damian. But even if he was the best stepfather ever, it wouldn't be him Damian confided in and depended on and took his troubles to.

It would be Hector.

Hector would have been the one to encourage his interest in wildlife. She could just imagine him saying, 'How about doing a nature column for the website?' and maybe Damian not being sure if he could, and Hector saying, 'Of course you can do it, you're practically a walking encyclopaedia of useless information about wildlife,' and ever since, Damian had been coming up with these funny little pieces, mainly about birds but also about other things – like the genetics of primroses, and how a wood ant colony was organised.

He was becoming really good at them. He was obviously exceptionally bright. And very sweet – although he'd no doubt be appalled that anyone could think so. And there was something about his sense of humour that reminded her of Hector.

Of course NatureDork could be any random person living on the Estate. But she liked to think he was Damian. She liked to imagine Irina standing behind her son to look at the screen, and draping her arms round him and resting her chin on his shoulder to read as he typed up the latest instalment, and laughing in all the right places. And maybe suggesting names for the birds. There was definitely something Irina-ish about Napoleon and Josephine.

She saved the latest NatureDork and sent it to the printer.

Then she navigated back to the News page and stared at Hector's signature.

And his words from eleven years ago suddenly came into her head:

I hope you're not still living in fear of that fucking little shit, Helen.

22

Eglinton Crescent was very West End – very fantoosh, as Dad would have said. A grand sweep of bay-windowed Victorian sandstone facing onto an acre or so of gardens – gardens maintained for the exclusive use of the residents of the streets around them. It was the kind of area that had a high density of consulates and bridge clubs.

The closest parking space she'd been able to find was three doors down from Number 31, but from where she sat in Stan, her little red Mini, she could see the door quite well because of the curve of the terrace. It was reached up four wide, shallow steps which gave onto an expanse of flagstones spanning the chasm between pavement and building. Beneath the flagstone bridge was the basement which in Victorian times would have been the servants' domain. Of course most of the houses had been turned into flats decades ago. There was a discreet row of buzzers set into the frame of the door.

The door was huge. In fact it was a double door, opening in two sections, with a heavy brass ring in place of a doorknob. Around the door were leaded stained-glass windows, and on either side flattened sandstone columns with acanthus-leaf corbels.

Posh.

She was perfectly positioned, as long as 'Moir Sandison' turned left, towards her, when he exited the building rather than right. But the chances were that he'd go left, towards the city centre. If he went right she wouldn't be able to get a good shot. The zoom on her phone wasn't great.

The other problem, of course, was that she might have missed him. Probably not – it was just half past seven, the early light cold and flat, the bare branches of the trees in the gardens stiff black fingers across a grey sky. But it was possible he started work at some unearthly hour.

It was also possible he worked from home.

Or that he wasn't here at all. He could have given the salon a false address.

It probably wasn't even him.

But what if it was? What if Suzanne – Sometimes people were kept prisoner for years. Decades. What if Suzanne was up there right now, looking down at her through a chink in a metal shutter?

She peered up at the windows.

Ridiculous.

She was being ridiculous. Suzanne wasn't up there. Even if it was Rob, Suzanne wasn't going to be here.

Two girls, probably Italian students or tourists judging by their colouring and the cut of their jeans, were coming along the pavement towards her with a slow, swaggering swing of the hips. She could use them as a dry run.

She lifted the map she'd spread across the wheel until it concealed most of her face. She was wearing the sunglasses she'd bought last time she was in France, and an ugly yellow sunhat. In March, for God's sake.

She picked up her phone, holding it half-concealed by the dashboard, and switched it on.

Nothing. The screen stayed black.

But she'd made sure she charged it last night! Or she thought she had. She mustn't have switched the charger on. Idiot! Well, but she had a camera… Her old camera, which she kept in the car in case of photo opportunities – a habit she'd developed when she and Jeff had been into photography. She flipped open the glove compartment and lifted it out.

But it felt too light in her hand.

The battery compartment was empty.

Right. The newsagent on West Maitland Street would have batteries. She grabbed her bag and, before she could let herself think what she was doing, had opened the car door and stepped out onto the pavement and locked Stan behind her.

She ran all the way to the shop.

Inside, feeling sweaty and a bit weak-kneed suddenly, she bought a pack of batteries, a bottle of water and a flapjack. She seemed to have forgotten to eat or drink anything before leaving the flat. She felt ridiculous in her sunhat and dark glasses, running back along Palmerston Place, but the people she passed didn't give her a second glance.

She ran across the road and back into Eglinton Crescent. Part of her brain was registering what a nice place to live this must be: Eglinton Crescent and the street opposite formed a long oval, with the gardens an island of green marooned in the tarmac between them. All the rest of her attention was on checking the pavement in front of her – no one there – and behind – just an elderly couple turning the corner into the street.

She was thirsty, her mouth dry. She stopped to pull the bottle of water from her bag. Head down, she was aware of movement between two parked cars, and someone moving in front of her. She stepped to the side to let them past.

But they stepped to the side too, blocking her way.

She looked up.

Moir Sandison smiled at her.

23

She squeezed the bottle of water. She stepped to the other side.

So did he.

The bulk of him filled her vision: a dark, expensive-looking suit; a very white shirt; a striped tie, blue and purple; a glimpse of gold cuff-link.

'Sorry,' he said, and cleared his throat: *cough-cough cough*.

She couldn't move and she couldn't speak.

He laughed, and stepped back; sketched a bow, and walked on past her.

She ran.

She ran to Stan, fumbled the key into the lock; dived inside and locked the door. She was going to be sick. Her hands on the wheel and her feet on the pedals were shaking, but she managed to make the car move out into the road and away, revving the engine like a learner.

24

There were two of them, sitting hip to hip on her sofa, making it look like a miniature version of itself. And she thought of the policeman in her hospital room long ago, dwarfing the chair he sat on.

The younger man was the one asking the questions, and writing down her answers in a notebook. She'd expected something higher tech. But no, she had to keep pausing while he laboriously wrote down what she said, while the older officer seemed bored, looking out of the window and about the room; at the painting of horses above the fireplace that used to hang in the dining room at the Parks.

They'd said 'No thanks' to Helen's offer of tea, so she hadn't felt able to have one herself. She sat on the pouffe by the window, facing them, feeling like a child whose lies had caught her out. She'd been so sure of her story before they'd arrived. She'd just say she'd seen him coming down the steps of Number 31 Eglinton Crescent and recognised him immediately.

She had two reasons for lying.

One, she didn't want to get Karim into trouble for giving out the address of a customer to another customer.

Two, the truth didn't make sense. Not to someone who didn't know Rob Beattie. Why would a man living under a false name, on the run for murder, not cross the street, or turn away, or at least hurry on past when he saw someone he knew in his previous life on the pavement in front of him? Not just someone he knew, but the girl whose cousin he'd murdered; the girl he'd attacked?

Why would he block her way until she looked up at him, and stare into her face, and smile at her?

It didn't make sense.

Not unless you knew him.

So she'd kept it simple. She'd told them she'd been walking

along the pavement and there he was – Rob Beattie, coming down the steps.

But then the questions had started.

What time was this? Where was she going? Why was she on Eglinton Crescent?

She'd blanked. Why *would* she have been there, on a residential West End street, that early in the morning?

She'd said she often went for an early morning walk before work, round the quiet streets of the New Town and the West End. It was virtually the only exercise she got. From there, she'd walk to the museum.

So, she often walked that route?

Yes, quite often.

But she'd never seen this man before?

No, she never had, but when she said she often walked that route, she didn't mean that *exact* route. Usually she'd go right round by Douglas Crescent.

The younger man had stopped writing after he'd put this answer down in the notebook, and now he was looking at her. Like he knew she was lying.

'Approximately how far away from you was the man?'

'Um – I was walking past on the pavement, and he was coming down the steps. So a few metres?'

'And how old would you say he was?'

'Well – mid to late thirties.'

'Height?'

'About average.'

The older man stood up. 'Compared with my height – taller or shorter?'

'Probably about the same.'

'I'm five-nine. Would that be about right?'

Helen nodded.

'What about his build?'

'On the muscular side. His shoulders and neck were very muscly. And his chest – and his legs. Almost like a body-builder.' She could feel herself flushing.

'Hair and skin colour? Hair length?'

'Brown hair, touching the collar at the back. Skin colour – well, white.' Obviously. 'Why do you need all this? You know where he lives. Can't you just go and – talk to him?'

The older policeman nodded. 'But first we need to finish taking your statement. Just so we have everything straight.'

The younger man consulted the notebook on his lap. 'What was he wearing?'

'A suit. Dark grey, I think. And a shirt and tie.'

'What colour was the tie?'

'It was striped. Blue and purple.'

'When you saw him coming away from Number 31 – did you see him actually exiting the building?'

'Yes.'

'Was there an interaction?'

'What?'

'Did you speak to him, or did he speak to you?'

'No. I – I think he might have recognised me though. He stared at me.' At least that was true.

'And how sure are you? That it was Robin Beattie?'

'It's not a face I'm likely to forget. It was him. His nose is a bit different, but – he must have had plastic surgery.'

'So there were some facial differences?'

'Yes. But his cough was the same too. Not a cough exactly, more of a nervous tic. Like – cuh-cuh *cuh*. In the back of his throat.'

'Right. Okay. I think we have all we need for now. I'll just get you to read this over and sign it…'

'And then what? You'll go and talk to him?'

'We'll visit the building and ascertain whether he's a resident. If we can locate him he'll be interviewed.'

'Rob Beattie – he and my cousin, Suzanne, they both just disappeared. We don't know for certain that he did murder her. He might not have. He might be… keeping her captive or something. In there. In the flat.'

The two men exchanged a quick glance.

Helen stood. 'Will you be able to search the flat? Would you have to get a warrant or something? You need to talk to Grampian Police – DI Murray was in charge of the case, but DS Stewart seemed to be the one doing most of the work. I don't know if he's still –'

'We'll have a chat with the force up there.' The younger man placed the notebook on the counter. 'If you could just read that through.'

She knew she must sound mad. She knew Suzanne wasn't in that flat.

'You've had quite a shock. Maybe you could call a family member or friend and have them come over?'

When they'd gone she switched on the computer, navigated through to the 'Contact' section of the Pitfourie Estate website and clicked on Hector's email address. When the blank email came up on the screen she typed 'Rob Beattie' in the subject field.

Then she closed the email and clicked 'No' when the box came up asking if she wanted to save it.

She really was mad. What sane person encounters a murderer, the murderer of her own cousin, and thinks: *Aha! An excuse to contact Hector!*

But she needed to tell someone.

She stared at the horses painting. It was of two shaggy horses on a hill, in the twilight, looking down into the glen far below; and if you peered closely you could see there was a tiny steam train there, its fire glowing red.

Mum, and worry her sick? Lorna, or Fiona, or Norrie?

Not Norrie, obviously.

She brought up the Favourites menu and clicked on Lorna's website name, *Damask and Delft*. On the homepage was a photo of the shop frontage, painted a tasteful dark blue, with displays of baskets and antique stone pots and a quirky cut-out cat on the pavement outside, and cushions and cards and pretty lamps in the windows.

It was where the butcher's used to be, next to the shoppie.

There was an email address on the contacts page.

But what would she say?

Hi Lorna, hope you remember me, your so-called friend who hasn't been in touch for sixteen years – just wondering if you could ID this man who I think could be your murdering psycho brother?

She went back to the Favourites list and selected the Aboyne Medical Centre.

Steve and Fiona McAllister both worked there as GPs, although Fiona was only part-time. When the website came up she navigated through to the 'Medical Centre Staff' section. There was a photo of Fiona looking 'trust me I'm a doctor'-ish in a lilac blouse, her hair falling in soft waves to her shoulders. Steve had put on the beef a bit. His hair was cut close to his head and he was grinning at the camera.

There was nothing about their personal lives – only stuff about where they qualified and their professional interests and specialties: Fiona's 'special interest' was 'initiatives to improve the quality of life of elderly people'. The website didn't even refer to Fiona and Steve being married.

She'd sent them a belated 'congratulations' card, after finding out from Hector that they were married. Fiona had written back to thank her, and said they must meet up some time soon.

That had been eleven years ago.

She shut down the computer.

There was no one she could tell.

25

'But – no.' She sat down on the sofa and brought the phone back up to her mouth. 'He's lying.'

'He's supplied us with satisfactory evidence that he's Moir Sandison.'

'Like what?'

'A birth certificate. A current passport. An old passport, which was obtained when he was nineteen and carries a photograph of himself at that age. A newspaper clipping showing him at eighteen in the school football team. Other documentary evidence of that nature. He also provided contact details for a gentleman who knew him in his youth – we've followed that up, and have had his identity confirmed to our satisfaction.'

'What about DNA? Could you make him give a DNA sample, or is that an infringement of his human rights or something?'

'He's said he's willing to supply a sample for DNA testing if need be, but the evidence he's already supplied is, we feel, overwhelming.'

'Right. So that's it? You're just taking him at his word?'

'Not at his word, no. We have documentation and corroboration from an individual who –'

'He could have had those forged. He could have got someone to pretend to have known him.'

'The individual in question is his former headmaster, who's been interviewed by officers from the Fife force and identified Sandison from a photograph. Apparently he was quite a football player.'

Helen got up and walked to the window, and placed the hot palm of her left hand against the glass. 'So – you're sure. He's not Rob Beattie.'

'No.'

'But then –' But then how did they explain him blocking her

way just like Rob used to; smiling at her like he used to; mocking her?

They couldn't explain it because she hadn't told them about it.

'I know it *is* him,' was all she could say.

'It's entirely understandable, in the circumstances, that you should believe that to be the case. But comparing this guy with photographs of Robin Beattie... I think most people would have to say the resemblance is superficial at best.'

'*Superficial?*'

'Miss Clack.' The voice was firm now. 'Our investigation has been thorough – I can assure you that we are one hundred per cent sure that this man is *not* Robin Beattie.'

When he'd rung off she set the phone back in the holder, picked up her bag and left the flat. She had to do this now, or not at all.

26

She walked quickly along Eglinton Crescent, her shoes slapping the stone of the pavement. Slap-slap, slap-slap. One of the doors she passed was open, and by the kerb a woman was strapping a child into the back seat of a car and telling him they would be having their supper very very soon but he could have some raisins if he liked.

Raisins. Oh yes, it would be raisins in Eglinton Crescent, not Jelly Tots or Smarties or fizzy juice.

The child, unsmiling, watched Helen pass by.

Slap-slap, slap-slap. She concentrated on the sound of her feet; watched them moving in front of her.

At Number 31 she went up the steps, crossed the flagstones to the door and pressed the buzzer that said 'Sandison'.

Eventually: 'Hello?' came a deep voice.

She'd thought that she'd know his voice. But people's voices changed over the years, didn't they? And the necessity of living under a false identity would be quite an incentive to change the way you spoke.

'This is Helen Clack.'

Silence. Then: 'I think maybe you've got the wrong buzzer? This is flat 1F1?'

She pushed her tongue around her teeth. Her mouth felt sticky and dry and when she said, 'I know it's you, Rob,' it came out much too loud.

'Oh God.' Then: 'You'd better come up.'

The door buzzed.

It would be stupid to go in. To go up there alone, when no one knew where she was. Like a stupid woman in a horror film.

She pushed the door open and stepped inside.

There wasn't just a passage like in her building. There was a proper big lobby, smelling of waxed wood and polished Victorian tiles, with an antique sideboard. And the stairs weren't cold stone like in a tenement; there was a thick wool carpet, cushiony under her feet.

He was standing at an open door on the first floor, wearing a light blue shirt tucked into suit trousers.

'So you're the mad bitch who's been telling the police I'm a murderer.'

'I know who you are.' She folded her shaking arms under her chest.

'Yeah, and do you know the name of the prime minister? Do you know what year it is?'

'I want to see inside your flat.'

'Huh?'

'Now. If you don't let me, I'll call the police.'

He turned on his heel, leaving the door open, and walked away from her into the hallway. His gait was lumbering but at the same time athletic, powerful. Like a bull. She could see a wide hall, and doors off it.

She stepped inside. He had disappeared.

'Suzanne?' she said, her heart bumping.

If Suzanne was here, would she be able to tell? Would there be miniscule particles in the air, atoms from her skin, from her breath, that her subconscious would pick up on?

Suddenly he was back, right in front of her, thrusting a piece of paper in her face. On it was a big photograph of boys in football strips.

'That's *me*, okay?' He stabbed a finger at it. 'Captain of the Menstrie High football team. And *that's* our coach, and *that's* our headmaster Mr McKillop who was a football nut and therefore keeps in contact with me rather than any of the kids in my year who actually achieved anything meaningful.'

Helen looked at the photograph.

Yes. It was a younger version of the man standing in front of her.

'Photoshop,' was all she could say.

'Oh right, and how do you explain Mr McKillop corroborating that I am who I say I am? Some huge conspiracy, all this, is it?'

She shook her head.

'You want my DNA? You want them to analyse my DNA?'

She shook her head.

It wasn't him. This man wasn't Rob Beattie. It wasn't the photo, or anything he'd said – it was the man himself. His face, his expression, that deep voice, the east Central Belt accent, the way his hair kinked round his ears.

It wasn't him.

Suzanne wasn't here.

How could she be? How could you keep a grown woman captive in a flat like this, with people underneath and above and through the walls?

'I'm sorry,' she said.

'You need help.'

'I'm very sorry. It must have been – horrible, to have the police come and ask you all those questions. But I really thought – My cousin... Suzanne... he killed her. He probably killed her. He attacked me and took her, and we don't know where she is, we don't know what he did to her –'

'Oh God.' He had a hand on her shoulder now, and she was gulping, sobs gulping up and her nose streaming, and she pulled a scrappy bit of tissue from her pocket and wiped at her face and he was saying, 'Oh God' again, and, 'I'm sorry. I didn't realise.'

She stepped away from him, and he dropped his hand and said, 'What if I *had* been him?'

'What?'

'What if I *had* turned out to be him? Coming here on your own –'

'Was stupid. I know.' She managed a shaky smile.

'I was going to say brave.'

She breathed. 'I'm really sorry.'

'No, *I'm* sorry. I'd no idea – of the background. The police didn't tell me much. Um... I'd offer you a cup of tea or something, but you probably want to just get out of here.' He smiled. 'My sister always says I'm an insensitive bastard.'

'I don't blame you for being angry.'

'I was well out of order. Look, at least let me take you to the Starbucks round the corner and buy you a coffee?'

'Thanks, but you don't need to do that.'

'You're shaking.' He reached out again and put his hand on her arm. 'Please. It's the least I can do. You need to sit down and have something to drink. Something to eat. Maybe something with chocolate?'

She looked up at him.

'Hey, the magic word. Not such an insensitive bastard after all, eh?'

27

She took a sip of hot coffee. 'So you're still in touch with your old headmaster?'

'Off and on. More off than on really. God only knows what he thought when the boys in blue turned up on his doorstep. He always said I'd come to a sticky end. Used to call me Psycho Sandison.' He shrugged, grinned, sat back a little in his chair. He was so obviously still proud of that, in a nice-teenager-trying-to-be-cool kind of way.

So she said, 'Why?'

'Well, I *was* a bit of a psycho on the football pitch. It has to be said.'

'But you were the team captain.'

'For my sins.' He reached for his coffee. His shirt was tight across the width of his shoulders. You could see the muscles flexing under it when he moved.

How could she have thought he was Rob Beattie? Rob had never had this sort of physical presence; this rather obvious, male-stripper type of attractiveness.

But wasn't it exactly the look Rob would have aimed for, given time, and access to a gym? The kind of look Suzanne would have loved? She used to have a thing for all those muscly action-hero types: Arnold Schwarzenegger and Sylvester Stallone and that other one. *Hunks.*

Outside on the pavement, he said, 'Look. I can see you're still not totally convinced. That I am who I say I am.'

'I am convinced. I know you're not him. Obviously, you're not.'

'Can we meet here again? Tomorrow maybe, after work? I'd like to show you some proper evidence.'

'Really, that's not necessary.'

'Please? I hate to think of you walking around wondering… well. If Psycho Sandison really is a psychopath.' *Cough-cough cough.*

So they met the next day, Moir with a briefcase of 'evidence' which he spread out on the table between their coffee mugs and the plates of cake. There were more team photographs, and programmes from Menstrie High School plays with Moir Sandison in the more minor roles ('Launcelot Gobbo: a foolish man in the service of Shylock'), and cuttings from the local paper featuring his exploits on the football pitch. There was an old letter from his mum from when he'd spent a summer in Germany, full of gossip from home.

He folded the letter and put it back in its envelope. 'My parents died when I was at uni.'

As Suzanne would have said: *Playing the dead parents card.* A grin was trying to twitch the muscles of her face. What would he think, if she started to grin?

She pursed her mouth. 'Oh, I'm sorry.'

'Mum had cancer. Dad couldn't cope after she died. Got up one morning, drove the car into the garage, ran a hose from the exhaust –'

'Oh – no!' Oh God.

He shrugged. 'A long time ago now.'

'But that must have been so – I just can't imagine –'

'It was tough for a while. My sister Rebecca – she blamed herself. She was meant to be going home that weekend, but decided to go to a gig instead.' He pushed a photograph towards her. 'That's Bec. She's a couple of years older than me.'

The photograph showed Moir and an attractive woman with long hair and fashionable narrow glasses, sitting in the sun outside a cafe in Greece or Italy or France, his arm round her as they leaned into each other and smiled for the camera.

'And that's us as kids.'

This one was of a mother and father and two children of about ten and eight, standing in front of a Christmas tree. The little girl was wearing a riding hat and beaming at the camera with exactly the same confident smile as her adult self, but the boy was standing disconsolately, a shiny red football shirt taut over his fat little chest, podgy bare legs white and sausage-like in the shorts.

'Dad's idea to get the weight off me was to enrol me in the local football club's youth programme. Nightmare for the first couple of months, but he made me stick at it, thank God.' He pulled a face. 'What do I look like?'

Morbidly obese?

At least it was okay to smile this time. To laugh. 'You're sweet!'

'Always was an idle little so-and-so. I'd be the size of a house by now if I didn't make myself go to the gym every day... There's more – but I think I've inflicted my life story on you for long enough.' As he reached to take back the photograph, his fingers brushed hers. 'So, do you reckon the evidence stacks up?'

She felt herself flushing as she met his eyes. 'Of course it does. I – don't know why I fixated on you like I did. I mean you don't even look like him, not really –'

'Not so sure about that. I checked him out on the internet last night. I can see there *is* a resemblance. I can understand how you might have wondered...'

'It wasn't that you resemble him, though – that wasn't what attracted my attention – it was – this'll sound ridiculous, but you know when you clear your throat, you do it three times? He used to do that. But even *that's* not the same really. He used to do two quieter coughs and then a louder one, but yours are all – well – more or less at the same volume.'

He laughed. 'You know, I wasn't even aware that I had a particular throat-clearing cough.'

'It's sort of – *cuh cuh cuh*.'

She laughed, and a woman at another table looked over, and Moir grinned and said, 'Captain Caveman, eh? Me Tarzan. Ungowa.'

He'd make a great Tarzan – a knife in his teeth, naked torso glistening with sweat, muscular thighs pumping as he chased down a lion in one of those ridiculously accelerated sequences –

She forked a piece of icing off the cake.

'Ahhhh-*ah*-a-ah-a!'

She giggled. 'Shhh!'

'Hey, look at my power over the animal kingdom.' He pointed his own fork at a tiny fly crawling across the table towards him. 'Moir Sandison: King of the Jungle!'

'Stop it!'

The woman was looking over at them again.

He squashed the fly with a napkin and leant back in his chair, smirking like a naughty child.

28

She went to the sideboard at the foot of the stairs and looked through the letters lying on its shiny surface. Whoever picked up the post from the mat left any letters for the other flats here, but there weren't any for her or Moir. Maybe that meant that Moir was home before her and had already collected them.

She carried on up the stairs.

How strange life was. The first time she'd climbed these stairs she'd been hoping to find Suzanne at the end of them. Now she was hoping to find the man she'd thought was her murderer.

She stopped at the door on the right and rummaged in her bag for her keys.

Eilidh said she was mad, moving in with him so soon; putting her flat on the market; 'committing' herself, when she'd only known him a few months.

And maybe she was. She didn't care.

It wasn't as if she was losing out financially. Quite the opposite. Moir wouldn't take the rent she'd offered to pay him. He wouldn't take any money for bills or Council Tax or anything else. His argument was that two could live as cheaply as one, and now he was eating in so much more, having Helen there was actually *saving* him money. In any case, he earned three times what she did and, call him an unreconstructed sexist pig of a caveman, but in his book the man should be the one bringing home the bacon.

But when her flat was sold, she'd insist on making a proper contribution. They could either stay on here or find a new place. Maybe a house, with a garden they didn't have to share with anyone else.

She let herself in and dumped her bag down on the marble-topped table by the door and called out: 'Helloooo-o!'

Moir appeared from the sitting room, and came and took her

face in his hands, and kissed her gently. She loved this moment, when they first saw each other after a day at work; she loved that she couldn't predict what he'd do. Sometimes he'd be desperate to get her into the bedroom, so desperate she'd find bruises later on her skin, in the oddest places; other times he'd be busy on his laptop and barely exchange a greeting; and other times he'd be like this, treating her like a china doll.

'How did it go?' He tucked her hair behind her ears.

'Quite well, I think. Interviews are always such a joke though, aren't they? Like there's an unwritten script you have to follow: "So, Helen, what would you say your weaknesses were?" "Oh, well, I'm a bit of a perfectionist. And a workaholic".'

He smiled. 'But in your case, both those things happen to be true. Those bastards don't know how lucky they are.' *Cough-cough cough*.

He immediately grimaced an apology. He thought the cough thing upset her.

It certainly upset Mum.

Helen had put off introducing him to Mum and Lionel for as long as she could. But when they'd moved in together, she'd bitten the bullet and gone to Penistone for a weekend on her own, with photographs of Moir, to prepare the ground. They'd all sat in the conservatory and Helen had passed Mum the first photo. 'Doing his Delia Smith impression.'

Mum had gone very still, and although this photo was one in which the resemblance wasn't, she'd thought, noticeable, she'd known at once what Mum was thinking.

He looks like Rob Beattie. Oh God, is Helen off her rocker, like those poor souls who're kidnapped and become obsessed with their tormentors? Going out and finding a man who looks just like Rob Beattie –

And so Helen had had to tell them how she and Moir had met. She'd tried to make a joke of it, and Mum had laughed and said, 'Poor Moir,' and then looked again at the photo and said he really didn't look like Rob at all. Lionel had shoved his oar in at that point – he seemed somehow to be an expert on Rob Beattie as well as everything else – and while he was pontificating about troubled teens Helen had focused past his bullet-shaped head to where she imagined Dad standing watching them, his expression completely deadpan apart from his eyes as they met hers.

Although what Dad's ghost would be doing haunting a market town in Yorkshire she didn't know.

Mum and Lionel had come to stay a couple of times since then. Moir had made a big effort, cooking his famous chilli and pretending he wanted to watch Antiques Roadshow, and losing to Lionel at Scrabble. Mum had made a big effort too, but Helen had seen her, sometimes, looking at Moir –

Now he was leading her into the sitting room. 'I've got something for you.'

It was a high-ceilinged room, almost square, with a lovely old fireplace. The first floor flats had been made out of what would once have been the grandest rooms in the old house.

But poor Moir! His taste ran to the minimalist – and the expensive – and now his cool bachelor pad was wall-to-wall junk shop finds and cute cross-stitch pictures of kittens and the old saggy sofa Helen hadn't been able to part with, set at right angles to his sleek leather one and looking ridiculous.

But when they snuggled in front of the TV it was Helen's comfy old rag-bag they always chose, not his beautiful designer 'piece'. He said he was becoming converted to shabby chic.

He led her to the sofa. She sat down with him, his thigh pressed against hers. He reached for a bag on the coffee table: a small maroon carrier bag with gold lettering. A bag from a jeweller's.

Oh God oh God!

He put his hand inside and pulled out –

A small silver picture frame.

She made herself smile. It was one of those hinged frames in three parts – for a bigger photo in the middle and two smaller ones on each side. In the middle section was a photo of the two of them, from the day they'd gone to Falkland Palace. Moir was handsome as ever, and she didn't look too bad herself – the week before, Moir had treated her to an expensive cut and colour at a salon in the West End, and she was wearing a fifties-style dress she'd never have chosen but which Moir had insisted on buying for her.

In the left-hand section was the photo of his family in front of the Christmas tree, the one he was so cute and fat and grumpy in. The right-hand section was empty.

'I thought you might like to put one of your family here. Maybe one with Suzanne in it?'

'What a lovely idea. It's lovely. Thank you.'

He made them both coffee, and she went and got one of her photo albums, and sat back down with it to look for a suitable photograph. Maybe this one of Suzanne, squatting by the burn, grinning at the camera with the sun in her eyes. It was one of those photos where you could almost see the person continuing to move on through the moment, hear the burn rushing, feel the sun beating down. It was hard to believe it was just some coloured ink on a piece of paper. Hard to believe that Suzanne wasn't there right this minute, and if you went down past the Mains to the bridge you wouldn't see her, eight-year-old Suzanne, turning back to the water to guddle that twig in the mud.

Funny, but as time went on she seemed to miss Suzanne more, not less. She no longer saw her in the street, but at odd times she'd be surprised by a memory she didn't even know she had. Like in a meeting at work yesterday, when she'd slipped off her sandals under the table, and a memory had come rushing. How old had they been – eleven? Twelve? They'd decided to give each other's feet a manicure, and got towels and nail clippers and scissors and pumice and lotions and potions and nail polish, and set everything out in Suzanne's bedroom like a beauty salon. Helen had imagined walking down the street in Kirkton in her flipflops with grown-up painted toenails, and Hector coming towards her, and doing a double-take, and thinking *Helen Clack is looking very glamorous these days.*

But they'd ended up drawing a face on each of their toes, and naming them, and giggling away at tea and annoying Auntie Ina and Uncle Jim with the toe people's voices – Helen's feet were in socks and trainers, and her toe people were suffocating, and Suzanne's, in sandals, had to mount a rescue operation under the table, undoing Helen's laces and pulling off her shoes and socks. No help from hands allowed.

'That's enough, now, the pair of you,' Uncle Jim had said at last.

That was what Dad had called them too.

The pair of you.

They *had* been a pair. Closer in age than any sisters could be without being twins; and twins, as Suzanne said, were unholy freaks of nature. Much better to be different. Much better to be cousins.

But as they'd got older, Helen had started to worry that they were too different in one vital respect: Rob. If they ever set up home together – she imagined a big cold Victorian manse (Suzanne, a minister's wife!) – would Helen be able to bring herself to go and stay in the same house as Rob Beattie? Would she want Rob coming to stay with her? Would they gradually stop seeing each other, all because of *him*?

But the weird thing was that being with Moir had let her begin to understand, a little bit, what Suzanne had seen in Rob. Not just physically. She was beginning to get why Suzanne, so assertive in other ways, had allowed Rob to dominate her. She suspected it was all about tapping in to your inner cavewoman; realising that there was something innately sexy about a man telling you what to do, however un-PC that might be.

She smiled.

In the end she decided on a photo taken in the garden at Parks of Clova: Mum and Dad behind, Suzanne and Helen in front, Helen holding a blurred Baudrins in her arms. They all looked so happy – well, apart from Baudrins.

'Good choice,' said Moir when she showed him. 'I see you were adorable from an early age.' He plomped himself down beside her and fitted her against him, snuggled under his arm.

'Look at my knobbly knees!' She leant over the coffee table to prop the photo against the silver frame.

'Hey, I love your knobbly knees.' He pulled her back against him and pushed his nose into her cheek.

She turned her face to his, breathing in the scent of him: masculine and animal and alien. The photo album slid off her lap, and Moir stooped to pick it up.

'This can go back in the cupboard now, yes?'

'Thanks. It goes in the box that's open, on the left-hand side.'

He got up and left the room with it. He couldn't stand what he called 'mess.' That was why most of her stuff was still in boxes.

She looked at the three photos in a row, wondering about his parents. So sad, what had happened to them –

'What the hell is *this*?'

Something came flying over the back of the sofa – a magazine, she thought at first, but no – as it landed on the carpet she realised what it was.

A scrapbook.

'Keeping tabs on your ex?'

He strode after it, snatched it up, threw it down on the sofa next to her.

The scrapbook had been in the same box as the photo albums.

She didn't touch it. She said, 'No,' and 'It's not important.'

'*Not important*! You've got a whole fucking scrapbook of stuff about this guy and it's *not important*? Who the *fuck* is he?'

'He's not my ex. We hardly even –'

Moir was standing foursquare in front of the mantelpiece, his face red. Behind him, where a cool film poster used to have pride of place, the horses in her painting looked serenely on.

'Please. Moir. I'll tell you about him, but not while you're like this. Not while you're so angry.'

'Oh, I've no business being angry when I discover my fiancée's obsessed with another man?'

Two, three beats.

'Your what?'

He put a hand into the pocket of his suit jacket; took out a small red box. 'I was going to ask you to marry me.' He opened the lid of the box. Inside was a ring.

Her heart thumped.

'I'm in love with you, Helen. I've never been in love with anyone before – I realise that now. But you obviously have. You obviously *still are*, or you wouldn't have kept this stuff –'

'Come and sit down. *Please*. Sit down and I'll explain.'

He sat, but not next to her. He put the ring in its box down on the coffee table, and sat on his own leather sofa, and looked at her.

And she told him everything: about Hector, and Pitfourie, and the cyberstalking.

'Ridiculous. I know it's ridiculous.'

He shook his head.

'You probably think I'm a complete lunatic.'

And then he was across the room, and holding her, and telling her he was sorry, that it was all right, that it was perfectly understandable, after all she'd been through. Probably there was a psychological explanation – post-traumatic stress syndrome or something. 'Regressing back to your life before the trauma, to your old home, to your crush on this Hector guy – that was probably your brain's way of coping with everything – Suzanne, the break-up with Jeff, and work, and your aunt... Taking you back to a happy place.' He rubbed her back. 'After Dad's funeral, Bec and I spent a week in a holiday cottage we used to rent on Skye when we were kids... Remembering the good times...'

She held on to the wonderful bulk of his shoulders. 'I'll get rid of it. The scrapbook.'

'You don't have to do that.'

'No, I do. I don't need it any more.'

And she didn't – she really didn't.

Because this was her happy place now.

'Hey. Shh. It's all right.' He wiped her face with a tissue, and kissed her, and said, 'Helen.'

She blinked.

'My sweet girl: will you marry me?'

He was snoring softly, right in her lug, one heavy arm draped across her. She was too hot. Carefully she started to pull away from him. He grunted, and the arm was suddenly tight around her ribs.

She moved back against him, and the arm relaxed.

The extent of his physical need for her, his passion, was something new. She'd never imagined it could be like this. Sex with Moir was like one of those fairground rides that hurtled you round impossible, vertiginous corners; a thrill that was all the more thrilling for the feeling that it wasn't quite right; that it wasn't something you should be enjoying.

How could she ever have thought Jeff was good in bed? It was like the difference between a rollercoaster and a merry-go-round.

But sometimes, when Moir was asleep like this and she lay awake, she couldn't help remembering... Another bed, and another man's arms. Not a birl on a merry-go-round or a rollercoaster ride, but a stratospheric soaring –

Daft Janet.

No. She was done with all that.

Moir was amazing.

The feeling of *not right* had nothing to do with him. It wasn't his fault that sometimes when he really lost control, really hurt her, she'd flash on Suzanne's narrow back in the firelight; the stalkers' path; the hand across her mouth.

And want him to hurt her again.

29

Stuart poked his head round the door. 'Helen. Do you have a minute?'

'Yes, come in.'

He walked to the cabinet in which she kept the finds she was currently working on, opened a drawer at random, looked into it, shut it again. Helen moved her mouse to close the document she'd been working on and sat back in her chair.

'I'm sorry Helen, but we've decided to give the position to Marc.'

'Marc.'

'I realise it's a disappointment. To lose out again.'

When the Section Head position had come up two years ago, just she and Eilidh had applied. She'd been pretty confident she'd get it as she was quite a lot better than Eilidh at the job, but they'd given it to Eilidh. And yes, it had been a disappointment, but at least she and Eilidh had roughly similar levels of experience –

'*Marc*?'

Marc Watkins. Living proof, as Moir said, that the British education system was in crisis.

The old Helen would immediately have blamed herself, assumed it must be because she wasn't good enough, that a Section Head had to be more than a good curator, that she didn't have the necessary social facility, wasn't enough of a team player.

The new Helen was angry.

'Why?'

Stuart blinked at her. 'Well um, there were a number of factors to consider, of course. For one thing, Marc has a PhD rather than an MA. And he has excellent people skills.'

'You mean he laughs at your dirty jokes.'

'Ha ha. Yes. But he's got the skill set we're looking for.'

'Really? What particular skill set *are* you looking for? Does it include any of the skills required to actually do the job? Because in terms of subject knowledge... the ability to apply that knowledge... the number of papers published in peer-reviewed journals... I think I just about have the edge.'

Oh God. Her heart was racing, her voice had gone shaky, but she'd said it.

And Stuart was staring at her like she'd grown another head.

'When another institution needs our opinion on something, who is it they ask for? Who was it had to go hotfoot up to Westray to do their instant analyses? Not Eilidh, not Susan. And certainly not Marc. *Me.*'

'Your knowledge is second to none.' He was almost simpering.

'But next to Marc's knowledge of the bars and clubs on George Street, it counts for nothing?'

'We felt that Marc's people skills were a fit for the Section Head post. But of course we value your contribution to the team enormously.'

'Stuart, if there was a problem with my performance in the "people skills" area, you should have told me so I could have worked on it. That's surely a basic management principle. You have to tell people where they're going wrong or they can't fix it.'

He smiled at her again and turned away to the window, and she only half caught what he said: '... to that issue in your yearly reviews.'

'No. You didn't. It looks like there *is* a problem with people skills, but I don't think it's mine.'

When he'd gone she opened the Word document back up and stared at the screen. She swallowed, and frowned at the black type on the white background. She read a sentence, and another. But she couldn't make sense of the words.

Oh God.

She found a tissue in her bag and blotted her nose, her eyes. She rummaged in her bag for her mobile.

'I didn't get it,' she choked when he answered. 'They've given it to Marc.'

'Are they stark raving *mad*? Hey, hey, it's okay. It's okay. I'm coming to get you, okay? Helen?'

She should tell him no. He was really busy at work. They had this horrible client they were designing a holiday complex for in Bulgaria, who kept making them change things. He was too busy.

'Okay.'

As she crossed the road, he got out of the Audi and came to meet her. He put his arms round her, right there in the middle of the road, and she clung to him, to the muscled solidness of him, and breathed the tangy smell of his aftershave – no, his *cologne*, that was what he called it – and pressed her face against his chest as he led her to the car and eased her into the passenger seat.

He got in at the driver's side and put his arms round her again and said, 'Stupid bastards.'

She couldn't stop crying.

He had a whole box of tissues in the well in front of the gear stick – had he bought them on the way? She grabbed a fresh one. He was saying something about an industrial tribunal.

'I can't take them to an industrial tribunal. In a way they're right about the people skills thing. I don't socialise with them. I don't sit talking to them in the staff room at lunchtime. I usually just work through with a sandwich in my office.'

'That's not a people skills issue, that's about not being in their pathetic little clique. That's about you being overworked because you're ten times better than any of them.'

'But they'll say I'm not a team player... Moir, I couldn't face it. I couldn't go through a tribunal. I'm just going to have to grin and bear it. Again.'

'Why don't you tell them to stuff their job?'

She stared at him.

She loved the way the hair grew at his temples. The way it almost curled. She loved twisting it and trying to *make* it curl, and watching his face, and he'd be smiling but trying not to, pretending to be annoyed, and then he'd go and look in the bathroom mirror and huff and puff, and flatten it with water.

'I can't just leave.'

'Why not?'

'There aren't exactly many job opportunities out there for curators of Iron Age and Roman collections.'

'There are always opportunities for the best people in any field.'

'I'm not one of the "best people".'

He sighed. 'Helen, have a bit of confidence in yourself. If those idiots don't appreciate you, there are plenty of others who do. People are always ringing you up wanting your opinion, aren't they? You could do consultancy work. Or go for a lectureship at a university –'

'I'd need a PhD for that. I can't just resign without anything else to go to.'

He took her left hand; turned the ring that still felt so strange encircling her finger. 'Look. It's not as if I'm exactly short of cash. I'm more than happy for you to live off me until you find something. I'm more than happy for you to live off me permanently, in fact – we want kids, don't we?'

It was the first time he'd mentioned children directly.

'I – yes.' Oh yes.

'You could go freelance in the meantime; look into doing a PhD.'

'I can't just sponge off you.'

'Why not? Hey, sponge away.'

And into her head, suddenly, the thought popped: did Suzanne feel like this, when Rob was egging her on to do something outrageous?

Back in her office she typed up a letter of resignation. She didn't even bother checking it for errors, she just shoved it in the first envelope she found and scrawled 'Stuart Gourlay' on the front.

He was with Eilidh in the conservation lab. They were footering about at the sinks, heads close together, obviously talking about Helen because when she came in they both stared at her like she'd caught them doing something disgusting.

She held out the letter. 'My resignation.'

Stuart wiped his hands on a paper towel and took the envelope from her, his already prominent eyes goggling.

'Helen. Don't be silly,' Eilidh said.

Stuart started to say something about Marc, but Helen cut him short.

'Yeah, good luck with Marc.'

Eilidh followed her back to her office, and while Helen emptied her desk drawers, shoving her folding umbrella and her little wooden box for paperclips and her knife and fork and spoon into the bag she kept in the bottom drawer, Eilidh told her she was behaving like a kid in the huff.

'You're being completely unreasonable.' And when Helen didn't respond, 'Have you something else lined up?'

'No.'

'This is a huge mistake. You won't be able to sign on, you know. Not if you resign from a job. Not for six months. And you have to work a month's notice anyway – you know that?'

'I've three weeks' holiday due.'

'That still leaves a week.'

'Considering all the unpaid overtime I've put in over the years, I think we can call it quits.'

'It doesn't work like that.'

'I don't care.'

'There has to be a hand-over period. It's not fair on whoever has to take over your workload.'

'Don't talk to me about what's fair.'

'If you want me to write you a reference –'

'You think *you're* qualified to write *me* a reference?'

Eilidh opened and closed her mouth. The skin on her face and neck had gone a mottled red.

And suddenly Helen felt sorry for her – this woman for whom climbing the greasy pole was everything. But not sorry enough to stop. 'Eilidh, I love what I do. I love holding something used by a woman who's been dead four thousand years, and feeling a connection to her. I love finding out all I can about what her life might have been like. I love that part of the job. What I don't love is having to stay late to finish a report because I've spent the whole day helping you or Susan or Donna or Marc with yours. What I don't love is having to always be the one to identify and classify new finds because no one else has a clue. And what I *really* don't love is being screwed over because I don't play the game. Just because I've never thrown up on Stuart's feet in the back of a taxi doesn't mean I'm not qualified to lead a team.'

'I didn't realise you felt like that.' Eilidh's lips were trembling.

'Of course you did.'

Carrying her bag of belongings down the stairs and out of the side door and crossing the road to the Audi, Helen felt like jumping in the air and clicking her heels and whooping like a lunatic.

'I'm a horrible person,' she said as they pulled away. 'I made Eilidh cry.'

He flashed her a smile. 'Feels good, yes?'

'Oh God. Yes.'

He flicked on the music system. Christine McVie's voice filled the car:

Cos I feel that when I'm with you...

'But Moir. What am I going to do?'

'You, my girl, are going to take a holiday.'

'A holiday.'

'Remember what one of those is?'

'Um… No. Not really!'

He started to laugh.

And I love you I love you I love you
Like never befo-o-o-o-ore.

And now she was laughing too.

30

Toilet. Before she went for a taxi, she should go to the toilet. She didn't need to empty her bladder – it was only two and a half hours on the train from York – but she did need to check that she looked okay. She was glad now that Moir hadn't been able to meet her because he'd been held up at work. It gave her a chance to do any repair work necessary.

As she was going into the Ladies a woman was coming out, wrestling with bags and carriers, one of which swung against Helen's hip. 'Oh, sorry, hen.'

She was home.

It had been wonderful, doing nothing for two weeks, spending time with Mum, being pampered, going for walks, stuffing her face in tea shops, even spending a day with Lionel's sons and their families – but it wasn't home.

Home was here.

Home was wherever Moir was.

Cheesy but true.

She put her handbag down on the counter that ran under the mirror and lifted a hand to her blunt fringe. She'd told the hairdresser she just wanted a 'tidy', but had ended up with this short, boyish, choppy style, and she wasn't sure it suited her. It wasn't nearly as nice as the West End cut. She'd loved the way she could shake her head and watch it fall into place.

She couldn't do that any more. And she had to keep wetting it to stop bits of it sticking out.

She'd say, 'I told her I only wanted a trim, but *look*. Isn't it horrible?' And Moir would say something like, 'On you, nothing could be horrible,' but his eyes would linger on the fringe. He probably thought he was being tactful and subtle, but when he didn't like something about her – her shoes or her skirt or her coat or her make-up – he had a way of looking a little too long.

Well, it would grow out, and then she could go back to the West End salon and get it cut properly.

She reapplied her lipstick and dusted her face with powder where it had gone shiny.

As she made her way to the taxi rank, she stroked her thumb across the inside of her ring finger, and the circle of metal around it that was Moir saying *I want to spend my life with you.*

She'd been walking around in the cocoon of that thought all the time she'd been away. It really was as if Moir's love was a cocoon; invisible protection from anything anyone could throw at her. There was enough of the old Helen left that she knew she *should* be worrying, about what she was going to do about getting a job, about whether she'd become a pathetic parasite, letting Moir take over like he had, arrange the sale of her flat, pay for everything, even the solicitor's fees for the conveyancing –

But the new Helen didn't care.

She hadn't felt like this since she was a teenager. But how could she ever have thought she was in love with Hector Forbes? She hadn't even known him, not really. And how sad had she been, cyberstalking him all these years later?

When she got back she'd burn that scrapbook.

As she waited for a taxi she checked her phone. There were two text messages. One from Mum, asking how the journey had been, and one from Moir:

Should be finished here soonish – see u at home about 6. Have teacakes! xxxxMxxxx

Teacakes. Looking at the words on the screen, standing there in the queue, she laughed out loud. Teacakes. And they'd be her favourites, from the baker on West Maitland Street.

She composed a quick reply:

Mmmmmmmm can't wait! xxxxHxxxx

'Thirty-one Eglinton Crescent, please,' she told the taxi driver, pulling her suitcase in after her, not quite able to repress the little feeling of satisfaction that came with giving that address.

Sitting back on the wide seat, she composed a reply to Mum's text.

Hi Mum. Back safe and sound but exhausted! Thanx for lovely time.
Will phone later. Love to Lionel. Helenxx

It was the rush hour. As they joined the back of a stationary queue of traffic on Queen Street, the driver said, 'It's not even the Festival yet,' and Helen said, 'Oh God, don't remind me,' and in the rearview mirror they exchanged a smile, one Edinburgh person to another.

He stopped at the door and got out to help Helen with her case. 'Nice part of town.'

She gave him £20 and told him to keep the change because he'd be expecting a reasonable tip, wouldn't he, from someone who lived in Eglinton Crescent?

'Thanks very much,' he said. 'Like a hand up the steps with that?'

'That'd be great. If you could leave it in the hall, my boyfriend will carry it up to the flat later.'

She opened the main door with her key and the driver put the case down on the Victorian tiles.

'Thank you.'

She shut the door behind him and just stood for a second, breathing in the cool air with its familiar smells. There was an arrangement of chrysanthemums and roses on the big mahogany sideboard.

Home.

The final contracts on the sale of her flat had been exchanged just before she left, so this really was home now. She climbed the stairs to the first floor landing, unlocked the mortise and then the Yale, and pushed open the door. There was another arrangement of chrysanthemums and roses on the hall table. Moir must have bought them specially. He wasn't a flower person, he wouldn't know a daisy from a dahlia, but he knew she loved them so he bought them for her all the time. He tended to go for red roses and bright, artificial-looking arrangements, and she hadn't the heart to tell him she preferred things with scent, things that looked more natural – but these roses were lovely. An old variety of some kind, the petals very pale peach and crumpled together.

She bent to sniff one.

And noticed the surface of the table. Wood, not marble.

It was a different table. Victorian, mahogany, with two drawers and legs that ended in claws. Nice, but she'd liked the other one better. She'd loved the fossils in the marble.

And there was a rug on the floor. Red, with blue dots.

Moir had been splashing out.

Well, it was his flat, wasn't it? Stupid to feel – left out?

Probably it was meant to be a big surprise. A make-over for the flat. Maybe there hadn't been hassles at work after all. Maybe he was in here waiting for her, waiting to jump out and say, 'Whaddya think then?'

She'd have to be convincingly enthusiastic.

But oh God, what was that on the wall? A huge painting of – what?

A woman's face, fractured and distorted and merged with a watermelon. Or was it a cabbage?

She opened the door to the sitting room.

Oh *God*.

There was a big orange sofa in place of their old ones. With chrome arms. And a new plasma screen. Moir's old TV had been big – too big – but this was a monster, completely dwarfing the fireplace.

On the mantel was a row of photographs. A wedding photo with people in it she didn't know, a big close-up of the bride and groom. And a kid in school uniform.

Everything in the room was different. All their old stuff had gone – their sofas, her pouffe, her desk and computer, the sideboard. The horses painting. And in their place – the orange sofa, two ugly leather chairs, a nest of tables with a pink lamp on top.

And who the hell were the people in the photographs?

Was she in the wrong flat? She couldn't be. She'd opened the door with her keys.

She could hear something.

She went back into the hall and listened. It was a chopping sound, coming from the kitchen.

She pushed open the saloon-style doors.

31

A sturdy woman in a yellow sweater was standing at the worktop, cutting something on a board. As Helen walked in she yelped and dropped the knife.

'What –? What do you think you're doing? How did you get in here?'

'I have keys,' Helen said, stupidly.

Could this be Rebecca? No. She didn't look anything like the pictures Moir had shown her.

A cold weight was settling in her stomach.

'If you want to enter the property you have to give us notice,' the woman was saying. 'That's in the agreement. You can't just let yourself in.'

'What?'

'The tenancy agreement? You're from Dunedin Properties?'

'No. I live here. With my boyfriend. My fiancé. Moir Sandison.'

The woman opened her eyes wide and pushed away the board. There were two whole potatoes on it and some cut-up chunks. 'Well not any more you don't. Moir Sandison doesn't live here any more.'

'Of course he does!'

'Dunedin are very interested in getting hold of your Moir. He owes them three months' rent, apparently, and a flat's worth of furniture.'

'Well that's not right. Moir's not renting the flat. He owns it.'

'That's what he told you, is it? Look, come and sit down.'

Helen stayed where she was. 'He just sent me a text message – just now – he said he'd meet me here.' She rummaged in her bag, hands shaking; found the phone and called up the text message: *see u at home about 6*. She pressed Call and put the phone to her ear.

The woman was looking at her.

She turned away.

Where the microwave used to be there was a row of cookery books. And there was a clock with poppies on it by the window, where their cork board had hung. Where Moir would leave funny drawings for her to find, and notes with his terrible spelling.

A buzzing in her ear, and then nothing. Dead air.

'I'm calling the police.' And before the woman could say anything Helen had pushed through the doors back into the hall. She wanted to just get out, to get out of the flat, but maybe if she did that the woman wouldn't let her back in again. Maybe the police wouldn't be able to get in either, without a warrant.

She stood in the middle of the hall and tapped 999.

32

She didn't know what she'd expected to happen. But surely this wasn't right?

'Isn't one of you going to stay?' She stood in the doorway so the woman in the yellow sweater – Kelly Reid, she'd claimed her name was – couldn't close the door on them.

The policewoman, who was already following her male colleague across the landing to the stairs, turned back to look at her but said nothing.

'Aren't you going to even search the flat?'

'For what?' The policewoman's hair was pulled back in a ponytail. She had fiercely plucked eyebrows and wore harsh red lipstick which made her look older than she probably was.

'For anything that could tell you what's going on. What's happened to Moir.'

Behind her, Kelly Reid said: 'You don't need to be Hercule Poirot to work that one out.'

The male officer hadn't even stopped. Now he was on the stairs.

'But he's *disappeared*.'

The policewoman walked back across the lobby and flicked a smile at Kelly Reid before saying to Helen, as if to an idiot: 'Yes. With the contents of the flat and three months owing on the rent.'

'How do you know these Dunedin Properties people are telling the truth? How do you know *she* is?'

'If there was some big conspiracy going on here, involving Dunedin Properties forcing your boyfriend to sign over ownership of the flat to them, do you really think they'd have reported his theft of the contents, and non-payment of rent, to us?'

Could it be true?

Could Moir have done all that?

She ran her thumb over the circle of hard metal around her finger.

No.

'Look, I don't know what's happened, but –'

'You think the conspiracy extends to the Land Register? Because Dunedin Properties are listed there as the owners of the property.' She shook her head. 'We'll do what we can to locate him. What you need to do now is come to the station and make a statement, and we can take it from there. Okay? You've just had a bad shock. Is there anyone you'd like to call?'

The room was in some respects like the ones you saw on TV: bare white walls, no windows, a squeaky vinyl floor; a table and some chairs in the middle. But there was also a line of tables with boxfiles and folders and computers along one wall. And she'd expected there'd be two of them, and a recorder of some sort, but there was just this one man, DC Powell, who wrote down everything she said in a notebook, as the policeman in her flat had done. Like what she was saying wasn't important enough to record.

Because she had to keep stopping to let him write down what she'd said, she kept forgetting where she'd got to, and he had to go back over what he'd written to remind her.

It was getting hard to think. A pulse of pain had started in her forehead and she wanted to close her eyes. She wanted to lie down on the floor and close her eyes and sleep. But she had to focus. She had to make this man understand that something had happened to Moir.

'Did you have a joint account?' He had very thick eyebrows. They made him look angry.

'Yes.'

'Have you checked the balance recently? Since you went away?'

'No.'

'I suggest you do so now. Do you have online banking?'

'Yes.'

He indicated the line of tables behind him. 'We've got internet access here.' And he got up from the table and switched on one of the computers. He pulled round a chair and placed it in front of the screen.

As Helen sat down in the chair he walked away across the room, looking down at his notebook. She logged into the bank's website and the account details popped up on the screen.

The number at the top of the right-hand column was £1100. With the letters 'OD' after it: overdrawn.

Her eyes jumped down the numbers in the balance column. On 5 July the balance had been £21 478.54. On 6 July, just before she had left for Yorkshire, the money from the sale of her flat had come through, bringing the total to £203 324.87. But yesterday the account had plummeted to £1100 OD.

'Someone's taken the money from the account. All of it. It's all gone.'

'Mind if I take a look?'

She pushed back the chair and stood.

He sat down in her place, swivelling to face the screen. 'I'm guessing £1100 is your overdraft limit?'

Helen nodded, staring at the dates and numbers. The money had been taken as a cash withdrawal.

'But – they let people withdraw that kind of money *in cash*?'

'As long as you give two days' notice and provide primary and secondary forms of identification, yes.'

'It couldn't have been Moir. Or if it was, someone must have been making him do it.'

'The bank's CCTV will show us who it was.'

Her head was pounding. Her whole body felt odd – weak, like she hadn't eaten for days and days. Her legs were wobbling and she needed to sit down *now*.

The nearest chair was the one DC Powell had been sitting on at the table. It was still warm from his bum. She dug her nails into the palms of her hands. She wanted Moir. She wanted him to be here, putting his arm round her and saying, 'Now what's all this,' in that very male, slightly patronising way he had – and how daft was that, because if he was here to help she wouldn't *need* his help, would she?

'There was this reconstruction once, on Crimewatch,' she said, 'where the criminals broke into a house in the middle of the night, and tied the people up, and made them give them the keys to a warehouse. Some gang might be keeping him locked up somewhere, making him give them money –' Oh God, please let him be safe. 'Or someone might be blackmailing him.'

'About what?'

'I don't know.'

DC Powell swivelled in the chair to look at her. 'Did Moir ever mention that he'd been involved in any illegal activities? In fraud?'

'No. Why are you asking that? Are you saying – that he *has* been?'

'No. As far as we can ascertain, he's got no criminal record. Do I have your permission to print off this online statement? And to contact the bank regarding this activity on the account?'

'Yes. Of course.'

'I'll just ask you to sign a form to that effect...' And as he opened one of the box files: 'So the money from the sale of your flat went into this account on 6th July.'

'Yes. Just before I went on holiday.'

'Was it you or Moir who suggested a joint account?'

'Moir. But it wasn't like you're thinking. It was so *I* could get at *his* money. I'd resigned from my job, I'd no income – so he started paying his salary into the joint account, and told me I mustn't be silly about it, I must take out as much as I wanted.'

'When did you open the account?'

'I can't remember. Why is that relevant?' This was just wasting time. 'The idea that Moir would take the money for himself – it's ridiculous. Apart from the fact that I *know* he would *never* do that, he earns three times as much as I did. And money, material things – they're just not important to him. He hates shopping. He hates all those property shows. What he calls "conspicuous consumption". He's *in trouble*, someone else is doing this and he's in trouble. You need to *find him*.'

Her bag with her tissues was on the floor on the other side of the table.

She went carefully round to the other chair, and sat down on it, and lifted her bag onto her knee.

'You've had one hell of a shock.'

She found the little pack of tissues and pulled one out. 'He's my *fiancé*.'

'Whatever the truth of the matter, the activity on your account is an important lead for us.'

'Yes. I'm sorry.' On the table top there were three little depressions in a row; as if they'd been made by one interviewee after another nervously drumming their fingers on the table. 'You want to know – I'm sorry, what was it you wanted to know?'

'When did you open the account?'

'It was after I resigned from my job. About three weeks ago.'

'Okay. Here's the form. I've put in the account details – if you could check them, and then sign and date it...'

While she did so, he said:

'Did he pressure you to have the money from your flat sale released to the joint account rather than your personal one?'

'No. We just decided it would be easier, because Moir was the one dealing with it, the sale of the flat, and as I was going away – in case there were any problems, it made sense to use the joint account. I can't remember which of us suggested it. It might have been me. The plan was that when I came back we'd decide what to do with the money: whether to invest it, or sell Moir's flat too and buy a bigger place.'

'Only the flat wasn't Moir's to sell.'

She pushed the form back across the table. 'No.'

That horrible policewoman had been right. It was the first thing Helen had asked DC Powell when he'd brought her in here – did they have proof that Moir didn't own the flat? – and he'd shown her the Land Registry details in black and white. 1F1, 31 Eglinton Crescent had belonged to Dunedin Properties since 2002.

He opened a folder, flicked through the papers inside it, removed two sheets and pushed them across the table. 'That's the tenancy agreement he signed with Dunedin Properties. And the application form he filled in initially. In the space for references, you see he's put the name "Ewan Mathers" and the address 16 Fountain Place, Dunfermline, and a landline number. And he's described this referee as his previous employer. Does the name mean anything to you?'

'No.'

'You never heard him mention Ewan Mathers?'

'No. But Moir worked in Manchester before he moved to Edinburgh. Not Dunfermline.'

'Apparently Mr Barnes at Dunedin Properties called the number and spoke to this Mathers, who was glowing in his praise of Moir Sandison. But the number is now disconnected, and when our Fife colleagues went to the address they found it wasn't even an office. It was just an empty house.'

'So do you think – could Ewan Mathers be involved? Could *he* be blackmailing Moir?'

'We're keeping an open mind at this stage.'

She had to *think*. She had to think what she could tell them that would be useful. But the pulsing in her head kept pounding and pounding on her brain, breaking up her thoughts and stopping the threads of them coming together.

'Anything you can tell us about Moir's friends and associates would be helpful.'

'Okay. Well. He moved to Edinburgh six months ago. Most of his friends live in Manchester.'

'Have you ever met any of them?'

'No.'

'Or spoken to them on the phone?'

'No – they all call him on his iPhone. He's practically welded to it.'

DC Powell nodded. 'And his family?'

'His parents are dead. He's got a sister who lives in France – Rebecca – we – we were going to stay with her this autumn. I've spoken to her on the phone, once or twice. Just small talk, before passing her over to Moir.'

And Moir would take the phone into the bedroom. But she did that too when Mum phoned. There wasn't anything sinister about it.

'You've never actually met her?'

'No.'

'Do you have an address in France for her?'

'She lives in Brittany, near the coast.'

'Do you have an address?'

She sighed. 'No.'

'Anyone else in the habit of phoning?'

'Not on the landline.'

'And what about his work colleagues? Did you ever meet any of them?'

'They don't really socialise.'

Cochran and Lyle wasn't like the museum. People didn't go out drinking together. Both the partners were in their sixties and their idea of a wild night out, Moir said, was Stravinsky at the Usher Hall. And the other architects and admin people were all married with young families.

'Right. Well, you've been a big help, Helen – I think we'll leave it there for now. If I could get you to read over this statement and sign it – and if you could leave us your phone. You said you had some photos of Moir on it?'

'Not very good ones.'

'Nevertheless. And we may be able to trace where he was when he sent you those last text messages.'

She took her phone from her bag and held it in her hand. Her last link to him.

'Do you have a number where we can contact you?'

'Not yet. I'll let you know.'

33

The receptionist blinked up at her. 'No Moir Sandison has ever worked here – at least not in my time, and I've been here twenty-five years. That's what I told the policewomen who were here before. Are you from the police?' Her eyes swept Helen doubtfully.

Moir had said that all the admin people had young families, but this woman looked like she was close to retirement age.

Helen pulled a photo of Moir from her purse. 'This is him.'

The woman lifted her glasses to her face without putting them on. 'No, I don't recognise him. Are you a private investigator?'

'Something like that.'

'What's he done? All they'd tell us was that he'd been making out he worked here.'

'Maybe he works in a different office?'

'We only have this office.'

And even if they'd had a dozen offices – it was this one Moir had told her he worked in. Sometimes she'd given him a lift in the morning, if she was taking Stan to the museum, and she'd always dropped him off here.

Outside on the landing she put her hand on the smooth wood of the banisters and looked down the stairwell to where a big Georgian window gave a view of Bernard Street, the main road through Leith, lined with elegant old buildings that had once probably been des reses for sea captains and harbour officials but were now full of dentists and architects and telecommunications people.

She headed down the sweep of the stairs and out of the main door.

It wasn't locked.

Anyone could walk in off the street.

Anyone could get out of their girlfriend's car and cross the pavement and push this door open and turn and wave, and wait until she'd pulled away into the traffic, and walk straight back out again.

In a newsagent on Constitution Street she selected a packet of crisps, a flapjack and a bottle of Sprite. Just the thought of putting anything into her stomach made her feel sick, but she had to eat. This feeling in her legs, in her arms, this weightless, weak feeling, like there was no substance to her – some food inside her would sort that out. She needed glucose and carbs.

The man behind the counter smiled at her and gave her her change as if she was just another customer, buying a snack the way people did every day of the week. And Helen smiled back and thanked him, playing along, pretending nothing was wrong, that this was just another normal part of a normal day.

She'd left Stan in a narrow lane off Mitchell Street. They were like ravines, the streets around here, the tall cliff-faces of the tenements looming overhead, pressing close, no space between them and the pavement.

She had to stop at one point, and put her hand against a wall, and take some deep breaths and stand straight so that her legs stopped wobbling. She opened the bottle of Sprite and swallowed some of the fizzy sweetness, and waited until the sugar hitting her bloodstream gave her a little spike of energy.

As she turned into the lane, her first thought was that Stan was gone. That he'd been stolen. She couldn't see him.

But no, there he was, his little red Mini rear coming into sight as she walked around the four-by-four that had been blocking him from view.

She put a hand on his roof. Stan. Her little bubble. And oh, the relief of sitting down behind the wheel. Sinking back against the seat. Closing her eyes. But she couldn't sleep. Not yet. She leant over to put the crisps, juice and flapjack on the back seat, next to the tiny carrier bag containing the new phone.

She took her purse from her bag and spread the notes from it on the passenger seat. Fifteen pounds in notes. Three pound coins, one two-pound coin, and small change. And she had the contents of her suitcase – some clothes, toiletries, her Kindle.

Plus £120, ish, in her own account and an overdraft facility of

£100. So – in total, that made about £240. And then there was the ring – not that that was going to be a real diamond. She took it from her finger and added it to the pile.

Even if the diamond wasn't real, it must be worth what – £30? In her suitcase in the boot were the cufflinks she'd bought Moir in a jeweller's in York. They'd been £86, but she wouldn't get that for them if she sold them. Maybe £40?

Say £310 in total – enough for a few nights in a B&B, plus food, petrol –

And then what?

Her credit card had been declined when she'd tried to use it to buy the new phone. When she'd called the credit card company they'd told her it was maxed out to the tune of £6500. Most of the purchases had been online – mainly jewellery. Small, portable items.

Moir must have copied down the number, the expiry date, the security code.

The woman on the help line had said that if Helen could prove she hadn't made the purchases herself, the debt would be written off as fraudulent activity and the card reactivated. But that would take time. And even when it was sorted out, all she'd be doing would be running up a debt.

She'd have to phone Mum and ask her to transfer money to her account.

Oh God.

What on earth would she say? Lionel would probably get Mum to put Helen on speakerphone, and Helen would have to tell them that Moir –

Oh *God*.

Maybe she could just say there was a problem with the money from her flat sale, and she needed something to tide her over? And tell them the truth later?

She'd need to sign on, she supposed, for benefits.

But she'd resigned, so she couldn't do that. She'd have to get a job in a shop or something for now, and use her contacts in other institutions, see what curatorship vacancies there were, or were likely to come up.

No way was she crawling back to Stuart.

Oh God.

Moir.

There was no mysterious gang making him do all this. No kidnapper. No blackmailer.

He was just some conman.

All the time he'd been smiling and joking and reaching for her, and holding her, and touching her face, and telling her he loved this place *here*, this soft place between her mouth and her chin – all the time, he'd been coldly calculating how much she was good for.

The man she'd loved had never existed. He was just a character invented to con her.

Like Hector and the letters.

Her 'Hector' had turned out to be a monster.

And so had Moir.

How could that be a coincidence?

She lowered her head to the steering wheel and shut her eyes. No. The police had checked him out, and he'd proved that he was Moir Sandison. And she *knew* he wasn't Rob. She didn't need anyone to tell her that.

So it was all just a coincidence?

Two men who happened to look alike, two men who got a kick out of making her think they were someone else, someone who loved her –

Two men who knew a mug when they saw one.

She wished she could pick up her new phone and press in some magic number that would connect her to Suzanne.

'Aw, Helen' she would say, and let her cry, but then she'd say something like, 'Although I think you'll find getting conned out of all your worldly goods and being left with a broken heart doesn't even get you to the starting blocks in the bad boyfriend stakes. I was *murdered* by mine?' And then: 'You mug, Helen. What did you ever see in him anyway?' and the two of them would go over all the things Helen had overlooked, or justified, or denied. The way he used to speak to her like a child when she didn't understand some boring technical thing on TV; the flashes of temper, when he'd throw things about and make her flinch; the obsession he used to have with really distressing human interest stories in the tabloid press and on TV, in an 'ironic' way, like he was laughing at the sicko journalists, but he would always read the article or watch the programme to the end. And in bed –

It had been just another fantasy world, hadn't it, that she'd constructed for herself? Fenced around with denial and wishful thinking.

He'd have taken Stan too, presumably, if she hadn't forgotten to leave the keys as they'd arranged. He'd said it might be best for her to leave the keys in the flat, in case he needed to move Stan for any reason, like for roadworks or removal lorries. And she'd agreed that that was a good idea. But then she'd forgotten.

And so he hadn't been able to take Stan. But she'd have to sell him. You didn't need a car in Edinburgh, when you could go everywhere so easily by bus.

How much would she get for him?

It had been a mistake to give him a name.

For God's sake, it was just a car. *Get a grip.*

She turned the key in the ignition.

Kelly Reid was waiting for her on the landing. Behind her, just inside the flat, was a man with a stubbly beard and glasses. Kelly's eyes were bright above the sympathetic grimace. When Helen had gone, she'd probably be straight on the phone to her mum or sister or best friend: 'She's been back. Just now. That poor woman. Apparently he took all her money and sold all her furniture and *everything!*'

'I'm sorry,' Helen said. 'For what I said before. It was just – I didn't know what to think.'

'You were in shock. Of course you were. Come in. This my husband Andy.'

'Hello.' She shook the hand Andy held out to her. It was big and damp. 'I'm Helen.'

'Helen, come on in. What a day you've had, eh?'

Ms Mug, meet Mr State-the-Bloody-Obvious.

'Would you like a coffee?' said Kelly.

'No, thanks, I won't stay. I just wanted to make sure – when you moved in – there wasn't anything left behind in the flat, was there?'

'No, there was nothing I'm afraid – the place was clean as a whistle. But then I guess Dunedin would have cleared out anything that was left. We've got their number here somewhere...'

'Thanks, the police have given me it.' She'd call Dunedin Properties in the morning.

'Are you sure you wouldn't like a coffee, or something stronger?'

'Thanks, but I've got to get on.'

Kelly dropped her voice sympathetically. 'He's sold all the stuff you left here?'

'It looks like it. Although most of it wouldn't have been worth much.' In fact he'd probably have had to pay someone to take her sofa to the dump. And he wouldn't have done that, would he? He'd have left the sofa and anything else of no value in the flat. Dunedin must have taken care of anything he'd left behind.

But, 'There wasn't anything in any of the cupboards?' Helen went past her into the hall.

'No. There wasn't anything at all.'

'I had – a box – a cardboard box, with photo albums in it and – scrapbooks and stuff.' And she didn't care how rude it was, she crossed the hall and opened the door of the big walk-in cupboard.

There were cardboard boxes, stacked up one on top of the other. But these ones had the removal firm's name on them in crisp blue lettering. Helen's had been scruffy old things, with graphics for tinned tomatoes and Cheesy Wotsits on them, scrounged from supermarkets when she moved into the student flat on St Mary's Street, and the veterans since of many moves into shared rented flats. Until eventually she'd saved enough for a deposit on her own place, and earned enough to be able to apply for a mortgage.

She'd paid off that mortgage with her legacy from Auntie Anne.

'There's nothing of yours here,' said Kelly. 'Sorry.'

Andy was looking at her like she had a terminal illness.

She made herself smile brightly at them both. 'Oh well, it was a long shot. Thanks anyway.'

34

In the B&B dining room, all shiny reproduction furniture and seersucker orange and pink tablecloths, Helen found she was unable to face the breakfast of boiled eggs and toast she'd ordered. She took one bite of toast and chewed it and chewed it but she couldn't bring herself to swallow. She lifted the paper napkin to her mouth and spat it out, and took a long drink of sugary tea.

She hadn't been able to face the crisps and flapjack yesterday either, although she'd finished the bottle of Sprite. She'd buy another today. She must have picked up a bug or something on the train; and all the stress had weakened her immune system, probably, so she hadn't been able to fight it off.

Her headache was worse, and her arms and legs still had that odd weak feeling. They ached with it. Coming down the stairs had been a challenge. Her throat was dry and scratchy, and when she'd first got up she'd had a fit of coughing from so deep in her chest she'd felt she was going to be sick.

And her nose was running.

She took a tissue from her jeans pocket. This was the last one from the pack. She'd need to take a wodge of toilet paper with her, and buy a box of tissues while she was out.

The B&B owner, a large woman in a green sweatshirt and what Helen was sure she'd call slacks, came in carrying a tray with two bowls of porridge on it. Helen's stomach turned over at the sight of them.

'Are the eggs not as you like them? I can do you some more.'

'No, they're perfect – I'm sorry, I'm just not hungry. I've got a bug or something, I think. I haven't been able to eat anything since yesterday morning.'

'Oh dear. Well, if there's anything you fancy, just say. If you'd like to stay in your room today, sleep it off, I'll put a Do Not Disturb notice on your door.'

The kindness had tears prickling Helen's nose. 'Thank you. A long sleep would be great.'

But there was something she had to do first.

Back in her room – a tiny single with a couple of square feet of free carpet between the bed and the wardrobe and the chest with the TV on it – she sat down on the bed and called the number for Mr Barnes at Dunedin Properties.

'Hello?' A Lancashire accent.

'Hello, my name's Helen Clack. I'm calling about the property at 31 Eglinton Crescent.'

'Ah. Been let, I'm afraid.'

'It's the previous tenant I'm calling about. Moir Sandison. He – well, he was my boyfriend. I just got back from holiday yesterday... to discover that he's gone, and all my stuff that was in the flat is gone, and – DC Powell gave me your name, he said you made a statement, about Moir taking your furniture, and not paying the rent he owed you...'

'That's right, yes. He absconded. Unfortunately that's not an uncommon occurrence in this business. He's your *boyfriend*?'

'Yes. Well – he was.'

'Do you know where he is?'

'No. But – the police are looking for him, obviously.'

A snort from the other end of the line. 'We'll never see that money again, even if they do catch up with him. He took your stuff too? Well forget it.'

'The police said he gave you a bogus reference? For his previous employer?'

'Yeah, I phoned the guy and it all seemed kosher, but the police have been round there and it's not even commercial premises, it's just a bungalow, and the fella who was renting it's also skipped out without paying what he owes. Seems like the pair of them were scammers.'

'Was there anything left in the flat? After Moir left?'

'That was the weird part. Usually when these low-lives skedaddle they leave the place in a right mess, you know? Fridge full of mouldy ready-meals, bathroom like nothing on earth, shit in the bath, rubbish piled everywhere. But the place was pristine. It was almost like he'd had cleaners in. That's why we could let it out again so fast. No clearing up required. At least that was something. Weird though.'

'So there was nothing at all? Nothing in any of the cupboards... I had a whole lot of boxes of stuff.'

'The place was picked clean. Literally. Oh, there was one thing though, a silver frame with a photo in it. The cops took it to dust for prints.'

Something was obviously wrong. DC Powell wouldn't meet her eye. He asked her if she'd like some water and then left the room, and the uniformed policewoman smiled at her and told her to take a seat.

It was the same interview room as before. She sat down in the same chair with the same blue plastic seat, moved her fingers across the same gouges in the table top.

The policewoman said, 'We're waiting on the DI. DI Blackburn. He's going to sit in.'

'Oh. Okay.'

When she'd called to ask if there'd been any progress, DC Powell had asked her to come by the station. All he'd say was that there'd been a development and they needed to talk to her in person. Like when doctors wouldn't give you test results over the phone. That always meant they were bad.

'Have they found him? Moir?'

The policewoman shook her head.

'So what's this "development" DC Powell was talking about?'

'I think we should wait for him and the DI.'

As if on cue, the door opened and DC Powell came in with a cup of water, which he set down on the table in front of Helen. Behind him was an older, grim-faced man who barely glanced at her before taking a seat opposite and slapping a folder down on the table.

'This is DI Blackburn.'

'Hello,' said Helen.

The man nodded.

DC Powell took a seat next to him, and looked across the table at Helen and then down at his hands. 'Thank you for coming in.'

'What's happened?'

'Well. It seems our guy – it seems he's not Moir Sandison.

That's not his real name.'

Helen shook her head. She was so tired. 'But you checked him out. Not you personally, but – your colleagues. They checked that he was who he said he was.'

'The *standard* checks we carry out are not, unfortunately, always proof against the determined fraudster,' said the DI. 'He'd gone to a lot of trouble to construct a false identity.'

'The real Moir Sandison,' said DC Powell, 'lives in Corstorphine, is married with two kids, and is five foot four.'

She couldn't speak.

The DI sighed. 'The passport he showed us – and which he used as identification when he withdrew money from the joint account – must have been forged, as the Passport Office has no record of having issued passports to two Moir Sandisons with the same date of birth – that would have been a red flag. Fraudsters don't tend to risk applying for a passport if the person whose identity they're stealing is still alive. Our man must have obtained a forged passport in Moir Sandison's name, and used it as proof of identity to get a copy of the real Sandison's birth certificate from the General Register Office; he then used the forged passport and the birth certificate as proof of identity in his scams. As for the photograph – we've obtained a copy of the original from Menstrie High in Stirling, and the name given under the captain of the team isn't Moir Sandison, it's David Clark.'

'So that's his real name?'

'If only it were that easy. No. The officers to whom he showed the photograph are both certain that the faces of the captain and the headmaster, Mr McKillop, differed in the photo they were shown from those in the original. Photoshopped, presumably, to superimpose the faces of the fraudsters, taken from old photographs of themselves.'

'So the real headmaster...'

'Died in 1997.'

'But they interviewed him.'

'Officers from Fife Constabulary interviewed a man who said he was Mr McKillop. At an address in Fountain Place in Dunfermline. The same address, by a strange coincidence, that was given for "Moir Sandison's" former employer Ewan Mathers, who acted as a referee when he rented the flat from Dunedin Properties.'

'So it was all fake.'

'These people often work in teams, running several scams con-currently – we're now looking into McKillop's activities in Dunfermline. Presumably he and Sandison provided cover for each other – references and so on.'

'But if you don't know who he is…' Helen dug her fingertips into the gouges in the table. 'Could he be Rob Beattie after all?'

DC Powell shook his head. 'Extremely unlikely. A murderer on the run is hardly likely to start a relationship with someone he knew in his past life.'

'But he'd proved that he wasn't Rob. As far as I was concerned, he'd proved it.'

She was going to be sick. She picked up the cup – it was heavier than she'd expected – and gulped some water from it.

'But what about your family – and old school friends? There'd always be the risk that one of them would tumble to him.'

'Mum lives in Yorkshire now. She's only met him twice. And all the other people who knew Rob – I'm not in contact with them any more. Well, apart from Uncle Jim. But I haven't seen him for years.'

When she and Mum had first moved to Edinburgh, Uncle Jim used to visit occasionally, but he'd never stay overnight. He had the farm to get back to, he'd say. And Helen and Mum would pretend to be disappointed, but really it was a relief when he'd gone. But then she'd think of him going back to that empty house – no Ina, no Suzanne – and feel guilty.

The DI said, 'How would the putative Rob Beattie know that, though?'

She stood. She really was going to be sick. Her throat spasmed and she put a hand to her mouth and swallowed bile.

'You've been close to him for weeks, months – if he really was Rob Beattie, don't you think you'd have realised it by now? Did the possibility even cross your mind, when you were together?'

'Of course not.'

She couldn't tell them that she'd almost started to seek out simi-larities to Rob. To *want* to find them so that, in some sick way, she could find a connection to Suzanne.

The girl he'd killed.

She couldn't tell them that.

'But he coughed like Rob used to. And sometimes – he had a short temper. And those text messages he sent me – when I got back from Yorkshire – pretending he was going to meet me at home, pretending he'd bought me teacakes – why would a common-or-garden conman do that? That's... that's calculated cruelty for no reason. That's exactly the kind of thing Rob Beattie would do.'

'Miss Clack, I know this is –'

'The first time I ever went to Eglinton Crescent, it wasn't true, what I told your colleagues, about just happening to see him coming out of a door – I first saw him in my hairdresser's and I got them to give me his address and I staked the place out – and...' She sat back down and took another gulp of water. 'And I had to go and get batteries for my camera, and on the way back he was suddenly there on the pavement, I think he'd been hiding between two parked cars and then he was suddenly there blocking my way, just like Rob used to in the school playground, and he smiled at me – I can't explain it, but it was *just like Rob* –'

'But again, why would Rob Beattie do that? He recognises a woman in the street as someone he used to know – the *cousin* of the person he *murdered* – and decides to have some fun reliving his childhood? At the risk of being identified?'

'It happens all the time, doesn't it?' The policewoman smiled at her. 'You go one way to pass someone in the street, and they go the same way. Then you go the other way, and so do they. Like a silly dance. And you both say "Sorry" and eventually you go one way and they go the other...'

'We'll have to take another statement, if the one you gave originally wasn't accurate,' said DI Blackburn.

'I'm sorry,' said Helen. 'I think I am actually going to be sick.' She pushed back her chair and lunged for the door and the policewoman was right behind her, saying 'There's a loo down the corridor –'

When they came back to the room the two men had paper cups of coffee on the table in front of them. The burnt smell of it filled her nose and mouth.

'I'm sorry,' she said. 'You must think I'm an idiot.'

'Of course we don't,' said DC Powell. 'It's a horrible situation for you.'

'It's just – even the slightest possibility –'

'Listen, Helen.' DC Powell set his coffee cup to one side and leant forward, forearms resting on the table. 'We *will* find out who he is. It might take a while, but we'll pin a name on him. And that name isn't going to be Robin Beattie. It's going to be the name of some rat of a con artist who's probably already done time for exactly the same sort of scam. A honey trap. These people are opportunists. You were just unlucky to stumble into the trap just as he'd finished setting it up. Maybe he had another woman in his sights, or maybe he got the flat before he started looking… Either way, when you turned up, accusing him of being Rob Beattie – I'm sorry, but he would've seen you as prime victim material. You were upset. Vulnerable, he'd have decided. But obviously educated, wearing nice clothes… I'm guessing it wasn't long before he'd elicited the information that you owned your flat outright?'

'I don't remember. I don't know.'

'These people are very good at what they do. I can virtually guarantee we're going to find a string of women he's scammed in exactly the same way.'

And that was supposed to make her feel better?

She almost laughed.

'Am I going to get any of my money back?'

The DI lifted his shoulders. 'That depends on whether, legally, the bank is in any way liable. Generally when money is withdrawn from a joint account by one party without the other's agreement, it's not a matter for the bank. But there's the false identity complication… You'll need a solicitor to look into it. You may qualify for legal aid, given your financial situation –'

'But *he* should be the one to give me the money back. Not the bank.'

'I'm afraid the chances of that are very slim.'

'But – you will find him? How long do you think it'll take?'

DC Powell smiled at her. 'We've got the photographs from your phone, which are going to be a big help. Chances are he's already in the database – the Police National Database. It's a case of plugging in what we know, his description, sending these photos round our colleagues in other forces… We'll get there.'

'He didn't like me taking his picture. He used to turn his head away.'

'I'll bet he did.'

'There were so many things… Things I should have picked up on.'

'Don't beat yourself up,' said the WPC.

'If we were going out after work, we'd never meet at his office – always at the museum, or in a café or a pub. Or a shop, if we needed to buy something.' Like a tin opener. When Helen had moved in they'd discovered that neither of them had a tin opener that worked properly, and the next day they'd met up in John Lewis to buy one. Moir had cornered an assistant and made the poor woman explain the pros and cons of all the various models, and Helen had laughed and apologised: 'I bet you don't get this many questions from people buying whole kitchens.' They'd decided that the one with pink handles was suitably celebratory, and carefully counted out exactly half the money each.

Was he still using it to open tins of tomatoes for his famous chilli?

'We're um, sorry about the confusion.' The DI was shuffling papers on the table in front of him. 'Over the Moir Sandison identity thing.'

Confusion. Right.

There had been no *confusion*. The policeman who'd phoned her – it seemed like years and years ago – had told her he was one hundred per cent satisfied that Moir Sandison was who he said he was.

DI Blackburn was here, she realised, not because he was concerned about her situation, or because he wanted to help catch a conman, but because he was worried she'd file a complaint or sue them.

As if she had the energy.

'The man in Dunfermline – you don't know who he really was either?'

'Not as yet.'

She took a long breath. 'The photograph. The photograph in the frame that he left behind in the flat. You said I could see it.'

'Ah. Yes.' DI Blackburn turned to the WPC.

The policewoman went to the row of tables behind the two men and lifted up a polythene bag. She took a pair of gloves from her pocket and wriggled her hands into them before undoing the top of the bag and bringing out the silver frame Moir had given her the day he'd proposed.

She set it on the table. The central photograph of the two of them and the one of his family were gone. The photograph that remained had been cropped to leave only Helen herself. Mum and Dad and Suzanne had been clipped away.

'There's writing on the back.' DC Powell had gloves on too now. He unclipped the hardboard at the back of the frame and lifted out the photo and turned it so Helen could see the back.

Moir's writing.

And Rob Beattie's words.

Smellie Nellie and her cattie

35

'Helen. Helen. It's okay. Take it easy.'

She was sitting on a hard, narrow bed. The WPC was smiling at her.

'I need to talk to DC Powell.'

'In a minute. Just lie back down for now.'

It was better when she lay down. She felt so woozy and strange – just like waking up in the hospital all those years ago. But no Mum to hold her hand. No anyone.

Her arms and legs were sore, as if she'd been running a marathon; her throat was dry and raw from too much talking; there was a tight band of pain squeezing her forehead – and she felt sick again. Her nose was running. She pulled the damp tissue from her pocket and sat up. 'I need to see DC Powell.'

'Okay. Just lie back down and I'll go and get him.'

She was in an empty room with a metal door. It smelt of bleach.

Had they put her in a cell?

There were sounds of people outside in the corridor. Echoey footsteps and voices.

When the door opened and DC Powell appeared she sat up and croaked at him:

'He's Rob Beattie. He *must be*.'

There was a cup of water by the bed. She lifted it and took a mouthful. The act of swallowing clawed against the raw place at the back of her throat, but she took another mouthful and that was better, slippery and cool.

'There are other possible explanations.' DC Powell leant back against the wall opposite. Keeping as far away from her as he could, evidently, in case she had some dread disease.

'Like what? I never told Moir that that was what Rob used to call me. *Smellie Nellie*. I never told him that.' She needed a copy of the writing. And copies of the photos that had been on her mobile.

'Are you sure? Maybe you had nightmares? Said it in your sleep?'

Helen shut her eyes. 'No. I don't think so.'

'My wife tells me I say all sorts of unrepeatable things when I'm asleep.'

'Even if I did say "Smellie Nellie" – and he realised what it meant – that Rob used to call me that – why would he write it on the back of this photo and leave it for the police to find? Why try to make out he's Rob Beattie, if he isn't?'

'To muddy the waters? To send us off on a false trail?'

'What, so you're not going to even *consider* that it might *not* be a false trail?' She pushed herself to her feet. Her legs shook. There were grey dots everywhere, growing and shrinking, growing and shrinking with the pulses of pain just above her eyes.

'Of course we are. The Grampian force are looking into obtaining a sample of Rob Beattie's handwriting – which will be compared with the writing on the photo by an expert.'

Just like last time, when they'd got an expert to compare Hector and Rob and Suzanne's writing with the writing in the letters.

'And meanwhile, what are you going to do?'

Water. She needed to rehydrate. She carefully turned and put out a hand and lifted the cup from the shelf by the bed.

'Meanwhile, we're continuing to look for him. "Moir Sandison", whoever he is. We have photographs, descriptions, a description of his Dunfermline associate – we'll get him, don't you worry about that. And when we do, it'll be a simple matter to compare his DNA profile to Rob Beattie's in the database and see if there's a match.'

She didn't understand about DNA. This was the kind of thing she'd always been careful to remember properly so she could repeat it to Moir, so he could explain it to her. But Moir was never going to look at her again and say, 'Are you sure you've got that right?'

Because Moir didn't exist.

She swallowed water. 'That's why he cleaned the flat.' She placed the cup back on the shelf and walked carefully to the door. Her head was still pulsing but the grey spots in her eyes had gone. And her legs were working as they should. 'The Dunedin Properties man said it looked like he'd had the flat professionally cleaned, and that was weird because people who skip out without paying the rent never bother. But Moir did. And now we know why. To eradicate any traces of his DNA.' A sudden shiver ran down her, from her shoulders to her thighs. She folded her arms round herself. 'Are you going to – put out a press release or whatever it is you do, telling people to look out for him, telling people Rob Beattie has resurfaced –'

'We'll alert our colleagues in other forces to the possibility. But at this stage –'

'Are the Grampian police going to interview his family? See if he's been in touch with any of them?' Another shiver went down her. She squeezed her arms against her ribs.

'I imagine they'll be speaking to the family.'

'You *imagine*. You still don't believe that he's Rob Beattie.' With her arms still crossed under her chest, she moved out into the corridor. Where it opened into the lobby at the end there was a fat woman in leggings bent over, laughing, and a policeman holding her elbow and turning to say something to another policeman.

'It's a possibility we're exploring.'

'Right.'

She started to walk down the corridor, towards the lobby and the laughing woman. The sound of the laughing was right inside Helen's head, fusing with the pulsing, unbearably loud at the peak of each of the pulses.

'Helen, we don't have a contact number for you. Can you –'

'I'm staying at a B&B.' She pulled her new phone from her bag, switched it on and pushed it at him. 'You can reach me on this number.'

He took a notebook from his jacket pocket, and a pen, and started to write it down. 'Right. Thanks. You don't think you'd be better staying with a friend? Someone who could...' He shrugged, smiled at her, handed back the phone. 'Support you through this?'

'I'm fine.'

'Have you thought about –'

'I need a copy of the writing. And the photos that were on my phone.'

'I'm not sure that's a good idea.' He sucked in a breath. 'Have you been in touch with Victim Support? They can –'

'I'll wait in the lobby if that's okay.'

He blinked at her.

'While you get me the copies of the photos and the writing.' She needed to sit down again. She didn't have time to be nice. 'Or do I have to do it through my solicitor? Because I really don't think you want a solicitor involved in this, do you?'

36

She parked opposite the wide space of the Green and wound down her window. Fresh air. She wished she was able to smell it. She breathed in and out through her mouth, sinking back in the seat, feeling the tightness and shivering ease. Like someone had put soothing hands on her shoulders, her stomach.

She reached for the bottle of Fanta in the driver's door. They'd kept her going on the nightmare drive north – bottles of sweet fizzy drinks. She couldn't get enough of them.

Probably she shouldn't be driving.

She'd had to stop five or six times because she just couldn't stay upright in the seat any longer. She'd been sick twice, once into some spiky shrubs behind a garage outside Brechin, and once into the verge on the Slug Road. She'd had to just stop the car and get out, even though there was a bend behind and she supposed it was dangerous.

She couldn't even remember the other places she'd stopped, and glogged down a couple more aspirin, wound her seat as horizontal as it would go and closed her eyes. Tried to tell herself she'd be fine after a rest and a sleep.

But she hadn't been able to sleep. Not properly. Her head hadn't stopped throbbing, and cars and lorries wouldn't stop whizzing across the backs of her eyelids.

A girl in skinny jeans was crossing the grass, phone clamped to ear, completely ignoring the dog on the other end of the bright red lead. She could have been anywhere, in some grotty city park, on a street in an inner city slum. At that age you never really *saw* the place you lived in. It was just *there*.

Aboyne, to this girl, would be just 'the Town.'

Nothing special.

In Edinburgh, when someone spoke about 'going into Town',

they meant of course into the city centre, but into her mind's eye always leapt a picture of Aboyne, the picture she was looking at now: the Green, the expanse of grass with its backdrop of trees and big Victorian houses, and behind them the hills of Birsemore and Craigendinnie, mist lying low over the dark green of the conifers. And the Huntly Arms Hotel, and the carpark between it and the road, where Dad had always left the car while they did the shopping.

And then they'd drive back through the Town and onto the Tarland Road.

Across the Green, under the trees by the gates, a man was standing facing her.

She squinted through the windscreen, the pulsing back in her head, in her eyes. He was too far away to make out any features – but he was the right height, the right build – and the way he was standing staring –

He turned and started walking towards the gates, and she let out her breath and closed her eyes.

How could that be Moir? How could he know where she was, unless he'd been following her all this time? How could he have followed her – to the police station, to the B&B, all round Edinburgh? All the way up here?

He wouldn't have needed to. He'd know where she was going.

So he hung around the Green on the off chance she'd stop by?

She fastened her seatbelt and started the engine. She drove slowly to the junction with the A93, scanning the area around the gates, the pavement, the grass, the car park, but there was no sign of the man.

Was she going to react like this every time she saw someone who looked vaguely like Moir?

She pulled out from the junction.

And there, on the other side of the road, was the bus stop – the one where she and Suzanne used to leave their bikes. They'd cycle all the way from home and chain their bikes to the metal pole of the bus stop, and get the bus into Aberdeen, with the limitless possibilities of £25 spending money each. A top from Dorothy Perkins, a magazine and a sandwich from John Menzies. And still money left over for a necklace or a pair of fluffy socks from Woolworth's.

And returning with their booty, they'd think nothing of the eight-mile slog back up the road.

Whenever she heard or read the words 'bus stop' it was this one she thought of, and the long road stretching back through the trees towards Ballater, and watching for the bus to appear at the end of it. And the wall – it was still there, still exactly as it was – where they used to sit and kick their heels against the loose mortar.

She smiled, and turned right at the crossroads.

She could actually feel the tension leaving her. Her arms weren't aching like they had been. Her foot on the accelerator wasn't shaking. Her brain wasn't jumping around all over the place.

Why had she been so afraid, all these years, of coming back?

This was the place that had been imprinted on her brain from when she was a baby. This was the landscape her mind would always move in, no matter where her body was.

And so of course it made her happy to be here.

Because what her eyes were seeing was matching up with the pictures hard-wired into her brain – as if her eyes had been searching and searching all this time for a match, and now finally here it was, and her neurons were firing off endorphins or whatever. Dopamine. Happy chemicals.

To say *Yes yes yes this is right.*

This is the right town, the right bus stop, the right hills with the cloud shadows moving over their heathery tops.

The right road home.

She turned off the Tarland Road and snaked down through Postie's Woodie, past the thirty limit and the sign in black and white: Kirkton of Glass. There was Miss Duff's house, just the same, except the row of pine trees behind the orchard were huge. Last time she'd seen them they'd been Christmas tree size.

And now into Kirkton, and already here was the shoppie, and opposite it the turn-off to the Estate Office; and 'Damask and Delft', just like on the website, except there was an old-fashioned pram outside with a big teddy bear in it.

From here she could see the road carrying on past the playground and over the bridge, and past the manse and the kirk, and off again into the trees.

When she was a little girl, Kirkton had been the centre of her universe. But it was just a tiny village on the most minor of B roads. Thirty or so houses, a primary school and a church, the Pitfourie Estate Office and a couple of shops.

Lorna's shop.

And the happy chemicals were gone, and her head was pounding worse than ever. What was she going to say? 'Hi Lorna! Could you just look at these photos and tell me if this is Rob? And is this his writing? You and your parents aren't secretly in touch with him, by any chance? You'll never believe it, but I think I was engaged to be married to him!'

She accelerated past the school and over the bridge.

Don't think about it.

His face, his hands touching her –

Her hands touching him.

Past the manse where the Beatties still lived, and the kirk. And here was the turn left, up the brae.

The road home.

She wanted to take the turn: over Worm Hill and onto the track, past the Mains – home, and Dad saying, 'Well, Hel'nie,' and getting between clean sheets and closing her eyes, and Mum putting a cloth on her forehead.

She kept straight on, past the farm track to Unthank, on into the trees. On to the gates of the House of Pitfourie.

She nudged Stan into the semicircle of road in front of them.

What if Hector found her here?

What if he was to appear now, driving out or in?

She pulled off her seatbelt and swung her legs out; walked to where the wall was lowest, just by the gates; leant on it. There was long grass on the other side, and those little white flowers she could never remember the name of.

A stream of orange sick, watery and acrid, came spilling out of her mouth and over the flowers. She waited for it to stop, her hands gripping the granite on the top of the wall.

Back in the car she reached for the Fanta, and gagged again as the sweet liquid filled her mouth, but she managed to swallow it down. She blew her streaming nose and turned the key in the ignition.

The gates were different.

Well, they were the same gates, but they used to be rusty, and multicoloured where the paint was flaking off to show all the layers underneath. Now they gleamed glossy black. And the East Lodge, which had had streaks of green damp down the wall by the door where the guttering was dodgy, and a saggy roof, and rotten windows – the stonework was clean, the roof straight, the windows trim and neat. There were sweet peas on wigwam things in the garden.

Could this be where Irina and Damian lived?

She couldn't imagine Irina putting up with dodgy guttering or a saggy roof. Or rusty gates that she'd be able to see from the little dormer windows upstairs.

She nudged Stan forwards so she could see round the back of the lodge, where there was a short driveway leading to the garage set into the trees: Victorian, with carved bargeboards along the lines of the gable, and a little arched window above the double doors.

The bargeboards didn't have gaps in them now. The doors weren't orra at the bottom where the wood was crumbling away. The whole garage had been painted a sludgy brown that was probably a heritage colour.

She revved the engine as she yanked Stan around and back onto the road. But when she reached the turn-off up Worm Hill, instead of going straight on she indicated right and accelerated up the incline. At the top of the hill she stopped. There was the Big Stone. And if she looked out across the fields – there was the Lang Park, and the plantation, and the low brown bulk of Craig Dearg.

Just the same.

She carried on down the other side.

There were the same old signs at the track end: two rectangles of wood, faded silvery grey, with the letters stamped in black into them: 'Mains of Clova' and under it 'Parks of Clova'.

She turned onto the track. It was difficult to judge the turn because everything was sliding to one side. The sky wasn't blue any more, it was pulsing pink and orange and grey. There were grey splodges over everything, getting bigger, joining together.

She slammed on the brakes.

If Moir really was Rob – if that really had been him on the Green – he could have driven ahead –

No. Why would he? If Moir was Rob, he'd had months to do whatever he wanted to her. Why wait until now?

Because it had been fun.

To take everything she had, and watch her suffer.

And then watch her suffer some more.

She pressed her foot to the accelerator, sending Stan bumping down the track and up into the yard at the Mains. Through the splodges she registered the changes – the weeds growing along the foot of the steading, the cracks in the concrete, the peeling paint on the windows – but suddenly nothing mattered except lying down.

She cranked her seat back.

Was she going to faint? What would happen if she did?

She closed her eyes.

She wasn't sure how long she'd been lying there when she heard a *click* at her ear, and cool air swept over her, and a rough voice said, 'Hel'nie.'

She opened her eyes.

The splodges had gone. An old man with tiny eyes and a big purple nose was bending over her. His lips were purple too.

'Hel'nie,' he said again.

'Uncle Jim –'

She lunged out of the car and felt his hand on her arm, his grip surprisingly strong. She pulled away and tottered across the yard to the high weeds at the end of the steading. She leant over and opened her mouth, and out streamed more orange cowk.

He hadn't followed her.

When it was over she walked carefully back. 'I'm sorry. I've got some kind of bug. I just need to lie back down in the car,' and he was holding her arm again and saying, 'Come on in to a beddie,' and then she was inside and up the stairs, and Uncle Jim was opening the door to her old room, the room next to Suzanne's where she used to sleep when she stayed over, and she was tugging off her shoes, and slipping between cool sheets, familiar pink Camberwick under her fingers. Closing her eyes.

And opening them again. 'Thank you. I'm sorry – for just turning up like this.' She had to tell him about Rob. Moir.

But not just now.

He was closing the curtains across the bright rectangle of the window. 'Na na,' was all he said.

She closed her eyes, and heard his steps cross the floor to the bed, pause, continue; and the door open and shut.

Even with her blocked nose she could smell something not quite right. Fooshty.

Auntie Ina's sheets had always smelt of too much washing powder. Helen used to worry in case she made a mess in the pristine perfection of this room. It was twice as big as her little room at home, and had a grown-up dressing table, and a boxroom off it with a big empty wardrobe for her clothes, and a double bed that she could roll over on four times without falling off the edge.

She opened her eyes.

In the dim light she could see the dressing table in exactly the same position as it had always been, against the opposite wall, and above it the only decoration in the room – a framed print of a ship, sails billowing.

On the bedside cabinet was a sweetie. A mint humbug.

When Uncle Jim used to find her crying in a corner of the shed or the steading or the byre, hiding her tears from Suzanne, he'd say, 'Eh, me,' and put his hand in his pocket and bring out a mint humbug: his cure for all ills, from a dollie's broken head to a little girl's broken heart. Sharp and salty and sweet.

She'd be sick if she tried to eat it. She put it under her pillow – in case he came back and saw it and thought she hadn't wanted it – and rolled onto her side, and knew nothing more until a voice said: 'Helen?'

A woman's voice, low and pleasant.

She opened her eyes.

37

Fiona Kerr was standing at the window. She'd pulled back the curtains. The light was far too bright.

Helen put a hand to her lips to check for crusts of sick.

'Hello!' Fiona smiled, as if her whole day had been leading up to this wonderful moment. 'Feeling a bit rotten?'

The photo on the website didn't, of course, do her justice. To get the full Fiona effect you had to see her in the flesh. You had to feel the *joie de vivre* – and it really was something you felt physically, whether you wanted to or not. It sounded so corny in English – the joy of being alive. But that was what she glowed with; that was what she gave you, diluted, to feel for yourself, like a passive smoker getting a little hit of nicotine.

Helen swallowed, and Fiona took a glass from a tray that had appeared on the bedside table. There was condensation on its sides – ice clinking. Helen propped herself up and took the glass and sipped. It was cool, delicious. 'Fiona – thank you. Are you – I'm sorry, but this is all… a bit surreal –'

'Your uncle called. Asked me to pop over and have a look at you.' Her hair was caught back in the sunglasses perched on her head. She reached up to adjust them. 'I'm a GP with the Aboyne practice now.'

'Oh. Right.'

'I couldn't believe it when he said you were back.' Her smile widened. 'We've all *so wanted* to know how you were getting on. For the past – how many years is it, anyway? Oh gosh, I don't want to think.'

'Sixteen.'

'Sixteen?' A little silence. Fiona fichered with one of the buttons on her shirt. It was a plain white cotton shirt, tailored at the waist, setting off the creamy skin at neck and cleavage. 'Well, but it's wonderful to have you back. But not feeling too good? Your uncle said you've been sick?'

She nodded. 'I think I picked up a bug on the train. Coming back from visiting Mum. A couple of days ago.'

'Okay, let's run through your symptoms. Have you been sick more than once?'

Helen nodded. 'I just feel generally yuch. Headachy, dizzy. Feeling sick. Being sick. I just want to lie down the whole time, and never get up again.'

'Horrid. And do you feel shivery?'

'A bit.'

'Achy?'

'Achy arms and legs.' Helen took another sip of water. 'And my nose won't stop running, and my throat's like sandpaper. Other than that I'm just fine.'

'And to add to your woes, do you have a rash?'

'No.'

'Okay. It sounds like you have a bit of flu. I'm just going to have a quick listen to your chest. Have you been having any problems with your breathing?' Fiona ducked down and reappeared with a stethoscope, hooking it into her ears and rubbing the other end between her hands. 'A mucousy crackling in your lungs?'

'No.'

'If I can just slip this under your T-shirt...'

Helen felt the smooth metal press into her skin.

'Take a deep breath in and out.' Fiona's face was intent as she listened, then moved the stethoscope to the other side of Helen's chest. 'And again... Good.' She smiled, and pulled out the earpieces. 'Your lungs sound fine. You don't have diabetes?'

'No.'

'Problems with any of your organs? Kidneys or heart? Liver?'

'No.'

'And have you been in hospital recently for any reason? Seeing your doctor for anything?'

'No.'

'Good. That's fine, then. It's just a case, I'm afraid, of waiting it out. Making sure you drink plenty fluids. Now, there's a Lemsip in the mug.' She indicated the tray. 'I've left the other sachets in the kitchen.'

'Oh – thank you.'

'But if you prefer straight Paracetamol, there's some here too.' There was a packet on the tray, Helen saw. 'Obviously, though, if you have the drink and then decide to take Paracetamol, adjust the dose accordingly. There's the equivalent of one Paracetamol in that mug.'

'Thanks. That's really good of you.'

'I know from experience that your uncle doesn't keep a well-stocked medicine cupboard.'

'Not exactly the ideal patient?'

'Not exactly, no… You know he had a little heart attack last year?'

A *heart attack*?

Just like Dad?

Fiona's hand was on her arm. 'Just a tiny one. A warning sign, really. I thought he might not have told you.'

'But – what do you mean, a warning sign?'

'He's meant to be following a new regime, healthy eating etc., but Hector says his diet still seems to consist of sandwiches, biscuits and alcohol.'

Hector.

Oh God.

'Maybe you can reform him while you're here.'

'Oh but I'm not staying. After I've had a rest, I need to see Lorna. And then I'll be going back to Edinburgh.'

'You're in no fit state to drive, Helen.'

'After I've had a sleep…'

Fiona folded up the stethoscope and bent down again. Presumably she had her doctor's bag down there, out of Helen's view on the high bed. 'You have to "Listen to your body", as they say. At least stay a couple of days. We've a lot to catch up on, haven't we, apart from anything else? I want to hear all about your work – I always think it must be so fascinating, like being a detective – and about your mum's new man and what she's been doing in Yorkshire.'

Her surprise must have shown, because Fiona laughed. 'Getting information out of your uncle is like getting water from a stone, but you know what Hector's like – you start off talking about the weather, and before you know it you're blurting out your deepest darkest secret. Or in your uncle's case, news about you and your mum, which he seems to regard as classified information. The rest of us have had to be content with getting it all third-hand through Hector.'

So Hector – Hector knew things about her. And felt they were interesting enough to tell other people. Like what? She tried to think what kind of things Mum might have told Uncle Jim, on the rare occasions they spoke on the phone. Boring stuff about her job. Boring stuff about her flat. Not so boring stuff about Moir?

There was a tentative knock at the door, and Fiona called, 'Come in.'

Uncle Jim edged himself into the room. Despite the heat he wore a thick, shapeless tweed jacket.

'Helen's got a dose of the flu, Mr Clack. I've just been telling her she's not well enough to drive back to Edinburgh. She can stay here a few days, can't she?'

He looked from Fiona to Helen, as if it had just been suggested he fly them to Mars. 'I'm not just sure… Hel'nie… I've not much in the way of provisions. And the house… I'm a muckit aald mannie, Doctor, and the place isna fit for folk.'

'Well maybe it's time that changed. And here's the perfect motivation. As for provisions, you can manage some invalid food, can't you? Some toast, maybe? A boiled egg? Some tinned soup? Jelly? Custard?'

Helen's stomach turned over. 'I really don't want anything.'

'It's not rocket science, Mr Clack.'

There was something ridiculous about Fiona lecturing Uncle Jim, but still calling him 'Mr Clack', as if doing that let her say anything she liked and still be respectful. Helen caught Uncle Jim's eye, and thought she saw a glint there.

'Do you have bread?'

'Aye. But nae a toaster.' This said with some satisfaction.

'You'll just have to use the grill on the cooker, then. How about a slice of toast with a bittie butter on it?'

'I'm really not hungry,' said Helen.

As Uncle Jim shuffled obediently off, Fiona said briskly, 'It's good to get something inside you, if you can.' And then, 'I really hope you'll be able to stay a while, Helen. Everyone will want to see you.'

Everyone?

'So how are you all?' Helen tried to make her voice normal. 'You and Steve –'

'Old married couple with three kids. Can you believe it? Lizzie – the youngest – is just three and a half. So I'm only working part-time at the moment.'

'You have three children? Wow... And what's Steve doing?'

'He's a GP too – in the same practice, actually. Talk about taking your work home with you... Our older two girls have had to impose a ban on "doctor talk" at the dinner table. How sad is that?'

Helen smiled. 'And Fish? Sorry, I mean...' What *was* his real name?

'Malcolm.' Fiona's eyes sparkled. 'Everyone still calls him Fish. Apart from Mum and Dad, and assorted aunts and uncles. And presumably people at his work. He's District Procurator Fiscal now. With a posh Georgian house in Old Aberdeen. Still looks like a startled haddock though.'

Helen laughed. 'And Lorna? I know she's got a shop – I've seen it online.'

'Yes, she's had that for – it must be two years now. Not the best time to set up a business, but she seems to be doing okay.'

'I bet she has it running like clockwork.'

'Gosh yes.' Fiona went to look out of the window, pushing a stray strand of hair behind her ear. Sunlight fell harsh on her face, and Helen saw that there was the faintest trace of a vertical crease in her forehead above her nose. The discovery was shamefully satisfying. 'And Norrie – he still works on the Estate – on the native forest regeneration thingy. His wife's just had a baby.' She flicked a look back at Helen. 'A little girl.'

This really was news. 'I didn't even know he was married.'

'He's been married a while now.' She spoke carefully, as if measuring her words against Helen's possible reaction. 'A girl he met on a chainsaw course, of all things. She's a lot younger than him. Mid-twenties.'

'Is she nice?'

'She's nice enough.' Fiona took the sunglasses from her head, pushed her hair back, and replaced them.

'And Hector?' She made her voice light. 'How's Hector?'

Fiona came back to the bed, bent down and straightened, holding what looked like a deep, stiff briefcase but which was presumably the latest in doctors' bags.

'Is he all right?' So much for keeping it casual. In her own ears the words sounded desperate.

'Why shouldn't he be?'

The temperature in the room had just plummeted.

Then Fiona grinned at her, and the sun was back. 'I can safely say that Hector enjoys what they used to call "rude good health". Doesn't even smoke now. He never darkens the surgery door – except when he has a suspect tick bite and needs a course of antibiotics. As a preventive measure for Lyme's disease. You know? Some ticks carry it now, so if you've been walking in long grass or heather you need to check yourself for them.'

'I don't think that's going to be an issue. When I'm well enough to go for a walk in tick-infested heather, I'll be well enough to drive back to Edinburgh.'

'Yes. Of course you will.'

There were a hundred things she'd like to ask, but she chose just one. As if as an afterthought: 'Is he married?'

'Hector? No.'

'But he's got a partner?'

'No.'

Silence.

Then: 'Hector's relationships seem to follow what we call in the medical profession a "self-limiting course". Average duration approximately three to four months. I don't think he's ever had what you could call a partner – although the women in question have no doubt felt differently. Poor things.'

Poor things.

Well, this was what she'd wanted to hear, wasn't it? That Hector was still single? That he didn't have anyone?

But how could she be glad that he hadn't found someone to love?

Fiona was swinging the case gently, back and forward, back and forward. 'Okay then, I'll leave you to –'

'I passed the gates to the House on my way here. They look very smart. And the East Lodge. Looks like it's had quite a make-over.'

'Oh, the whole Estate's had a make-over – although we're talking sash-and-case window renovation at £400 a time, and lime repointing, and flagstones, and native species, rather than uPVC, decking and water features.'

'So the Estate's doing well?'

'Seems to be.' Fiona took a step away from the bed. 'Now. You get plenty of rest, and I'll come back and see you tomorrow.'

'Thanks Fiona. But you really don't need to –'

'And you can tell me all about what you've been doing.' She opened the door. Oh-oh. I smell burning.'

38

The vinyl on the bathroom floor was sticky under the soles of her shoes. Glancing into the loo was a mistake – the sides of the bowl were encrusted with brown and yellow keech. There was no toilet brush or any sign – unsurprisingly – of toilet cleaner. It stank.

She tore off a piece of toilet paper and wet it at the sink, and wiped the toilet seat. The paper turned yellow. She chucked it into the toilet and lifted the seat, electing to hover as if it was some grotty loo in a nightclub.

What would Ina say? Probably: *Get me the Vim.*

Did Uncle Jim ever hear from her? Had they ever got divorced?

As she washed her hands at the sink, running the tips of her fingers along the sides of the bar of soap, where it wasn't quite so clarty, she noticed on the top of the cabinet next to the door, covering a spare roll of toilet paper, the knitted form of Frank.

The white poodle Grannie had made, Grannie who had died before she and Suzanne were born. There was dust lying thick on his nose. Ina had always been scathing about Frank, but she and Suzanne had loved him. They used to add him to their gang of soft toys and dollies. Helen had felt sorry for him because he didn't have a proper body, just a big floppy space where the toilet roll went, so Suzanne used to roll up a scarf and stick it up his bottom.

Or a blouse, if they wanted to make him a little fat-arse.

She crossed the landing not to her own room but to the one next to it.

She opened the door and went in.

Suzanne's room, but not Suzanne's room. All the posters and photos and gonks and the huge cut-out vampire were gone. The walls had been repainted a bilious shade of green. Everything was neat, and covered with dust.

The bedspread was the same, though. Camberwick, like in Helen's room, but green instead of pink. The walls had been painted to match, presumably. The sun slanting through the window highlighted the names scratched on one of the lower panes of glass: *Helen* and *Suzanne*, hopelessly crooked. She smiled, and walked to the window on weak legs, and traced the letters with a fingertip.

They'd done them with a belt buckle, on a winter day with snow thick on the ground outside, cold through the thin glass. Uncle Jim had not been impressed. He'd told them the window wasn't theirs to deface, it was the Laird's, and did they want to go and explain to *him* how this had got there?

Suzanne's response had been a classic:

'It wasn't us.'

Instead of going back to bed, she made for the stairs. She needed a drink of water, and the idea of supping from the bathroom tap wasn't appealing.

She hung onto the banister as she made her way down. The front door was standing wide open, and a dog was clicking across the flagstones of the hall, ignoring her, intent on its progress along the passage towards the kitchen.

She was reaching for the door to close and lock it when Uncle Jim appeared, stooping to put a hand on the dog's head in passing. 'Now, Hel'nie. Back to bed with you.'

'You shouldn't leave the door open like this. Anyone could just walk in.'

He smiled, as if at the daftness of the idea. 'Will I get your gear in from your car?'

'Oh – well. Yes. Thank you.'

'Up to bed with you.'

'I'm sorry to be such a nuisance, but could I have a drink of water too?' And as she had a mental picture of the probable state of the kitchen: 'Or actually there are some bottles of drinks in the car. Could you bring them in? Thanks, Uncle Jim. I feel awful, landing on you like this. Making you fetch and carry for me.'

'Na na.'

'Fiona was saying you've had some heart problems.' Actually, she probably shouldn't have done, but Uncle Jim was hardly going to sue her for a breach of confidentiality. 'You should have told me – I could have come and looked after you after you got out of hospital.' Could she? She was only here now out of necessity, and as soon as she could sit behind the wheel she'd be off again.

Uncle Jim was moving out of the door. He turned back with a smile, and waved a hand as if to say *It was nothing.*

The dog followed him.

'Not the great big suitcase,' she called, on second thoughts, having visions of him struggling, red-faced, up the stairs. 'Just my handbag, if you can find it. Thank you!'

She needed to phone Mum at some point. She'd just say she and Moir had split up and she was visiting Jim. And she'd also have to call DC Powell in Edinburgh to tell him where she was.

But right at this moment she needed to lie down.

When Uncle Jim appeared with her handbag and two bottles of Sprite, she was half-dozing, half-wondering if she needed to be sick again.

'Oh, thank you. Just dump them anywhere.'

He set her handbag on the bedside cabinet, carefully, as if it was the latest must-have designer bag rather than the scuffed, bauchled old thing she'd had for years. She reached for it and opened its flap. She'd put the photos of Moir in the centre pocket, ready to show Lorna.

'Uncle Jim – could you sit down a minute? I need to tell you something.'

All through her story he sat frowning, shaking his head and sucking in a breath occasionally, but not saying anything until she'd finished. 'So you think this mannie was Rob Beattie.'

'I don't know. That's why I'm here. I wanted to show these photos to Lorna.'

He brought a pair of filmy reading specs from the top pocket of his jacket and perched them on his bulbous nose. As he examined each photograph in turn, his face gave nothing away.

He handed the photos back and shook his head. 'I dinna think it.'

'But he's a grown man, remember, now. And he could have had cosmetic surgery... As long as it's even a possibility, you see why we have to be careful? Keep the doors locked? Be on the look-out for him?'

He sighed. 'You've had a sair time of it, Hel'nie.'

She gulped air. 'When the police catch him they'll be able to do a DNA test, and that'll tell us one way or the other – but they have to catch him first. And meanwhile he could be anywhere. He could be out there *right now*.' She gestured at the window.

'That DNA's a great invention, eh?'

She blinked.

She'd just told him the psychopath who'd killed his daughter could be prowling round the house, and he wanted to talk about DNA?

A bubble of hysteria rose up her throat. 'Oh Uncle Jim. It's good to be back.'

'Well, well.' He stood. 'If you'd like a gander round the Parks, when you're feeling better, it's empty just now. I've the keys.'

As if she was going to want to go wandering about a deserted house. 'No one's living there?'

'It's a holiday let. Empty just now – the Laird's to have the place rewired.'

For a second Helen thought he'd lost it – that he'd forgotten the Laird was dead. And then she realised he meant Hector.

Uncle Jim didn't know about what had happened in London – she hadn't even told Mum. But he knew about the letters: about Suzanne and Rob writing them, about Helen thinking they were from Hector. So she couldn't bring herself to ask him any of the questions she wanted to. Instead: 'Fiona was saying the Estate's doing well.'

'Aye.'

'I've had a quick look at the website. There seems to be a lot going on, with holiday lets and shooting parties and everything.'

'Aye.'

'There must be money in that sort of thing, then. Although I was under the impression that most rural estates find it hard to make ends meet these days.'

He didn't say anything.

She sank back against the pillows.

'You get some shut-eye, lass.'

After dwaaming and dozing through the day, she found she couldn't sleep when night came. She lay on her side, on her back, on her front. She tried to force her mind to think of practical things: what sort of job she'd look for in Edinburgh; where she might live; what she'd say to Mum and Lionel tomorrow.

She closed her eyes.

Had he watched her while she slept? Moir? Rob?

Don't think about it.

London. Another bed, and another man.

A man who had come upon her on a dark road, and crept into her shadow, and carried her off to Corrachree. And when she came back –

When she came back, she was nae use to naebody.

Practical things. Practical things.

She was going to have to persuade Uncle Jim to get a cleaner, and someone to come in and cook him a decent meal at least once a day. Someone to help on the farm.

To do the heavy work. The lifting. To manhandle the beasts... Jostling and barging... Big thick tongues and strings of saliva... The smell of them... The byre... The byre at the Parks, and the calfies...

Horses, not calfies.

Horses, galloping.

She had to hide. She couldn't outrun them. Galloping horses, bells jingling on their harnesses. Three of them – four, five – and on their backs... instead of faces there was just blackness, and their hands were reaching for her, stretching, their thin fingers twining in her hair –

She jolted awake, her whole body tense under the covers.

The Sith.

First the Ghillie Dhu, and now the Sith. Oh God! She laughed, shakily, and stretched out a hand to the bedside lamp.

And froze.

She could still hear it. The tuneful sound of little bells.

She got out of bed and padded to the window and edged inside the curtain. Crouching, keeping her head below the level of the sill, she eased up the window's bottom section.

The nutty smell of ripe barley came drifting in.

And the tinkling of bells.

Could it be something loose in the wind – a chain, or pieces of rusty metal chittering against each other? Wind chimes? Was it likely that Uncle Jim had wind chimes?

The sound was moving. Coming closer.

She looked over the sill. In the light of the moon she could make out the steading, the byre, the shapes of Uncle Jim's old pick-up and Stan – but nothing moving.

What was it?

Where was it?

A jaunty jingling. Getting louder and louder. And she realised that she couldn't see what it was because it was right under her. Moving against the wall of the house. To see it she'd have to put her head out of the window –

Instead she shot away from it on her bottom, crawled to the door and out onto the landing, jumped to her feet and then she was at Uncle Jim's door, knocking and saying his name, and he was opening it, wisps of hair sticking up in a halo around his head.

'What's the matter?'

'Can you hear it?'

'Eh?'

'There's someone outside.'

'Eh?'

'Someone – moving around in the yard.'

At the window she shushed him. But the sound had stopped.

'What was it you heard, Hel'nie?'

'It sounded like – bells. Someone jingling little bells.'

She couldn't see his face in the dark. 'Well. I'll let Fly and Ben out to have a yowf. You get back to bed. There's naebody coming in about – that pair'd have the arse off them soon enough.'

As Fly and Ben barked and yelped in the yard below, she rummaged in her bag for her mobile, and the piece of paper on which she'd written down the number of the local police station. But she had no bars. No reception. She'd have to use the landline downstairs.

With her foot on the first step she stopped.

What was she going to say?

It's an emergency – send a squad car – I think I heard bells.

Ridiculous.

Just like everything else.

Everything he'd done – from dodging in front of her in the street, to worming his way into her life, to following her up here and jingling bells under her window – they were things nobody would believe. Nobody would believe that Rob Beattie, a murderer supposedly on the run, would do any of those things.

She went slowly back to her room.

She was remembering the riddle he'd made up, the riddle he'd told her the night before he'd attacked her and killed Suzanne.

I am the dagger in the night...

Outside the dogs were still barking, but it was a general *We're here, this is ours, keep off* kind of noise – not the purposeful, snarling sound they'd be making if they'd actually found someone out there.

He'd gone. By the time the police got here it would be too late anyway.

39

'You're looking better!' was the first thing Fiona said when she arrived the next morning, swinging a colourful rectangular shopping bag instead of her doctor's case.

Helen smiled from the pillows, dabbing her nose with a soggy tissue. 'I bet you say that to all the patients.'

'Nope – I've just been telling your uncle that some fresh fruit and vegetables would do wonders for his digestion. I've told him to get some decent food in. Meanwhile...' She perched on the bed and delved into the bag. 'I thought you might like your own supplies up here.' There was a big thermos, a box of oatcakes, a bag of nuts and raisins, a tupperware box with something inside, some Babybel cheeses and some fruit – a bunch of grapes, dusky purple, three apples and two fat peaches. 'There's iced water in the thermos.'

Like she was a heroine in a costume drama, visiting the sick and needy with a basket on her arm. Fiona would have made a perfect Regency heroine, all sparkling eyes and pert remarks.

'Fiona, this is – so kind of you. You'll have to let me pay you.' Helen reached for her handbag.

'Oh poof!' Fiona set the plate down on the bedside cabinet and started putting the fruit on it. 'Don't be daft.'

'Thank you.' She closed her hand on her purse. Under it were the photographs of Moir. She pulled them out. 'Fiona – these are – could you have a look at these and tell me what you think?'

She laid them on the bedspread between them: Moir at the beach at Yellowcraigs, squinting into the sun, hair blown half across his face; Moir in the flat –

'Who's this?'

Helen reached for a fresh tissue. 'Do you recognise him?'

'No. Should I?' Fiona picked up one of the photos – the one of Moir in the kitchen, turning away from the camera, laughing. 'He looks a bit like –'

Helen waited.

And waited.

'Like who?' she prompted.

Fiona was looking at her as if she was an unexploded bomb. 'I was going to say... oh Helen, I was going to say Rob Beattie, but –'

'Do you think it's him?'

'Oh God! Helen! No. Where did –'

'Is it him?'

She was frowning at the one of Moir admiring the frontage of Falkland Palace – the best one, showing his whole face. 'No. I don't think so – but there's certainly a resemblance. Who is he?'

Helen wheeled out her story, watching Fiona's eyes widen and her mouth twist in dismay at the appropriate places. She kept saying, 'Oh my God. Oh my *God*.' At several points she reached out and touched Helen's arm.

And when Helen had finished, she said, 'Let me see the writing that was on the photo.'

Helen handed her the photocopy. 'DC Powell – my police contact in Edinburgh – says Grampian Police went to see Mr and Mrs Beattie yesterday.' She'd phoned him first thing for a progress report, such as it was. 'To get samples of Rob's writing, and show them these photos of Moir. The Beatties say it's definitely not him. But... sixteen years is a long time. And he could have had plastic surgery. And the Beatties...'

'May have their own agenda?'

'Exactly. If he *is* Rob... He could have been in touch with them. They could have been helping him, all this time.'

'They're certainly still convinced of his innocence. And Mrs Beattie – well. She's gone a bit loonie tunes.'

Helen smiled. 'Is that a medical term?'

'In the absence of a more definitive diagnosis... A psychiatrist would probably say she's within the normal spectrum and her "lacunae" are the result of the traumatic events she's experienced. She's not certifiable or anything. But boy has she some strange ideas.'

'Like what?'

'Oh, accusing all and sundry of murdering Rob.'

'Murdering *Rob*?'

'Yup.'

'Who's she been accusing?'

'Just about anyone who was there that night. Hector, primarily.' Fiona was looking back down at the photocopy. 'All I can remember about Rob's writing is that it was terrible. People with dyslexia often have dysgraphia, especially as children – virtually illegible handwriting. This isn't exactly copperplate, but it's not terrible, is it? I wonder, though, if someone with dyslexia – would their writing maybe change more than the average person's, as they're starting from a lower base? I don't know. I'll check.' She handed the photocopy back. 'But Helen –' She was looking at the photos again. 'I really don't think this is Rob.'

'But he could have had plastic surgery.'

'I guess so.' She frowned. 'Did this – Moir – have problems with reading and writing? Or any other symptoms of dyslexia? Was he uncoordinated? Did he get motion sickness? Did he confuse left and right?'

'His spelling was pretty bad. I don't know about motion sickness. But he definitely wasn't uncoordinated. It was completely believable that he would have been the captain of his school football team. But sometimes I used to think Rob exaggerated his lack of coordination. Before he was diagnosed with dyslexia, I don't remember him being particularly uncoordinated. It was almost as if he found out that lack of coordination was a symptom of dyslexia, and then pretended to have it as an excuse for dunting into people and breaking things.'

'Boys, in particular, can become uncoordinated for a while once they hit puberty, whether they have dyslexia or not. Even if it was genuine, Rob's lack of coordination could have been just a temporary thing.'

Helen blew her nose. 'He has to be Rob. Otherwise how could he know about me being called "Smellie Nellie"?'

'Maybe you told him, but you've forgotten? Or maybe the policeman's right with his talking-in-your-sleep theory?'

'Maybe.' She scrunched up the tissue. 'I think he might have followed me up here. Last night I heard – a tinkling sound outside. Moving under my window.'

Fiona looked dubious. 'Tinkling.'

'Like the Sith... Like he was pretending to be the Sith.'

Fiona's dubious expression didn't alter.

'The police think I've lost it too.'

She'd told DC Powell – not about the bells, but about seeing 'someone' in the yard last night. Maybe she hadn't been convincing. Or maybe it was a common thing for victims of crime to 'see' shadowy figures in the dark. His promise to alert the local force had been distinctly lacklustre. He'd said the local boys would 'keep an eye on the place', which probably meant they'd drive by a couple of times a week.

Fiona shook her head. 'Helen, I don't think you've *lost* it! God, if it was me –'

'What I need to do is get back on my feet, talk to Lorna, and go back to Edinburgh. And while the police are looking for him, whoever he is, I need to find somewhere to live where I can lie low, and see about getting a job. Look into recovering the money from the bank.'

'Fish could help with that. He'll be here tomorrow, staying with Mum and Dad for a few days. Why don't I bring him to see you? If you feel up to it?'

'He won't want to be bothered with work stuff on his holiday.'

'Don't be daft. He'll be champing at the bit.' Fiona was gathering up the photos spread out on the bedspread. 'What a nightmare.'

'Yes. But enough of my tales of woe – tell me about you and Steve and the girls.'

Fiona put the stack of photos face down on the bedside table, and launched into a series of stories. Helen let them wash over her, until:

'... When I was eleven my hair either did its own thing or was contained in a ponytail. But it's all so different these days. The girls in Cat's class are all little fashion-plates.'

'Talking of which – where's Irina living now?' She didn't care that it was a conversational gaff – that she hadn't shown sufficient interest in the children. There were things she needed to know.

'Irina? No idea. Somewhere in Europe. France, I think.'

France? 'Oh. I just assumed – Has she remarried?'

'I've no idea.'

'Is she not in touch with Hector?'

'Hardly.'

But how could they not be contact, if Damian was still at Glencoil? Well, but the last mention of Damian online in connection with Glencoil was a few years old. She'd assumed that was down to schools becoming cagier about revealing information about pupils, but the simple explanation must be that Damian wasn't there any more. That he lived in France now.

'That's a pity. For Damian, I mean.'

Fiona was looked at her oddly, as if she'd made an even worse faux pas than not talking about the children.

'What's he like? Damian? Is he like Hector?'

Fiona's mouth relaxed in a smile. 'Yes and no.'

He was like Hector, probably, in all the ways that mattered. And unlike him physically, and in his rather geeky preoccupations.

Fiona said, 'Hector knows you're here. Everyone in the parish knows by now. He'd like to come and see you, but he wanted me to ask you if that was all right. He seems to feel you might not want to see him.'

There was hot dampness under her arms.

Very gently, Fiona said, 'Do you blame him, for what happened?'

'No! Of course not.'

'But you don't want to see him?'

'There's not much point, is there, if I'm leaving in a couple of days.'

'But you're happy enough to see me, and Fish, and Lorna. What is it between you and Hector, then, if it's not that you blame him?'

How like Hector not to tell anyone, even Fiona, about London.

She shook her head. 'Nothing.'

40

She woke in the dark to the knowledge, the certain knowledge, that there was someone in the room.

She lay completely still, all her senses straining.

Could she hear something? The door, very slowly opening?

She turned her head on the pillow.

Was that a shape? A blacker shape against the door?

Her breath trapped in her throat, she shot upright, fumbled for the switch on the bedside lamp – and as light blazed from it she scrambled off the bed and into the corner of the room furthest from the door, her eyes frantically scanning from the door to the bed to the window and back.

The room was empty.

41

She slept fitfully and woke late to a bright blue sky, promising a
scorcher. She had a thorough wash at the sink – there was no
shower, and the bath was grey with scum – and dressed, and found
Uncle Jim in the kitchen, sitting at the table with the *Press and
Journal* and a packet of custard creams. At his elbow was a hideous
mug half full of stewed tea.

'Aye aye.'

'Morning.'

Fly, chewing on an old tennis ball, rolled his eyes up at her.

There was a throat-catching smell of dog, and tea and old grease,
and something less savoury. Every surface was piled with opened
letters and torn envelopes, and newspaper with bits of machinery on
it, and boxes and, on top of the cold Aga, four huge sacks of dog
food and an orra pair of old boots. An electric cooker stood next to
the Aga. There wasn't room for it to go back against the wall so it
stood at an angle to the worktop, as if the tradesman fitting it had
left it there temporarily and never come back. The hob was encrusted with burnt spillages, and the once-white oven door was grey, with
streaks over it of brown and orange and – oh God – *green*. The floor
around it was similarly encrusted and spattered. The worktop –

She went closer. Yes, it *was* the same worktop as she remembered: there were a few places where the marble-effect surface was
visible, where the layers of grease and grime were absent – by the
sink, where water erosion had presumably prevented build-up. Dirty
dishes and cutlery were piled on the draining board. A stained tea
towel hung from the rail of the Aga.

'Uncle Jim.' She pointed to the worktop; the floor; the cooker;
the tea towel. 'This is *gross*.'

'Good clean dirt, eh, Ben?' He poked at the dog with the toe of
his boot, and Ben brushed his tail across the filthy floor.

'Do you have cleaning stuff?'

He pointed at the sink. There was a bottle of washing-up liquid next to the taps, its sides smeared black.

'Sit you down, and I'll get you a cup of tea.'

'Do you have a clean mug?'

He went to a cupboard, and brought out a mug with a cartoon figure of a woman on it, up to her elbows in suds. 'Make yourself at home' was written in red above her, and 'Wash some dishes' underneath.

Helen took the mug from him and looked inside. It was gleaming, white and pristine.

'Christmas present from the Laird,' said Uncle Jim.

Her hand tightened on the smooth glaze.

'I'm under orders it's for visitors. The Laird himself's the only one uses it, mind. And the Doctor. She gets her tea in it, when she comes. Or her man – he's a doctor too. Sometimes it's him that comes.'

Helen set the mug down on the draining board and filled the kettle.

'The Laird's aye on at me about getting the wifies that do the holiday houses to come and gie the place a dichting. But I'm nae for it. We like it homely, Fly and Ben and me.'

'Uncle Jim, that's *ridiculous*. A place can still be *homely* without being...' She waved a hand wordlessly.

Uncle Jim looked smug. 'That's what he said.' He got up and rummaged in the bits of paper piled on the dresser, and came back with a leaflet. 'Said I should *get my act together* if I want the Council keeping their nebs out. Wifie from the Council left this two, three weeks since.'

It was a leaflet about sheltered housing.

'I told her she needna come back.' He chuckled. 'Laird says what I need is a gate across the track end: *Mains of Clova – And May the Lord Be Thankit!*'

She smiled.

'You winna remember Jessie Mitchell.'

'I remember Dad talking about her.'

Jessie Mitchell had been a cousin of her great-grandfather. She'd lost her husband and brother in the First World War, and her two children to a childhood illness – scarlet fever? But she'd insisted on living on alone at Altmore, scraping by on what she made when her beasts went to market. She'd put up a locked gate at the end of the track, with that written on it: *Altmore. And May the Lord Be Thankit.* 'Aye, Jessie,' Dad would always say at the end of any story about her, shaking his head with a smile.

'Altmore' said Uncle Jim. 'Nothing but a ruckle o' stanes now.'

'Yes, well, and the Mains will be going the same way if you're not careful. This house is getting cleaned whether you like it or not.' She filled the mug, dropped in a tea bag and fished it out with her fingernails. She sat down at the table opposite him, and he held out the packet of custard creams with a placatory look. She took one and dunked it in the tea. Maybe that would sterilise it. Fly sat up, eyes on the biscuit. 'We'll need to go into Town for cleaning things.'

Uncle Jim's little eyes blinked at her. Then: 'There's all that at the Parks.'

'But we can't use Pitfourie Estate things.'

'The Laird said I was to help myself. To that, and the fruit. The blackcurrants when they're ripe, and the whitecurrants, and the gooseberries.'

'The bushes are still there?' A row of prickly bushes against the back wall of the garden, heavy with sharp fruit that she and Suzanne would stuff their faces with when it was still hard, forgetting the griping stomachs of the year before.

'And your ma's roses.'

Well, they could get the stuff, and she could blitz the bathroom and kitchen at least. Then talk to Fish, talk to Lorna… And go. Back to Edinburgh. Tonight.

As she came downstairs after brushing her teeth, Uncle Jim appeared from the kitchen. 'Are you riggit?'

'All set.' It was perfectly safe, after all, to go up to the Parks with Uncle Jim and the dogs. In broad daylight.

A sudden jangling noise had her heart jumping in her chest, even as she realised it was only the doorbell. She missed a step and had to clutch at the banister. Fly gave a piercing yelp, and he and Ben threw themselves at the front door. Uncle Jim grabbed Fly, chucked him bodily into the dining room and slammed the door. He pointed a finger back at the kitchen, and Ben, with a token yip, slunk back in there.

He opened the door.

Mr Beattie was standing in the yard, some distance from the door, his bouffant grey hair lifting in the breeze. His eyes scanned the area around Uncle Jim's legs before he moved forward. 'Helen,' he said, with the little droop of the mouth that had always reminded her, for some reason, of Rob. It was a look that said *You don't deserve it, you know, but Jesus and I still love you.* 'I wonder if I could have a word?'

Uncle Jim, without offering even a greeting, made for the kitchen.

'Um – would you like to come in?'

Would the front room be a possibility? She hadn't looked in there yet, but surely it couldn't be worse than the kitchen.

He had a folded sheet of paper in his hand, blindingly white in the glare of the sun. 'I won't, thank you.' He unfolded the paper and held it out to her.

It was a print-out of an email.

Dear Mr and Mrs Beattie

I know it's too late now, but I need to tell you that Rob didn't kill Suzanne. I lied. I made it all up.

    I hope you can find it in your hearts to forgive me.
    I'm so sorry.
    Helen Clack

She thrust it back at him, her hearth thumping. 'I didn't write this.'

He didn't reach out for it, he just carried on looking at her with that sad-dog expression.

She knew her face was beetroot.

'I didn't write it!' The paper trembled in her hand. 'How could I? "Moir Sandison" took my laptop along with everything else, and there's no computer *here*.' She agitated the piece of paper in the space between them, as if he was a dog she was trying to interest in a toy.

He finally took it from her. 'One can send emails these days, I understand, from mobile phones.'

'Not mine.' Because her new phone was the cheapest, most basic one you could get. 'I *did not* send this.'

'So who do you suppose did?'

'Well obviously *he* must have. Moir. Rob.'

'Helen.' His jowls drooped even further. 'I'm going to have to take this to the police.'

'I was about to suggest the same thing.' She took a breath. 'The police have spoken to you about Moir Sandison, haven't they?'

'They have.'

She didn't say anything more. She just looked at him.

He sighed. 'They showed us the photographs…. Helen, that man is not Rob.' He dropped his voice suddenly, as he used to in sermons. 'Is what it says here true? Was it an invention, what you said about Rob attacking you and Suzanne? A deliberate lie?'

'Of course not!'

This time it was Mr Beattie who kept silent.

She shook her head. 'In the face of all the evidence – you *surely* can't *still* think he's innocent? If he didn't attack me, if he didn't kill Suzanne – why did he take off like he did? Why didn't he stay to prove his innocence – and help with the search?'

'Perhaps he was unable to come forward because he himself was by that time no longer… alive.' The last word was no more than a breath.

'I'm sorry. It must all be very hard for you. But – he did it. He did.'

'And what *evidence* is there of that, Helen?'

'*I was there!*' She reached behind her for the edge of the door. 'Excuse me. I have to –' She stepped back into the hall and shut the door between them.

42

As she stepped into the dim end room of the steading the old smells hit her: slightly mouldy packed earth, old wood, creosote and oil. Soothing her jangled nerves. Amazingly, Dad's tools were still hanging from their nails on the wall. The big graip and the little graip, and the mallet and the hammer, and all the others. She touched the scarred end of the mallet.

Moir must have sent that email. So Moir must know. He must know that she'd lied about remembering the attack.

But she'd never told a living soul.

Was it possible that Rob really had been innocent, and had disappeared for some other reason than that he'd killed Suzanne? And now he was back, to wreak his revenge on Helen for falsely accusing him?

But it *was* Rob who'd attacked her. It had been his hand, grabbing her out of the dark. She might not be able to remember consciously, but deep down she knew. Yes, she'd made up the details; yes, she'd probably got some of those wrong...

And the only person who could know that was the attacker himself.

Rob Beattie.

'Aye,' breathed Uncle Jim. She'd half forgotten he was there. 'What we need'll be in the house, most likely.'

They crossed the yard, hot and bright in the sun, the dogs bounding ahead to scatter a group of spurgies from the dust. A crow cawed.

And the happy chemicals were back, and despite it all she was grinning like a feelie. Uncle Jim got the key from his pocket and unlocked the door, and stood back, smiling, and she took the doorknob in her hand and turned it.

Even the smell was the same. An indefinable smell that had to do, maybe, with the air off Craig Dearg, filtering through the fabric of the house, the Victorian plaster and tongue-and-groove linings and sooty old chimneys.

Home.

The table and chairs in the kitchen were different. Well, of course they were. Theirs had been 1970s pine, orangey and unconvincing, whereas these chairs looked like real Victorian ones, and the table with its scrubbed top and painted legs had probably come from some expensive interiors shop. Lorna's, maybe.

She walked through the house, still with her feelie's smile. She touched the mantelpiece in the sitting room, and the shelves in the pantry, and the pitted glaze of the old Belfast sink.

Home.

She found a scrubbing brush and a wooden trug of cleaning products under the sink, and a mop and dustpan and brushes, and some unopened packets of cloths, in the cupboard in the pantry. As they loaded it all into the cab of Uncle Jim's pick-up he shook his head, as if at the folly of a world in which such things existed.

Back at the Mains, they found Fiona sitting on an upturned plastic crate in the shade of the steading wall. She stood as Helen and Uncle Jim got out of the pick-up. Uncle Jim raised the mop in greeting and headed for the back door.

'It's hot to be humphing all that about, isn't it?' She had a stainless steel water bottle in one hand.

'I feel fine.' Helen dumped the cleaning stuff down. 'Well, a bit pathetic and snuffly, but other than that, more or less back to normal.'

Fiona handed her the bottle – she must have been staring at it longingly.

'I don't want to give you germs.'

'I think I'm immune to most things by now. Go on, have a swig.'

Helen swigged. 'Thanks. Oh, that's lovely.'

'Have some more. You've to keep hydrated.' And as Helen drank: 'I've brought some more supplies. And Fish. And the girlies. Steve's had to go with a patient to hospital, so I'm on child-minding duty. And talk of the devil – or devils in this case...'

Running towards them were three children. In the lead was Cat, a mini-Fiona, hair flying, thin legs scissoring, arms flung out to the sides, laughing and squealing as Ruth aimed a stream of water at her from a fluorescent-yellow pump-action water pistol. Ruth was smaller and darker and plumper, hair tied back from a face that would have been chocolate-box sweet if her mouth hadn't been wide open and shouting: '*Die!*'

Little Lizzie brought up the rear, all dark curls and trembling lower lip.

'Mum, tell her to stop it!' squealed Cat, grabbing onto Fiona and using her as a human shield.

'Ruth!' bellowed Fiona, making Helen jump out of her skin and spill water on the ground.

Ruth skidded to a halt, the water pistol dripping in her hand as she looked consideringly at Helen. Fiona disengaged herself from Cat and hurried across the yard to where Lizzie was running towards them, tears spilling over, a wailed *Mummeee!* preceding her.

Helen smiled at the two older girls. 'Hello. I'm Helen. You must be Cat, and you must be Ruth?'

Cat nodded. 'Hello.'

Ruth said nothing.

Helen tried, 'I hope I'm not in the firing line.'

Ruth grinned, and shouldered her weapon.

'Ruth,' said Cat. 'Don't you dare.' And to Helen: 'She's a problem child. Her behaviour's "challenging".'

The barrel of the gun swung round, and Cat squealed again, and ran down the slope of the yard and across the track, Ruth in pursuit. Helen laughed.

'I'm sorry,' said Fiona, coming back with her youngest child in her arms. 'Mayhem.'

'Is she okay?'

'Just feeling left out as usual. Although why she'd want to join in *that* beats me.' She nodded to where Cat and Ruth were wrestling with the water pistol. 'Come and talk to Fish and then we'll get out of your hair... Where's your Uncle Fish, Lizzie? Did he go inside?'

In the scullery, Fiona set Lizzie down on the kist and, squatting in front of her, began to use a tissue on her face. 'Are you going to say "Hello" to Helen?'

'Hello.'

'Hello, Lizzie. That's a lovely badge.' On her pink sweatshirt she had a badge with a cartoon face on it. 'Who's that?'

Lizzie pulled it out from her chest towards Helen as far as the sweatshirt material would allow. 'Ariel.'

'The Little Mermaid,' said Fiona. 'She's a very girlie girl, this one. Thank goodness. Ruth's made me appreciate gender stereotyping. Lizzie's been brainwashed, haven't you, Pettie, with princesses and ponies and all things sugar and spice?' And as Lizzie smiled at her mother uncertainly: 'You love the Little Mermaid, don't you?'

Lizzie nodded. 'Sometimes she's naughty,' she told Helen. 'Doesn't listen.'

Behind them, a shadow fell across the doorway. Helen whipped round.

A man in a bright white polo shirt, with thinning hair slicked back from a high brow, stood looking at her.

This was really Fish? This suave man with the cool smile and the polite kiss on the cheek? He smelt of something expensive, and the watch he wore on one tanned wrist was probably a Rolex or something; but as he listened to her thanking him for taking the time to come and see her, she noticed that his mouth hung very slightly open.

'Of course I'll do anything I can to help,' he said, but perfunctorily, as if she was someone he had to deal with in the line of duty but didn't much care for. Well, why should he want to put himself out for her, when she hadn't been in touch with any of them for over a decade?

'Thank you,' she said again.

'What I suggest is that you come over to Fi and Steve's, maybe later today or tomorrow – I'm guessing you don't have internet access here?'

'What do you reckon?' Fiona giggled.

'We can take a look at the account you had with the bank, the terms and conditions and so on. I know someone in the legal department at the Bank of Scotland – you're not with them, are you?'

'No.'

'Well, these things are pretty standard across the industry. I'll email him the details, ask him to take a look. And if the bank –'

'I need a pee,' said Lizzie.

'Oh, okay, lovie.' Fiona took her hand. 'Is it all right if we use the bathroom?'

No. No no no. 'Of course.'

She supposed Fiona must have seen it before – but oh God. That lovely little girl, having to use that loo… having to wash her peachy-soft little hands at that sink…

When they'd gone, she got straight down to blitzing the bathroom. The physical exertion had her coughing and her nose running, but the mindless activity felt good. And when she'd finished, she ran a bath in the newly white tub and lay back to admire her work.

Frank was snowy-white after a good soak in handwashing liquid in the sink. The porcelain of the sink and toilet gleamed. The vinyl on the floor was several shades lighter green than it had been, although the marks from the floorboards underneath had resisted all her efforts, as had the black mould in the grout between the tiles around the bath. And she didn't want to think about how many silverfish might be squirming around under the vinyl, moving more troops up to the front line along the skirting board and at the base of the loo, where she'd gone Rambo with the Dettol skoosher.

The vinyl would have to come up. Here, and in the kitchen.

No time now, but tomorrow she'd rip it up (so Uncle Jim would be forced to buy new stuff) and get into all the nooks and crannies. Blitz the kitchen, see Lorna, and go.

She dressed in a fresh top and skirt and set off in Stan, the sheet of paper with Fiona's directions angled towards her on the passenger seat. They lived in Ardie, a tiny hamlet in the shadow of Tom na Creiche. All the way there she kept checking in her mirror, but the only two vehicles she encountered were going the other way.

The house was an old manse, with a beautiful, flower-filled garden, screened from the road by a line of oaks and sycamores. And actual roses round the door. Well, the door of one of the outbuildings.

Fiona brought her laptop outside to a table under a tree, and while she and Helen sipped iced elderflower cordial Fish took down all the relevant details of the joint account, and the recent transactions, and phone numbers and email addresses of people at the bank.

Steve still hadn't returned by the time she left, refusing Fiona's offer of dinner but accepting, gratefully, a Tupperware container of tuna pasta.

She and Uncle Jim ate it at the kitchen table, Helen drinking water from Hector's mug, Uncle Jim glugging whisky.

When they'd finished, Helen washed up while Uncle Jim sat back with his drink. 'You're a good lass.'

Helen made a face into the sink. 'I'm sorry I haven't been to see you before.'

'I didna think you'd just be awful keen to come back. But now you're here –nae as bad as all that, eh?'

She smiled over her shoulder at him. 'No.'

'But you've money troubles, until the Doctor's brother can mend them. Why don't you stay until you've seen to it? It'd be good to have another pair of hands about the place. I could pay you a wage – not much, mind, but a fair wage. You can handle the beasts, and a tractor.'

She turned to lean back against the sink, wiping her hands on her skirt. Tears were prickling at the back of her nose. 'I'd love to stay, but if I'm going to sort things out, I really need to be in Edinburgh.'

'Well, well. But you've a beddie here as long as you want it.'

'Thank you. But – I need to see Lorna, and then I have to go.'

He didn't argue with her. But as she turned back to the sink, he said, 'It was a hell of a thing she did to you. Suzanne.'

'You mean the letters.'

'She could be a coarse bitch of a quine, that one.'

When she was little she used to secretly think that maybe Uncle Jim liked her best – he never tutted at her like he did at Suzanne. He never told her she was coarse.

She left the dishes; dropped into the seat opposite him; shook her head.

He shook his. 'Nae her wyte. We spoilt her, Ina and me. Never a skelp or a scauld, though she'd need of it.'

'But would you have wanted her any different? I wouldn't. She saved my *life*.'

Uncle Jim shook his head again, and tipped back his glass. 'Maybe she did. Maybe she did at that... Well well. She was my ain dearie, but I never could faddom her.'

'If she hadn't come to help me, she'd be alive now.'

For a while they just sat there, saying nothing more. Then Uncle Jim stood, and said goodnight, and she heard his heavy steps on the stairs. And then silence.

She knew she wouldn't sleep.

She could make a start on the kitchen.

First, the piles of things cluttering the worktops and dresser. It seemed mainly to be junk mail, and this went straight into the recycling box she'd unearthed from the scullery. Almost all the rest was bills, with the payment slips torn off them, which hopefully meant he was up to date with paying; these she put in a pile on the table.

Near the top of the third stack of envelopes was a Jiffy bag. It had a courier's sticker on it and when she felt it her fingers encountered two hard knobbles.

There was a sheet of paper inside. A letter from McIlraith Bridger, Solicitors, Glasgow, informing Uncle Jim that their late client, Mrs Clementina Clack, had made him a small bequest in her will, and they were accordingly enclosing the two items: viz. one solitaire diamond engagement ring, and one 18-carat gold wedding ring. The letter was dated February this year.

Auntie Ina.

Auntie Ina, sitting at the table with *The People's Friend*, and milky tea in a cup and saucer covered all over with big dark-pink roses; capturing Suzanne as she ran past, and making her stand still as she retied the laces on her shoes.

Auntie Ina, dead.

She tipped the contents of the Jiffy bag onto the table.

Uncle Jim hadn't even taken the rings from their bubblewrap, which was still held tightly in place with Sellotape. Auntie Ina's rings; digging into her face as she lay, half conscious, in a hospital bed.

She pushed the letter and the squashy little packages back into the Jiffy bag.

Had he told anyone that Ina had died? Maybe not. He couldn't have told Mum, or she in her turn would have told Helen. It would be like him, she supposed, to keep it private. Not to want people making a fuss. What should she do? Confront him?

No. When she'd sorted through everything, she'd give him the 'Don't know' pile, Jiffy bag on top, and see if he said anything.

The phone in the hall trilled, and she jumped her height.

'Hello? Ms Clack?' A man's voice.

'This is Helen Clack.'

'Sorry to be calling so late. DCI Campbell Stewart from Grampian CID. You probably don't remember me, but I was part of the investigation into your cousin's disappearance.'

She took the phone to the table and sat down. 'I remember.'

The man with the rugby player's thighs, sitting by her hospital bed. The man who'd told her that the letters from Hector weren't from Hector, and that the blood on her jersey was Suzanne's.

'Have they found him?'

' "Moir Sandison"? No. But our colleagues in Lothian and Borders have made some progress in identifying the man he appears to have been working with. The bogus headmaster in Dunfermline – we hope to have someone in custody imminently.'

'Oh. Well, good. Who is he?'

'I don't want to say too much until it's been confirmed – but that should happen tomorrow morning. I wonder if it would be possible to come out and see you in the afternoon?'

'Yes – of course.'

'We'd like you to look at a photograph; and I'd like to touch base with you generally. I'm the point of contact here for the "Moir Sandison" investigation – given the possible connections with your cousin's case, which is still in my remit.'

'Her case? But – you mean you've reopened it?'

'We never close unsolved cases. Any new information that comes in on your cousin's case automatically comes to me... Such as the email Mr Beattie has received.'

'I didn't send it.'

'So he said. In fact it was sent from a disposable email address. And the IP has turned out to be an internet café in Aberdeen, so no joy there.'

'In Aberdeen? So if he sent it – that means he was in Aberdeen yesterday?'

'It wasn't necessarily "Moir Sandison" who sent it.' A pause. 'The suggestion it contains, that what you told us wasn't the truth –'

'I only wish it wasn't.' She didn't have to feign the weariness in her voice.

'I'm sorry. I had to ask.'

'Yes.'

'So – can we say five, five-thirty?'

'That would be fine.'

43

She wasn't asleep, this time, when she became aware of it.

The sound of bells jingling.

She flung out of bed to the window. The moon was huge and high in the sky, casting an unreal half-light over everything. A figure, a man, was walking across the yard. Away from her, away from the house, down the side of the steading until his dark form merged with the shadows –

She ran to the bedroom door, hauled it open, ran across the landing.

'Uncle Jim!'

She grabbed him when he appeared; pulled him to the window. 'Look!'

The yard was empty and still.

'He was out there. Moir. Rob. *I just saw him.*'

'There was an aald gangrel mannie a year-two since –'

'I'm phoning the police.'

In the harsh overhead light the kitchen looked like something from one of those TV shows where council workers go into a dead mad person's house with masks over their faces. The two young officers in their bulky black waistcoats, one ruddy-faced, one pale, didn't turn a hair. They sat down at the table and accepted her offer of tea. One could have Hector's mug, but the other would have to take his chances.

'Aye,' the ruddy-faced one said. 'A professional job.'

How could he possibly know that?

In their search of the farm, they'd discovered that Stan's wheels had been removed. Her initial feeling of relief that at least she'd be believed, at least they wouldn't think she was a hysterical female hallucinating, had been replaced by frustration.

Because why would Rob Beattie do that?

She said, 'But if it was just thieves – there's all sorts of other stuff, more valuable stuff, lying around on a farm. Machinery and equipment.'

'Everything of value's under lock and key, yes, Mr Clack?'

Uncle Jim nodded. 'Steading and sheddies are aye locked.'

'They were probably hoping for easy pickings, found everything locked up, decided to cut their losses and take a set of wheels.'

'He must have done it to try and keep me here.' Even to her own ears it sounded ludicrous. 'I'm going to have to get a garage to come out and replace them – and meanwhile I'm stuck here.' She set their mugs down on the table and pulled her thin cotton robe closed over her chest.

The ruddy-faced man piled sugar into his mug. 'You could hire a car, couldn't you?'

Of course she could.

'We'll come by again in the morning. Make sure everything's OK.'

His colleague had a pad on the table in front of him. 'If we can just get your statements?'

When they'd gone, Uncle Jim said, 'There's a fair bit of it now. Tinkies coming out from the towns, raking round. Folk lock their doors now that never would have thought of it, twenty-thirty year back. Aye.' He sucked in a breath. 'That noise you heard the other night. That'll have been them "casing the joint".'

Had it been? The jingling sound – had it just been thieves, with a bag of tools?

She took the crockery to the sink, and swirled water into Hector's mug. 'Could we leave the kitchen door open? So Fly and Ben can get out into the rest of the house?'

Back in her room, she unhooked the ship picture from the wall and propped it against the door. If anyone opened the door, she'd hear it clatter over. Then she got a nail file from her bag and put it under her pillow, getting a sudden flash of Suzanne, Suzanne making a daft face:

I've got a manicure set and I'm not afraid to use it.

44

At the top of Worm Hill she slowed the pick-up to look back across to Craig Dearg and the Lang Park. There were stirks in the field, toy-sized from this distance, heads bent to the grass.

When she'd phoned the garage and arranged for them to come out to replace her wheels – which Uncle Jim had insisted on paying for – and the policemen had been and gone, she'd directed her nervous energy to battle with the kitchen. And overdone it. Her legs felt weak, her head woozy. The afternoon sun was fierce on the windscreen.

She carried on down the brae to Kirkton, and past the kirk and the manse and the playground, empty in the sun. From the gates she could just see the block of toilets. She needed to go to the loo, in fact – she'd forgotten to go before she left. Well, she might be glad of the excuse to interrupt the conversation, if it got awkward.

If?

She carried on into the heart of the village, to the apron of tarmac in front of the shoppie and what used to be the butcher's and was now 'Damask and Delft'.

Lorna's shop.

She opened the door on air that was unpleasantly cloying with the scents of candles and spices. There were two spaces separated by a doorway to her right. Mr Jappie used to have the counter in front of that door, and he'd disappear into the inner sanctum, as Dad used to call it, if you asked for something that wasn't set out in the chilled display area of the counter.

Now the inner sanctum, what she could see of it, contained antique furniture, and lacy things hanging on towel rails, and shelves with little pottery birds.

In the front bit of the shop, where she was standing, there were whirly stands with cards in them, and tables with books and candles and a basket of little polished fossils, and at the right of the door stacks of wicker baskets, and a glass cabinet with Celtic jewellery, and another with pretty etched wine glasses and beakers.

The counter was at the back of the shop.

The girl perched behind the till smiled at Helen. 'Hi.'

'Hello.'

The girl was wearing a scoop-neck black top and an orange cotton scarf with gold and silver threads through it. Her jet-black hair conformed to the current teenage fashion for dead straight. Spiky, clumsy false eyelashes adorned her lids.

'I'm looking for Lorna.'

The girl nodded, slid off the stool and opened a door behind the counter.

'Lorna!'

Helen stayed where she was. She didn't move forward towards the counter.

A woman came through the door: small and neat in a white blouse and fawn skirt and sensible flat shoes; mid-brown hair styled in a glossy bob.

'Helen,' she said. She didn't smile.

'I'm sorry – to just turn up like this.'

'That's okay.'

'I wondered if I could talk to you. Just for five minutes.'

'Come on then.'

Through the door was a little room with floor-to-ceiling shelves and a table and chair and computer, and a staircase leading up. Lorna stood facing her.

'I'm sorry,' Helen said. 'I'm probably the last person you want to see.'

'Is this about the email?'

'I didn't send it.' And it just occurred to her: 'Whoever it was knew your dad's email address.'

'So it must have been Rob? Dad's email address is on the church website.'

'Oh. Right.'

'Not that Rob would need to look it up, because we've secretly been in touch with him all these years, haven't we? That's what you're alleging, isn't it? Sending the police round to harass us, demanding a handwriting sample, and that we look at photographs of some man who obviously isn't Rob.'

'Are you sure?'

'I think I'd know my own brother.'

'I'm sorry.' She put her bag down on the table. 'But could you just have another look? *Please*?' She spread out the photos.

Lorna glanced down. 'It's not Rob, Helen.' But there was a new note in her voice.

Next to the photos of Moir, Helen set the photocopies of the photo of herself and Baudrins, and what had been written on the back. 'If he's not Rob, why would he – the police have told you what happened?'

Lorna nodded.

'Why would he write this? How would he know I was called *Smellie Nellie* when we were little? And don't say I must have told him, because I know I didn't. Why would I tell anyone that?'

'He must have found out somehow.'

'And why would he send your dad that email, if he wasn't Rob?'

'How should I know? He's obviously a headcase.'

'Yes.' Helen gathered the photographs back up.

'Why didn't you answer my letters?'

'What?'

'When you went away to Edinburgh? Didn't you get my letters? Do you think it was easy to write them?'

'No.'

'No, you didn't get them?'

'I got them, but I couldn't –'

'You didn't want to know me any more, because of what Rob did? Or was there another reason? Is it true, what was in the email? Was it not Rob at all? Was it someone else?'

Oh God. 'It was Rob.'

'How can you be so sure? It was dark under the trees and you were all wasted. You've always had it in for Rob. You just *assumed* it was him, didn't you?'

'It *was* him.' She snatched up her bag.

'It's only on your say-so that he's been blamed all these years. Only on *your say-so* that no one's ever tried to find out if maybe something else happened that night. What's the point, when everyone knows it was Rob? Can you imagine what it's been like for Mum and Dad? For Mum, having to face all those cows in the

Women's Institute? For Dad, having to stand up in front of the congregation every Sunday and preach at them when they all think he brought up a murderer? A *psychopath*?'

'He *is* a psychopath!'

And she grabbed up her things and fled: back through the doorway, past the wide-eyed girl, round the counter, past the pretty useless things and out.

She was going to wet herself.

Smellie Nellie.

She ran along the pavement and across the tarmac of the playground to the passage open to the sky that led to the girls' toilets. She ran along it, realising too late that the door would probably be locked, but she couldn't wait any more – if it was locked she'd have to squat here like a dog.

But the door came open under her hand. She dived into a cubicle, snibbed the door and sat down on the cold black plastic seat. They had been wooden before. As she emptied her bladder she shut her eyes and they were back – the ghosts of her childhood, out there in the empty playground.

She could hear footsteps.

She really could. Rapid steps, purposeful, coming closer. Coming very close.

Bang.

The door of the cubicle shook.

Bang bang.

Her fingers tightened on the toilet paper. She sat perfectly still, perfectly quiet, her eyes jumping about the cubicle. Was the gap between the bottom of the door and the floor big enough for a man to wriggle through?

Bang bang.

The door bowed inwards with the force of the blows.

45

She took in a long breath and shouted:

'Help! Help me! *Help!*'

She screamed it, the sound bouncing back off the walls. She screamed until her throat was raw, and she kept screaming, her eyes fixed all the time on the door. But it didn't move again. And when she finally stopped screaming there was no sound from outside.

He had gone.

Had he? Or was he standing on the other side of the door, waiting?

And then from outside, distantly, a girl's voice: 'Be careful! Damian!'

And a little nearer: 'I think it came from the toilets,' and it was Hector's voice of twenty years ago, and somehow Damian wasn't in Europe, he was out there, his chubby little face turning to Moir inquiringly –

She tore at the toilet paper, cleaned herself, pulled up pants and jeans, didn't stop to flush; fumbled with the lock on the door and yanked it open, ran out of the toilet and into the passage –

And straight into not Damian, not Rob, but a stranger who said, 'Whoa,' and smiled at her, steadying her with a hand on each of her shoulders, and Helen couldn't do anything but stare back at him.

The sunlight glancing into the passageway lay across his shirt and the line of his jaw, and struck a sheen of gold from his hair.

And maybe it was the incongruity, the feeling she'd stepped straight from a rerun of her childhood hell into one of those male fragrance ads, all sundrenched Mediterranean and gorgeous, narcissistic youth, that had her yipping, suddenly, with mad laughter.

'Are you okay?' said Narcissus, dropping his hands from her shoulders, and Helen, absurdly, wanted to stop him, to tell him not to speak, that his kind didn't speak, not ever. Smouldering looks, yes. Sensuous hands on yielding flesh, yes. Speaking – no. No no no no *no*.

She covered her mouth with her hand. Why couldn't she stop this ridiculous yipping? Like a dog?

'We heard someone shouting. Was that you?'

We?

She looked past him. A plumpish teenage girl in cropped jeans was standing at the end of the passage. And as Narcissus turned his head to the girl, as the sunlight fell full on his face in profile, she saw that he was much younger than she'd thought – that there was still a softness to his cheek and mouth and jaw, an adolescent fragility to the collarbone visible at the open neck of his shirt.

Then he looked back at her, and raised his lovely eyebrows. He had asked her a question.

'Yes. There was someone – did you see anyone, out here?'

He shook his head. 'What happened?'

She hadn't washed her hands. The thought hit her as she saw herself, suddenly, through his eyes – a middle-aged woman with chopped-short hair and a pasty fluey face, no make-up, in a wrinkled shirt and creased jeans; and with unwashed hands hanging at her sides.

How could he possibly know they were unwashed?

She couldn't stop staring at him: at the straight, classical lines of nose and brow and jaw; the subtle athleticism of the lean young body; the pale blue shirt, the chinos, the expensive-looking leather belt and polished brown leather shoes; the hair that, in shadow and sunlight, was all colours from nut-brown through ochre to gold. And no way had he got that haircut at Tanya's Tresses.

The girl had arrived at his side: rosy-cheeked, with layered messy hair and bright purple eyeshadow. Trainers with no socks. She looked terrified.

Helen took a breath. 'I – someone was in there. Banging on the door. Of the cubicle. I'd gone in to – to do the obvious, but then someone started banging on the door. I thought it was going to give way.' She swallowed. 'I'm sorry – I probably completely overreacted – it was probably just kids.'

'That's horrible,' said the girl.

'I'd have been screaming too,' said Narcissus.

'You didn't see anyone?' Helen said.

'No.'

'You didn't see a man...? I've got a photo – It's in my bag – can you wait a minute while I –'

She'd left her bag in the cubicle. She hurried back into the toilets, but before going into the cubicle she stopped at the sinks and quickly turned on a tap and held her hands under the water. There was no soap. No towels. She shook her hands and wiped them on her jeans, leaving damp streaks that made it obvious what she'd been doing.

They hadn't followed her along the passage. She could hear them talking in low voices. She couldn't make out what they were saying, but she could imagine: *Nutter.*

She flushed the toilet, grabbed her bag and hurried back out into the sun. She pulled out one of the photos of Moir. 'You didn't see this man?'

'No...' the girl said. 'But we've just remembered that when we were parking –' she waved a hand in the direction of the road '– Connor Sinclair and his pal were messing about at the Buchans' gate. It could have been them.'

'Did it sound like ten-year-olds?' said Narcissus.

She shook her head, her hand closing round the photograph. 'He could still be out here.'

'Safety in numbers,' Narcissus said, absently, as if his attention was already wandering. But then: 'You think he's followed you here from Edinburgh?'

And as she blinked in confusion –

'I'm assuming you're Helen.' He smiled, and Helen could do nothing else but smile back, and think how unfair, how unequal the world was, that he should have that smile on top of everything else.

'I – yes –'

'You're Helen Clack?' said the girl.

'Sorry,' said Narcissus. 'This isn't a mass break-out of stalking or anything. I'm Damian Forbes. Hector's brother. Fiona told us what happened. What that bastard did to you.'

No.

No no no.

You're not my little Stinker. You're not my little cushie-doo.

'And this is Anna,' he said.

'Anna Tait,' said the girl.

'You're *Damian*?'

No. Damian was a sweet, chubby-faced boy – rather awkward, rather puppyish – who loved watching birds and grubbing about doing nerdy things in the woods. He was in the school chess club. He wore old sweaters and cargo pants and muddy walking boots. He probably still had a skull collection. He was NatureDork.

He wasn't *this*. This escapee from the pages of a glossy magazine.

The smile had returned full force. 'Yes, I think the last time we met I was probably dribbling all over you. Shall we get out of here? I always thought there was something creepy about these toilets.'

He stepped back to let Helen and Anna precede him.

Anna said, 'You think this guy is really *Rob Beattie*?' and Helen answered something, and all the while she was thinking: *this* is Hector's little brother?

The shock of it had momentarily displaced every other conscious thought. It was like the shock, almost, of a bereavement. The Damian she'd had in her head all this time – he was gone. Hector's sweet little brother. Her darling baby boy. And in his place was –

Irina's son.

Well of course. Much more than he was Hector's brother, he was Irina's son. And so *this* was what he was like. Irina would have made sure of that. She'd send him to her father's tailor in the Rue de Whatever, and buy him designer shirts, and pay hundreds of pounds for his haircuts. And show him off at dinner parties with aristocrats and politicians and filmstars and all the beautiful people.

What on earth must Hector make of him?

What would Suzanne have said?

Probably: *Way to go Stinker.*

'Are you on holiday?' she said, turning to him, searching his face for any trace of their Damian. His lashes, maybe – he had the same long brown lashes that baby Damian had had, but apart from that – *nothing*. Their Damian's eyes had been bright blue, like Irina's – this Damian's were a smoky blue-grey. The Laird's eyes.

'Yes, we go back in August.'

For his last year of school. It was ludicrous to think of him as a schoolboy. But maybe in the poshest, most sophisticated parts of Paris they were all like this.

But he was here, at least. Visiting Hector, presumably. So she'd been wrong about them not being in contact. And they must get on, to some extent, if he came for holidays.

She carried on walking, across the playground, and at her side he said, 'I gather the Beatties are saying it's not him? That Moir Sandison isn't Rob?'

How did he know all this? 'Yes. I mean, yes, that's what they're saying.'

'Although we are talking people who believe in supernatural beings, so their opinion isn't maybe the most reliable.'

'Tch,' said Anna, on his other side. 'Believing in God isn't believing in a "supernatural being".'

'What is it then?'

So Irina had let her son grow up an atheist?

They'd reached the gates. Impostor Damian held the right-hand gate open, and snibbed it behind them, and looked down at his hand, as if wondering what it was doing messing about with school gates when it should have been caressing the curves of bee-stung-lipped girls. There were some rusty flakes of paint on it, she saw, but instead of just wiping them off on his clothes he took a perfect white square of handkerchief from his trouser pocket, and opened it, and used that. Then he shook the handkerchief, folded it again, and replaced it in his pocket.

'OCD,' said Anna to Helen in a stage whisper.

'Yes,' said Damian, looking up the road towards the shops. 'Relative to someone who considers a compost heap a snack opportunity, I'm practically Howard Hughes.'

She looked where he was looking. Had he seen something? No – there were just two women outside the shoppie. She looked the other way. No one.

'Um, hello, bananas have *skins*? And they weren't even *on* the compost heap.'

'No, sorry, that's right – the rats had dragged them to one side.' He looked at Helen. 'He's not going to try anything here, is he? Not in full public view.'

'No.'

'We have to pick up our friend from Lorna's shop, then we'll be going back your way to Anna's, so we can give you a lift if you like?' He waved a hand at a car parked at the curb just beyond the school.

And yes, of course it would be a sleek convertible, metallic midnight blue, top down, gleaming, pristine. *Irina* written all over it.

'Thanks very much, but I've got my uncle's pick-up.'

'He can collect that later, can't he? You won't want to go back on your own.'

'Well – thank you. I don't, to be honest.' She took a breath. 'It's a wonderful car. And isn't it immaculate.'

He smiled and shrugged and said yes, he was pretty much OCD about that too.

The dashboard was shiny wood of some sort, the seats beautiful soft-looking black leather. Inside and out, it was showroom spotless. But Impostor Damian hadn't stopped. He was already half way up the apron of tarmac outside the two shops. Bored already, it seemed, with the conversation. *Their* Damian wouldn't have been. Their Damian would have been all eager and enthusiastic about his car, and all happy that she was interested. Although he might not keep it so clean. There'd be mud all over it, and a tank of toads on the back seat.

'Birthday present,' said Anna. 'I considered myself lucky to get a laptop – he gets a Mercedes convertible... Are you OK?'

'I feel a bit... light-headed. Maybe if I could sit down.'

And then she was upstairs in Lorna's little kitchen, sitting at the table looking across the fields as Lorna ran the tap and shook shortbread onto a plate. From downstairs the teenagers' voices drifted in and out of audibility.

'It'll've been that little thug Connor Sinclair,' said Lorna, fussing about with glasses and ice. She set two coasters down on the table, and on each a glass of water. 'But you think it was Rob. Banging on the door of the toilet, in some bizarre re-enactment of what happened thirty-odd years ago?'

'I don't know. But last night, there was someone prowling round the Mains – They took the wheels off my car –'

'And that was Rob too. Helen, listen to yourself! You're *obsessed* with Rob, with the idea that he was some kind of... evil psychopath. But he wasn't.'

Helen put the cool glass to her forehead.

'He could be really nasty. Of course he could. I was his sister. I know what he was capable of. And what he *wasn't*.'

'No you don't.'

'I wouldn't be surprised if it was Damian, banging on the door to freak you out.'

'*Damian*?'

Lorna gave a sudden, weary laugh and sat down, turning her glass on its coaster, running a finger through the condensation. 'I suppose you think that because he's Hector's brother he can do no wrong.'

'I don't think anything of the sort. I've only just met him.' Helen took a long gulp of cold water. 'Why would you think it was him?'

Lorna carried on wiping the condensation from her glass. 'He was there, wasn't he?'

And he and Anna obviously knew all about what had been happening to her.

'Damian's very like Irina, isn't he?'

'Mm. Bit of an elephant in the room, that one.'

She felt light and queer and floaty. Maybe she just needed some food. She took a piece of shortbread from the plate. Lorna was looking at her as if she expected a reaction, so Helen said, 'Elephant in the room?'

'We all just pretend she never existed. We're good at that sort of thing round here.'

It took a moment to penetrate, the sense of it. 'Irina's *dead*?'

46

'Oh no. Much as certain people might wish she was. She high-tailed it off back to France or Italy or wherever after the accident, never to be heard of again. Not exactly Irina's idea of fun, being lumbered with a disabled child.'

'She had another child? So what –'

'No no. You really are out of touch, aren't you? I mean Damian.'

'Damian, downstairs?'

'Well, there is only one. Thank God.'

Helen's hands were shaking. She put down the shortbread. 'But he isn't disabled.'

Lorna laughed. 'It doesn't tend to be the first thing people notice about him.'

'But –'

'The old Laird was killed in a car crash nine years ago – you knew that? Well, Damian was in the car too. His leg was mangled. The foot had to be amputated – you can imagine Irina's reaction to *that* – and it was obvious the rest of the leg wasn't going to function properly. She'd have sent him back for a new one if she could, but that not being an option, she threw her toys out of the pram and ran back home to Mummy and Daddy. Mrs MacIver and all that lot claimed it was a "nervous breakdown", but she obviously just didn't want the hassle.'

For a long moment Helen couldn't say anything. Then: 'Irina... *went off and left him?*'

'She went mental when the surgeon said they'd have to amputate the foot, and wouldn't give her consent – the surgeon went ahead anyway, he had to, and while the operation was going on Irina flounced off. There was no one else there. I think friends had been with her initially but Irina had told them to go. The hospital staff didn't think to try and contact anyone else because they didn't realise that Irina had just up and left. Hector was abroad at the time – it took him a while to get back. So there was no one there when Damian woke up. Apart from nurses and people, obviously. Like a headline in one of those awful magazines: *Model Mum Dumps Disabled Child.*'

So all the time she'd had them living in the cosy little world she'd constructed for them – All the time –

'It was Hector to the rescue, naturally. There's an aunt and uncle on the west coast with children not much older than Damian – they offered to take him to live with them – but oh no, Hector has to play the martyr. Has to give up his glamorous lifestyle in Rio de Janeiro or wherever to stay at Pitfourie and nurse him – although he'd never shown much interest in the kid up till then. And never mind what would have been the better option for Damian. That was of secondary importance.' She took a sip of water. 'It's always been a power thing for Hector, though, hasn't it, this compulsion to control people's lives? One big ego trip.'

'Hector's been looking after him, all this time?'

'What *else* he's been doing, of course, is another question.' Pause for wide-eyed *What do you mean?*

But there was no room in Helen's mind for anything but the horror of what she'd just been told, and abhorrence for the woman sitting opposite.

Rob Beattie's sister.

She was saying now, 'Have you met any of his more – *unusual* employees?'

'I haven't met any of them, usual or unusual.'

A wail from downstairs, and laughter, increasing in volume as steps pounded on the stairs and the door came open and Anna was beaming at them, and saying, 'We'll get off now. Is that okay?'

Lorna looked at her watch. 'No, it's not "okay". Karen has ten more minutes to work before she can leave.'

'She says she was in ten minutes early this morning.'

'It's not flexitime. This might come as a shock to Karen, but the world doesn't revolve entirely around her social life.'

'No. Okay.'

'Or am I supposed to leave an ill person up here and staff the shop myself for the remaining time? Even though it's *meant* to be my day off?'

'No. Right. Sorry.'

The footsteps retreated back down the stairs.

'They've just got no idea, these girls. They think a holiday job in a shop's going to be a right laugh. If she was left to her own devices, Karen would spend all her time on i-thingummies of one sort or another. Regardless of whether there were customers. I'm *paying* her at this moment, out of my own pocket, to lounge about talking to her friends. They're always in here. Like I'm running a youth group.'

Helen would have liked to reach with both hands across the table and take fistfuls of that perfectly groomed hair and yank it.

Who had told him? About his father? About his injuries? A nurse? Some sort of counsellor? Or had they waited for Hector to get there? How long had it taken, for Hector to find out what had happened and get home? What must that journey have been like? And when he got to the hospital and found out that Irina had gone, and Damian had been alone all that time –

Lorna, she realised, had stopped speaking and was expecting a response.

Helen said flatly: 'That's teenagers for you.'

'Yes, but I'd rather not be subsidising it.' She shrugged. 'Damian often buys something. That's the problem. So Karen can say they're "customers".'

'What does he buy?'

'Oh, anything at random. A basket, an artificial plant. Sometimes something expensive, like one of the lamp bases. So I can hardly complain. That's presumably their logic. At least I'm making some money out of them.'

'I wonder what he does with the stuff.'

'It generally reappears in the shop. At first I thought I had a stocktaking issue. Then I realised it was the things he was buying that seemed to be multiplying.'

'Do you give him his money back?'

'What?'

'For the things he returns?'

'Why should I? It's not like he doesn't have money to burn.'

Helen breathed. 'Is Anna his girlfriend?'

'Depends on the day of the week, from what I can make out.'

She stood. 'Thank you, for the water and the biscuit. I'll get out of your hair. I'm sorry that you've had all the Rob business raked up again, because of me.'

Lorna sat back and folded her arms. 'You're sorry.'

Pounding footsteps up the stairs again, and Karen's head round the door: 'Can I go *now*? It's five o'clock.'

'Yes Karen, and don't take that tone with me. Five o'clock is your finishing time, and it is now five o'clock, so you can go.'

A lift of the lip, and a look flicked at Helen. 'Damian says we're giving you a lift? So we're going *now*?'

She didn't thank Lorna again, or say anything else at all. She just picked up her bag and made her way down the stairs. Lorna didn't come after her.

Karen was standing outside the door of the shop, saying, 'Oh come *on*. *She* can do that,' hands on hips, huge bag slung from one shoulder. Anna was pushing the pram with the teddy and mini blackboard and jack-in-the-box in through the door, and behind her Damian was carrying the sandwich board that said 'Damask and Delft: Interiors, Antiques, Gifts'.

Anna parked the pram by a stand of cards.

Helen couldn't look at Damian. She said to no one in particular: 'Are you sure it's not out of your way? I'll be fine going back on my own.'

'Don't worry,' said Anna. 'It's on our way.'

From the corner of her vision, she was aware of Damian propping the hinged boards up against the far wall. 'It's no problem,' he said.

She made herself smile at him as he came back to where she and Anna were standing. And she saw that there was a catch in his walk, a transferring of his weight too soon from his right leg – and he seemed to swing the leg under him more than push off with it. But even so there was a smoothness, an ease to the sequence of movements, as if God had intended *Homo sapiens* to walk with exactly this kind of loping limp.

Maybe that was why she hadn't noticed it.

But that couldn't even be a real foot, inside the beautifully polished shoe; it must be an artificial one, and –

She was staring.

She risked a glance at his face, but he wasn't looking at her, he was looking out through the plate glass window. The light falling across the perfect lines of nose and cheek brought back Irina so strongly that she couldn't stop her breath juddering in her throat.

As they left the shop: 'You're being stalked by the maniac brother?' said Karen. '*Her* maniac brother?'

'Subtle,' said Anna.

Helen blinked. 'Yes. I think I am.'

'You could sue the police, if – you know. If he attacks you, and they've not done anything to protect you even though you've told them –'

'Ever feel like you're trapped in an episode of *Little Britain*?' said Damian.

The car beeped at them as they reached it. Damian didn't get in, he limped quickly round to the far side and opened the passenger door, and smiled at her, as the two girls plomped themselves in the back seat.

'Thank you.' She smiled back at him as he held the door while she settled herself in the soft leather seat, and then shut it with an expensive-sounding *clunk*.

Before he turned the key in the ignition he glanced round into the back seat and Karen said, 'Check, and check,' and then, presumably for Helen's benefit: 'Seatbelt OCD.'

Didn't she know it was a car crash that killed his father, and crippled him, and lost him his mother?

Maybe Irina really *had* had a breakdown? Her husband had just been killed. Her child horrendously hurt. Maybe she just couldn't cope?

'I've never been in a convertible before,' she said.

'It does for your hair,' from the back seat.

'I think mine's "done for" already.'

Neither of the girls contradicted her, but Damian said, 'I like your hair,' and pulled out into the road.

She had been doing calculations in her head. 'You're... not seventeen until December, is that right?'

'I know!' Karen wailed from the back. 'It's like, why should you be safe to drive at sixteen if you've got a disability but not if you haven't? It should be the other way round.'

Damian was smiling. 'It's political correctness gone mad.'

'It is,' said Karen. 'It so is.'

There was a gear stick. Surely he couldn't be using the artificial foot on the pedals? That wouldn't be safe, would it? Or even possible?

She must have been staring again because he said, 'Don't worry, it's a semiautomatic clutch,' and pointed to the pommel of the gear stick. 'That little button thing's an infrared detector. When you touch the gear stick, it activates a computer system that operates the clutch pedal. The computer monitors your speed, revs per minute, acceleration. Don't ask me how. The great thing is, though, it's impossible to stall.'

'I could do with one of those.'

The air swirled round her neck. As they passed the kirkyard, she could almost have reached out and touched the railings. It was a disorientating sort of feeling, not to be separated from the landscape you were moving through.

As Damian indicated left at the Worm Hill turn-off, he said, his voice pitched low so that it was covered by the chatter from the back seat: 'Why don't you want to see Hector?'

She shook her head, and turned to watch the verge blur in the film of her tears. He didn't say anything more after that.

As he slowed for the turn-off to the track: 'Stop here,' she said. 'I'll get out here.'

He didn't stop. 'I'll take you to the door.'

The girls in the back were shrieking now about something.

'Could you tell him I'm sorry?' She rummaged in the bag on her lap.

As they powered up the incline to the yard at the Mains, gravity pushed her back into the softness of the seat. She found a tissue, finally, and wiped at her face. The garage people must have been – Stan, parked over by the steading, now had a full complement of wheels.

They'd stopped at the door. And before she could start to thank him he was out of the car, holding Helen's door for her and picking something up from the ground – Fly's horrible slimy tennis ball – and throwing it right over the roof of the byre.

Fly, tongue lolling, bounded after it.

The handkerchief was already out of his pocket as he made for the open door, calling out, 'Hello, Mr Clack?' and disappearing into the house.

'We'll stay here,' said Karen.

Uncle Jim wasn't in the kitchen. Only Damian, shaking his head, and laughing, and saying, 'Oh my God. Did you do this? Well of course you did. Oh my God, you deserve a medal.'

And she realised he meant the cleaning. 'I do, rather, don't I?'

She hadn't done the cupboards yet, or taken up the vinyl or even washed the floor, so there was still an unpleasant odour underlying the fresh scent of the Ecover cleaning stuff. But the worktops were clean, and the cooker and the Aga and the dresser; the piles of mail had gone, apart from the one awaiting Uncle Jim's attention, Jiffy bag on top; and she'd washed all the shelves above the sink, and everything on them. She'd taken the chairs outside and washed them down. And scrubbed the table. It had once been varnished, but most of that had peeled off. It would have to be stripped and redone.

'Maybe I'll be able to revise my nil-by-mouth policy,' said Damian. 'This is actually quite a nice dresser, isn't it?' He ran a hand down the smooth curved edge of the shaped side-panel joining the base and the top. Helen had been doing that a lot – there was something very tactile about that particular piece of wood. Strange, and oddly unsettling, that he should go straight for the same bit.

'It's very shoogly,' she said. 'Watch that you don't bring it over on top of you.'

He stood back, grinning. 'How undignified a way to go would that be? Like something from a cartoon.' Now he was looking at the worktop. 'I had no idea this was white.'

'It probably won't be for much longer.'

'So you're not staying?'

'I'm going back to Edinburgh tomorrow. Please tell Hector I'm sorry. But he doesn't need to worry about me. Fish has very kindly offered to handle the legal side of things, with the bank... And the police are dealing with the rest.'

He was moving about, absently touching surfaces. 'Are you going to tell the police about what happened in the toilets?'

'There's someone coming over later – a DCI, to update me on progress and – he wants me to look at a photograph – they think they've identified Moir's accomplice. They've probably arrested him by now, in fact.' Why was she telling him this? 'I can make a statement to the DCI, presumably, about what happened.'

'They won't bother their arses. They've already dismissed what happened last night as petty theft.'

'How –'

'One of the PC Plods who came out used to work on the Estate.'

'But it's surely meant to be confidential?'

'Mark Howden doesn't know the meaning of the word. Literally. I think, you know, it might be a good idea to speak to Hector about all this.'

Click-click-click through the door. Fly's nails on the floor. He went straight to Damian and dropped the ball at his feet.

'Thank you.'

Fly's tail moved. Damian tapped the ball with his right foot – the foot that wasn't a foot – sending it bouncing under the table, and Fly after it.

And she wanted to cross the room and take him in her arms, this beautiful boy who wasn't what she'd wanted him to be, and tell him she was sorry; to hug him like she used to when he was a baby.

What would he do, if she did?

As hysteria rose, she blurted: 'I don't want to see Hector.'

The words were out before she could moderate them.

'You don't want anything to do with him, because of what happened to your cousin? Because it was his fault you were all out of your skulls?'

'Why does everyone just assume that? Hector knows that's not the reason.' But it seemed he hadn't even told his brother the truth about why Helen couldn't face him. 'I was in love with him. I thought – Rob got Suzanne to write me letters, supposedly from Hector, while he was away in the Army. I thought they really were from Hector, and I thought he was in love with me too. They weren't, and he wasn't. Then five years later we met up in London, and – I was in a right state, crying all over him – and he felt sorry for me... And I made an idiot of myself all over again. Got it all wrong as usual. That's why I don't want to see him. Okay? Satisfied?'

He was laughing. He was actually laughing.

'But I suppose it's a common enough occurrence for both of you, stupid little no-hopers and their unrequited love? The two of you have some good laughs about it, do you?'

'No. I'm sorry. It's just – Hector's so useless about that kind of thing. There's no need to be embarrassed. He's probably feeling much worse about it than you are.'

That kind of thing. 'And that's supposed to make me feel better?'

'It does happen fairly regularly. Women falling for Hector. Norrie's wife propositioned him in the shrubbery. Like something out of P. G. Wodehouse. I mean – the *shrubbery*.'

'But if you just said "the garden" it wouldn't be nearly as funny, would it?'

His eyes widened a little, but not, she thought, in embarrassment. 'Not nearly.'

'I thought Norrie and his wife had just had a baby?'

'That was her excuse. Hormones all over the place.'

'Does Norrie know?'

'Let's hope not.'

Fly nudged Helen's leg with the ball. She took it, with the tips of her fingers, and rolled it out of the door into the hall.

'So you'll see Hector, yes?'

'What? No… No.'

He followed Fly into the hall. She heard him speaking to the dog, then silence. Then he was back. He was holding the cordless phone to his ear.

'What are you doing?' Fly pressed the slimy ball against the back of her hand. She pushed it away. 'Damian?'

He smiled at her, as he said into the phone: 'No, not yet. I'm at Mains of Clova. With Helen.' A pause. 'Well, I've been working on persuading her to speak to you. Here she is.'

And he was holding the phone out to her with a question in his face. A question that had only one possible answer, if you knew Hector – if you knew him as she'd just revealed she did. If you knew what he must be to this boy who was giving into her hands the power to hurt him.

It was the worst kind of emotional blackmail.

'Hello?' From the phone, the voice that she'd never thought to hear again. 'Helen?'

47

She put the cool smooth plastic to her ear. 'Hello.'

'God, I'm sorry. It seems to be a family failing – sticking our noses in where they're not wanted. Give him a wallop from me.'

It was hard to speak. 'I would, but he seems to have made himself scarce.'

The scullery door was open, and Fly and Damian were no longer in the room.

'Look, Helen – I get that you don't want to see me, of course you don't, but – this chap Moir Sandison. It seems he may have been in Aboyne. I've just been speaking to Mr Findlay, who says someone strongly resembling him bought some gear from the shop two days ago. Including a camping stove and canisters.'

She stared at the calendar, ten years out of date, that was hanging on the opposite wall.

'Helen?'

'Yes.'

'Can you hear me?'

'Yes. What do you mean, "strongly resembling him"?'

'Hmm?'

'Resembling him, going on what?'

'The photographs. The ones you gave the police.'

'Oh. So Rob – Moir – he really is here. It really has been him –'

'Well, Mr Findlay could be wrong. But I think we need to talk.'

She took a breath. 'Isn't that what we're doing?'

'Properly.'

She took another breath. 'The police didn't tell me they were showing people those photographs. I thought – I got the impression they didn't believe me. About him being up here. But they've been going round asking about him?'

'No. Not exactly... Some copies of the photographs you gave

the police came my way, and we've been circulating them. Locally, I mean, and on the internet.'

'*Came your way?*'

'Can't reveal my sources.' There was a smile in his voice.

'Do the police know? That he's been seen?'

'Not as yet.'

'Campbell Stewart – he's coming to see me. About Rob. He was the detective sergeant – before. He worked on the case. He's a DCI now.'

'Yes. I know him.'

'Will I tell him to speak to you?'

'God no.' The smile was back in his voice. 'No, I'd rather you didn't.'

'Why not?'

Silence. Then: 'A lower key approach might be more productive – initially at any rate. I was thinking of going into Aboyne later, talking to Mr Findlay. Maybe having a look round some of the campsites.'

'Hector –'

'You could come along, if you like.'

A mad yip came out of her mouth. 'You make it sound like – a trip to the seaside!'

'Bring your own bucket and spade... At least let's talk. Can you come over? After Stewart's been?'

'I'm not sure exactly when – I'm not sure how long he'll stay.'

'Doesn't matter. Come when you can.'

'All right.' She swallowed. 'Thank you. For... taking the trouble. To help me.'

'It's no trouble. It's the least I can do.'

The reaction set in as soon as she'd finished the call. She dropped into a chair, her hand gripping the phone, her armpits damp and sticky. She felt trembly and sick. But adrenaline was pumping too.

She'd spoken to him. She was going to see him.

And at the back of her head, Suzanne's voice: *You sad cow.*

Outside, Damian was standing by the fence with Uncle Jim, looking across the barley. Fly and Ben lay on the grass, bellies pulsing. Uncle Jim was saying, 'Aye,' on an indrawn breath. 'Backend of the week, gin there's no rain.'

'So?' said Damian. 'Has Hector worked his magic?'

She looked at him, and he at least had the grace to grimace an apology before the smile broke through, wider than ever.

And she couldn't help smiling back. 'You were such a sweet baby, too.'

'Really? That's not what Hector says.'

Detective Chief Inspector Campbell Stewart dealt with the problem of Fly and the tennis ball simply by pretending neither existed. He took a seat at the kitchen table, unbuttoning the suit jacket stretched a little too tight across his chest, and as his eyes scanned the room Helen felt suddenly conscious of the bits of the kitchen she hadn't got round to – the splattered walls, the grey marks all round the cupboard handles, the filthy floor – in a way she hadn't with Damian.

Uncle Jim, sitting at the head of the table, gave a sudden deep sigh.

She tried to concentrate on what DCI Stewart was saying, about Lothian and Borders Police, about how they'd been working with the Fife officers who'd interviewed Moir's supposed headmaster 'Mr McKillop' in Dunfermline as part of the identity checks on him four months ago. But her thoughts kept flying off to Hector. What was she going to say? What was *he* going to say?

And what on Earth was she going to wear? She only had two clean tops left in her suitcase: the yellow shirt, which would be Crease City, and the blue crossover thing that flattened what little boobs she had.

What did it matter what she wore? Hector wouldn't care. And it was about time she got over this ridiculous teenage infatuation.

'One of the Fife lads was able to identify "Mr McKillop" from photographs in the PNC – the Police National Database – as a certain Peter Laing, who was picked up at his home in Glasgow last night.' DCI Stewart reached into the inside pocket of his suit. 'This is the gentleman in question.'

He set the photo on the table. It was a head and shoulders shot of a startled-looking elderly man, weak-eyed and trembling-jowled.

'He doesn't look like much of a desperado.'

'Fraudsters seldom do. Not the successful ones, anyway. He's a nasty piece of work all the same. Have you ever seen him before?'

'I've no idea. He's not what you'd call memorable.'

'But he's not familiar? You never saw him in Moir Sandison's company?'

'No.'

'I imagine they made sure of that. He's a slippery customer. His last contact with the system was when he was released from Castle Huntly eight years ago. It was assumed he'd "retired".'

He turned over the photograph, on the back of which were written four names:

Michael Dee
Ewan Mathers
Peter Edwards
Peter Laing

'Any of these ring a bell?'

'No. Sorry.'

'Peter Laing's his real name. The others are aliases.'

'And you've arrested him?'

'He's in custody at Drymen Police Station in Glasgow – being questioned as we speak. Hopefully we might learn something about Sandison.' He returned the photograph to his pocket. 'But there's another bit of news. The graphologist reckons the writing on the back of the photograph left in the Eglinton Crescent flat doesn't match the sample we obtained of Rob Beattie's handwriting. These things are always couched in probabilities, but for all intents and purposes, I think we can say it isn't Rob Beattie's writing.'

'Oh. But – you know he was dyslexic? That could mean his writing might have changed a lot. Or he could have deliberately changed it.'

Uncle Jim moved in his chair.

Helen frowned. 'Did you tell the graphologist that Rob was dyslexic?'

'I don't know how much of a difference dyslexia would make.'

'So could you tell them?'

'I'll mention it.' As if he was doing her a favour.

'Last night – I suppose you've heard about what happened from your colleagues who came out.'

'I've seen your statement about that, yes.'

'Something else has happened.'

Uncle Jim gave her a sharp look.

'Oh?' said DCI Stewart.

'I'd like to make another statement, please.' And she told him what had happened in the toilets.

He wrote it all down, swiftly, in shorthand. 'But you didn't see who it was.'

'No. But Rob – when we were at school, I used to hide in the toilets to get away from him. And once – once he came inside the girls' toilets, and started banging on the cubicle door. Just like today. How would Moir know about that unless he's Rob? I never told him about it.' And it suddenly struck her: 'I never told *anyone*.'

'Right... But –'

'I know it seems unbelievable, I mean why would he follow me up here, why would he mess around doing these things to scare me – but you have to understand what he's like. His mind doesn't work like a normal person's. He gets his kicks out of torturing people. The email; stalking me –'

He looked down at the notes he'd taken. 'When you came out of the toilet block, Damian Forbes was right outside.'

'Yes. He'd heard me shouting. His girlfriend was there too. She can vouch for him.'

'Why would he need vouching for?'

'Just – the way you said he was "right outside". As if you thought he might have been the culprit. I'm sure he wasn't.'

'Well. I don't suppose we should hold his family connections against him.'

Even such an indirect reference to Hector had the heat, ridiculously, rushing to her face. She smiled. 'Ha. No.'

He didn't smile back.

Was it not a joke, then?

He clicked his pen, and dropped it and the notebook back into his pocket. 'I'll have this typed up for you to read and sign.' He stood. 'Thank you. You've been very helpful.' And for the first time, he addressed Uncle Jim: 'Some people don't have their troubles to seek, eh?'

Uncle Jim grunted. He didn't get up.

Helen showed him to the door. 'When you said Damian's family connections shouldn't be held against him – were you implying something – about Hector?'

He smoothed his tie. 'It's a cliché that gets used a lot in our line of work, but in this case it's apt: a leopard doesn't change its spots.'

'It was sixteen years ago. We were all young and stupid –'

He didn't say anything.

'What exactly have you got against him?' Her face was burning.

He patted the pockets of his suit jacket. 'What have we got against Hector Forbes?' He was looking off over the roof of the steading to the wooded slopes of Craig Dearg. 'Not enough. Not quite enough.'

48

The drive had no potholes. The yews in front of the house were neatly clipped, and the flowerbeds a mass of colour – lupins and geraniums and lavender. The old rose garden spilled over with heavy blooms, pink and white and peach and dark purple.

All this she noted with the part of her brain that wasn't freaking out. And that part went absent without leave when she looked at the house and saw the man standing at the front door.

He had a hand up, shading his eyes, and as she turned the car onto the gravel he moved the hand palm-outwards in a greeting. By the time she'd swung to a halt, and opened her door and stood, straightening the cross-over-y bit of the top, he was coming towards her, saying, 'Helen!' and grinning as if he'd been waiting there in anticipation of this moment for days.

And he was just the same: the thick, dark, neatly barbered hair; the tanned, handsome face; the warm brown eyes alight with the smile that made all the rest irrelevant.

And she knew in that moment, as she had always known, that for her there would only ever be this one man. It wasn't something she had a choice about. It was part of her, like the colour of her eyes or the shape of her nose.

The fact that she loved Hector Forbes.

He was going to touch her. He would feel that she was trembling, like a silly schoolgirl.

She tensed her muscles; clenched everything.

But when he did touch her, his hands on her arms, warm and firm, there was nothing she could do about her reaction. It cut straight through her and she put up her hand, reflexively, as if to defend herself, flat against his upper arm; hard muscle under the crisp shirt. He bent his face to her, and his lips, cool, still smiling, touched her cheek. She didn't turn her face to touch her own lips to his skin.

She just stood there, smiling desperately, and said something. It might have been, 'Oh, Hector – hello,' as if it was a surprise to see him here outside his own house.

And now his hand was on her back, and surely he must feel it, her reaction, a shock against his hand as he gently guided her towards the door, as if she might not know where to aim for. As if she might try to climb in through a window.

'Have you eaten?' he said. 'Don't worry. I'm not proposing to force-feed you any of Mrs MacIver's culinary delights. I was thinking more in terms of a sandwich and something to drink.'

'Thank you. That would be nice.'

He had taken his hand away, but its imprint remained on her skin like a wound.

Could something this strong, this visceral, this hardwired into her be *completely* one-sided? Such a connection – surely he had to feel *something*? In London... It hadn't all been play-acting, had it?

Or was that just wishful thinking?

As they came into the hall the familiar baize door opened and a man came through it; in his forties, maybe, compact and muscly, tattooed biceps bulging from a khaki T-shirt, hair a stubbly fuzz over his skull. He didn't say anything, just stood there, and Hector said, 'Helen, this is Chris McClusky.'

The man nodded at her.

'Hello,' she said.

Hector said, 'Why don't you make yourself at home in the library, and I'll see what I can scavenge?'

She climbed the stairs on automatic pilot: the broad, shallow steps to the long half-landing with its windows overlooking the courtyard at the back of the house, from which a double sweep of stairs rose in a horse-shoe to the first floor. She took the right-hand set of steps, up to the wide landing, its Persian carpet bright in the early evening sun. There was a smell of beeswax and wood fires and flowers. On the table in front of the three Georgian windows was a big arrangement of roses in a blue and white jug, echoing the glimpses of the gardens beyond.

And she had to stop, and grasp the edge of the table, and breathe.

She turned slowly on the spot.

It was just as she remembered.

To the right, a wide passage ended in a Victorian bay window – that was the Scottish Baronial part of the house. The passage was panelled to the picture rail in waxed mahogany, and from the rail hung the familiar lines of paintings, mostly dark old portraits and huge prints of battle scenes – horrendous things, full of dying horses and cannon smoke and whiskery men running each other through with sabres. The passage to her left was much narrower, and the panelling, painted a light mossy green, less regular and extending right up to the ceiling. The paintings here ran more to little oils of dead hares and partridges, and vases of flowers that somehow managed to look sinister, the bright blooms arching on their stalks against a pitch-black background; and if you looked closely you could see insects crawling over the petals, as if they'd come off a corpse just out of the picture.

She climbed the two steps into the narrow passage. On the left was the door giving on to the back stairwell which cut right through the house, from the basement to the second floor, where the nursery used to be, and Suzanne's little room. On the right was the door to the library; squat, 17th century probably.

She pushed it open and went in.

The Laird and Irina used to sit here in the evenings, by a fire in the winter, and sometimes watching the little portable that had been the only TV in the house. Until Suzanne had persuaded them to let her have one in her room.

Where the portable once sat, on the Pembroke table to one side of the fireplace, was a plasma screen. Otherwise the room was the same. She'd always liked it. It was coothie. The ceiling was low and its plasterwork eccentric. The fireplace was made of stone, plainly carved. All round the walls there were bookcases, and three windows looked down over the formal gardens and the fields in front of the house.

The chairs on either side of the fireplace were monsters, with deep seats and high backs and lugs that stuck forward for you to rest your head against. The one facing her, the one that had been the Laird's chair, still had the squashed, thin leather cushion she remembered. Irina had had the other chair reupholstered, in a tapestry style with twining vines, but now it was covered in tweed.

The sofa was exactly the same, though – a big old saggy purple velvet one with a low back. The dogs always used to try to get up on it.

And there was Black John, still hanging on the wall between two of the windows. And under him the glass-topped display table and its collection of geological samples and artefacts: bitties of stone and polished rocks, with faded labels under them saying things like 'Feldspar' and 'Gneiss' in spidery writing; and what she now realised were early mediaeval spindle whorls, and a fragment of a Roman button-and-loop fastener, and some late Mesolithic flint knives and arrowheads. Fairy darts, those used to be called. People would find them lying in the fields and think they'd been left by the fairies, creeping about in the night shooting darts at the beasts.

She sank down onto one of the window seats, onto the familiar faded chintz.

So here she was.

Sitting on a windowseat at the House, waiting for Hector to make her a sandwich.

He hadn't said anything about London – other than that oblique reference on the phone. But – she couldn't help it, his words from that long-ago email kept looping round her brain:

You are, and have always been, one of my favourite people in the world, and I'll always remember our weekend together.

There was a pile of magazines next to her. She glanced at the top one, and saw that it wasn't a magazine, it was the scientific journal *Nature*, dated last week. The cover promised papers on microRNAs, bumblebee gut parasites, genomic analyses of cancer tumours, and a luminous quasar.

She stood, and walked once, twice round the room.

On the little side table between the Laird's chair and the sofa was a square tin of toffees with a chipped picture of the Houses of Parliament on the lid, and an elastic band round it, and under it a scuffed green rectangle that looked like a folded chess board. She opened the tin. The lid had lost its hinge – hence the elastic band. Inside were not toffees but chunky wooden chess pieces.

She replaced the lid of the box and the elastic band.

He was going to help her. That was why he'd asked her here. He was going to sort out the Moir thing. The Rob thing. Whatever it was. Because he felt sorry for poor Smellie Nellie, in a bind as usual? Or because he felt some sort of obligation? Or because –

Pathetic. She was *pathetic*. Moir – Rob – had been seen in

Aboyne, and all she could think about was *Hector Hector Hector*.

She made her way back downstairs and through the baize door. In the corridor beyond, set into the wall immediately on her left, was a flush grey sheet of metal, and next to it a lighted panel. A lift. And there were sturdy wooden handrails fixed to the walls on the steep stair descending to the kitchen.

For Damian. For their little Stinker.

And Mrs MacIver must be a fair age. She'd seemed ancient twenty years ago – how old must she be now? Surely she should have retired long ago?

The kitchen was empty, and there were no signs of sandwich-making, but she could hear voices outside. She crossed the scullery to the back door, and stepped out into the courtyard.

The man with the tattoos was squatting in front of a large white van. He was in the process of tightening a screw holding the van's number plate in place. Another number plate was lying face-down on the cobbles. A younger man stood over him – this one could have been an architect or a surveyor: tweed jacket, shirt and tie, document folder. The brutal haircut, though, had something of the military about it.

He smiled at Helen, and said, 'Hi, it's Helen, am I right? Are you looking for Hector?'

She nodded.

He offered his hand. 'Gavin Jenkins.'

The van, she noticed, was completely plain. There was no Estate logo on the side. No nothing.

'You're changing the number plates?'

'No no, we're just putting new ones on. The old ones were getting so grotty they were nearly illegible.'

The van wobbled, and Hector emerged from the back of it. 'Does your stomach think your throat's been cut? Let's see what's in the fridge.'

There was ham, and pickle, and tomatoes. A wholemeal loaf from the breadbin. She buttered the bread, badly, tearing it, and watched him cutting the tomatoes. This would be a good time to say something. About London. Or maybe his father. Damian.

What had it been like, what *was* it like for him to be stuck here, looking after the Estate and a disabled child, when he could have been doing – well.

Anything at all.

His shirt sleeves were rolled up a few times, revealing tanned arms, hard-muscled but not like Moir's. Moir's physique was the kind you got from two hours' sweating in a gym every day, but Hector's gym had been Pitfourie – its mountains and rivers and fields – from the time he was a half-wild little boy, with no more thought of heart-rate recovery time or VO_2 max than a wild cat quartering its territory.

There were two little scars by his right wrist bone, and another on the back of his hand. He hadn't had those in London. How had he got them?

He was talking about Uncle Jim. Uncle Jim and his diet. And now he was looking at her, expecting her to contribute something.

'Ina's dead,' she said, as if she was about thirteen and not quite *au fait* with adult conversation.

He stopped slicing.

She bit her lip. Giggling with hysterical laughter during a conversation about her dead aunt wasn't going to help. 'Jim didn't tell me – I found a letter from a solicitor –'

'I see. Well. I'm sorry.'

Oh God. She really was going to start giggling.

Chemistry class.

Double chemistry last thing on a Friday afternoon. She and Suzanne had shared a workbench, and Suzanne would get more and more hyper as it got closer to the weekend, and they'd end up in hopeless giggles, and have to write sad things on the covers of their jotters to show each other, to stop themselves exploding and getting sent out to the corridor.

Helen used to write things like 'A little toddler starving in a locked room'. And Suzanne would write 'Hector's parachute not opening'.

And now they were sitting down at the kitchen table. And he was pouring her a glass of wine – water for him – and oh God, she'd never needed it more. But she made herself sip it like a normal person as she told him about Moir. All the reasons why she thought he was Rob. Sometimes it was hard to breathe and she had to stop talking, but he'd put that down to having to recount her ordeal. He was looking at her with those brown eyes of his, like what she was saying was the most crucially important thing he'd ever heard.

By the time she'd got to the incident in the school toilets, she'd finished her glass of wine and he'd poured her not a refill but a glass of water.

She glugged it. 'Maybe it was just some kids, but I'm very glad Damian was there. He's –' And the silence stretched on, and she couldn't think, she couldn't think what to say, and to her horror she had started to cry.

'Mm, I can think of several ways of ending that sentence,' said Hector, and as she found a tissue and gulped and sniffed, he continued as if they were still having a normal conversation, saying that he understood that Fish was going to help her get her money from the bank, and how it was the sort of thing Fish did in his sleep – but as for the question of whether Moir Sandison was Rob Beattie – he'd studied the photographs and he wasn't convinced.

'I don't suppose we're going to settle the question other than with a DNA test. But regardless of who this bugger is, we need to get hold of him. And to that end... I've been having these fliers handed around.'

He got up from the table and came back with a print-out – a montage of three of her photos of Moir, and along the bottom, 'If you've seen this man, please contact: Hector Forbes' and then two phone numbers and his email address. 'And we've put it on the local community Facebook page. It'll be interesting to see what Mr Findlay has to say. He and Maggie still live in the flat over the shop. I told him we'd be down there around seven.'

'Okay.'

'I also think it might be a good idea if you came to stay here rather than at the Mains. Just until all this is sorted out.'

'*Here*?'

He smiled; nodded.

'But... What about Uncle Jim?'

'I wouldn't have thought he'd be in any danger, but what I'm also proposing is having someone stake out the Mains, as from tonight, to see if your prowler returns. And I'm having all the likely places he could be hiding out searched. Empty houses, derelict steadings – and Gavin's going to do the rounds of the guest houses and hotels and B&Bs, while we concentrate on campsites.' He looked at his watch. 'Right. Eat up. We can call in at the Mains en route, pick up anything you need, explain to Jim –'

'Hector.'

It was a strategy he'd used, she realised, from childhood – acting as if something had already been agreed, when you hadn't even started to formulate your arguments. And before you had a chance to do so, or even to realise that no, you hadn't agreed to this, he'd already moved on.

He looked at her, and she looked at him. He smiled.

'You don't really want me staying here. I'm just a big nuisance. I've always been just a big nuisance.'

'What rubbish. Of course I want you to stay. Although I should warn you that there will be some consumption of Mrs MacIver's food involved, and you'll have to listen to Damian holding forth on various subjects of incredible tediousness – "That's very interesting" is a much-abused phrase in this house – but on the plus side, we have a new HD television.'

A stupid little giggle came out of her mouth. 'So I saw.'

'You haven't lived until you've watched *Bargain Hunt* in HD.'

49

Findlay's hadn't changed one bit, from the Victorian brass thumb-latch on the door to the polished mahogany counter, to the smell of grass seed and Jeye's Fluid. Even Mr Findlay himself hardly seemed to have changed, except for more white in his hair. He was still the definition of 'dapper', in an immaculate green shop-coat, a perfectly sharpened maroon pencil and a tiny notepad in its top pocket.

He waved away Hector's thanks for opening the shop up specially.

'You remember Helen Clack.'

Mr Findlay looked at her. 'Never! Helen Clack!'

She grinned.

She used to love coming here with Dad. She'd been particularly fascinated by all the different-sized nails and screws and things in the little drawers behind the counter – sometimes Mrs Findlay would let her go up the steps, and find the right drawer, and count out however many nails Dad was wanting.

'How are you, lass?'

'Oh. I'm fine. Thank you.' It would be polite to ask him now how he was, and his wife, but that would have seemed wrong. Presumptuous. As if she was still a child, and a child didn't ask an adult something like that.

Hector was speaking about Moir, and telling Mr Findlay that he'd defrauded Helen of a lot of money, and there was a chance that he may have followed her up here. That he may be stalking her. Hence the flier.

'What a terrible thing,' said Mr Findlay. 'But the police are involved, surely?'

Helen nodded. 'But they don't seem to believe me – about the stalking part. I mean, I'm not a hundred per cent sure myself...'

Of course he wanted to hear all about Moir. As Hector gave him an edited summary, she moved round the shop. She was finding it hard to stay still; to concentrate. She looked out of the window, past the mops and brushes and tins of paint. The shops across the street were shut, but there was a new Indian take-away with the lights on and its door open. A group of teenagers were standing outside.

Hector's van was parked a few yards down to the right. Chris was sitting in the cab with the window open, one tattooed arm sticking out of it, a cigarette held between thumb and finger.

'I don't suppose you have CCTV?' said Hector.

'No no.'

'How sure are you, that this was the man?' There was one of the fliers, she saw, lying on the counter. Hector picked it up.

'I'm fairly certain. He made some large purchases and paid in cash, so I did take note.'

'Can you take us through what you remember? What time was this?'

'I've the till receipt here.' Mr Findlay removed a sharply folded slip of paper from his top pocket. 'Eleven-twenty-one. He was in the shop maybe ten minutes, no more. Came in and past the counter, without an acknowledgement, and through to the back.'

'What was he wearing?'

'Now. What was he wearing.' He shook his head. 'Just ordinary clothes, I'd think, or else I would have remarked it. I left him to it for a whilie, and then I went back after him. Asked if I could help. He said he was after a camping stove, so I went through the options. He chose a Campingaz Chef. Good little stove.'

'What sort of accent did he have?'

'Not local. Scottish, but not local.'

'Could you pinpoint it at all?'

He shook his head. 'He was well spoken. Not a strong accent.'

'Did he have a funny cough?' said Helen. 'Like a nervous tic?'

'Not that I noticed.'

'How did he seem generally?' asked Hector. 'What were your impressions?'

'I can't say I warmed to him. Tried to start up a conversation, asked him if he was camping in the area, but he just said "No" and that was the end of that. I took the stove and the canisters for it to the counter while he chose some other things, and then he paid – in cash – and left. *But.*' Mr Findlay smiled from Hector to Helen, as if about to produce a sweetie for each of them. 'I saw him again, a few minutes later, while I was helping a customer out to her car with her purchases. He drove by in a motor home. One of those smart modern ones. With "Swift" above the windscreen – would that be the make of it?'

Helen looked out of the window, as if he'd be driving past right that minute.

'That's extremely helpful information,' said Hector. 'I don't suppose you got the registration number?'

'I'm afraid not. All I can tell you is that it was white, and had a sort of bulbous bit above the windscreen, with, as I say, the word "Swift". Other than that...'

'Was there anyone with him?'

'No, I don't think so.'

Hector had taken his phone from his pocket. 'What we need is the website for Swift motor homes...'

He put the phone on the counter, and Mr Findlay looked on in amazement as he navigated the internet until he'd found a webpage with various models of Swift motor homes on it.

'Could it have been one of these?'

Eventually they had a shortlist of three possibilities. While Hector continued asking questions – Was the vehicle clean or dirty? Did he notice anything in the cab, anything on the dashboard or the passenger seat? What time was this, approximately? – Helen paced, across to the stand with seed packets, along the aisle, back to the window.

Flu and feeling yuchy was a distant memory: she fizzed with energy. It was like being a kid again, off on some ploy with Norrie and his brothers, pretending they were the Famous Five, following suspicious-looking men round Kirkton. Off on an adventure, and back home in time for tea.

Only with Hector.

Now he was holding the phone over something on the counter: the till receipt. He was taking a photo of it. But before she could get close enough to read it he'd picked it up, and folded it, and handed it back to Mr Findlay.

'Can I see that?' she said. 'What else did he buy?'

'Just some other camping things.'

She didn't want to make a fuss in front of Mr Findlay, but when they were back in the van – Helen on the seat in the middle, perched between the two of them – she said, 'Can I see your photo of that receipt?'

Hector started the engine. 'Yes, of course – just a second.' He had the phone to his ear. Now he spoke into it. 'Gavin. Where are you?... Okay. I'm sending you a folder called 'Swift Motor Homes' – could you add the three photos in it to the Facebook post and the flier? With text along the lines "May be driving..." Print off another couple of hundred fliers, and meet us at the campsite at Ballater in... can you do half an hour?... Okay... Right, thanks.' He frowned down at the phone's screen, navigating through a menu. Then he put it back in his pocket.

'Hector.'

'Mm?'

'Why don't you want me to see that receipt?'

He took the phone back out of his pocket. 'All right. But bear in mind that it may not even have been him.'

She looked down at the screen.

Campingaz Camping Chef	£78.99
Butane/propane gas canisters (2)	£21.00
Polypropylene twine 50 g	£4.69
Gerber LHR fixed blade knife	£210.00
Subtotal	**£314.68**

'He bought a knife.'

Hector was pulling the van out into the street. 'Let's not read too much into it. And in any case –' He shot her a smile. 'You're perfectly safe. We're not going to let anything happen to you.'

She smiled back. He didn't have to tell her that.

She knew she was safe as long as she was with him.

'First thing tomorrow,' he was saying across her to Chris, 'you and Mick can get on to Alan Anderson, ask if you can check out his CCTV footage for between, say, ten and one. Any motor homes on it, try and get clear images, showing the drivers, and if possible registration numbers.'

Chris grunted.

'But can't the police do that?' she said.

Hector raised his eyebrows. 'Eventually, yes, they'll probably get round to it.'

She glanced at the profile of this man called Chris who was presumably one of Hector's 'unusual' employees: a flattened nose; cold blue eyes intent on the road ahead; bare forearms with dirty-blue tattoos of snakes and a stag with spreading antlers entwined, incongruously, in ivy leaves. He smelt strongly of cigarettes.

He was smirking.

'What happens if we find him?' she said.

The smirk got bigger. Hector said, 'That depends.'

'On what?'

'On where we find him, for a start.'

She was very conscious of Hector's hands on the steering wheel; on the gear stick. She turned away, to the flow of air coming through the open window, to the street outside. At the edge of the pavement there was a bow-legged little Westie on a lead, trotting jauntily. The teenagers who'd been at the take-away were slouching along at the next corner, the girl and one of the boys jostling each other as they went.

Loch Deer was a sheet of silver, the water still and clear, reflecting the low-dipping branches of the beech trees that ringed the carpark, and beyond them the pines, and beyond them the humps of Ben Aven and Tom na Creiche and Monadh Caoin.

The motor home parked up facing the water looked similar to the ones on the website, but it was a Romahome, not a Swift. There was a table set up outside the open door, and a man and a woman of about Helen's age sitting on folding chairs. Two mountain bikes were hung on a rack attached to the side of the van.

When Hector approached them, the man stood, and said, 'Sorry, are we not supposed to be here?', as if Hector had 'Landowner' tattooed on his forehead.

He said, 'No no, you're fine,' and 'Lovely spot, isn't it?' And he handed them one of the fliers, and started asking about Moir.

Helen went to the water's edge. Two mallards were bobbing about, the male's plumage iridescent in the slanting evening light. The water made a sucking, plopping sound against the peaty bank.

Might Suzanne be here? Somewhere under all this cold water?

Hector was at her shoulder. 'No joy.' He was holding a map, folded into a rectangle. They'd done the rounds of the large campsites at Tarland by Deeside and Ballater, and smaller places like this, and although they'd found two Swift motor homes, one had been full of kids and the other, according to the people camped on the neighbouring pitch, belonged to a couple of pensioners.

'He could be anywhere,' said Helen.

Hector looked off over the water. 'Okay. You're driving one of those things. You're trying not to attract attention. Do you stick in one place, or do you park up somewhere different each day? A big campsite, amongst the herd, or off the beaten track? Literally? The majority of tracks are pretty much passable just now, even for a motor home – we've had such a run of dry weather.'

She shook her head. 'I don't know. I think I would want to move around, park somewhere out of the way...'

'And how has he been getting to the Mains? To Kirkton, if that was him in the toilets? On foot, by bike, what? Does he bring the vehicle, park nearby while he does his prowler routine...?'

'If it's Rob, he'll know the area round Kirkton as well as we do. He'll know all the good places to hide a big vehicle.'

'Would he risk it, though? Isn't it more likely that he'd base himself further afield – not too far, but far enough to be off the radar?'

'Maybe.' She shrugged, watching the ducks.

For a little while there was silence. Then he said, 'This must be very hard.'

She didn't turn to look at him. She said, 'Was it just that you felt sorry for me? Was that all it was? Please tell me the truth.'

As soon as the words were out, from the slight movement she sensed at her side, she realised that that hadn't been what he'd meant at all. He'd been talking about Moir, Rob, Suzanne – not what had or had not happened between them in London.

She could feel her face heating up. And Suzanne's voice was back in her head: *Daft Doris.*

'No,' he said. 'Of course not.'

'What was I like?' She tried a laugh; a glance at his face.

He smiled. 'Those were a wonderful couple of days. I'm just sorry... well, that I wasn't much of a gentleman about the whole thing. That it ended the way it did.'

And what on earth did he mean by that? Did he mean he was sorry it had ended *at all*?

'Oh, Hector, really, it's fine. I was an idiot. I was very young. We both were.'

Good.

That had sounded mature and sensible and sane. Philosophical, even.

But her heart was thudding, and her arms and legs felt weak again, like the flu virus was rallying, taking advantage of her stupid heart going haywire. For no reason. She knew he didn't want her. Not then and not now.

But but but thudded her heart.

But maybe the problem had been his lifestyle. His mysterious – and presumably dodgy – job in South America. Things were different now. He was a landowner with responsibilities; with a proper home. There wasn't any reason now why he couldn't have a proper relationship.

So why didn't he?

He said, 'I was old enough to know better.' And then: 'Did you and Martin ever get back together?'

'Oh God no!' How odd, that he remembered Martin – Martin, coming to the flat, worried about her, and finding her with Hector. She herself hadn't thought of him in years.

She didn't know how he was navigating. The track kept splitting in two, or even three, and all she could see was trees, to the sides, in front, behind them. Sitka spruce and pine and beech and birch and oak and sycamore, and the occasional line of larch. Sometimes they'd come to a clearing with a vista out across the hills, but mostly it was trees, their canopies absorbing the evening light where it didn't fall warm on the track, or in a slanting shaft of green cutting through the murk of the understorey.

'Would he have come this far in?' said Helen. 'He'd never find his way out again, surely. I mean, I know psychopaths are supposed to lurk in the undergrowth, but isn't this taking it a bit far?'

It was wrong on all kinds of levels that she was starting to feel...

not happy, exactly, about what had happened. With Moir. Rob. Whoever he was. Of course not.

But OK with it, if it had to happen to bring her here.

'No excessive lurking required,' said Hector. 'We've looped round the contour of the hill – another quarter of a mile or so and we'll come out onto the road just past the Knowiemuir Crossroads. So if he came in from that side...' He slowed to a stop, frowning out of the windscreen. And then he had his door open and was jumping down, and saying, 'Get the cutters.'

A deer shot away from them down the track and into the forest. But there was another one, a little fawn, in the trees by the side of the track. There was something wrong with it. It was twisting and leaping about – having a fit?

No. It was caught by the neck in the running noose of a wire snare.

'Oh God.'

Chris got down, and Helen followed him. Hector had a rug in his hands. While Chris headed for the back of the van Hector approached the deer. It froze. She could see its little chest heaving. Its mouth was white with thickened saliva; its eyes frantic.

As Hector got nearer it started to leap and twist again, and Helen put her hands to her mouth. Then the rug was over its head, and Hector was holding the struggling little body while Chris cut the wire noose.

Hector set the fawn down on its feet, and twitched away the rug, and it bolted into the trees. He took the cutters from Chris, and used them to remove the other end of the wire from a branch above his head.

'I suppose it was meant for foxes.' Helen's mouth was dry. 'Whose land is this?'

'Ours.' And as her face must have registered her dismay: 'We don't snare. But a wire snare intended for a fox would be lower, pinned to the ground. This is poachers after deer.'

'There might be more.' Helen walked slowly on down the track, scanning the trees.

'There will be. I'll get the boys to do a sweep.'

'It's so – barbaric.'

He was twisting the wire round his hand. 'Poachers don't tend to be big on animal welfare. Okay – let's go.'

But they'd only gone another hundred yards or so when Hector stopped the van again, and put his head out of the window, and said, 'Smell that?'

She sniffed. 'Woodsmoke?'

'Stay here, both of you.' And he was off again, jogging down the track and then striking off it, ducking under the low branches of the trees.

'Go with him,' said Helen. 'I'll be fine here.'

Chris shook his head but didn't look at her.

'Do you think it's the poachers?'

A shrug.

'But they could be dangerous –'

A smirk. Still he didn't look at her.

She wriggled across the gear stick and onto Hector's seat, and opened the door, and jumped down onto the track. But she hadn't got five yards when a hand, suddenly, was hard across her mouth, and a muscled wiry arm was around her waist, lifting her off her feet.

50

Chris manhandled her to the passenger door, pulled it open and tossed her up onto the seat. The air whoofed out of her lungs as she fell against the dashboard. Distantly there was a shout, and then another. She twisted to look out of the windscreen – a man was running out of the trees ahead, and Hector after him.

Chris slammed the door on her. Before she could reach for it he was in at the driver's side, firing up the engine. She shouted something. The man was swinging what looked like a mallet over his head – swinging it at Hector, who dodged, not away but in close under the man's arm, as if in a bizarre dance, turning him around and abruptly down.

There was another man. Running out of the trees. At Hector. Helen screamed his name, and screamed again, and then she saw that the mallet was in Hector's hands, arcing towards the man's face. It connected with a crunch, and the man flipped backwards and lay still.

Chris cut the engine and got out.

'Oh God oh God.' She fumbled at the door; stumbled to the ground.

Chris had one of them on his feet – just a boy, in dirty jeans and camouflaged jacket, eyes wide, mouth contorted, snot on his face. His right arm hung limp.

'This isn't him, is it?' Hector bent over the other man, who was lying face down in the dust of the track, and yanked up his head by the hair. The man spat blood, and a tooth, and swore.

Helen could only shake her head.

It was obviously the boy's father. They had the same body shape, broad at the shoulder and skinny at the bum. The same caved-in looking cheeks.

'Too much to hope for.' Hector dropped the man's head and

grabbed hold of his jacket, hauling him upright.

'Broke ma... fucking nose...' It was a Lowland accent.

'Oh, I'm sorry. That was careless.' Hector grinned at her as he pushed the man in front of him to the van.

Its rear doors were standing open. Chris helped him shove the man inside. Immediately inside the doors there was a rack of tools, but beyond that there was a grill, dividing off the inner space. The middle section of the grill was hinged, opening outwards.

Behind the grill there was only a bench, running along one side of the van, on which the boy was slumped. They pushed the man in beside him, and then Chris shut the hinged part of the grill and locked it with a key.

A cage.

It was a cage.

Chris settled himself on a coil of rope under the tool rack, and Hector shut the doors on him.

'Sorry about this.' He put a hand on her arm.

She shook it off. Her legs were trembly again; her knees, and the backs of her thighs. 'What are you going to do to them?'

'Dump them the other side of Aboyne. They'll have a vehicle nearby, but we'll dispose of that. And their gear. Chris will have a little chat with them, explain the procedure.'

'You're not taking them to the police?'

He raised his eyebrows.

'Hector –'

'The police... All right, yes, we could take them to the police. But to what purpose? This way, their assets are seized, they're, um, disincentivised... and all at no cost to the taxpayer.'

'How can you – It's not *funny*. They could have *killed you*. Or you might have killed *them*.'

'Could try harder?' His hand was back on her arm. 'It's okay. I'm sorry you had to see it. Shh. It's okay.'

He pulled her against him, and she breathed the familiar clean, sharp smell of his shirt, his skin. She put her hands on his back; felt the slight movement of his ribs as he breathed. He wasn't gulping air like she was; he was breathing perfectly normally.

He wasn't sorry about what had happened. He was sorry she'd had to see it.

He patted her shoulder – like she was a child, or a daftie.

She pulled back. He dropped his arms, and she stepped away.

'What is – *this*?' She opened her palms, encompassing him, the van, the track behind them.

He shook his head, and raised his eyebrows again in the expression she knew so well, that she'd known all her life.

But she didn't know him.

Her stupid fantasy about them, Hector and Damian and Irina – it could hardly be further from reality. The real Irina wasn't swanning about some neighbouring stately home, playing the lady bountiful and doting on her son – she'd abandoned him because he was disabled. The real Damian couldn't be further from her imaginary version. And the real Hector –

'When I asked DCI Stewart what he had against you, he said: "Not quite enough". What did he mean?'

The smile was back. 'He's convinced I'm running some sort of criminal enterprise.'

'And are you?'

'Helen –'

'I don't want you going after Rob like this. You have to leave it to the police. Please. Hector. Not for his sake, I don't care what happens to him, but this is just – It's not right. You shouldn't be doing this.'

'All right. If that's what you want.'

They drove into Aboyne, and through it, and up into Glen Tanar. Helen closed her eyes and pretended to be asleep, forcing herself to breathe deeply, regularly, as her mind whirled, until the van slowed and stopped.

'I'd say this is as good a place as any to drop our passengers.'

There was a mossy dyke on either side of the road, the fields beyond poor, boggy, full of rushes.

'They'd lit a fire,' she said.

'Uh huh…?'

'They must have been intending to camp overnight. There'd have been plenty of time for the police to get up there and arrest them.'

'The police would have arrested them, would they?'

She took a long breath. 'If we *had* found Rob – what were you going to do with him?'

Silence. Then: 'You'd be happy to hand him over to the police, and let justice take its course? Whatever that may be?'

'I'd rather that than...' She took a shaky breath. 'Whatever alternative you've got in mind. That doesn't mean I'd be "happy" with the outcome of the judicial process – Rob in a nice warm cell with TV and the internet and courses on basket weaving? Of course I wouldn't be *happy* about it.' Another breath. 'I've no aspirations to the moral high ground.'

'Well, if we're getting metaphysical – I think you'd find it already a bit crowded.'

'Is it? I can't say I've noticed.'

'What do you think would happen to our friends back there, if the so-called justice system was given the responsibility of dealing with them? No hard evidence... Do you think they'd even end up in court? And do you think they don't know it, and aren't laughing up their sleeves at it all? At all the suckers up there on the moral high ground?'

'So your solution is to go in swinging a mallet.'

'It wasn't my mallet. Actually I think it was a sledgehammer.'

And suddenly he laughed, his head flung back against the seat, and sitting there beside him in the cab, with a tattooed thug and two beaten-up poachers in the van behind them, she had to bite her lip to stop from laughing too. Laughing, and crying, for the ten-year-old girl held tight in the circle of his arm, swinging up, and up and up, over the river's peaty depths.

51

It was almost dark by the time they got back to the House, the distant hills soft against a dramatic sky in which bank upon bank of elongated clouds, underlit by the last, pinky-purple glow of the sunset, stretched into infinity. Hector parked the van in the courtyard and Chris jumped down. As Hector got out, Helen shuffled herself across the seat to the passenger door but she wasn't quick enough; there he was, reaching up a hand to help her down.

Ever the gentleman.

'Thanks,' she said. 'I can manage.'

He unlocked the back door and a beeping started, cutting off when he keyed in a code on a pad on the wall. In the kitchen he said, 'You could embark on an archaeological dig through the contents of the fridge, if you like – I think there's some ratatouille Damian made that's half edible, if he hasn't scoffed it. I'll be back in a sec – I'll just take this up to your room.' He was carrying her suitcase.

'Thank you.'

But when he'd gone, when she was standing alone in the middle of the big kitchen and a little thrill was running through her, a thrill at the thought of sitting down to a meal with Hector, she knew that it was wrong.

That she couldn't – shouldn't – do this.

She ran up the stairs, aware as she did so of muffled music. She yanked open the baize door and stepped through to the delicately falling notes of a classical piano recording, Chopin or Brahms or Liszt, cascading through the dimly shadowed hall. And she was brought up short, memories assailing her, memories of when she used to come to the House to see Suzanne and linger here at the baize door on a summer night like this, not liking to intrude any further into the family's domain but thrilling to be almost a part of it, standing here breathing the scents of the big flower arrangement on the table just beyond the door, lingering to listen to the distant strains of Beethoven or Mozart or Chopin or whatever the old Laird had selected from his vast collection of classical music records.

So many ghosts.

Was Damian playing one of his father's records? How well would you remember your father, if you were only seven when he died? But you would remember, surely, the house being filled with his music; there would be a response to it hard-wired into you, evoking – what? A feeling of security, maybe; of being a child drifting into happy slumber, knowing that your parents were just downstairs and all was right with the world.

Her suitcase sat at the foot of the stairs, seemingly abandoned there.

Hector was crossing the hall away from her, to the corridor that led into the Victorian part of the house.

'Hector?' As she went after him, she realised that the music was coming from the end of that corridor, through the open door of the Terrace Room, from which yellow light spilled.

He stopped and turned, and she said, 'Thank you, but I really think I should get back to the Mains.'

In the dim light she couldn't see his face properly.

'Oh?'

'I just – I don't think...'

'Look... Helen. I'm sorry things didn't quite pan out today as – well, as I would have wished.'

As if what had happened had been completely beyond his control.

She could just see the outline of his face. The piano notes tumbled, filling the high space above them with a dizzying, dancing lightness that confused her senses, that shivered suddenly up her spine as the melody reached its climax and then took her where she wasn't expecting to go, all the lightness turned to cool shadow, measured and austere, but with something unbearably tender in it, something agonising that clawed at her insides, and it was suddenly not possible to stand here and look at him and listen to it any more.

She turned away and walked quickly to her suitcase, pulling up the handle and starting to wheel it over the Persian carpet towards the door, and he was saying 'Helen...' and then she was struggling with the huge key in the lock on the front door, and he was reaching past her to release a bolt and the Yale, to key in the code to deactivate the alarm, and she was out into the night air, saying, 'Thank you. I'll...' and struggling with the wheels on the gravel, and he was taking the case from her, the piano music pursuing them faintly, and she said, 'No,' and she could hear the smile in his voice as he said, 'At least let me help you with this beast of a thing.'

And so she walked with him to Stan.

She pulled the key from her pocket and walked behind the car to open the boot –

And stopped and stared at the back windscreen.

L I A R was scratched on the glass in huge big letters.

That hadn't been there when she'd driven here. She'd have seen it, surely?

Rob must have –

Rob had been here.

And now she was running, running back to the door and shouting *'Damian! Where's Damian?'* because Rob knew, he had always known how to hurt her –

And he had always hated Hector.

How better to hurt Hector, and so Helen, than by hurting his brother?

'Damian!' she shouted again as she ran through the hall and down the wide corridor to the Terrace Room towards the music, images rushing through her mind of Rob having found Damian there and – what?

And smiling as he heard the van returning, and placed a record on the turntable.

She was running through the open door, registering the changes to the room with one part of her brain, the grand piano in front of the four big windows looking onto the front lawn, the table against the wall with instrument cases on it, the table next to it with an incongruously modern sound system, but now the music had suddenly cut off and Damian was getting up from the long green velvet piano stool –

And Rob wasn't here.

It hadn't been a recording.

Stupidly, she said, 'You're very good' as Damian looked beyond her to Hector; and as Hector put a hand on her back she pulled away, she ran across the expanse of wax-polished floorboards and the twining foliage of the beautiful Victorian carpet to the windows and the French doors giving onto the terrace at the end of the house, and then to the four big windows on the side of the room that overlooked the courtyard.

All these windows.

Almost the whole of three of the walls of this massive room, the biggest room in the house, were windows.

'He's out there. He's going to try to get in, he might already be... Hector, he's *Rob*. He's Rob.' A draught of air, sweeping through the room, shivered on her skin. 'Damian, you can't stay here – this room, it's too exposed, all these windows, he might –'

And Hector said, 'Come on then' and he had his arm round her, warm across her shoulders, and he was guiding her from the room, and telling her that all the windows were covered by the alarm system, and then she was sitting upstairs in the library and letting Hector talk her into staying until 'all this is resolved', barely able to answer him, to nod pathetically, while Damian fastened the shutters on the windows.

And then Hector had gone to check round the house, and Damian was sitting on the arm of her chair and taking her shaking hand in his steady one and saying, 'You don't need to worry. I hope he *does* try something. Bring it on, knobhead.'

And on the wall behind him Black John looked down on them and it occurred to her to wonder what it did to your genes to have so many ancestors, going back seven, eight, nine hundred years, who had wrested what they had from their neighbours by force, by sheer bloodyminded strength of will.

She wished that she had some of whatever Black John had passed down running in her veins.

'I wonder how he knew you were here,' said Damian.

'He must have followed me, I suppose.'

'But how? If he was watching the Mains, and saw you drive off – he couldn't have had the motor home parked anywhere near, could he, or it would've been too much of a risk that someone would see it. Maybe he's got a bike.'

'Maybe.'

'But then he wouldn't have been able to keep up with you in your car.' He was looking at her speculatively. 'And why "liar"?'

She was so tired.

'I don't know.'

And to prevent him asking anything more, she said, 'So you're a musician?'

He looked at her. 'Right. By all means let's talk about our hobbies. TV. The weather.' And he lifted his eyebrows.

'Rob,' she said in the end. 'He seems to be trying to make out I lied about him killing Suzanne. I think he's trying to frighten me into changing my story, but – why would he want me to do that? It's obvious he killed her. Why disappear if he didn't?'

Was that really why Rob was doing this? He wanted her to say he hadn't killed Suzanne? Had that been his intention all along – first of all to punish her, and then to get her to change her story and say he was innocent so he could reappear, so he could be exonerated?

He shrugged. 'Might there have been another reason for his disappearance?'

She just shook her head. 'I don't see what other reason there could be.'

But what if he really was innocent?

What if someone else had killed Suzanne?

52

She woke very late, to the birds and pagodas and chrysanthemums that rioted across the yellow walls of the Chinese Bedroom. She hadn't closed the curtains the night before – she'd barely had the energy to go to the loo, and splash her face at the sink – and light fell across the bed in a hot rectangle.

She could smell flowers. On the bamboo stand beside the bed there was a little pewter jug with pink and white striped roses crammed rather haphazardly into it, and stalks of lavender sticking up, bizarrely, from the centre.

She pushed back the covers and padded over to the en suite. It had an Art Deco-style sink and bath and loo and shower, all so sparkling clean she was nervous about using anything. And it had its own window, draped in crisp antique lace, overlooking the terrace and the lawn and, behind a bank of rhododendrons, the tennis court and walled garden.

She stared at her face in the mirror over the sink.

Liar.

What sort of sick game was Rob playing? *He* killed Suzanne. She may not be able to remember what had happened, she may not be able to remember it in the conscious part of her brain, but she knew that must be what had happened.

And he was never going to make her say otherwise.

It was almost twelve by the time she made it downstairs. Mrs MacIver, rolling pastry on the kitchen table, cast her eyes up to the clock before favouring Helen with a tight smile and a 'Now then, Hel'nie Clack.' She wore her hair in the same uncompromising bun. And Helen could have sworn she recognised the dress, plain navy, teamed with navy shoes.

'Hello, Mrs MacIver.'

'Lunch winna be long, but if you're wanting your breakfast –'

'No no. If I could just have a glass of water?'

'There's the tap.'

There were two glasses draining next to the sink. She took one and ran a splash of water into it.

'Thank you, for putting me up at such short notice.'

Mrs MacIver's attention was back on the pastry. It had split, and she was pressing the tear together with her fingers. 'None of my doing.'

'I'm sorry for the extra work –'

'It's the chiel you have to thank for it. For your room.'

Damian then, not Hector.

'Oh. Right. That was kind of him.'

'What's all this about some mannie you think is Robin Beattie?'

'Hector told you…'

'He's told me I've not to leave the house unless one of the men's with me. And the same goes for Damian and Hel'nie Clack.' As if Hel'nie Clack was another person entirely. Maybe she was. 'In case this mannie comes in about.' Her mouth pursed in contempt – for 'the mannie', Hector or Helen wasn't clear. 'Himself and the chiel are in the garden – I've to get Gavin to take you, if you're going.'

It was more of an instruction than a question.

'Right. Thank you.'

And so she set off across the courtyard with Gavin Jenkins, smart and scrubbed-looking in a lightweight grey jacket, and tried to concentrate on what he was saying about the changes since she'd last been at Pitfourie, the renovation of the coach house and outbuildings, the garden, the old laundry.

They crossed the lawn, and passed the tennis court with its pristine terracotta surface, and then her sandals were crunching on the gravel of the path to the old kitchen garden.

The maroon door set into the wall was the same as she remembered, with its oversized Victorian latch. Gavin flicked the thumbpiece and pushed it open, and she followed him through.

She'd expected a transformation like those she'd seen everywhere else: neat rows of vegetables and flowers, and box hedges, and tilled earth. But although one of the far corners was under cultivation – with raspberry canes and cabbages and potato shaws, and carrots, and were those sprouts? – the rest was nature run riot, great high elder bushes and brambles and ivy, and in the middle a swathe of long grass and wild flowers.

The greenhouses against the far wall, though, had been repaired, and inside them she could see neat rows of plants.

A voice spoke – Hector's voice – and someone else laughed.

Then silence.

Tendrils of honeysuckle hung over the path, and a nettle nodded against the thin linen of her trousers. Moving from the shadow of the high wall, finished with brick for the ripening of fruit for a long-ago Victorian table, they passed into the sunlight and she was conscious, then, of the sounds around her – bees and other insects, and a thrush singing, trailing its song across the garden.

The wild garden.

That was what this was.

Hector was standing with his back to them, arms folded, in the middle of the long grass. He was looking down at something which also held the attention of his brother – the chiel – who was sitting on one of those cheap collapsible chairs made of green nylon slung over an aluminium frame, a clipboard on his knee.

Damian saw them first. He stood, and smiled, tucking the clip-board under his arm and pushing his hair off his forehead. The hair was tousled, and he wore jeans and trainers and a faded, if spotlessly clean, brown T-shirt. The sophisticated young man of yesterday had gone, you might think, until you met his eyes.

And she supposed it was all very amusing – another infatuated female, spinning in orbit around his brother.

But as Hector turned to her she couldn't help it, she couldn't not look at him, she couldn't not drink him in: the firm, tanned skin over cheek and jaw; his beautiful eyes; the way his lips lifted a tiny bit at the corners before he gave her the full force of his smile.

'How are you feeling? Did you manage to sleep?'

'Yes, thank you. Eventually. Hector... Thank you so much, for...'

Where to start?

He just kept smiling, and said to Gavin: 'I think you've just squashed one of the subjects.'

Gavin looked at his feet, and stepped back. 'Oops. Sorry.'

Damian said, 'If it hasn't got a stake with a number beside it, it's expendable. For my purposes, anyway.'

'I won't ask what those are.'

'No, best not,' said Hector. 'Not unless you've an hour or so to spare.'

It was a dismissal. With a quick smile for Helen, Gavin turned and started back the way they'd come.

'Sorry about the oversized nanny. But I don't want you leaving the house on your own. Not unless I'm with you, or one of the men.'

'I'm causing so much trouble. I don't think I should stay. I could be putting everyone here in danger.'

His lips became a straight line, and he shook his head slightly; impatiently. Why had she said that? He must know that *she* knew fine there was no way he'd agree to her leaving. Which was why she was safe to suggest it.

She babbled: 'The man who was watching the Mains last night – Is he still there? Uncle Jim…'

'Yes, don't worry, we'll keep an eye on the Mains. Jim came over earlier to see you but we decided not to wake you. I said we'd call round, maybe tomorrow…'

'Oh. Will he be all right on his own at the Mains, though?'

'He won't be on his own.'

Damian, dropping the clipboard onto the chair, grinned. 'What really freaked him out was Hector's suggestion that he, Ben and Fly might want to join you here.'

She smiled, trying and failing to imagine Uncle Jim, Ben and Fly installed in one of the bedrooms at the House – the Regency Room, perhaps, with its gold silk wall coverings and elegant Georgian furniture. Or – oh God – the White Room.

'He's quite enthusiastic about staking out the Mains,' Damian went on. 'Still a reasonable shot, apparently, with that shotgun of his.'

'Oh.'

'Quite,' said Hector. 'As if Postie's not traumatised enough by Fly.'

Damian flicked a greenfly off his arm. 'I've been thinking… If this man really is Rob, he must have engineered the whole thing. Your encounter in the salon. Everything.'

Hector put a repressive hand on his arm.

The possibility hadn't occurred to her. 'I suppose he must have done.' She turned to Hector. 'I need to convince the police that I'm not some mad time-waster… I need to convince them he's out there and he's going to... I don't know what he's going to do, but I need to convince them that he's Rob, that the man who murdered Suzanne is back and they need to catch him. But they're not going to take any notice of what I say any more. I need... I need corroboration from someone credible. I was thinking maybe Norrie... Maybe Norrie could have a look at the photos sometime and if he thinks it could be Rob he could make a statement or something... I don't know. Do you think he might?'

'Well, I thought I'd ask him, and Fish, and Fiona and Steve, to dinner tonight. It might help to thrash things out between us.'

Us. It had been so long since she'd been part of *us*.

Fresh tears threatened.

'If that's okay with you?'

She nodded. 'Thank you.' She held his eyes. Or he held hers. And her face was suddenly too hot, and he looked away.

She looked down at the clipboard on the chair. The paper clipped into it was covered with columns of tiny figures. Along the top of the columns was written 'Plant no.', 'Time', 'Pollinator group/species' and 'Visit duration'.

So here they were, Black John's boys, carrying on as if nothing had happened, as if a woman stalked by a psychopath hadn't just dumped herself on them, as if he might not still be lurking out here somewhere. While she and Hector had been off looking for Rob and his motor home, he'd been here, maybe looking in at Damian in the Terrace Room, prowling around, before defacing her rear windscreen. And they weren't in the least bit worried about it.

Or did they not, after all, believe her? Did they think she'd scratched 'Liar' on her own car? Were they humouring her? Humouring poor mad Helen? Did they think she'd finally flipped her lid?

Well, if they did, she had to convince them otherwise. She had to convince them that she was a hundred percent sane and normal.

She said, 'This looks...'

'Very interesting?' suggested Hector. 'Are you agog to know all about the evolutionary implications of the markings on the petals of the common spotted orchid?'

'I'm agog to know how a stopwatch figures.' She'd just seen it, in the net cup hanging from the arm of the chair. 'I wouldn't have thought evolution worked quite that fast.'

They both laughed, and Damian said, 'I'm trying to find out whether there's an association between flower morphology – the patterns of the spots – and the duration of visits by different types of pollinator. I watch each flower for fifteen minutes and note down which pollinators visit it, and for how long. Then on the following day I switch the order to account for temporal effects, so in the analysis –'

'Yes,' said Hector. 'Personally, I can't get enough of the statistical analysis.'

Helen bent to peer at one of the orchids. Each stem had dozens of frilly white flowers, lined and spotted with purple, clustered together on a heavy spike. 'The patterns are really beautiful, aren't they?'

'And they do vary quite a bit.' Damian bent too, and slid his fingers under one of the individual flowers, turning it up so she could see. 'Some pollinators have vision in the UV spectrum, but –'

Hector hooked an arm round Damian's neck. 'Enough.' And to Helen: 'You've had breakfast?'

'No. But that's my own fault for having such a long lie.' She straightened, and said to Damian, 'Thank you for doing my room.'

'You're welcome. Do you like the flowers?'

'Love them.'

'Mm.' Hector adjusted the headlock. 'You'd think a budding Charles Darwin would be a dab hand at all things botanical. You'd also think that anyone who expends so much time and energy on their own appearance would have a highly developed aesthetic sensibility. But ask him to put some flowers in a vase and you end up with something that looks like it's been arranged by a colour-blind marmoset.'

Damian wriggled. 'Actually, colour vision in marmosets *is* a bit weird.'

Hector released him. 'Most females can see blues and greens and reds, but some females and all males can see only blues and greens.'

Damian blinked, and put a hand through his hair. 'How do you know that?'

Hector's gaze rested on the boy in a sort of tender scrutiny identical to the way Fiona had looked at Lizzie. 'The same way I know lots of bits of useless information, presumably.'

The thrush sang, a sweet tumbling and trilling of notes above their heads, and Damian looked up, and Hector smiled.

So she'd been wrong about him not finding someone to love.

Romantic love – why was the world so obsessed with it? It was a poor thing next to the other kind – the kind that wasn't jealous, or needy, or selfish; that was given without any conditions; that asked nothing of its object in return.

'Well,' said Damian. 'You might thank me one day. You never know when it might come in useful. Say the world was overrun by rabid marmosets –'

'– I'd know that my best chance of survival would be to dress as a giant tomato.'

'Um, no, that wouldn't do you any good. Most of them would just see you as a big juicy bluey-green prey item instead of a red one.' And into the expectant pause: 'Okay, I'm sketchy on the finer details, but knowing the enemy's weakness is the first step to defeating them, isn't it? According to any rabid-primates-on-the-rampage type films I've ever seen.'

'Right. So actually it is a *completely* useless fact, even in the event of marmoset world domination.'

'Pretty much.' Damian was looking at Helen. 'Would you like some rasps?'

Her head was spinning. 'What?'

'To make up for no breakfast?' He waved a hand at the cultivated corner of the garden. 'Wait here and I'll get you some.'

'Good idea,' said Hector. And as they stood watching him, Helen unwilling to take her eyes from him in case Rob was lurking somewhere among the overgrown vegetation, he went on: 'Last night... I've had a report from one of the Estate workers that there was a car parked up the track past Milton, which is just quarter of a mile or so from here if you cut through the wood... this was at half past eight, quarter to nine. He didn't, unfortunately, take the registration number. It's a popular place for dog walkers, so he didn't think anything of it. Dark blue Fiat.'

'So you think Rob parked it there and came through the wood? He's using a car to get about and the motor home is hidden away somewhere...? That would explain how he was able to follow me from the Mains without me noticing. He could have been staking out the Mains from the trees, with the car parked maybe up the road... And when he saw me leaving he ran back to it and followed me.'

'It's possible.' Hector shrugged. 'As far as the motor home line of enquiry goes, the CCTV outside the jeweller's didn't pick any up at the relevant time.'

'Oh... So you think Mr Findlay might have made a mistake?'

'There's a first time for everything, but I'd say it's more likely our man turned off before that point. Took a short cut up to the main road.'

'Which would suggest he knows the town.'

'Maybe.' He pulled seeds off a high stem of grass. 'And I'd a call this morning from Shona Robertson. Shona Morrison as was. She and her husband Brian were on the back road to Logie Coldstone a couple of nights ago, and met a tractor, and Brian had to reverse for "miles" because a motor home and, interestingly, a car were parked in the passing place at the corner in Habbie's Wood. When they came back past it, Shona made Brian stop, and got out to remonstrate. No one in the car. There were lights on inside the motor home, but the curtains were drawn and no one answered her shouts. Well, you wouldn't, would you? She thinks it could have been a Swift like the ones in the flier.'

Helen grimaced. 'Shona...'

'Mm.' He let the grass seeds fall from his hand. 'But I talked to John Donaldson this morning – at Balnamoon, just down from the wood. He remembers seeing a motor home there, on Wednesday night, although not a car.'

'Could Shona describe the car?'

'"Dark".'

Helen took a breath. 'You have to go to the police and tell them all this.'

'Well, yes, that's the plan. In fact, Campbell Stewart wants to "have a word" with us both later. I said we'd meet him at the Estate Office at three.'

'Has something happened? Has Peter Laing – has he told them who Moir really is?'

'I imagine you'd have heard directly if that were the case. No, I think it's "a word" in the sense of a bollocking. Seems Mr Findlay has been on at the local boys, complaining about ordinary citizens – that's us – having to take up the slack where the police force leave off.'

'Oh.'

'Bit of a red rag to a bull. Poor old Campbell.'

The birds sang. A bee floated past her face. Across the garden, the sun was bright on Damian's hair as he reached a hand into the raspberry bushes, then swung round and stretched across to another red clump. There was an easy grace to all his movements, as there was to Hector's; an obvious inborn athleticism.

'What have you told Damian, about yesterday? About... trying to find Rob... About those men... The poachers...'

'I've rather been putting off that conversation – but I'll fill him in before we go. He'd only get it out of Chris eventually anyway.'

'Chris?'

'Mm. The Spanish Inquisition could learn a thing or two from my little brother.'

53

The Estate Office had originally been a Victorian villa, and in the lobby there were still things like a gothic fireplace with a mottled red marble mantelpiece, and next to it a curved brass and ebony handle for summoning servants. But above the mantelpiece, instead of an ornately framed mirror or a stag at bay, there was a map of the Estate. She used to stand on her toes to try and read the names of the farms. They were all marked on it, even the ones that were just ruins now like Altmore.

Set into the opposite wall was a sliding window through to the office where Mrs Gordon used to work, with a little bell beside it to ring if she didn't see you – which she always used to pretend she didn't.

The woman sitting in there now was presumably Gillian Webster, solidly built and cheery, chattering away to a man standing by her desk.

DCI Stewart.

Hector opened the door next to the window and said, 'Campbell – punctual as ever – please come up.'

Hector's office was the one his father had had, upstairs, with a view through the branches of a sycamore to a tattie field and, over to the right, the back of Miss Duff's garden. It was hot, sun streaming in across the faded Persian carpet. Hector went to each of the two windows in turn and flung up their lower sashes, letting cool air drift in.

The old Laird had had the desk positioned facing in to the room, but Hector had it facing a window. There was a PC on it, and on a table in the corner a printer. And in front of the fireplace was a coffee table with a comfy sofa and chairs round it. There were more maps on the walls, and above the filing cabinets a group of framed photographs – mainly of estate workers, but the one she wanted to go over and peer at was of the old Laird, in this room, leaning back against the desk and smiling at the camera in that way he'd had, as if he found life and everything about it faintly ludicrous. Behind him, in the process of clambering from the desk chair onto the desk itself, was a blurred blond toddler, one fat little hand clutching something that might have been a soft elephant. He was looking up at whoever was taking the picture with a wide conspiratorial smile. Was he about to launch himself at his father?

Who'd been behind the camera? Irina? Hector?

Hector. It'd hardly be here on the wall if Irina had taken it.

Lorna had been right: it was as if she'd never existed. The only evidence to the contrary was Damian himself. It had been pure Irina, the way he'd said, as they'd left, 'Have fun,' lightly, but with such a black look at Hector... Irina's death ray, Suzanne used to call it. And: 'We will,' had been Hector's breezy response.

'Take a seat,' he invited DCI Stewart now.

Stewart chose one of the chairs, took a folded piece of paper from his pocket, opened it out and set it on the coffee table. It was one of the fliers. Moir's smiling face looked up at them.

Hector waited until Helen had taken the other chair before sitting down himself on the sofa.

'I've just come from talking to James Findlay,' said DCI Stewart.

'Yes, I was about to call you about that, in fact, when you phoned this morning.' Hector leant back. 'So what do you think? Could it be your man?'

'This stops. *Now.*'

'Of course.' Hector smiled. 'I'm sorry for any embarrassment caused. It certainly wasn't my intention to suggest that the local police force was in any way... apathetic. I can personally attest to that not being the case.'

DCI Stewart suddenly leant forward. 'Hector, if this man in Findlay's yesterday turns out to be some perfectly innocent person – and chances are, he *will* – and you've been going round suggesting he's a *stalker*, you may be laying yourself open to legal action.'

'Uh huh. You know, the great thing about being a private individual is that you're not obliged to follow the cover-your-arse guidelines you "public servants" invariably work to.'

DCI Stewart's face was going red. 'It's not a question of "covering your arse"! It's a question of not slandering an innocent man!'

Helen might as well not have been there, for all the attention either of them was paying her. She said, 'He bought a knife.'

DCI Stewart blinked at her.

'The man in Findlay's. He bought a knife.'

'It's a hardware shop.' He sighed.

'And last night someone scratched "Liar" on my rear wind-screen. Rob – he obviously wants me to say I was lying about him killing Suzanne. First the email Mr Beattie supposedly received, and now this.'

'Helen. You have no evidence whatsoever, first of all that Moir Sandison is Rob Beattie, and second that he's within a hundred miles of here. Anyone could have vandalised your car. Anyone could have sent that email.'

He turned to Hector, like a headmaster, having dealt with one miscreant, tackling the next. 'Even professionally planned and executed appeals of this kind throw up far more false sightings than genuine ones. In fact, it very often turns out that *none* of the supposed sightings are genuine.' He set a hand on the flier, fingers splayed over Moir's face. 'This kind of amateur nonsense only serves to muddy the waters. I don't want to see any more of these in circulation. Although if anyone does contact you with information, obviously, you tell them to call us.'

'Obviously. In fact...' He told DCI Stewart about the car parked near Milton the night before, and the motor home at Habbie's Wood a couple of days ago, and DCI Stewart took down the estate worker's name and address, and Shona's, and the farmer's.

Then he set down his pen. 'Now.' He looked at Helen, almost warily. 'Peter Laing has had a bit of a story to tell about Sandison. Whether it's true or not, of course, is another matter.'

'He's Rob Beattie.' Helen's mouth was suddenly dry. 'I know that.'

'We still don't know who he is. Laing claims not to know him-self.'

The Gillian woman bustled in with a tray, which she set down on the coffee table with a smile for Hector. There was a pot of tea, and cups and saucers, milk and sugar, and a plate of little rock cakes that looked homemade.

When she'd gone, Helen asked: 'What *has* he said?'

'He claims they encountered one another in Glasgow a year ago, when he helped Sandison out with another scam. All he's admitting to as regards their latest venture is that he agreed to supply references and pose as Sandison's old headmaster if need be. He claims neither knew the other's real identity. That he was only peripherally involved, and knew none of the details of the actual scam.' He pushed a hand into his suit jacket pocket.

Hector was pouring the tea.

'Do you think that's true?' Helen said.

'Who knows?' DCI Stewart produced a photograph, then two more, which he placed on the table between the tray and the flier. 'He's been charged with conspiracy to commit fraud; these are the mug shots that were taken when he was being processed. He looks a bit different now from the photos in the database.'

He looked older: doddery and benign.

'Goodbye Mr Chips,' murmured Hector, handing Helen a cup and saucer.

Helen quickly repressed a smile – but not quite quickly enough, judging by the way DCI Stewart was looking at her.

'You still don't recognise him?'

'No.'

Hector lifted the plate of rock cakes. 'What else has he to say about Sandison?'

'He claims that, for the duration of the scam in Glasgow, Sandison was going by the name James Johnstone.' DCI Stewart shook his head impatiently at the plate. 'The target on that occasion was a woman called Lisa Greig. Name ring a bell?'

Helen set her cup and saucer down. 'No.'

'I think only the Glasgow papers carried the story. Last year, after the Fatal Accident Inquiry into her death.'

'Oh God – he *killed* her?'

'No. No no. The Sheriff in charge of the Inquiry found there was insufficient evidence to indicate whether the death was accident or suicide, but there was never any suggestion of foul play. Her body was found in the Clyde. Tangled up in river detritus under the Tradeston Bridge. Whether she'd fallen into the river while under the influence or jumped, the Procurator Fiscal was unable to determine, but the death wasn't suspicious. There were no pre-mortem injuries or defensive marks on the body. She simply drowned. What came out in the Inquiry was that she was in a very fragile state of mind – had been for some time. Very high levels of alcohol were found in her bloodstream.' He paused. 'Witnesses said that she'd moved in with a boyfriend – "James Johnstone" – and then split up with him at around the same time that the investments she'd made with the proceeds of her flat sale went bad, leaving her with no money to buy another place. She'd moved back in with her parents shortly before her death. The police never did locate Mr Johnstone. Her friends thought he may have gone abroad.'

'It's the same,' said Helen. 'The same as he did to me.'

'Laing's version of events suggests that may have been the case.'

Another photograph appeared on the coffee table. And this time she did recognise the face in it: a woman in trendy glasses, a mane of dark hair falling to either side of her face.

'It's Bec. Rebecca. That's what he told me. He told me she was his sister. Oh *God*. This is her? This is Lisa Greig?'

'He said she was his sister?'

'He showed me a photo of her, the two of them together – and there was one of them as children, at least that's what he said it was – with their parents... Did Lisa Greig have a younger brother?'

'I don't know –'

'He did the same to her. He took everything. Her photos, everything... He got her to sell her flat and took the money... There were no *investments* that went bad, were there? That was just what she told her family. She couldn't bear to tell them what had really happened. What an idiot she'd been.' Just like Helen still hadn't told Mum and Lionel. 'Can you tell me about her?'

'She was a solicitor. Lived in the West End of Glasgow – beautiful penthouse flat, roof terrace, the whole shebang. But James Johnstone persuaded her to sell up and move in with him. Laing claims he became involved through a mutual acquaintance. "Johnstone" needed someone to play the role of his father – Lisa had been pressuring him, wanting to meet his family –'

'She killed herself because of what he did to her.'

DCI Stewart sighed. 'We don't know that for sure. This is only Laing's story.'

'But it all fits.'

He picked up the pen. 'I'd like to take yet another statement, if I could, about these photographs of his "sister". And the vandalism to your car.'

When they'd finished, and he was getting to his feet, she said: 'Have they asked Peter Laing about Rob Beattie? Whether he ever came across the name in connection with Moir? Whether he knows if Moir might be dyslexic?'

'I don't know, but I'll ask them to do so, if they haven't already.'

'Have you told the graphology expert about the dyslexia?'

'I will,' he said. 'First thing on Monday morning.'

Of course – it was Saturday.

When he'd gone, Hector spooned sugar into her tea and made her drink it. She drew the line at a rock cake.

'She didn't want to live. Lisa Greig. After what he did to her.' After her whole world fell apart. And then she was telling him, of all people: 'Sometimes he used to hurt me.' She set down her cup and stood. 'And he used to enjoy watching human interest documentaries, you know, about people who'd been burned and had to have skin grafts, that kind of thing – People suffering.'

His eyes were the softest of dark browns. Soft with pity, or sympathy, or –

She couldn't stop her mouth wobbling, but presumably he'd ascribe that to Moir. She closed her eyes, and felt his arms around her.

'It's all right.'

She pulled away; lifted her face to look at him. He smiled down at her. She moved her hands on his shoulders –

And under her right hand, she felt a muscle contract.

The pit of her stomach responded.

And then he stepped back, putting her gently away from him, holding her by the arms and saying, 'He's not going to hurt you again.'

'I know. Thank you – thank you, for helping me.'

What had just happened? Had he been shrinking from her touch, or responding to it? Or just moving his shoulder? She didn't want him to let go her arms, but he did. He started to turn away to the window. To keep him where he was she said, 'It's Rob. I know it's Rob. It has to be. There are too many things that are the same. The – the cruelty –'

'Rob Beattie never had a monopoly on that.'

She shook her head. 'But things like the cough... *Smellie Nellie* –' And most of all the email to his father and the word LIAR scratched on Stan last night, revealing that he knew she'd lied about the attack – that she didn't actually remember it. But she couldn't tell Hector that.

'Conmen always research their victims' backgrounds. After you saw him in the salon, you confronted him because you thought he was Rob – of course he'd then have gone off and found out all about Rob, you, Suzanne... There's a lot of information, presumably, out there in the public domain. Even trivial things like the way Rob used to cough – all that's probably out there.'

'But it was the cough that drew my attention in the first place, in the salon – and that was *before he'd even met me*. He couldn't have been researching my background *before he'd even met me*. So he *has* to be Rob.'

'There are other possibilities.' He took two paces back, and perched on the desk.

He was putting space between them. Was he? Did that mean he felt something, but didn't think it was a good idea to pursue it given all the trauma she was going through at the moment? Or had he been removing himself from her touch, and was withdrawing himself now from her reach, because he didn't want to give the poor little nymphomaniac bunny-boiler the wrong idea?

'Damian may be right about the whole thing having been engineered,' he was saying. 'But that doesn't necessarily mean that he's Rob.'

Her bare arms were cold. She rubbed them. 'A conman who just happens to look like Rob Beattie decides to target me in a scam – and to freak me out by planting little hints that he *is* Rob – Is that what you're saying? That's ridiculous! If he did manipulate me into spotting him in the salon, and finding out his address, and going after him – that only makes sense if he really is Rob.'

'His fascination with TV programmes about people suffering – I imagine that probably extended to a fascination with true crime. Let's assume for the sake of argument that Moir Sandison isn't Rob – don't you think he'd have *known* about Rob, and his own resemblance to him? There've been two books written about Suzanne and Rob's disappearance, and doubtless plenty of articles;

plenty of stuff on the internet. Maybe he became obsessed with Rob. It wouldn't have been hard to track down the Helen Clack involved – half an hour on Google would have done it. Your name was on the museum website, presumably? All he'd need to do would be follow you home from work.'

'But was it in those books that he used to call me *Smellie Nellie*? The way he used to cough?'

'Possibly not. But he could have done his own digging – rung people up pretending to be a journalist, wanting details about Rob's childhood.'

'Have you read them? The books?'

'Oh, years ago.' He stood. 'One of them concentrated on the Beattie family, as I recall – its thesis seemed to be that Rob was the way he was because of his upbringing. Son of the manse kicking against the traces. Weak father, overindulgent mother. The other – well, the other painted Suzanne as the ultimate wild child.'

'What, you mean, as if it was *Suzanne's fault*?'

'No. The authors took the view that it was her wildness that made her vulnerable.' He went past her to the coffee table and started putting things onto the tray. 'The police may well get more out of Laing yet. They've already got a whole new line of inquiry in the Lisa Greig thing – that could bear fruit.'

'Yes.'

'Who knows, he may have left a trail as "James Johnstone" that'll lead them to his real identity.'

'So you don't think he's Rob.'

'No,' he said. 'I don't.'

54

There was rain coming, in a grey bank of cloud darkening the sky from the west. Watching the car approaching down the drive, Helen buttoned her cardigan and agreed with Damian that yes, maybe lighting the fire would be a good idea.

So here she was: standing on the doorstep at the House, with Hector so close that the wool of her cardigan sometimes brushed the sleeve of his shirt. Ready to welcome their guests.

'I take it yesterday's little escapade didn't happen?' said Damian. He was lounging back against the dressed stone of the doorway, casually gorgeous in dark khaki chinos and a thin navy jersey that had to be cashmere, pale shirt collar just visible at the neck.

Hector altered his stance, putting cold air between his arm and Helen's. Deliberately? 'I don't want to get into this again now.'

'Neither do I.'

'There's no point telling any of them about it.'

'Well, no. It would only *upset* them, wouldn't it?'

Hector glanced across Helen at Damian, and away again.

A little silence developed, and then Damian said, the edge gone from his voice: 'Steve would go mental.'

Hector smiled.

Almost before the car had stopped Fiona was out of it, tottering across the gravel in elegant strappy sandals and a floaty dress with a wrap over it, wailing that she was *frozen* and wasn't it *Arctic* all of a sudden, and she hoped they'd lit a fire.

'There's no such thing as bad weather,' Hector said as she reached up a hand to his shoulder and he bent to kiss her cheek.

'Only inappropriate clothing. I know.' Fiona broke away from him, almost before their kisses had connected, to squeeze Helen, and give her a bright smile, before turning to Damian and saying, '*Is* the fire lit?', and grabbing him for a hug and a kiss.

'Very nearly.'

Then Fish and Steve were there, and Steve had his arms round Helen, a big bear of a man in a rugby shirt, telling her he was sorry to have missed her the other day, and he was sorry about all her troubles; and everyone was talking at once and then Norrie appeared from somewhere, and Helen was being kissed again, awkwardly, and asked if she was all right.

She'd forgotten how small Norrie was. Small and a bit ferrety about the face. He was fingering his tie and not looking at her; shooting looks at Steve, as if worried he'd overdressed for the occasion.

'I'm sorry I –' She felt herself flushing. She could hardly say she was sorry for not keeping in touch. The last thing he'd want was to be reminded of her rejection of him, all those years ago in Edinburgh. Oh God. Was this how Hector felt about *her*? 'I hear congratulations are in order. You have a little girl?'

'Aye.' And he started talking about the baby – her name was Annabel but they called her Beryl the Peril – and the awkwardness fell away. Norrie. How strange it was, to be talking to Norrie, to be moving at his side through the hall after the others, as if all the years of her absence had never been. As if, if she turned quickly enough, she might see Suzanne, scooting off down the passage; hear Irina calling after her: '*Suzanne!*'

Steve was handing one of the fliers to Hector. 'These are all round town. What the *hell*?'

'Make yourselves comfortable and we'll fill you in. Who wants what to drink?' And to Damian: 'Are there nuts or something?'

Fiona was holding her hands to the first fierce flames of the fire. 'I've been hearing all sorts of things from patients.'

Steve plonked himself down on one of the sofas. 'So what's the story?'

She let Hector tell it – or rather an edited version of it, in which the flier was nothing more than an attempt to 'gather information'. When he got to the bit about LIAR being scratched on Helen's car, everyone was suddenly talking at once, and Fiona was sitting at Helen's side with an arm round her and interrogating Hector about what he was doing to keep Helen safe, and Fish was raising his voice over everyone, asking questions; and then they were quiet as Hector told them what DCI Stewart had said, and the new information about Lisa Greig.

'Christ's sake!' said Norrie. 'So what are they doing about it? What are the police doing?'

'Bugger all,' said Hector.

Helen sighed. 'They're doing all the usual things. At least they now know he was calling himself James Johnstone at one point, when he scammed Lisa Greig.'

'Tracing someone like that – it's not easy,' said Fish. 'They shed their identities like skins.'

'But I'm sure they'll catch him.' Fiona squeezed Helen. 'In the meantime... You have to make sure you don't go anywhere alone, you have to –'

And then Norrie was on his feet, his face red, and saying, '*We* have to *do something*,' and Steve was telling him to sit down and have a drink, and Norrie sat, but kept on: 'If he's driving a motor home, how hard can it be to find him?'

Hector set a bowl of crisps on the ottoman. 'Problem is, the place is crawling with walkers just now, climbers, canoeists, Druids, you name it. One more nutter in a motor home isn't going to attract undue attention.'

'There's plenty of us would help look.'

'That's a job for the police.' Hector sat down in an armchair and stretched his legs across the rug. His mouth quirked as he looked over at Helen, at Damian, then down into his whisky.

Damian widened his eyes at her, as if to say *What can you do?*

'Aye,' said Norrie. 'But – God almighty. He's out there somewhere –'

'Mm,' said Fish. 'But as Hector says, going after this character has to be left to the police. He could be dangerous –'

'Of course he's *dangerous*. He's a bloody *psychopath*.' Norrie blinked at her. 'You really think he could be Rob?'

She nodded. 'But – I'd like to hear what you all think.'

And so they looked at the photographs of Moir. Hector had found some old ones featuring Rob, and they spent a tense five minutes contrasting and comparing. Were the eyes different colours, or was it just the light? Moir's hair had a kink in it and Rob's hadn't, but Moir wore his hair longer – if Rob had let his grow, maybe it would have curled a little. The chins were very similar, but were they the same? Norrie thought he could be Rob; Steve and Fiona weren't convinced; Hector and Fish thought there was no way. For one thing, Fish couldn't believe that plastic surgery could so radically change a person's nose; Fiona started on about all the amazing work that was possible now, on the faces of people who'd been in accidents or who had congenital deformities –

'Yes, all right,' said Fish. 'But what about this?' He tapped the photocopy with the writing on it. 'It doesn't match the sample of Rob's handwriting the Beatties supplied.'

'Who knows what they supplied, though,' said Helen. 'And the graphologist wasn't told about Rob having dyslexia.'

She wished she could tell them why she knew Moir *had* to be Rob. But she couldn't admit to them that the email to Mr Beattie had been right; that she really was a liar.

Fiona was still sitting close. 'I've done a bit of research, and it seems that people with dyslexia *are* more prone to changes in their handwriting.'

'Well, DCI Stewart is going to mention the dyslexia to the expert.'

'The only way of knowing for sure, of course, is a DNA test,' said Fish. 'They didn't get any DNA from the flat in Edinburgh? Did they do any forensics – look for hairs in the plughole, that kind of thing?'

Behind them, rain skittered suddenly against the windows.

'No,' she said. 'Because they don't believe he can possibly be Rob. They only had the writing checked, I think, to get me off their backs. There was no way they were going to do a CSI job on the flat. Although there probably wouldn't be any point anyway. He had the place professionally cleaned, apparently, before he left.'

'Because he didn't want anyone finding his DNA,' said Norrie. 'So he *is* Rob.'

'No,' said Hector. 'Not necessarily. It could be that he wants Helen to *think* he is. He wants her to *think* he had to have the flat blitzed to obliterate his DNA.'

'But why would he want her to think that?'

'Because he's a sick bastard.' Hector glanced at her, just briefly, but with such concern –

She shouldn't be enjoying this. She shouldn't be basking in his attention, in the attention of all of them, in this wonderful feeling of being back in their world, of being protected and worried about and fussed over.

Smellie Nellie and her ridiculous problems.

She frowned; tried to focus. 'But if he *is* Rob... He wouldn't want to leave any actual *proof* that he is, DNA or anything, but he'd get a kick out of letting me know who he was in other ways... unprovable ways... like writing "Smellie Nellie" on the photo. Like his cough. Like banging on the toilet door. Like, when I first met him, standing in front of me so I couldn't get past... remember at school, Rob used to ambush me at the gates and not let me past?' She'd been looking, she realised, all the time she'd been speaking, at Hector.

Steve grunted. 'Why didn't anyone ever take the little shit in hand? If it'd been nipped in the bud by his parents...'

'Mm.' Hector swirled the whisky in his glass, first one way, then the other. 'They'll probably be saying the same about Ruth in twenty years' time.'

Fish grinned.

Fiona said, 'If his dyslexia had been diagnosed early enough, things might have been different.'

'Plenty of people have dyslexia,' said Norrie, 'and don't become psychopaths.'

'No, but if a person has issues anyway, the dyslexia on top of those could be enough to push them over the edge.'

'Bollocks,' said Hector. 'There was something fundamentally wrong with him. Something –'

'Evil?' suggested Steve. 'Original sin, and all that?'

'I was going to say, something in the structure of his brain. It was as if he was wired up to take pleasure in things a normal person would find abhorrent. As if his wires had been pulled out and crossed over.'

'A well-known medical phenomenon,' said Steve.

'I don't know that Rob Beattie was necessarily a *psychopath*,' said Fish.

'What was he then?' said Norrie. 'Misunderstood?'

'Well,' said a brittle voice from the door, 'that's dinner ready, Mr Forbes.'

Hector stood. 'Thank you, Mrs MacIver. It smells wonderful.'

She didn't crack a smile. 'If we could have some help to carry it up. And I've said Charlene can go once we've served the main course.'

'Yes, of course. And you can finish up too, if you like. We'll load the dishwasher and tidy up.'

'The silver and the good plates and glasses dinna go in the dishwasher.'

'Come on, Mrs Mac,' said Damian. 'Where's your sense of adventure?'

'I'll give you a sense of adventure,' was the response, 'if I find anything in that dishwasher in the morning that shouldna be.'

When she'd gone, Hector said, 'Shall we shelve all this until after dinner?'

'Yes,' said Fiona at once. 'I'm sorry, Helen – you must just say when you want us to shut up. When it's getting too much.'

'It's fine. I'm really grateful, to you all, for – well. Wanting to help. But, yes, let's talk about something other than me me me and my problems.' As they moved into the hall, she asked Damian, 'Can I help carry things up?'

'Got it covered,' Fish spoke over his shoulder, following Hector down the hall.

The table in the dining room was set with a snowy white damask tablecloth and gleaming silver: three sets of candelabra marching down the middle, and an array of silver cutlery at each place; and a forest of glasses in which each of the candle flames was multiplied, over and over.

On the massive Victorian sideboard was a selection of bottles of wine and soft drinks, and a big glass jug of iced water. Steve inspected the wine while Damian hefted the jug. 'Everyone want water?'

Rain was streaming down the panes of the long Georgian windows. Fiona went straight to the fireplace, struck a long match and held it to the paper under the pyramid of sticks and pine cones.

The room was so familiar – the huge table, the dark Victorian furniture, the picture over the sideboard of some long-dead, pantalooned, serious-faced Forbes children with a thin dog in an Italianate landscape – and yet different. There wasn't that heavy smell of boiled meat and damp. The wallpaper wasn't coming away in the corner above the little cupboard. The gilded frame around the mirror above the mantelpiece had been repaired.

As she took a chair next to Norrie in front of the windows, she realised that this was the first time she'd ever actually sat down at this table.

Hector came in just then with a tray, and behind him a pretty, curly-haired bap of a girl – Charlene, presumably – and behind her, Fish. They set the trays down on the sideboard and Charlene and Fish distributed the plates – a nest of salad leaves with smoked salmon, mussels and prawns – while Hector went round with the wine.

'This looks edible,' said Fish, when Charlene had gone.

Hector, taking his place at the head of the table, examined his plate. 'So it does.' He looked down the table; flicked a glance to the windows; shifted slightly in his chair, picked up a platter of brown bread and offered it to Helen with a smile that didn't reach the odd, intense expression in his eyes.

She took a piece of bread. He used to get restless like this at school, she remembered, like a wild creature eager for its freedom – but that had been a happy, anticipatory sort of restlessness, while this was –

What?

She wasn't imagining it, was she? The tension in the air between them?

Fish speared a prawn and chewed. 'Definitely acceptable.'

'Hector's new strategy,' said Damian, passing Helen a blue dish of butter, 'is to request a menu that consists of strictly separate elements. So, for the main course – sole fillets, new potatoes and broccoli. His reasoning is that turning that into brown sludge will be beyond even Mrs Mac's powers – but as I pointed out, we know it *will* end up as brown sludge, so the closer the request is to the finished product, the less we have to worry about in terms of what the hell happened.'

Steve grinned. 'So taking that argument to its logical conclusion...'

'Soup,' said Hector. 'Damian's strategy is to ask for soup.'

'Which she's actually not bad at,' said Damian. And as his brother raised his eyebrows: 'Not *too* bad.'

When the main course did arrive, presided over, this time, by Mrs MacIver herself, it came in a large shallow dish with a lid. Hector set it in the place of honour in front of him, and Damian lifted the lid.

Various shapes lay concealed under a thick, glutinous brown gravy.

'Ah...' said Hector. 'Sole fillets...?'

Fish found the hallmarks on the napkin ring by his plate of sudden interest. Norrie noticed something out of the window, and Helen turned to look.

'The potatoes and broccoli are in there too, are they?' said Damian.

'Aye.'

'Keeps everything hot,' said Hector, 'having it all together.'

Damian began to cough.

Hector said over him: 'Thank you, both of you, for all your work tonight. We'll manage from here.'

As the door closed behind the women, one of Damian's coughs became a yelp, and Hector shooshed him, and that started everyone else off. Shouts of laughter hit the ceiling as Hector dipped the serving spoon into the sludge, and at last Helen was able to let the hysterics out.

55

Fiona, carrying the glass dish with the remains of the profiteroles, bumped the baize door open with her bottom and Helen, balancing a tray, walked through after her. She felt giddy. She'd had too much wine.

Fiona jabbed a finger at the lighted panel next to the lift doors.

'This is an innovation,' said Helen.

'Well, those kitchen stairs are a death trap. And it goes right up to the second floor too – up the middle of the stairwell.'

Norrie followed them into the lift with some empty bottles. It disgorged them into the big storeroom at the back of the kitchen, now fitted out with shelves on which were stacked enough tins and jars and packets to stock a shop, and a huge American fridge, and two chest freezers. There was a sink, too, and a dishwasher, standing open, and a table in the middle of the room.

Fiona dumped down the dish. 'If you think that's smart, come and see this.'

They were opening the back door, Fiona having keyed in the code to deactivate the alarm, when Norrie caught up with them. 'Hope you weren't thinking of going out there on your own.'

The rain had stopped. They crossed the slick courtyard, and walked out through the arched tunnel under the clock tower, and under a copse of dripping pine trees to the old laundry.

Helen remembered the laundry as being more or less a ruin. Now the roof was straight and the walls repaired and repointed in lime mortar. The rows of Georgian windows were painted a soft green. Fiona opened the big door at the end of the building and flicked on the lights.

They were in a passage, panelled in grey tongue-and-groove, with black-and-white photographs on the walls showing the laundry in Edwardian times, women in white aprons standing outside.

Fiona opened a door onto light and space, and air, and a faintly chemically smell. Stretching in front of them was a swimming pool, its gently moving surface bouncing the light to ripple along the walls and the rafters high above.

It was beautiful: very modern and sleek, the tiles round the sides a pale oat colour, the chrome handrails at the steps sparkling silver. Over the Georgian windows, translucent, Japanese-style blinds were pulled.

Fiona had gone to stand right on the edge, looking down into the water as if she might just jump in. Norrie had disappeared.

'The girls practically live here. Although where Cat's concerned, the pool's not the main attraction.' She stopped. 'Sorry. You don't want to hear about Cat's nonsense.'

'I do. Please tell me about Cat's nonsense.'

Fiona smiled, and said, too lightly: 'She's hopelessly in love with Damian.'

Helen stiffened. Did she know, then, after all?

Fiona stepped back from the edge. 'Blushes furiously whenever he speaks to her, and can hardly get out a reply. Damian of course is oblivious. "Have I done something to upset Cat?" he asked me the other day. Maybe I should tell him – Hector thinks we should – but I promised Cat *on pain of death* not to.'

Helen knew she herself was blushing furiously. 'If Cat doesn't want him to know, I don't think you should say anything.'

'Oh, I won't. And if she has to have a crush on anyone, I'm glad it's Damian. Isn't he a sweetheart?'

And for the rest of her life, Cat would measure every other man against him.

'He is. I don't know how Irina – I can't understand how she could have –'

'Oh God, I know, don't ask me.'

'She seemed such a doting mother.'

'Well. Yes. And Damian adored her. I used to think they couldn't be true, the stories we used to hear – the nanny they had after Suzanne was best friends with one of the nurses in the practice, and she used to regale us with – well. All sorts of stories.'

'Like what?'

'A lot of it was probably exaggerated. But – I was walking be-hind them once, Irina and Damian, when she'd just picked him up from school, and he was all excited, telling her he'd made her something, and he produced this bizarre – *thing* – from his bag, made out of papier-mâché I think. Brown and rather faecal-looking, with odd green excrescences sticking out of it. He said it was a tree for her to put her rings on – to put on her dressing table. And she hooted with laughter, and hugged him, and said, "Oh darling, I think *this* is the best place for it, don't you?" And she plucked it from his hand and dropped it into the bin outside the shoppie. I don't suppose she knew I was behind her. I could have slapped her.' Fiona coloured slightly as she said this, as if having a desire to inflict violence might be in breach of her Hippocratic Oath.

'The worst thing was the way Damian reacted. Or *didn't* react. He just took with it. Laughed. But when she went ahead of him into the shoppie he looked back at the bin, and the expression on his little face –'

'That's horrible.' She didn't want to hear any more. 'What's through there?' She pointed to a door next to the one they'd come through.

'Oh, changing rooms and showers and stuff.'

'This building isn't alarmed – or even locked?'

'Well, no. There's nothing to steal, is there?'

'But isn't it the kind of thing Rob would do? Let himself in and go for a swim, right under our noses?'

'And pee in the pool.'

They looked at each other. And before Helen could stop her Fiona had walked to the other door and flicked on a light just inside it.

A big, tiled space, with slatted shelves under high windows along one wall, and, opposite, three tiled shower cubicles, their curtains all pulled neatly to the same side.

She followed Fiona through a doorway, past a row of changing cubicles, to a final door which she pushed open to reveal a pristine toilet and sink.

'Well phew,' Fiona said, starting to laugh. 'No one hiding behind the curtains?'

The curtains of the cubicles were all pulled to one side like the shower curtains had been, and you'd have to be stick-thin to hide behind them, but Fiona batted each one with her hands, like a kid playing a game of hide and seek, and Helen felt a prickling of irritation.

Now nice it must be to be Fiona, to have the courage of someone to whom bad things just didn't happen; to live such a charmed existence that searching for a psychopath in a deserted building was just a bit of a lark, an after-dinner game, a Famous Five adventure to tell the kids about later.

In one of the cubicles a pair of crutches was propped in a corner.

Did that mean Damian couldn't even walk without crutches, when he wasn't wearing the artificial foot? She had imagined that he'd be able to use the stump of his ankle to balance on, if he bent the other leg a little bit. But maybe not.

And as they returned to the showers and Fiona repeated her curtain-batting exercise, Helen saw that the middle cubicle had bright yellow grab rails, two on each side, and the floor of the shower was different from the others: creamier, and textured. There was a large white plastic rectangle set into the tiles of one wall.

'Clear!' Fiona announced like an American cop, giving the end curtain a final pat.

Helen smiled perfunctorily.

Fiona must have seen where she was looking because she reached out a hand to the plastic rectangle and said, 'Now this is really nifty.' It was a seat. She showed Helen how it could be adjusted, pulled out from the wall and turned round and moved up and down. 'Sorry. I'm a bit of a gadget freak.'

A seat for Damian, because he couldn't stand properly.

Helen said, 'Damian likes swimming, then.'

'I think so, although he moans about Hector getting him out of bed to do it on winter mornings. It's good non-load-bearing exercise. Not that he doesn't get enough exercise otherwise – more than enough, in fact. He – well.' She smiled. 'Straying into doctor/patient confidentiality territory here.'

'You're his GP?'

'No, thank goodness. Steve is. Not that Damian's a difficult patient, really – it's Hector that's the problem, with his shelves of medical textbooks and online subscriptions to every relevant journal there is. And his tendency to check every little thing Steve says with his tame private consultant at the Royal London. And – well. You can imagine.'

'Yes.' Helen smiled.

'The pool was finished two months after Damian came home from hospital that first time – right on schedule for his first hydrotherapy session. His whole rehabilitation was run like a military campaign.'

'But – where did Hector get the money? For the pool, for everything – all the improvements on the Estate... Where has it come from?'

'He's really turned things round. With the holiday lets, and building up the sporting side –'

'So the money comes from the Estate?'

She lifted her shoulders.

'Fiona?'

'You know Hector. He plays his cards close to his chest.'

'DCI Stewart said an odd thing. When I asked what he had against Hector, he said, "Not quite enough." And that man Chris who works for him... It all just seems... He's not involved in anything actually *criminal*, is he?'

Fiona laughed. 'I did wonder why he bought up the entire stock of balaclavas at the last WRI sale of work.'

'No, but seriously... Hector's always been... a bit of a law unto himself, hasn't he?'

Fiona's eyes were suddenly bright with – what? Not anger? – as she turned away. 'Actually, I think Hector's probably the most moral person I know.' She was moving to the door. 'They should have finished in the kitchen by now, so hopefully that's us neatly avoided the wimmin's work. Where's Norrie got to?'

He was in the passage, looking at the old photographs.

'Raining again,' he said, and removed his jacket to act as an improvised umbrella for the three of them.

In the drawing room, there was a cafetière, a thermos and three remaining mugs on a tray on the ottoman. Coffee this late always kept her awake. But she didn't want to make a fuss and ask for something else.

She lifted the cafetière. 'Fiona? Norrie?'

Fiona shook her head. 'Not for me, thanks.'

'Your peculiar tastes have been catered for.' Hector took the thermos from the tray.

Helen was about to ask for some of whatever was in the thermos too, but as Hector poured the contents into one of the mugs she saw it was only hot water, and he was stirring it into something that was already in the mug – some sort of malted drink.

'I feel I should be offering you Fairy Liquid with this,' said Hector, handing Fiona the mug.

'I know – Cat says it *tastes* like dishwater too.'

Helen poured coffee for herself and Norrie, added milk, and sat down in her place on the chintz sofa. Fiona passed her a box of chocolates.

Fish said, 'Surely the most compelling argument against this guy being Rob, Helen, is that he'd never jeopardise his liberty by getting so close to you. I mean, why would he?'

Helen sighed. 'Rob always got a kick out of tormenting me. The night before Suzanne... Before she disappeared... before he attacked me... he even hinted what he was going to do. He came up Craig Dearg to find me and he told me this riddle. This stupid riddle.'

Fish raised his eyebrows encouragingly.

'*I am a garden of delights. I am a desert* – no, that's wrong – *I am a wasteland frozen. I am the dagger in the night. I am the sweetest poison. What am I?* And the answer was obviously *Rob Beattie*. He was talking about himself.'

'Really? Would anyone, even someone as narcissistic as Rob, describe themselves as a *garden of delights*?'

She was still holding the open box of chocolates in one hand, and the little menu card in the other. Bile rose in her throat at the thought of putting a chocolate in her mouth.

'Could the answer be *cruelty*?' suggested Norrie. 'Or maybe *sadism*? A garden of delights as far as he's concerned.'

Helen set the box and its card down on the little table next to her. 'Or *hatred*. I think he really must hate me.'

Damian said, 'Mm,' with an odd sort of grimace. He was sitting on the sofa opposite, an elbow resting on its arm, the light from a lamp highlighting the contours of his face.

Hector, straightening from throwing another log on the fire, looked round at him. 'Out with it, then.'

'Well.' The grimace became apologetic. She was beginning to know that look of his, but even so she wasn't prepared for: 'I was wondering if it could be the opposite. Could it be *love*?'

For a beat, two beats, no one said anything.

Then:

'But Rob didn't love me,' she got out. 'You mean – he was using love against me, as a sort of weapon…'

Everyone except Hector was looking blank.

And before she could get her mind properly in gear, she'd already blurted: 'So that fits too.'

Hector had gone to stand at one of the windows behind her, and she was glad she didn't have to see his face as she told them about the letters. 'I thought they were from Hector. But it was Rob. He made Suzanne write them, pretending to be Hector. And then that night on the Knock – they left me a note, from "Hector", asking me to meet him down at the vehicles. That's why I was on the stalkers' path. And Rob was lying in wait. To – rape me, I suppose. Suzanne must have tried to stop him, and – he killed her.'

'Jesus Christ,' said Norrie.

'Oh Helen,' said Fiona.

And Hector's voice: 'We don't know that Rob *forced* Suzanne to write the letters.'

'But he must have done. He must have been the one behind it all.' She didn't turn to look at him. 'That day at the party here, before we went up to the Knock, he was always there, butting in, making sure we didn't have the opportunity to talk too much.' She met Damian's gaze.

He said, 'And you think Moir Sandison, whoever he is, must have known about the letters, and have set out to repeat the process of –'

'Humiliation,' she said. 'Yes. It all fits.' She looked away from him, from them all, to the flames of the fire. 'With the riddle, he was telling me what he'd done, I think – telling me about the letters.' And that he knew what *she'd* done? 'Or not telling me, exactly – amusing himself at my expense. That's another reason why Moir has to be Rob. Otherwise, it's too much of a coincidence, isn't it? Two different sadists decide to pretend to be someone else, and make me fall in love with them, and then humiliate me, and – do things to hurt me.'

'Coincidences do happen more often than people think,' said Fish.

'Or Moir could have found out about the letters,' said Damian.

'How? No one knew about them. Apart from Mum, and Uncle

Jim and Auntie Ina. And Hector.'

'And the police,' said Hector.

'They kept it all confidential.'

'Supposedly.'

'You never told anyone else?' Fish was speaking to Hector, who came round from the window, at last, to sit down in the wingchair next to Fiona.

'No. But who's to say who Rob and Suzanne might not have told?'

'Have you ever all compared notes?' said Damian. 'On exactly what happened that night?'

Hector shook his head. 'What would be the point?'

'If Moir Sandison *is* Rob, maybe the reason he's been out to get Helen is that the accepted version of events isn't right. That email to Mr Beattie, accusing her of lying about Rob attacking her... "Liar" scratched on Stan...'

How did he know about the email?

But of course they must all know about it. She'd forgotten how efficient the bush telegraph was around here.

Fish's mouth was hanging open. '*Stan*?'

'Helen's car.'

She dug her nails into her palms. 'You think I did lie? You think it must all be my fault?'

'Blame the victim, eh?' Norrie's eyes, fixed on Damian, were cold. 'Two sides to everything? What a load of crap! How can any of this be *Helen's* fault?'

'That's not what he's saying,' said Hector, his eyes meeting Helen's.

Was it her fault? Had she started it all? Rob *must* have known what she'd done, all those years ago in the playground. He must have seen the laburnum seeds in his vomit – or more likely his mother or father had, and given him a row for eating them. Told him how dangerous they were. He could hardly tell them what he realised must have happened – that Helen had put poison in her own sandwich because she knew he'd take it from her.

It would have been quite a shock, the realisation that she could fight back. And that was why he'd pretended to be her friend.

Of course it was.

56

Norrie was on his feet. 'He *attacked* her and *killed* her cousin. It's like – blaming the Jews for the Holocaust! But you lot, you can't faddom it, can you, how folk can be victims and not able to do anything about it? That's not the way the world works for you. You get your leg smashed to buggery and the end of it cut off –'

'*Norrie*,' said Fiona.

'– and four months later you're back in the playground using your crutches as offensive weapons. Two bloody nebs and a summons to Mrs Mackay's room later, and you're back at the top of the Infant Class pecking order. That's just the way things work for you, but not for the rest of us. That's *not normal*.'

Three mouths had stiffened in objection; two had lifted in identical grins.

'Mrs Mackay would certainly agree with you,' said Hector.

Damian prompted: 'What was it she said?'

' "He seems to have anger issues." I think she'd been on a course.'

Norrie sat back down with a bump. 'Aye, and that's my point made for me. What do they put in your milk?'

Damian said, 'Helen – I'm sorry. I didn't mean to suggest that you were in any way to blame.'

She smiled at him. 'I know.'

That hellish playground; a traumatised little boy, swinging a mutilated limb between crutches; and instead of helping him, being kind to him, the other children closing in for the kill.

But Norrie was right: Damian Forbes wasn't Helen Clack.

'Maybe I am to blame.'

Hector leant back in his chair. 'How could you be?'

I lied about remembering being attacked. And when I was eight, I tried to poison him. She shrugged. 'Maybe if I'd done something

342

to get Suzanne away from him –'

Fiona puffed. 'Like what? She was infatuated.'

'I think she was scared. Deep down. She was scared of him.'

'No,' said Norrie. 'She should have been, but she wasn't. Or if she was – she got a buzz from it. Because that was the kind of quine she was. She got a buzz from things that were – twisted. Not that *you* could ever see it.' He turned to face her. 'A week or so before that night, we were all of us in the Forbes Arms, Rob and Suzanne and me and my brother, and some other folk – and Rob pulls me aside and says Suzanne will have sex with me for fifty pounds.'

Helen's stomach clenched.

'I didn't really want to. But I paid up, and she took me to the old laundry. Put a bittie tarpaulin over the pigeon shite, and a blanket...'

Complete silence.

'She said I was to think of it as a private school – a fee-paying school – and her the teacher.'

'My God,' said Fish.

Norrie looked at the carpet.

'She was a limmer,' Helen managed to say. 'I know that. I know she was – wild. Outrageously so, at times. But she could be so sweet.' She looked round the circle of dubious faces, and suddenly it was very important that she make them understand.

Fish said, 'She could, actually. She once came to school with this big marble her dad had given her – I can see it yet, white china with red swirls in it. But she wouldn't play it in a game to give us a chance of winning it. She just rolled it around the playground in some stupid girls' game. I followed like a feelie... And at lunchtime she slipped it into my hand and said I could keep it.'

This prompted other, less complimentary Suzanne stories: money disappearing from Fiona's bag at the Youth Fellowship; Suzanne being thrown off the bus for blowing smoke into an old woman's face; Suzanne sneaking in to the Kirkton Flower Show before the judging to pull petals off the dahlias.

'Of course Ina spoilt her rotten,' said Fiona. 'No control at all.'

Hector said, 'It seems Ina's dead.'

Fiona's eyes widened, and her mouth opened a little, like her brother's. She turned to Helen. 'But... When?'

'A few months ago. I only found out when I was clearing up in the kitchen. There was a letter from her solicitor.'

'Oh, your poor uncle.' Fiona pulled her wrap closer. And after a little silence: 'Did he have any contact with her, after she left?'

'I don't think so.'

Fiona sighed. 'What happened to Suzanne – it must have put a huge strain on their marriage. Although maybe there were cracks before then – maybe that would explain why Suzanne... Children from troubled marriages are statistically more likely to end up in dysfunctional relationships themselves.'

' "Dysfunctional" is putting it rather mildly, isn't it?' said Hector.

Fiona pursed her lips, as if she was trying, suddenly, not to smile. 'I just meant – I can't understand how she could have felt anything for Rob.'

'Love isn't *logical*,' Helen blurted.

'Of course it isn't,' Steve, unexpectedly, backed her up. 'There's nothing to say that the object of a person's affection is necessarily deserving of it.'

Fiona made a face. 'But *Rob Beattie...*'

'What I've always wondered,' said Steve, 'is whether he felt anything for Suzanne in return. Or was it all a sham?'

'Maybe it was,' said Fiona. 'Psychopaths can be extremely plausible. He had a lot of people well and truly fooled. Our parents, for a start. They thought he was a lovely boy. Always so polite.'

'Did a lot of good work for charity,' added her brother. 'Oh yes, the adults all thought he was wonderful. With the exception of your father.' He turned to Hector. 'He never liked him.'

'No, but then he was prejudiced against the Beatties generally. Felt obliged to attend church, for some reason, and spent the whole time inwardly fuming and fantasising about Christians and lions. If he saw either Mr or Mrs Beattie coming towards him in the street he'd always take evasive action – hide in a shop or something.'

'Have you heard about Mrs Beattie's theory?' Damian asked Helen. 'She thinks Hector, in a drug-crazed homicidal frenzy, attacked you, killed Rob and Suzanne and hid their bodies. And he terrorized you into concocting a story about Rob being the attacker. God knows what she'll have made of that email.'

'Yes, well,' said Steve. 'Mrs Beattie has some mental health issues.'

'It's better than EastEnders once she gets going. She –'

'Do you really think,' said Hector, 'that this is a topic Helen, or anyone, come to that, finds remotely amusing?'

'No – sorry.'

'I think it's time you were in bed.'

'But it's only ten o'clock!'

'Maybe if you hadn't drawn attention to yourself with that little piece of puerility, you could've stayed up a bit longer with the grown-ups.'

Damian stood smoothly. 'Looks like I'll be saying goodnight, then.'

Fiona got up to kiss him. 'Well, darling, sleep tight.'

He looked at Helen. 'I didn't mean – I hope you don't think –'

'I know. It's okay.' She wanted to jump up and hug him too. She looked at Hector. 'It's – The alarm system's activated, isn't it? There's no way he could get into the house?' And be lying in wait up there for Damian?

'Yes, it's activated,' said Hector. 'We're safe enough. And I've taken what other precautions I felt necessary.'

She didn't ask what those were. She didn't have to. If Hector said they were safe then they were safe.

When Damian had limped to the double doors, and closed them behind him, Steve said, 'All right, so what's the secret? We tell Cat and Ruth to go to bed, and an hour later they might start making a move.'

'Guests,' said Hector. 'Best behaviour – such as it is.'

'Oh God, no, that just makes ours worse,' said Fiona. 'Playing to the gallery.'

Steve looked across at Norrie. 'You've all these delights still ahead of you.'

Norrie was the first to leave, half an hour later, to walk home by the back path, and then Fiona couldn't find her bag, and Helen and Fish helped her look. Returning from a fruitless search of the dining room, Helen, pausing at the half-shut drawing room doors, heard Steve say, 'The banging on the toilet door – the *bells jingling*, for God's sake – all now seemingly substantiated by this "identification" of Mr Findlay's –'

'And how do you explain away the email to Mr Beattie?'

'She probably sent it herself. And scratched "Liar" on her own car.'

'Of course she didn't.'

'There's no "of course" about it. What she's been going through would be enough to unbalance anyone, let alone someone with Helen's history. She's obviously incredibly vulnerable. Having *you* back in her life is the last thing she needs. What is it with you? Why can't you ever just *leave well alone*?'

She wanted to fling open the doors and run at Steve and tell him to shut up, just *shut up* – what did he know about any of it? What did he know about what she needed?

And then Fish was coming in at the front door, waving the bag and grinning at Helen and saying, 'In the car all along' and 'I suppose I'd better tell Hector he can rearm the guided missiles or whatever he's got trained on the door' and she put a smile on her face, and they went back into the room together.

57

'Good morning.' Hector was in his shirt sleeves at the massive Aga, stirring something in an old pan. He was wearing lightweight stone-coloured trousers – the kind serious walkers wore – and a Tattersall shirt tucked in at his flat stomach.

'Good morning.'

Damian got up from the table. 'There's tea in the pot. Or coffee. Or juice. What would you like to eat? We can do porridge, eggs, bacon, sausages, tomato, um, fried bread –'

'I think I'll have some of this muesli, thanks.'

Hector tipped the contents of the pan onto a plate and handed it to Damian. Scrambled eggs. Damian sat back down at the table, pushing a sheet of paper to one side to make room for the plate. As he did so, he looked at Hector, who came over and picked up the paper.

'Got this last night.'

She took it from him. It was a print-out of another email:

Dear Hector

You know that I lied, don't you? That it wasn't Rob. That he didn't kill Suzanne. That the person responsible is someone else entirely.

Could I be any more of a pathetic loser? How many more lives am I going to ruin? I'm sorry. I'm so sorry about everything.

Love
Helen

'I've forwarded it to Stewart,' said Hector. 'For what that's worth. I don't imagine they'll have any more luck tracing it than they did the last one.'

She pushed the email away. The thought of him, of Rob, Moir, hunched over a keyboard chuckling as he typed those words –

Damian ground pepper over his eggs. 'It's definitely not possible that Rob *didn't* kill Suzanne?'

Helen reached for the carton of juice. 'Of course it's not.'

Damian's eyes on her were cool, considering. She looked down at her glass as she poured the juice, and he stood, and said to Hector, 'I'm going to get your laptop. See if I can trace the IP address.'

'Okay, go for it.'

As Damian headed for the stairs, Helen said, 'What if the email Mr Beattie supposedly got – what if he sent it to himself? And sent you this? Or maybe Mrs Beattie did... What if they're in collusion with him? With Rob?'

Hector sat down on the chair at the end of the table, almost as if he was settling down to hear her line of defence. Almost as if he might believe that Helen was responsible for the emails.

She breathed. 'If you were Rob – right after it happened – after you'd killed her – you'd need help, wouldn't you? To disappear. You'd need money. He had a savings account with a building society, but the police said he never tried to withdraw what was in it. The building society would have been alerted to look out for him, I suppose – it would've been too risky for him to try to withdraw his money.'

He nodded. Thank God, he nodded.

She took a swallow of juice. 'Don't you think he'd have gone to his mother? She would've helped him. No matter what he'd done.'

'But her behaviour argues against that theory.'

A clatter on the stairs announced Damian's return as he half-hopped, half-jumped down the last two steps, swinging from the hand rails as if from a piece of gymnastic apparatus. 'Where the hell *is* your laptop?'

'Oh – it's in my room. Sorry. I'll get –'

But Damian was already jumping back up the stairs.

'– it,' Hector finished, smiling as he met Helen's eyes.

So she ventured: 'He copes very well, doesn't he, with – everything.'

The smile widened. 'Yes, and this is where we hear *thud thud thud* from the stairs.'

Thus far, and no further.

He reached across the table for Damian's plate. 'If Rob did go to his family for help, why has Mrs Beattie been insisting he's innocent so vocally all these years? If she knew him to be guilty – if she was secretly sending him money, helping him with his new identity, whatever – wouldn't it make sense for her to keep her mouth shut rather than draw attention?'

'But the two things aren't incompatible, are they? She could have been helping him, *and* believe he's innocent.'

He shrugged, dipping a fork into the eggs. 'It's possible.'

'I'd like to go and see the Beatties. And check on Uncle Jim.'

He glanced at his watch. 'If you really think it'll do any good, we could ambush the Beatties after church.'

'You don't have to come with me.'

'Wouldn't miss it for the world.'

Hector pulled in at the end of the line of cars stretching from the kirk almost to the manse gates. 'Should be finished in five minutes, if he's running true to form.'

The clock on the dashboard said 12:25. The service always used to finish at 12:30 sharp, unless there was a christening. Mum had always suspected that this was because Mr Beattie got his sermons from a book – God by the yard, she used to call it.

She opened her door and got out. From here, you could just see the grey slate roof of the manse amongst the trees. All along the top of the high garden wall was glass, cemented in place, cruel jagged triangles of it to repel invaders. When she was a little girl she used to hope that Robin Beattie might climb up on his own garden wall, miss his footing, and fall so that his neck landed on a shard of glass, severing an artery.

'So what's the plan?' said Damian, as they headed back up the line of cars towards the kirk.

He'd had no luck tracing the source of the email sent to Hector. The IP address was for a mobile phone, and the chances were that the phone would turn out to be an unregistered pay-as-you-go, but Hector had sent the details to DCI Stewart in the hope that the police might be able to turn something up.

'I suppose we wait for the service to finish and people to disperse...' She shrugged.

'No chance of that, once they've seen you and realised that for once there's going to be a performance worth coming to church for.' Damian shot a smile at her over his shoulder. 'It'll be pass the popcorn and quiet in the cheap seats. Although with Mrs Beattie's powers of projection –'

'So we'll make ourselves inconspicuous until people have left,' said Hector. 'If you can manage that for ten minutes.'

'I can give it a go.'

As they approached the little gate a car passed, a bit too fast considering there were vehicles parked on each side of the road and no pavement at this point, and Hector's hand went suddenly forward to Damian's arm, before dropping back without actually touching him.

It was instinctive, for Hector, this compulsion to protect.

But when was the last time anyone had reached for *him* like that? He'd always been the one everyone came to with their problems and woes and insecurities – but what about *his* problems? *His* woes? *His* insecurities?

He couldn't let himself have any, because he had no one to take them to.

She wished –

She wished she could be that person? But how could she wish herself on him, when she didn't even have the guts to tell him the truth about what she'd done? How could he ever trust her?

From the kirk the muffled strains of *All Things Bright and Beautiful* were drifting through the graveyard. At the top of the steps Hector said, 'I hope you're ready for some fireworks.'

'Fireworks is what we want, isn't it? We want her blurting things out without thinking. We don't want a measured response.'

'In that case, I think I can safely say you'll get your wish.'

They sat on one of the table graves at the back of the kirkyard to wait for the end of the service. Not the one she and Hector had sat on long ago – this one was plain, with only the inscription and some curlicues – no emblems of mortality. No angels, no scythes, no hour glasses with the sands of time run out.

Damian leant over the stone to pick at the lichen. 'This is the kind of place, isn't it, where you *might* get jumped by a psychopath?'

'Yes, thanks for that,' said Helen.

A blackbird flapped up from behind one of the gravestones.

Damian straightened, flicked away the bits of lichen, and took his handkerchief from his pocket. 'Did Rob Beattie torture animals? That's meant to be a sign of a proto-psychopath, isn't it?'

'He certainly used to torment that poor mutt they had,' said Hector. 'What was its name?'

'Scamp,' said Helen. 'And...' She ran her finger along the edge of the stone slab. 'He killed my three cats. I'm pretty sure he did.'

They both looked at her.

'God,' said Hector.

'I've no evidence, but –' She told them about Baudrins and Susie and Fergus. 'I'm not absolutely sure it was him. Or anyone, for that matter. It could have been a series of accidents.'

Damian frowned. 'And what about Lorna? Did he used to hurt her?'

'Actually, no. I don't think so. I think he was all right to her. She must have – well, loved him, I suppose. She must have done, to keep believing in his innocence.'

The stone was cold through the thin cotton of her skirt.

'There's her mother too, of course,' said Hector. 'Dripping her mad theories into her head.'

'Do you want to hear my mad theory?' said Damian.

'No,' said his brother.

'Helen, you're not going to like it. I apologise in advance for any offence caused.'

'In that case,' said Hector, 'we definitely don't want to hear it.'

'What if *Suzanne* killed *Rob*? And attacked you?'

'Am I speaking to myself? I said we *don't want to hear it.*'

'It's been suggested before,' said Helen wearily. 'I think people must have come up with every possible permutation of who did what over the years. Suzanne killed Rob and attacked me because we'd been having an affair; my memory of events was clouded by the concussion, and I got it wrong. That was one of the variations.'

Damian's grey gaze was wide. 'But maybe you did get it wrong. Maybe you're "remembering" what your brain is telling you *must* have happened. What if Rob had started to fall for you, in the course of your correspondence? And Suzanne realised it, and under the influence of a cocktail of drink and drugs went for you both? She kills Rob, disposes of his body and makes her getaway in his car. The police are looking for Rob, not Suzanne. So it's easy for her to elude detection, set up a new life –'

'Bollocks,' said Hector. 'For one thing, Suzanne was – what – five feet tall? And built like a ten-year-old. She'd never have been able to 'dispose' of Rob's body. Not on her own – and who'd have been her accomplice?'

Damian shrugged. 'Ina?'

'And I suppose Moir Sandison is Suzanne in disguise?' said Helen.

'If he's a professional scammer, like Peter Laing says, Suzanne could have paid him to target you – to get back at you for stealing her boyfriend. That would explain why he knows so much about you.'

'And she waits sixteen years to do so?' said Hector. 'And why would she blame Helen, in any case? Helen – well.'

'I didn't know it was Rob I was writing to,' she finished for him. 'Suzanne would never have killed Rob.' She stood, and turned to face them both. 'She worshipped him.' She met Damian's eyes. 'You don't remember her, do you?'

'No.'

Of course he didn't. 'She used to take your cot into her room when you were teething, and cuddle you, and sing to you – and tell you stories about that soft elephant you were obsessed with.'

Damian was looking at her with a slight, faintly dismissive frown, as if the idea that he could ever have been six months old, and teething, and obsessed with a toy elephant just wasn't credible.

It was the exact same look Irina would give you when you'd said something particularly stupid, and just for a second the charm slipped and you saw what she really thought. But then you'd be deciding you'd imagined it, as she nodded and smiled and made out like you were the most wonderful person she'd ever met in her life.

She wanted to say something about Irina. About how Suzanne had been more of a mother to him than she ever had. But she said only, 'Little did she know that sixteen years later you'd be casually discussing whether she was a murderer, like it's a game... like she doesn't even matter... like she wasn't even a real person.'

The frown became a grimace: apologetic and rueful and self-deprecating and completely charming.

She turned and walked away, back towards the kirk, where people were spilling out into the sunshine, yattering, laughing; children running through the gravestones.

Mr Beattie was standing at the door, a benign expression on his doughy face as he patronised two elderly ladies – one of whom, she realised, was Mrs Smart who used to have the shoppie. Mrs Smart, but old.

She advanced up the path, digging in her bag for a photo of Moir, passing faces unfamiliar and familiar and everything in between; faces that turned to follow her progress; voices that dipped in excited speculation, or disapproval, or put-on pity.

'Is this Rob?' she said, and thrust the photograph at him.

He blinked, his smile fixed in place.

'Is it him?'

58

He made no move to take the photograph. He said to the two women, 'I'm sure it will be a great success,' and to Helen, in a rapid, soft, lilting voice, almost a whisper, as if reciting a prayer: 'You have our sympathy my dear but what do you think can possibly be gained by persisting with this fiction this is not my son.'

Amen.

'You haven't even looked at it.'

'I've been through all the material shown to us by the police.' His eyes darted behind her, and then back to the people still coming out of the kirk.

'It's Rob, isn't it? *This is Rob.*' She shook the photograph at him.

He moved abruptly towards the open door as a large woman in a pink jacket came striding out, pushed past him and lunged at Helen, snatching the photograph and flinging it to the ground.

'Robin is *dead.*'

Hector was beside her.

'*As you well know.*' Mrs Beattie pushed her face up to Helen's – and for a moment she was back in a hospital bed, Auntie Ina's face huge in her vision.

There was something weird about Mrs Beattie's mouth – the lipstick. It wasn't contained within the borders of the top lip, but made jaunty excursions into the faint moustache above.

Mr Beattie muttered, 'Now, now, Caroline.'

'How could it have been Robin who took the bike from the shed? If it'd been Robin, he'd have taken the money. Didn't know about that, *did you*?' She turned on Hector. 'Didn't know what was in the tin? But *he would have done*. You slipped up there!'

Hector raised his eyebrows at Helen. 'There was a tin in the shed, apparently. With money in it for the gardener. Hidden in its usual place amongst the kindling. Rob knew about the tin, so Mrs Beattie's argument is that, if it was Rob who took the bike, he'd also have taken the money in the tin.'

Helen took a step towards Mrs Beattie. 'He'd just *murdered Suzanne*! Not exactly a huge surprise that he wasn't thinking straight enough to remember some small change in a stupid tin!'

Mrs Beattie stepped back, her hands to the sides of her cheeks as if Helen had slapped her.

'Come on, Mum.' Lorna; glaring at Helen and putting an arm up to her mother's shoulders. 'Come on.'

Helen walked away from them all. She walked round the back of the kirk, between the pair of yew trees, down the mossy path that led to the gravestone: a sturdy slab of speckled grey granite with her grandparents' names incised in black – the grandparents she couldn't remember – and under them, Dad's.

She put her hand on the top of the stone, and closed her eyes.

'Helen. I'm sorry, but – I don't want you going off on your own just now.' Hector was standing on the grass a little distance away. 'Your uncle will be expecting us.'

She nodded. They had a cool-box in the car, packed with soup and sandwiches and a chicken pie to take to Uncle Jim for lunch. And a raspberry pavlova Hector had found in the freezer.

He handed her the photo of Moir.

They walked back down the path in silence. The headstones here were arranged companionably in family groups that spanned the generations, from the early 1800s to the present. The family names that she'd known all her life: Gordon and Smart and Hewitt and Duff.

She stopped at a small, polished black granite stone set alongside a substantial Victorian one. The name on it was William Duff.

'Keeper who used to smoke foul cigars in confined spaces? Moustache and prominent ears? Morose old bastard?'

She smiled. 'I don't remember him.' But something had caught her attention. She went closer to the stone. Not the name, but the date under it.

She touched the numbers incised into the granite. The date of his death, sixteen years ago: just ten days before Midsummer's Eve. Ten days before Suzanne.

'She should have something. Suzanne. Does a person have to be buried here, to have a memorial put up?'

'I don't think so. If you're cremated you can still have a stone put up, or your name added to an existing one, I think. And there are plenty of names of local lads who died in far-flung outposts of Empire.'

But would Suzanne have wanted a big slab of granite with her name on it? Maybe one of those tacky ones, with doves and sunbeams. Something ridiculous like that. Something funny.

They carried on down the path. Even thinking about Suzanne being dead wasn't completely unbearable when she was with him. Even if all they were doing was walking along a path in silence.

On the gravel track beyond the back gate to the kirkyard, by the wall of the manse garden, several cars were parked, and Steve was there with Fiona's parents, strapping Lizzie into a car seat. Damian was standing by the gate talking to Fish, who was grinning in an I-shouldn't-be-finding-this-funny sort of way.

As Hector and Helen joined them, Fish turned to her. 'I've been having a think about the business with your account. Rather than concentrating on his using a false identity when the two of you opened the account – which is complicated by your joint signing of the declaration – our best angle of attack will probably be to contend that, because he used a forged passport as a form of identification to withdraw the cash, and a birth certificate that wasn't his, the bank shouldn't have authorised the withdrawals and is therefore liable.'

'But surely – proof of identity when you're withdrawing money is just to prove that it's your account? And it *was* his account.'

'I know it seems back to front. But –'

'Why can't you just *leave us alone*!' a woman's voice shouted.

Lorna: striding towards them in her sensible black lace-ups.

Fish's mouth dropped open.

Lorna strode right up to Helen until they were face to face.

Helen stepped back. 'I'm sorry.'

'No you're not. You don't care about us. About what you've done to my family.'

'Oh for God's sake,' said Hector. 'It's rather the other way round, isn't it?'

'Is it?' Lorna was breathing fast, as if she'd been running. '*Is it, Helen?*'

Fish said, 'This isn't –'

'Have you asked her? About what was in that email?'

'Lorna –'

'Ask her. Ask her if she told the truth about Rob.'

'Why would I not?' Helen was gripping her bag so tight the raised stitching was digging into her palms.

'You hated him.'

'For no good reason, I suppose,' said Fish.

Lorna looked from him, to Helen, to Hector. And she opened her mouth and began to cry, like she used to when she was little, without restraint, not trying to stop it or hide it.

'Oh God,' said Damian, without sympathy.

Helen opened her bag and found a tissue. She held it out to Lorna, who looked at it as if Helen was brandishing a weapon at her. The sobs had become a wailing noise that sounded on one continuous note, as if drawn from deep within her, from a place where no comfort could reach.

Hector put his hand on Helen's back and started to guide her away.

She shrugged him off and turned back to Lorna. 'All right. No. I wasn't telling the truth.' She didn't look at Hector.

The wailing stopped, abruptly. Lorna stared at her, her face frozen in its misery, and Fish's voice behind her said, sharply, 'What?'

'I don't remember what happened. But it must have been Rob. I knew it must have been him. So I told the police I remembered him attacking me. And Suzanne.'

'You lied,' said Lorna.

'But I'm sure it was him.'

Silence. Then:

'You bitch, Helen,' Lorna gulped. 'You *bitch*.'

'It must have been Rob. He made Suzanne write me a note, pretending to be from Hector, asking me to meet him – he must have been intending to – attack me, rape me –'

'How do you know that? He *made* Suzanne write you a note? How do you know?'

'I don't.' And now Helen was the one choking on tears.

'Tell me what happened,' said Lorna. 'Tell me everything.'

'I don't *remember*!' Helen pushed her hand against her mouth.

'God, Helen,' said Hector. He didn't touch her.

'I'm sorry.'

'I'm going to pretend I didn't hear all that,' said Fish. 'But you'll need to go to the police and amend your statement.'

'They've been working on a false assumption all this time,' said Damian, absently.

'A reasonable assumption,' said Fish.

Hector shook his head. 'Once Helen told them it was Rob, they obviously never bothered their arses to seriously consider any other possible scenarios. Did they ever take you through the events of that night?'

Fish shrugged. 'Not as such. Asked me if I'd seen Rob, when was the last time I saw Suzanne... But no – they never sat me down and took me through what I remembered, minute by minute, as would be done now.'

'Then – we need to do that,' Helen got out. 'And I have to try to remember what happened. I have to.'

Lorna was still staring at her. 'Now. We do it now.'

'Yes,' she said. 'All right.'

'Christ,' said Fish.

59

The air smelt of pine resin and peaty earth; the sharp, clean, sweet smell of the hills in summer, except when they passed what had to be either an animal's corpse, decomposing somewhere in the undergrowth, or a stinkhorn, thrusting phallus-like from the black soil, reeking of rotting flesh.

She thought a few times she wasn't going to make it. Her legs were weak, her heart fluttery-feeling in her chest, the voices of the others coming loud and then distant in her ears. She should have eaten some lunch. But she'd managed to push only a few mouthfuls of soup past the blockage in her throat. She'd told Uncle Jim she'd had a huge breakfast at the House, all the time conscious of Hector's unsympathetic presence across the table.

He despised her now.

Even the stalkers' path under her feet seemed different. She'd walked it in her head how many times? But she hadn't remembered it quite right. She'd forgotten this whole section, where it traversed the hill, following the contour, before climbing up to the stone circle.

Maybe she'd got everything wrong. Maybe it hadn't been Rob at all.

Maybe she deserved his hatred.

At her elbow, Fiona said, 'Where – have we passed the place yet, where –'

'It was back there. I think.' A shiver went through her arms, and she hugged them round herself. She was wearing a long-sleeved T-shirt and jeans. After lunch, they'd gone back to the House to change and drop off Damian. Only Damian had somehow ended up coming with them.

He and Hector had dropped out of sight, far back down the path.

Damian's presence had been yet another source of friction.

When Steve and Fiona had pulled up at the end of the track, and Steve had seen Damian all kitted out in walking trousers and boots, sitting on the tailgate of the Land Rover with a pair of hiking poles next to him, he'd blown up at Hector.

'Putting aside all the other reasons why it's inappropriate for him to be here – There is *no way* he's climbing that hill. Not on that path.'

Hector was putting a pad of paper into a rucksack. 'Tell him that.'

'It's not up to *me* to tell him anything.'

'Um – *he* is right here?' said Damian.

'Hector –'

'For God's sake!' Hector, uncharacteristically, had suddenly snapped. 'It's his look-out, isn't it!'

When they reached the stones, Helen sat down next to Fish on one of the long recumbent ones. Steve, sweaty in an oversized T-shirt, walked past them to look down across the clearing and the tops of the trees to the west, and said, 'Nothing changes, does it?'

She thought he meant the view – the softening outlines of the Grampians receding to the horizon. Morven and Tom na Creiche and Monadh Caoin. Then Fiona said, 'That's not fair.'

'Isn't it? You think it's perfectly reasonable to let that boy attend this – *whatever* it is – and break his neck on that path? Just as it was perfectly reasonable to push Class A drugs on a bunch of kids? Some of them no older than Damian? How old were you?' He turned to Lorna, who was standing on the other side of the circle.

'Fourteen.'

'*Fourteen.*'

'You know what Damian's like.' Fiona's voice was tight. 'Once he sets his mind on something.'

'Oh please.'

A tense silence descended.

None of them wanted to be here. Of course they didn't. They must all despise her. And the childish part of her longed to be poor Helen again, the object of their sympathy and concern, not – whatever it was they thought of her now.

'I'm sorry,' she said. 'I've tried so hard to remember –'

'Well try again,' said Lorna.

What *did* she remember?

Hector, walking round these stones, delivering his performance. His story about Sandie Milne and the Sith. And then the sound of bells, coming jingling through the trees in the dark –

'He must have been here.'

'Hmm?' said Fish.

'When Hector was telling the story about the Sith. When you were footering about with the bells in the trees – Rob must have already been here. That's how he knows about the bells. And it must have been Rob who spiked my drink with cocaine.'

'That could have been anyone,' said Steve. 'Hector –'

He stopped as Damian appeared, grinning as he limped past Steve to sit on the stone next to Fiona, and calling back to Hector: 'Come on, what's the hold up? I want juice.'

Hector, unsmiling, tossed a little carton of juice at his brother and dumped the rucksack on the ground in the middle of the circle.

'Let's just get this over with,' said Steve.

'By all means.' Hector turned to Helen. 'You and Suzanne stayed here by the fire, yes, when the rest of us went off into the trees with the torches? That would have been – some time before midnight?' His tone was brisk.

'Yes.' Helen stood.

'Where exactly were you sitting?'

Steve snorted. 'What does *that* matter?'

Shloook, shloook, shloook – Damian, sucking juice through the straw.

'Come and sit where you think you were.'

She dropped down onto the grass.

'... And *you* can make yourself useful and be Suzanne.'

Damian scrunched up the empty juice carton and threw it at Hector, who caught it one-handed and dropped it into the rucksack.

'Where was Suzanne?' he asked Helen.

'Here.' She touched the grass next to her.

Damian limped across and lowered himself into place, setting the hiking poles down next to him and using his hands to adjust the position of his right leg.

Steve said, pointedly, 'Are you all right there?'

'Mm.' Damian lay back. 'At least I'm going to make a convincing corpse.'

'*That*,' said Hector, 'is your most offensive remark *yet* today.'

Damian raised his eyebrows.

'And that is not a fucking *compliment*!'

Damian turned his head to look at Helen, and smile an apology. Close up she could see there was a heaviness about his eyes, about the place on his brow between them.

'Can we just *get on with it*?' said Steve.

Hector folded his arms. 'You, Fish, Fiona, Norrie and I – we were all up there in the trees. Lorna – where were you?'

'I don't know about timings, but –' She came into the circle of stones. She had scraped her hair back into a scrunchy, and her white face looked naked, exposed. 'While everyone was still gathered round the fire, I decided to walk down to the phone box on the road and call Dad to come and pick me up.'

'On your own?' said Fiona.

'Yes. I'd asked various people if they'd drive me back, but no one was sober enough. I had a little torch I'd brought with me – and it was only really dark under the trees. I got as far as the track, but then I saw Rob's car.'

'You're sure it was his?'

'Of course I'm sure. I knew he hadn't been invited, but I wasn't surprised he was gatecrashing. I decided to go back and find him. I thought if I caught him before he'd had a chance to drink too much, he could drive me home, and then come back to the party. But when I got to the fire, there was no one here. I could see the flames of the torches in the trees. Helen – you weren't here. Neither was Suzanne.'

'So that must have been just after midnight?' said Hector.

'I don't know. I followed the torches, hoping Rob would be with the rest of you. But he wasn't. I never found him.'

'You asked me if I'd seen him,' said Fish.

'But you hadn't. No one had.' Her voice cracked.

'I remember you – uh – getting a bittie blootered,' said Norrie.

'Someone gave me a bottle of something. The rest of the night's just a blur. I remember clambering down the hill with Norrie and those girls; and sitting in a car... Then I woke in the morning in my own bed at home. By then everyone had realised that Rob and Suzanne were *both* missing – and I told the police about seeing his car on the track. By then it was too late. To be of any use. And then *you* told them he'd attacked you –' She turned to face Helen.

'Okay,' said Hector. 'We can take the rest as read. Fish?'

Fish was looking at Helen too. 'You know it was Tom and I who found you?'

She nodded.

He walked across the grass, back towards the path. 'We were going back down to the vehicles for some booze that got left behind by mistake.'

'Tom had been meant to carry it up,' said Hector. 'I made him go back for it – a crate of beer, I think it was.'

'And Tom said it was too heavy for one person, so I went with him.' Fish walked a little way down the path, and stopped. 'Are we going to go back down to where we found Helen?'

'In a bit,' said Hector. 'Tell us what happened first.'

'Well,' said Fish. 'We'd taken one of the torches with us – of the flaming variety. It was a bit of a bugger because it kept knocking against the branches of trees. So we were going pretty slowly. Because of that, and the fact we were smashed and could hardly walk in a straight line... If we'd been going at a normal speed I don't suppose we'd have spotted you.' He came back up the path and stood looking at Helen. 'I saw something light-coloured through the trees, on the ground. It was your top. You were wearing a light-coloured top...'

'Yes.'

He'd been carrying around this memory of Helen Clack lying there in her light-coloured top all these years. Strange to think that they all featured in each other's versions of that night, but never as quite the same person.

'I thought at first it was literally that – someone's shirt or sweater. But as we got nearer we saw it was a person. Someone passed out drunk, was my second assumption – until I saw the blood. And your face – it was in quite a state. It was obvious you'd been – assaulted. Tom lost it, screaming that you were dead – but I could see you were breathing – I tried to get you to hear me, but you were unconscious. Meanwhile Tom was screaming blue murder, literally –'

'Bringing us all running,' said Steve.

'You arrived first, I think,' said Fish. 'I remember you checking her airways or something – I was so relieved that you were there and knew what to do.'

Steve grimaced. 'I hadn't a clue.'

'We carried Helen down the path...' Hector turned to Norrie. 'While you followed behind –'

'I ended up with Lorna and Perdita and that other quine – she'd lost a shoe, and Lorna was in a gey state, and Perdita would suddenly take off running – by the time we made it to the track end you and Steve and Fiona had got Helen into a Land Rover and were starting off for the hospital. I was relatively sober, so I took Fish in my car and we followed. I say *relatively* sober – I doubt I'd have passed a breathalyser. We left Lorna and Perdita and her friend with the others at the track end.'

'I remember sitting in a car,' said Lorna. 'I suppose someone realised Suzanne was missing, and started a search. And then some of the men from the Estate got here, and eventually the police... Someone must have taken me home at some point.'

Silence.

Helen said, 'Right. So now it's my turn.' She looked at Damian lying on the grass beside her. 'Suzanne – when I last saw her she was lying face down...'

Damian rolled onto his front, with a suspicious look at the grass before he lowered his face onto his arms.

'She – she'd tried to stop me. To dissuade me from keeping what I thought was... an assignation... with Hector.' She could feel her face flushing scarlet. 'But she was very drunk. I think she was asleep when I left her.' She got to her feet.

'Okay.' Hector slung the rucksack over one shoulder. 'You started down the path. Were you conscious of anything behind you? Suzanne moving, maybe?'

'No.' She walked over to the path. 'I didn't look back. I thought I was going to be late – I was hurrying... Do you want me to –'

'Do whatever you remember doing that night.'

So she lengthened her stride on the path and tried to think herself back. She'd been hurrying, her feet slipping about –

'I lost the path quite soon.' Then: 'Here, maybe?' The path turned sharply to the left – in the dark, it would be easy to go wrong. She went straight on into the trees and they all trooped after her, ducking under the thicker branches, pushing aside the thinner ones. 'I carried on down the slope until I found the path again...'

'It chicanes back round,' said Hector. 'If you go straight down here you'll come onto it again.'

Back on the path, when they reached a place where it dipped down and then curved gradually to the right, she stopped. 'I think it was here.'

Hector, Fish and Lorna were behind her. There was no sign of the others.

'No,' said Fish. 'A bit further on. It was just past that big pine with the branch sticking out.' And when they'd passed the tree: 'Here. Wasn't it?'

Hector nodded. 'Yes, I think so.'

She wanted to run – on down the path and away.

But: 'So you're walking down the path...' Lorna prompted her.

'Shouldn't we wait?' said Helen. 'For the others?'

'Why?'

She couldn't think of a reason.

'Maybe you should sort of half-shut your eyes,' Lorna suggested. 'As if it's dark.'

She didn't want to.

'Helen?' said Fish.

'Okay.' She half-shut her eyes, and let her mind free.

She'd had no warning. No sense of anyone being there before she'd felt herself grabbed from one side – from the right. Hands grabbing her – her arm, her head – a hand across her mouth, and being pulled off the path, stumbling against him, a smell of sweat –

'He smelt,' she said. 'Of sweat. Like Rob did.' She opened her eyes and walked off the path and into the trees. 'He pulled me in here. His hand was over my mouth so I couldn't scream. I couldn't breathe properly – the hand was over my nose too – Maybe I blacked out because I wasn't getting enough air? And came to later, when he was hitting me –'

No one spoke.

She lay down on the mossy ground. The sky, where it showed between the trees, was searingly bright in her eyes. She closed them.

She'd tried to remember so often: to remember lying here in these woods, and Rob on top of her, punching her – but that wasn't a memory – was it? It was her imagination filling in the gaps. It was the version of events she'd constructed.

Or was there really something, a memory of a weight on top of her, a knife cool against her skin –

She sat up. 'I think – he had a knife.'

'Who's *he*?' said Fish.

'Rob. I'm sure it was Rob.'

'But *do you actually remember*?' Lorna was standing very straight, her hands locked in front of her. 'Or are you just guessing?'

'I don't remember seeing him. No. But –'

'The injuries you had were consistent with someone using their fists on you,' she said. 'Not a knife.'

'Yes.' Helen took a long breath. 'I'm sorry. I don't really remember... I just thought...'

'You *must* remember.' Lorna was suddenly on her knees in front of her. 'There were defensive injuries on you. That means you must have been aware of what was happening to you. That means you must be able to remember. Lie back down and put up your arms – hold them out as if you're trying to stop me hitting you.'

She lay back and lifted her arms, forearms parallel to one another above her face. And suddenly Lorna hit her, quite hard, just below her wrist and again on the elbow.

'Lorna,' said Hector, and pulled her away.

'You must remember,' said Lorna.

'The mind's a funny thing.' It was Fiona's voice, suddenly near. 'If you're in a life or death situation, your system diverts all your resources to your muscles and the fight-or-flight part of the brain and away from the part that lays down memories. That's why people often don't remember traumatic events.'

Helen sat up. Fiona was squatting next to her. Hector still had hold of Lorna, who was taking ragged breaths. Behind him were Fish and Norrie.

'I'm sorry. I don't remember. I just don't.'

When Steve and Damian had caught up they continued down the path, at a slower pace to accommodate Damian, although he was very knackie with the poles, only seeming to have problems where the path dropped steeply, when Steve or Hector would help him. At one very steep place, treacherous with scree, his right foot slid out to the side and he would have fallen if Hector hadn't been holding onto him.

'Thanks,' she heard him mutter as Hector half-lifted him down the worst of it. 'Sorry. Bit of a pain in the arse.'

'You're a *bloody* nuisance.'

Fiona grinned round at Damian, as if to reassure him that Hector was joking. But the look that passed between the brothers had no levity in it.

As they returned to the vehicles Hector's phone beeped, and he turned away to take the call. 'Well, it was a long shot,' she heard him say. And then: '... past Rotmachy...'

Fish was saying, 'So that's that then. We're no further forward. Although I suppose we've eliminated ourselves from the inquiry. Everyone has someone to vouch for them for the time Helen was attacked.'

'Well,' said Lorna. 'I can vouch for Norrie, and vice versa. Tom, I suppose, can vouch for you. But I don't know that we've established anyone else's innocence.'

Hector shut his phone, and Helen said, 'You're still looking for him. You've got them out looking for him.' But she couldn't summon any righteous indignation. What was this lie, compared with hers?

'Oh no,' said Fiona. 'Don't tell me. *Hector –*'

'Um.' He grinned. 'It's a fair cop.'

'Great,' said Steve. 'And when your thugs catch up with this guy, who's probably a perfectly innocent tourist – then what?'

'My "thugs" will call the police.'

Steve snorted, but Norrie rounded on him. 'Of course he's not a "perfectly innocent tourist"! Rob's back, he's running around out there –'

'He's not Rob,' said Lorna.

'Of course he's not,' said Steve.

An inimical silence.

Then Lorna looked at Hector. 'I suppose you were with the torchlight procession up until the time we all heard Tom screaming? I suppose there are lots of people who can verify that?'

Hector shrugged.

'What's that supposed to mean?'

'I was with everyone else for part of the time. For the rest – I was with one other person.'

'Oh, right.' Lorna wrinkled her nose. 'So who was the lucky girl?'

'I don't think that's important.'

'Oh for God's sake,' said Steve. 'Don't hold back on my account.' And as Hector just looked at him: 'I'm not a complete fool. I know you were with Fi.'

60

With Fi. Fiona.

He'd been with Fiona.

Her stomach spasmed.

All the time she'd been counting down the minutes until they could be together – all the time she'd been strung up so tight, so aware of him across the fire, wondering what it would feel like when he touched her, wondering what would happen when her whole world changed – all the time, he'd barely given her a passing thought. All the time, it had been Fiona.

Had he held her gaze across the fire? Had their hands brushed as they both reached for another log?

'What?' said Fiona, her face blank.

'The two of you vanished at the same time,' said Steve. 'Didn't take a genius to work it out.'

Everything looked suddenly different – the colours of the trees more intensely green; Fiona's top startlingly blue, her lips a perfect Cupid's bow; Hector a tall stranger. As if she was seeing the world as it really was for the first time since that night.

And discovering herself a ghost in it, a spectator, insubstantial and irrelevant.

Fiona said: 'You knew?'

'You weren't exactly subtle about it, were you?' There was no anger in Steve's voice. No bitterness. He just sounded very tired. 'You're not exactly subtle about it now, you know.'

Damian leant back against Hector's Land Rover, as if settling down to be entertained.

Norrie said, 'Jesus.'

'We didn't plan it,' Fiona said. 'We didn't *mean* it to happen.'

'You know the state we were all in,' said Hector.

Steve's lips twitched in a tiny smile, his eyes unmoving on Hector. 'It didn't mean anything? That's your next line.'

'If you like.'

'Look,' said Fish. 'Don't you think you three should be having this conversation in private?'

'Yes,' said Steve. 'I'm sorry.'

'We were just *kids*.' Fiona's mouth contorted around the word.

'Not any more you're not.'

'It never happened again.'

'Next you'll be telling me you're not still in love with him.'

The words dropped into the dead air between them.

Too late: 'Of course I'm not.'

'One thing I've never understood.' Steve's voice was still perfectly calm, but the hands he pushed into his trouser pockets were shaking. 'Okay so now we've got the girls and he's got Damian and you don't want to rock the boat – but before – why stay with me, when you could have had him? Why, come to that, did you ever split up in the first place?'

Fiona just shook her head.

'I'm guessing it was something suitably juvenile – like you caught him smoking a joint, and prim and proper little Fiona Kerr was shocked and disgusted and didn't want anything more to do with him?'

Hector looked up, at the sky above them, as if for inspiration from the God he didn't believe in.

'Yep,' said Steve. 'I've hit the nail on the head, haven't I?'

'It was cocaine,' said Fiona.

Steve hooted. 'Cocaine. Yes. Of course it was.'

'And I'm still *shocked and disgusted*, actually.' Her voice was wobbling all over the place. 'Hector and I – we're not right for each other. We never were.'

'And that's what you've been telling yourself for sixteen years.' Steve took something from his pocket and handed it to Fiona, very deliberately. A car key. 'I'm going to walk home. I'll see you there.'

'But it's – it must be six miles…'

'So it'll take me a while.'

'Steve,' said Hector.

'Whatever you have to say to me I don't want to hear it. I'm sorry if I'm overreacting – it's not like it's a revelation or anything. But right at this moment, whatever you've got to say, I don't want to hear it.' He turned and started walking, stiffly, away down the track.

He was a ludicrously dignified figure, in the oversize T-shirt and huge walking boots, overweight and lumbering, sweat marks under his arms and down his back.

Fiona just stood, looking after him, turning the car key over and over in her hand. She didn't look at Hector, and he didn't look at her.

And now it all made sense.

Of course it did.

The tension she'd picked up on last night – Hector's contained restlessness all through dinner – it had had nothing to do with her at all.

'Are you all right?' said Lorna, but she was speaking to Fiona, not Helen; her eyes sweeping her from head to foot.

A silent banshee scream filled Helen's head.

Fiona ran. She dropped the car key and ran down the track after Steve, and caught at his T-shirt, and he stopped and said something and then carried on walking. Fiona fell in a couple of paces behind, like an Oriental wife from the 19th Century.

Fish picked up the key.

'Nice one,' said Lorna.

'Oh for God's sake,' Fish puffed. 'A drunken fumble sixteen years ago? Who bloody cares?'

'Steve seems to.' Lorna looked from Fish to Hector.

'Awkward,' said Damian.

'Bloody Steve,' said Fish.

'I'm sorry the purpose of our coming here has been – rather overshadowed,' said Hector, whether to Helen or Lorna, or both, she wasn't sure.

She couldn't speak and she couldn't move.

She hadn't really screamed, had she?

She looked at him, at the man she loved, the man who had stolen her senses away, long ago, and carried her off to Corrachree.

But he didn't want her.

She had always known that, really.

It's not like it's a revelation or anything.

'Nice deflection,' said Damian. 'And I can help you out with that, because I've been thinking.'

Hector raised his eyebrows.

'About the sequence of events, after Rob killed Suzanne – if we assume that's what happened. The accepted version is that he drove down to Kirkton for the bike, put it in the boot, then dumped the car on the Hill of Saughs and made off on the bike – having disposed of the body either before or after going to Kirkton. Yes?' It was like he was talking at the end of a tunnel. Such a long tunnel that his lips and his words, by the time the light and sound waves reached her, weren't quite in sync. 'But why go to Kirkton? If it was just a bike he wanted, he could've nicked Melvin Bain's easily enough from just up the road. At least I'm assuming Mr Bain kept a bike in that shed back then too?'

'Oh aye,' said Norrie. 'In that same sheddie by the roadside. Track to the house is that rutted.'

'And he's recently put a lock on the shed after his bike was stolen,' said Damian. 'Which I'm assuming means that, sixteen years ago, it *wasn't* locked.'

'I imagine not,' said Hector.

'And everyone knew about Mr Bain and his bike. Rob would have known.'

'Yes.'

'So why did he have to go all the way to Kirkton? Why run the risk? The only relatively populated place for miles?'

'Maybe it didn't occur to him to get Mr Bain's bike.'

'Or maybe Mum's right,' said Lorna. 'Maybe it wasn't Rob who took the bike at all.'

'Or maybe there was *some other reason* for him to go there,' said Damian. 'And taking the bike was secondary.'

Fish shook his head. 'What other reason could there be?'

'Maybe to enlist his mother's help?'

Lorna's lip lifted. 'Oh yes, very likely. He could have called her from the phonebox, couldn't he, rather than running the risk of going home?'

'True.'

Hector was frowning. 'Willie Duff... Helen and I were looking at his gravestone earlier. He died what, a week, ten days previously? When was he interred?' He turned to Lorna. 'It wasn't the next day, by any chance? There wasn't an open grave lying ready and waiting on Midsummer's Eve?'

Lorna shook her head. 'No. At least, yes, a grave *had* been dug

371

for Willie Duff. His funeral was scheduled for the next day, but it was postponed because of all the police activity round our house, and in the kirkyard and the church – and because obviously Dad couldn't take the service – they had to draft in another minister. The grave was one of the first places the police looked. I know that for a fact, because I watched them from my bedroom window. They were down in the hole poking about.'

'And when did your family realise the bike was missing?' asked Damian.

'A few days later. It could just have been a random theft. One of the searchers could even have taken it.'

Hector said, 'When was Willie Duff's funeral actually held? The day after?'

'I think so. What does it matter?'

'Did the police examine the grave *again* on *that* day, before Willie's coffin was put in it?'

'I don't think so. Why would they?'

Norrie shook his head. 'It's not like he was going to hang on to the body for two days before disposing of it and making off.'

'Isn't it?' Hector appealed to Fish. 'Isn't it actually rather common for psychopaths to keep the bodies of their victims a while?'

'It happens.'

'Or maybe – well. Maybe when he took her she was still alive.'

Someone said something else after that, and another person answered, and the conversation continued as the trees swayed and Helen put out a hand to steady herself but there was nothing, just air, and then Norrie was catching hold of her. And then she was sitting on the grassy bank, and Lorna, in another universe somewhere, was berating Hector.

'That's her *cousin* you're talking about, and *my brother*?'

'Yes – I'm sorry.'

Helen took a long breath. 'We should tell the police. They could – look, couldn't they? In Willie Duff's grave?'

Fish pushed out his lips. 'No way would an exhumation order be granted on the basis of this kind of wild speculation. We'd need a hell of a lot more than that.'

61

Something had woken her. Noises, from through the house.

She got up, pulled on her cotton robe, and looked out into the dark passage. Right at the other end of it, on the other side of the landing, light spilled from two half-open doors – the one at the end which used to be, and presumably still was, the door to Hector's room; and the one next to it on the right.

Fiona.

Steve had thrown her out, and she was here.

Her cold bare feet silent on the Persian carpet, she made her way along the passage, across the landing, up the two steps until she was standing outside the door of Hector's room. She could see a tub chair against the wall on the left, and a bedside table with a book and a glass on it, and a small section of an austere-looking mahogany bed – part of the dark headboard, and a snowy-white pillow and duvet cover.

Hector's voice: 'Of course not.'

'What, so you won't get even the slightest bit of a sick thrill from it?' Not Fiona: Damian. 'And there's the added frisson of the possibility of being hauled off to prison. Again.' There was something different about his voice – it sounded like a bad recording of itself, flattened out and blurred at the edges.

'Hardly. A few hours' community service at worst.' Silence. Then: 'Do you want this back on?'

'Uh. No. Too hot.'

'How about I put it on the low setting, just for twenty or thirty minutes? Just till you get back to sleep? Were you asleep?'

So this was Damian's room now, not Hector's.

'Until you started blundering around out there. Why didn't you put on the lights?'

'Because, ironically, I didn't want to wake you. So do you want it or not?'

Silence. Then, so low she could hardly hear: 'I don't know.'

'You can always take it off again if it does get too hot.'

'Okay.'

Hector appeared in her line of vision, wearing a dark sweater and dark trousers. He bent to fit a plug into a wall socket, and turned back to the bed. 'Let's shift you over, then.' He pulled back the duvet and leant over the bed, his head and shoulders disappearing; and then reappearing, the boy's arm slung across his back, pale head next to his dark one.

Damian's hand on the wool of the sweater tightened as Hector lowered him onto the mattress, and Hector was still for a moment, and said something she couldn't make out. Then the hand loosened its grip, and Damian lay back.

'Right.' Hector moved again, out of her sight, but she could see Damian's face now against the pillow, eyes shut, skin blotched ugly red and white. She wouldn't have recognised him. 'So I'll put it to three? For how long – maybe better make it an hour?'

'Okay.' Damian opened his eyes. 'Hector.'

'Mm?'

'Is there anything going on between you and Fiona?'

She closed her eyes, steeling herself for the reply.

'No.'

She reached out to the wall and put her palm flat against it.

The sound of Velcro being pulled apart. Then:

'There? Or a bit further down?'

'That's fine. Thanks.'

She opened her eyes. Hector was pulling the duvet up the bed; pushing the hair from Damian's forehead and asking, 'Is that better?'

'Mm-hm.' Damian looked up at him with a twist of the lips that was less a smile than a desperately placatory grimace. 'Thank you.'

Hector sat on the edge of the bed and put his hand over Damian's. 'I'm not going to say I told you so... Well, obviously I just have. But I'm not going to labour the point.'

'Good.' And, the words starting to slur: 'Don't you have a grave to desecrate?' But she could see that his fingers had gripped Hector's hand.

She wasn't sure how long Hector sat there, speaking in a low voice about inconsequential things, like Norrie's idea for a new fishing hut and his ever more ludicrous suggestions for its location; and then falling silent, watching the tense face on the pillow; how long she stood at the door, watching him. When Damian's mouth relaxed and his breathing deepened Hector let go of his hand and got up slowly, and straightened the duvet where he'd been sitting, and turned and came to the door. Before Helen could gather her wits he was there, switching off the light and leaving the room and –

'Helen,' he said, and shut the door behind him.

He was angry.

She knew it from the way he stood; the way he said her name, however softly; the way he closed the door, blocking it with his body, as if to protect what was behind it.

'I'm sorry – I heard something – something woke me.'

'Fell over the hoover. Sorry.'

'Is Damian all right?'

'Yes.'

'But – is his leg –'

'He's fine.'

Nothing to see here.

Like when Tip had died. Nasty old Tip. His breath had smelt of jobby and he would nip you for no reason, on the leg or arm, as he ran past. When Dad had told her Tip had died she'd been secretly glad, even though he'd died in agony because he'd eaten rat poison, and gone into fits, and the Laird had had to shoot him and Hector had nearly cried. That was what Dad had said. At school the next day she'd wanted to tell Hector she was sorry, but couldn't pluck up the courage – she'd never seen Hector cry before and didn't want to.

But Norrie's brother Craig had said, 'That's a shame about Tip – what happened?' and Hector had told a lie. He'd said, 'He just died of old age,' and shrugged, and said he was getting a new puppy and this time he'd teach it not to bite.

He hadn't wanted anyone's sympathy – for himself, or for his nasty old dog.

And he didn't want it for Damian.

He didn't want anyone scrabbling at the edges of his privacy – least of all the ghost of Helen Clack.

He hadn't once mentioned Irina; and neither had she. He hadn't told her anything about what had happened; and she hadn't asked.

She hadn't asked him any of the questions she'd been longing to have answers to – what had happened when he'd got to the hospital and found Damian abandoned there? How had he managed living day to day, with a child who'd needed so much care, and an estate to run? Why hadn't he let the aunt and uncle step in? Was Damian the reason he was still single? Or was Fiona?

But one question, at least, she was entitled to ask, although it would betray just how long she'd been standing here.

'Are you going to look in that grave?'

She couldn't see his face properly – only, in the light spilling from the open door of the other room, the planes and angles of it. She thought for a moment that he wasn't going to answer – that he was too angry to speak – but then he said, 'Yes.'

'Then I want to come.'

This time, he didn't say anything.

'If Suzanne's in that grave, I want to be there.'

'All right. Wear something warm. We're leaving in five minutes.'

She couldn't stop shivering. Hector had got her an extra jersey from the Land Rover, a thick Norwegian one that came down over her hips, but she was still cold. All the muscles in her shoulders and back and arms ached, although she'd been doing nothing but standing holding the torch. The clouds against the dark sky were unnaturally bright in the moonlight; against them, the branches of the trees moved, every so often, with a creak or a sigh. And, ludicrously, there were actually bats – their tiny bodies like winged bullets, whizzing over their heads.

Emblems of mortality.

Of death.

Suzanne, dead and cold in the ground.

There were three of them digging: Hector and two men she hadn't met before, introduced as Mick and Chimp, like a comedy double-act from the 1950s. Mick, a stringy man with short grey hair, had explained the procedure on the drive from the house: cut out the turfs, line them up on one side of the grave in order so they can be fitted back into their place in the jigsaw, and mound up the earth on the tarpaulin on the other side. He'd dug many a grave in his time, he'd told her; and added, with a grin: 'For Aberdeen Council, when I was a loon.'

They worked in silence, apart from the occasional muttered swear-word when a spadeful of soil went astray, and Hector's stinging remarks on the work rate. He himself was digging like it was a race.

'Where's the fire?' grumbled Chimp at one point.

'Under your arse if you don't step it up.'

Mick and Chimp exchanged a look.

Hector wanted to get this done and get home, not because there was anything wonderful waiting for him there – Fiona, drowsy and warm in his bed – but because there was a boy with a maimed limb, lying awake, maybe, and in agony.

At last: 'Now then,' said Mick, and tapped his spade on something that rang hollow.

The coffin was intact, from what she could see when they lifted it with ropes and set it on the grass at the foot of the hole. As soon as they'd put it down, she moved the torch away.

'Okay,' said Hector, lowering himself back into the hole. 'Ca' canny with the spades. Helen, do you want to go and sit in the Land Rover, and if we find anything –'

'No. I'll stay. You need me to hold the torch.'

'We can prop it up on something.'

'I want to stay.'

But when all three of them suddenly stopped digging, and Chimp looked up at her and pointed to indicate where she should direct the beam of the torch, she froze. He put up his hand, and Helen gave him the torch, and he knelt and shone it onto the earth, and scraped with his fingers at something white.

'That's a skull.'

'Got a boot here,' said Mick.

Helen turned and walked away into the dark, the air shivering across her face.

'Helen? It's not Suzanne. It's someone much bigger.'

She walked back to where Hector was standing, a tall figure fitfully illuminated by the moving light of the torch.

'It's a man, I think, judging from the size of the feet.' He took her arm, and guided her to the edge of the hole. Chimp shone the torch on the toe of a thick black boot.

'And check out the belt.' Mick took the torch and angled the beam to show them a thick belt with a square buckle on it.

'Helen?'

'That's Rob's belt.'

Mick was holding something up to the torch. 'This was loose in the soil.' He handed it up and Hector put it on his palm.

It was a ring, a silver ring, in the form of a snake eating its tail.

'Suzanne's,' she said. And: 'I'm all right,' as Hector put an arm round her. She took the ring from him and rubbed it between her fingers to remove the soil. Then she closed her hand round it and held it until it was warm.

62

'But it makes sense,' said Damian.

'Just because Suzanne's body wasn't there, doesn't mean she wasn't also killed. By whoever killed Rob.' Hector sat back in his chair. 'If it *is* Rob. We'll have to wait for the police to do their stuff before we can be sure about that.'

Morning sun streaked the end of the table. Another lovely day. She had her hands round her mug, but what was radiating from it seemed to be an unpleasant prickling feeling rather than warmth. She was cold all the way through, as if there was nothing left of substance of her at all; nothing that could think or feel or care.

'But the ring...' Damian brushed toast crumbs from his finger-tips onto his plate, and then set his empty porridge bowl in its exact centre. 'If some hypothetical psycho killed them both, why would he bury Rob there, with Suzanne's ring, but Suzanne somewhere else?'

'Not enough room in the grave for two bodies plus Willie Duff?' Hector shrugged. 'The ring could have fallen out of his pocket.'

'Or maybe it came off Suzanne's hand when she was shovelling soil back on top of him. Suzanne wouldn't have had the strength to carry Rob's body to some remote place up a hill to bury it. But if she knew about Willie Duff's grave, she could have parked at the back gate, dragged – or even rolled – the body to the grave, tipped it in and covered it up, losing her ring in the process. Then she got the bike from the shed, put it in the car –'

'But she couldn't have got Rob's body down the stalkers' path in the first place. Not without help.'

'She *could* have had help.'

As if they were discussing some abstract problem (Hypothesis A: Suzanne is dead; Hypothesis B: Suzanne is alive), she said, 'No. Suzanne could never have killed Rob. She loved him too much.'

Damian pushed himself to his feet, both hands on the table. It was only then that she noticed a stick, a sturdy wooden one, hooked over the back of the chair next to him. But he left it where it was as he took his plate, bowl and mug to the sink.

There was nothing graceful about his limp now – it was more of a hobble, so obviously painful that she wondered at Hector not doing or saying something. But Hector was gazing off, abstracted. And as Damian hobbled back to his chair and she met his eyes, she registered a flash of antagonism. A challenge: *want to make something of it?*

And a little part of the hollow inside her filled up.

'Maybe it was an accident?' His mouth tightened as he sat back down. 'Maybe he attacked her and in the struggle...'

'In which case, why would she conceal the body? Why run off?' Hector shrugged, and looked at Helen. 'One thing at least we can be pretty sure of – Moir Sandison is not Rob Beattie.'

'No.'

'The question is: why did he want you to think he was?'

The phone on the worktop trilled. Damian started to get up, and Hector said, 'Sit down for God's sake,' and rested a hand briefly on his shoulder as he passed behind his chair.

'Hello?... Have you – Okay, so what can I do for you?... Well, that's interesting... Really?... Yes... No, I don't mind in the least. No. No... I can come over now, if you like... Yes.... All right. Goodbye.'

As he put down the phone:

'Campbell Stewart,' said Damian.

'Requesting my presence at the station.'

'They traced the "anonymous" call about the grave?'

'Give me some credit: I used an unregistered pay-as-you-go. Some insomniac curtain-twitcher saw the Land Rover last night, turning onto the track at the back of the kirkyard.'

'So what's the story?'

'Simple denial. There's no CCTV or anything. They can't prove it was one of our Land Rovers. Still less who was in it.' He put both hands on Damian's shoulders. 'Right. Shouldn't be long.'

When he'd gone, Helen stood. 'Would you like more tea?'

'No thanks.' And then: 'You still think it was Rob who attacked you, on the Knock?'

She put her hands on the warm top of the Aga. 'Yes.'

'What if Suzanne did follow you? What if she found him attacking you... You remember a knife, but there were no knife wounds on you – what if Rob had the knife, but Suzanne managed to get it off him, and stab him –'

'She was so little. How could she get a knife off him? How could she get his body all the way down that path to his car?'

'Maybe she got the knife off him, he chased her down the path to the track – caught her as she was trying to get into his car – and *then* she stabbed him.'

Her hands, her whole body, were suddenly burning hot. She walked away from the Aga on legs that shook.

Suzanne could still be alive.

'Well,' said Damian. 'If she is – don't you think her parents would know it?'

She must have said it out loud.

'Don't you think they'd have helped her? All those times your aunt went off supposedly following up leads – couldn't she have been with Suzanne? Helping her establish a new life?'

The kitchen was tipping. She locked her hands on a chair back.

'Although why would she need to, if it was self-defence – or defence of you? She was injured too – it was her blood on your clothes, wasn't it – there would have been plenty of forensic evidence to back her story up. But maybe she didn't know that.'

And now she could speak. 'I have to see Uncle Jim. I have to ask him –'

'Wait till Hector gets back and he can take you over there. He shouldn't be long.' He put the top back on the marmalade jar. 'They're not going to arrest him or anything.' *Are they?* was unsaid in his quick look up at her.

She sat down on the chair. 'Of course they're not. But I don't want to wait for Hector. Can one of your tame gorillas take me?'

63

'It's locked.' Helen tried the doorknob again to make sure. 'And his car's gone.' Uncle Jim always parked his Volvo in the same place, in the shelter of the steading.

Damian reached behind the downpipe and pulled the big Victorian key from its hiding place on the bracket holding the pipe to the wall. 'We can wait for him inside.'

Chris looked at his watch.

'You can come back and get us later. Hand over your nannying duties to Dod in the meantime.'

'Wherever the fuck he is.'

'Well he won't have gone far.'

Chris had left the Land Rover next to its twin, in identical Pitfourie Estate livery – presumably Dod's mode of transport.

'Boss'll have a Hairy Mary if he has,' said Chris. And, without warning, he gave a piercing whistle.

An answering whistle came from somewhere behind the steading.

'Gorilla mating call,' said Damian, putting the key in the lock.

'Dod!' Chris shouted. 'Get your fat arse to the house!'

'Gimme two seconds!' was the response.

Chris brought a mobile phone from his pocket. 'When do you want picked up then?'

'About an hour?' Damian raised his eyebrows at her, and she nodded. 'If Mr Clack's still not turned up by then, Helen can come back later.'

Chris was frowning at the phone.

'You won't get reception here,' said Damian. 'You'll have to go back onto the road, or up to the Parks.' He opened the door and stood back for Helen to enter first.

The hall seemed different. As if everything had shifted a little.

The phone on the table – had Uncle Jim lifted that phone to his ear and dialled a number and waited, and then Suzanne's voice –

But if Suzanne was alive and living her life somewhere, if she'd killed Rob and had to disappear – wouldn't she have let Helen know? If it had been the other way round, Helen would never have let Suzanne think she was dead.

'Okay?' said Damian.

'Yes. Sorry.' She walked past the table, down the passage to the kitchen. The stack of correspondence was where she'd left it on the dresser. She could go through it while she waited, couldn't she? See if there was anything significant she'd overlooked?

Damian hadn't followed her. She turned back into the hall, half expecting him to have found something on the table, a phone number written on a piece of paper with 'S' next to it or a cryptic note scribbled in the phone book – but he was just standing, one hand on the stick, the other lightly touching the wall. When he realised she was there he smiled and started to move, with an odd, rapid sort of lurch that had her hurrying back to him.

The look he gave her – full-strength death ray – banished any thought she might have had of taking his arm, of offering help.

'Do you have the letter from Ina's solicitor?'

She went ahead of him to the dresser and pulled it from the Jiffy bag. She didn't watch his progress into the room, to her shoulder. She didn't suggest he sit down.

When he'd read it: 'You could phone them. Ask them about Ina's will – who the beneficiaries were. Although that stuff's probably confidential. You're a relative though. Maybe they *would* tell you. If Suzanne's alive and Ina knew it, she'll be the main beneficiary, won't she? Under whatever name she's using.'

Helen set the letter back down on the dresser. 'Of course. Yes.'

'And look at all these coincidences.'

'What?'

'If this letter was written a few weeks after Ina died, that means she must have died in January or February this year. Just a month or so before Moir came into your life. And Ina was living in Glasgow – where Laing lives. Where he met Moir. Where Moir scammed Lisa Greig.'

'But how can those things be related?'

'Through Suzanne, somehow, if she's alive?' He picked up and then discarded the next item of correspondence on the pile – an invoice from a seed merchant. 'Where would your uncle keep stuff he wouldn't want anyone to find? His bedroom?'

'I'm not going to pry round his room. I'm going to just wait and ask him.'

'Right, and he's always so forthcoming with information.'

She pushed the letter back into the Jiffy bag. 'When he finds out about Rob's body being found, maybe he'll open up.'

'How about we compromise? We could confine our search, initially, to the public rooms. Kitchen, sitting room...'

There were steps in the hall and she looked round, straight into Moir's smiling face.

64

She shot backwards away from him, tripped over Damian's stick and fell. The stick clattered away under the table. Damian grabbed the dresser and hauled at it, bringing it crashing down across the doorway, between them and Moir. China exploded, shards bouncing over her legs, over the floor.

'Go! The back door!' Damian was grabbing her, pulling her up; pushing her. '*Go!*'

Moir jumped up onto the back of the fallen dresser, easily, casually, not hurrying.

Helen ran.

She ran into the scullery, to the back door, and pulled it open. Shouted:

'Help! Help us!'

She turned back into the kitchen, but Damian was right behind her, reaching past her and jiggling the key from the door, and then they were outside and he was slamming it behind them and locking it.

'Go!' he pushed her. 'Get Dod – if you can't find him just go, run – not on the track, cut through the fields to the road – I'll hide.'

He had a curved, triangular shard of pottery in his hand.

He didn't have his stick.

'Go!' And he shouted: 'Dod!' And started to hobble across the grass of the Bleach Green. 'I'll hide in the shed. *Go!*'

Yes. She had to get Dod. She was running before the sense of it got through to the front of her brain, as if her limbs had some primitive survival instinct her brain lacked. She ran round the side of the house, shouting something, eyes leaping from steading to byre to yard.

Oh God. Oh God.

Chris's Land Rover was gone. The other was still there. But

where was Dod?

Not here.

She carried on running, past the byre to the dyke and scrambling over it, into the field of barley, running through it like a sprinter. But still it was too long before she reached the other side of the field, and the dyke that separated it from the next one, pasture, easier for running. Then she'd be on the road.

How could he hide?

The shed would be locked. And so would the gate into the steading courtyard. How could he climb it to get to the steading? The byre was too far.

Where was there for him to hide?

Nowhere.

But she couldn't do anything to help him.

Her mobile was in her bag. And her bag was in the kitchen.

When she got to the road she'd stop the first car that passed and make them help.

But an hour could go by without a car on this road.

She stopped, and turned, and looked back down the slope, across the barley, to the byre, to the house looming beyond it.

There was nothing I could do. Was that what she'd say to Hector?

He must have known the shed would be locked. He must have known there was no way – but he'd pretended that he could hide. Not to make her leave him – there was never any question about that – but to make her feel all right about it.

She started to walk, back to the dyke – and then she was clambering back over it, running down the trampled path through the barley, the dusty scent of it rising in her nostrils, her feet slipping on the smooth stalks.

A weapon. She needed a weapon.

The tools were all in the shed, or in the steading room.

Over the other dyke, and she was grubbing wildly amongst the grass-tangled remains of the binder at the end of the byre, pulling at the rusty metal. Finally a piece came loose in her hand, a long length of rusty steel.

She ran back across the yard, on round the side of the house.

65

He hadn't got far.

He was lying on the grass of the Bleach Green.

His lips were parted. There was blood in his hair, on his forehead, streaked down the side of his face. One hand was curled in the grass, as if he'd clutched it.

The slate-grey eyes were open and empty.

She dropped to him and took the curled hand in both of hers. It was cool.

'Damian.'

She willed his eyes to move. She squeezed his hand.

'*Damian.*'

Moir said, 'Oh, Helen.'

And before she could react he'd dropped down next to her, and put an arm round her, the smell of his cologne choking her throat.

'I'm sorry.' He was looking at Damian with a slight rueful pout. There was a red line down his cheek, seeping blood.

'Why?' She didn't know what she was referring to, or who, even, she was addressing.

He reached past her. His hands were encased in clear gloves, the kind surgeons wore. He took the hem of Damian's trouser leg between finger and thumb and began to lift it up over his ankle, revealing smooth flesh-coloured plastic above the blue sock. 'Shall we call it euthanasia?'

And Helen's hands were at his face, her fingers howking at the line down his cheek, the side of his eye – and then she was hurling herself the other way, falling, scrambling up, grabbing for the rusty spike, whirling to bring it down on his head.

But he'd moved too. Body-builder arms came round her, pinning her own arms, and as she kicked her heels back against him he flung her, hard, to the grass.

She dropped the spike and he kicked it away.

His breath was ragged in her ears. He wrenched both her arms up behind her back. She wriggled under him but he was too heavy. She managed to turn her head.

There was blood on his face. He wasn't smiling now.

She turned her head again, to Damian. He hadn't moved.

How could he move?

Moir was wrapping something soft and stretchy around her wrists.

'Right.' He pulled her to her feet, and she screamed, and he pushed her against the wall of the house. Then there was cloth in her mouth, and he was wrapping a bandage – yes, it was a bandage – across her mouth, round her head. And now he had binder twine, pulling it tight over the bandage. And all the time the pressure of his body, pinning her to the wall.

She sniffed desperately, swallowed mucus, air whooshing in through her nose – Oh God. What was he going to do?

He pulled her round and she felt him wrapping more twine round her wrists, on top of the bandage. And some detached part of her brain wondered, Why the bandage? Why the concern for her comfort?

When he'd finished he made her walk, holding onto the wrists bound behind her, supporting her when she stumbled – across the grass and behind the steading to a dark blue car whose passenger door he opened for her.

He eased her, quite gently, into the seat and fastened the seatbelt across her. He patted her shoulder with his gloved hand.

'Excuse me for a minute, Helen – I just have to make a call from the landline. Back soon!'

He shut the car door. She watched him walk back to the house and in through the open back door.

She wriggled round in the seat, wriggled to the side so that her hands could feel for the thing the seatbelt clipped in to – but she couldn't find it. But it had to be here! Her fingers fumbled for the belt itself, found it; moved down it until the plastic casing was shaking in her hands.

She pushed at it until with a click she'd released the belt.

Opening the door was harder. She twisted the other way and pushed her back against the door, running her hands up it to find the handle, lifting herself off the seat awkwardly.

Her eyes met Moir's through the windscreen.

He shook his head.

He opened the door and she half fell out of it. He pulled her all the way out and pushed her, face down, to the ground. He sat on her legs. She couldn't see what he was doing but she could feel the slippery gloved fingers on her ankles, bandaging them, tying the twine on top. When he'd finished he got up, leaving her trussed on the ground. She could hear him walking away. She was going to choke on the cloth in her mouth. She couldn't swallow. Her mouth was too dry –

She wasn't brave.

She'd always known that. She couldn't be brave about this.

Footsteps. He was coming back. She rolled her head to look.

He was moving backwards, quickly, almost jogging, pulling something along the ground. At first his body was between her and what he was pulling. And then she could see.

Damian. Moir had him by the wrists. The sleeves of his shirt, rolled up a few times at the cuffs, had fallen back to his shoulders, exposing the length of his arms. They were thin – the muscles defined but without the bulk that would come with maturity. That would have come. The skin was lightly tanned where it had caught the sun, but the insides of his arms were pale and smooth-looking, milky-white, like a baby's.

There was blood in his hair, on his face, on his shirt.

The heels of the polished shoes bounced on the dusty ground.

She closed her eyes.

One thud. Two. The clunk of the boot shutting.

'Helen? You okay?'

She hated herself for shaking her head – for pushing out her lips against the cloth, trying to move it, trying to make him see what the problem was.

He stooped and put a knife flat against her cheek, hard and cold – then whipped it away, slicing through the twine, and with his gloved hands he was pulling the cloth from her mouth, and she was coughing, choking, gasping –

'That better? You're not going to scream again, are you?'

She shook her head.

'That's my good girl.'

He lifted her against his chest. She held her breath, not wanting to breathe him, the smell of him as he carried her back to the passenger seat and dropped her into it. This time he didn't fasten her seat belt, or his own, as he started the engine.

At the track they turned not right to the road, but left.

Left, to the Parks.

66

He had to unbind her feet so she could walk in front of him, past the motor home, in at the back door, through the kitchen, up the stairs to her old bedroom. To the woman sitting, small and calm, on the bed under the eaves.

'Have you checked to see if she's got a phone?' It wasn't Suzanne's voice. The accent was Glaswegian – apart, oddly, from the *o* in *phone*.

'No – good point.'

'Suzanne?'

The woman stood, and walked towards her. She was wearing the same clear gloves as Moir. Her eyes were heavily made up with kohl and smoky eye shadow. She stared at Helen as she pushed a hand into each of her jeans pockets. The small hands were quick, deft. She was so close that Helen could smell the garlic on her breath.

Garlic bread. Suzanne had always loved garlic bread.

'Oh come on, girls.' Moir encircled them both with his arms, pressing them against each other, chuckling as Suzanne wriggled free, her pixie face contorting –

'*Suzanne.*' Joy, uncomplicated and primitive, flooded her mind, to be replaced at once by pain. Anger. '*Why –?*'

In a flash Suzanne had lifted a hand and slapped her, hard. Grabbed her hair.

Slammed face-first into the wall, Helen's head banged on the plaster – once, twice, three times. Suzanne had a hand in her hair and a hand squeezed round her neck. The hard point of her shoulder was pressed into Helen's back.

And then she was released.

Pivoting against the wall, she met Moir's eyes. He was holding Suzanne from behind, grinning past her at Helen. 'Uh uh *uh.*' He lifted Suzanne bodily and tossed her onto the bed.

Suzanne immediately jumped up again, but Moir turned and pointed a finger at her. 'No.' Like she was a dog he was training. 'Don't mark her.'

Suzanne sat down on the bed, her eyes never leaving Helen's.

She was wearing black leggings and a red shirt and red shiny high-heeled boots. Her hair was short. Very short, almost clipped, and dyed black. Her eyes looked huge in her pale face.

'I thought you were dead,' said Helen, as the tears came.

'You hoped.'

'No!'

Suzanne turned her mouth down at the edges and half-shut her eyes and trembled her lips, mimicking, Helen supposed, her own expression.

And they were eight years old again. 'Does Uncle Jim know you're –'

'Alive and kicking? Of course not.'

Oh God – '*Where is he?*'

Moir laughed. 'What do you take me for, Helen? A psychopath? Unc and his minder were off at the crack of dawn. Where to, I've no idea.'

Of course. Dod had gone with his charge, with Uncle Jim. When Chris had whistled, it'd been Moir who'd answered. Moir had been watching the watcher; learning his habits. His whistle. His voice.

Moir put his hands on her shoulders and pulled her to a hard chair by the window; forced her down onto it. On the floor were more rolls of bandage and twine.

'Please – not in my mouth. I won't scream.'

He untied her wrists, but before she could even think about how she could turn this to her advantage he had gripped them in his hands, and Suzanne was wrapping bandage round and round her body and upper arms. Like a game they might have played as children: Suzanne going too far as usual; Helen crying.

But no Mum and Dad downstairs to come and put a stop to it.

Suzanne. Suzanne was *here*. She was *alive*. But –

'What are you going to do?'

'Well,' said Moir. 'That all depends. Are you going to be a good girl?'

He had orange twine in his hands. But he only handed it to Suzanne, who tied it round Helen's ribs and arms, over the bandage, round the back of the chair.

Her hands were free. She could move her arms from the elbows. But what good was that, when she was tied to the chair, and her ankles were tied together?

She said, 'Did you kill Lisa Greig?'

'Lisa?' Moir stuck out his lower lip. 'Poor Lisa took her own life.'

'I don't believe you.'

'It was either suicide or an accident, according to the inquiry. Take your pick.' He slid something onto her lap – a magazine. As if she was waiting to see the dentist. And then a sheet of paper on top of it, and a pen.

'Write this,' said Suzanne. 'Write "I killed Rob Beattie." '

'What?'

'Write it. Write what I tell you.'

And so Helen wrote:

I killed Rob Beattie. He was lying drunk by the stalkers' path and I stuck a knife in him until he was dead. Suzanne tried to stop me and I half killed her too. When the others came I pretended to be unconscious. But then I told Hector and Norrie that Rob had attacked me and I'd killed him, and they hid the body until Norrie could come back for it and take it to Willie Duff's grave. Hector told Suzanne that she had to disappear and not come back, or else we would all say that she killed Rob.

Tears were plopping onto the paper. 'No one's going to believe this.'

When Moir turned up in my life I didn't know what to think – whether it was possible that Rob wasn't dead after all. So I got Hector to dig up the grave.

'It doesn't even make sense!' Helen flung the pen across the room and started to scrunch the paper in her hands, but Moir wrenched back her fingers and pulled the paper away.

'It's not meant to *make sense*.' Suzanne clipped across the floor in her high boots. 'Poor little Helen hasn't thought it through logically. The poor little murderer, haunted by her victim. She doesn't know what way's up any more. She doesn't know if Moir

Sandison is Rob Beattie, or the ghost of Rob Beattie, or the Sith, come jingly-jangly-jingly through the veil...' She laughed. 'We were pretty good Sith, don't you think? Were you scared? Did you have *baaaaad* dreams?'

This was real? This was Suzanne, grown-up Suzanne, playing some terrible game she didn't understand? Some demented game?

'And hey, I was a pretty good Rob.' Moir smirked. 'Did you notice I said "Hey" a lot? Like he used to? No? Pearls before swine.' He smoothed the paper in his hands and placed it back on her lap. 'Sign it.' He retrieved the pen from where she'd thrown it, under the washstand which stood where her chest of drawers used to be.

Shakily she signed her name.

'Good girl.' He handed the paper to Suzanne.

Suzanne just looked at her.

Suzanne. She'd been alive, all this time. Buying those boots and that top. Getting her hair cut like that so she looked more like a pixie than ever.

She made a sad face. 'And now you kill yourself.'

67

Helen tried to stand. She did manage to get to her feet, the chair tied to her like a snail's shell, but when she tried to move she fell sideways to the floor, banging knee and shoulder on the hard boards. She had wet herself.

Suzanne clipped over to the window. The red patent leather boots gleamed in the light falling on them. 'I don't think it's high enough.'

'Maybe not onto packed earth – but we can take her round the back – the front, whatever – why do you call it the front when it's at the back?'

Suzanne shrugged. 'The kitchen door's always been the back door.'

'Whatever. There's concrete at the "front", isn't there, between the house and the lawn?' Moir took hold of the chair and Helen's arm and set her upright again. 'Okay. I'll get the stuff into the van.'

He left the room. Helen heard his steps on the stairs.

'Why are you doing this?'

Slowly, Suzanne spun on a heel. 'I don't see them.'

'What?'

'The audience you're playing to.'

'*What?*'

Suzanne sat down on the bed and crossed her legs. 'He took a whilie to die. But not long enough. He managed the stalkers' path. He managed to make it to his car. Leaning on me, he managed it. We got about half way to the cottage hospital. We left the knife in him. That's what you're supposed to do, isn't it? So there wasn't blood pouring out of him or anything. But there must have been internal bleeding. He stopped breathing just after the Tarland crossroads. So I stopped the car and did all the first aid stuff I'd been taught on the childcare course. But I couldn't get him to breathe.'

Helen's own breath was shuddering in her throat.

'We drove up Greenhill. I – Maybe you'll think this is twisted, but I held him in my arms. While the sun came up. And all through the day. I washed him. I combed his hair. We listened to the car radio. I talked to him. Got a bit soppy, telling him all kinds of mushy stuff. Stuff I'd never have said when he was alive. Daft cow, eh? Then at night I drove him down to Kirkton. Used the wheelbarrow from the shed in the manse garden to move him from the car to Willie Duff's grave. And you won't believe it, but I said a prayer.'

'You left your ring with him.'

'I left my ring with him. I took the bike from the shed, dumped the car, cycled to Aboyne. Got the bus into Aberdeen.'

'And you phoned Ina.'

Suzanne's eyes narrowed.

'Damian worked it out. She took you to Glasgow?'

'First to A&E to get stitched up, under a false name of course – our story was that my injuries were the result of "drunken horse-play". Mum playing the shocked parent – convincingly, as you can imagine. They'd no reason not to believe her. They'd no reason to involve the police.'

'Was it – how did the knife get in him?'

'Well I didn't put it there, did I?'

'So why didn't you go to the police?'

'How could I? By the time I was in any fit state to do anything, you'd told your little story. Heard it on the car radio – how poor little Helen Clack had been attacked and Rob Beattie was being sought 'in connection' with that and my disappearance. If I'd popped out of the woodwork with his body in tow, how would that have looked? You'd have "remembered" me stabbing him, wouldn't you? And who'd believe my version of events over poor little Helen's?'

'I wouldn't have done that. How could you think I'd do that? Suzanne!' Why on earth would she think Helen would do that? 'I'd have told the truth – that I didn't remember.'

Suzanne just looked at her.

'Why didn't you hide his body and then come back? You could have said he attacked you, and you'd been lying unconscious somewhere... And you didn't know where he was...'

'Like I'd let Rob take the blame, when *he* was the one murdered?'

'Murdered?'

Suzanne just stared at her.

Eventually, she tried, 'Where have you been?'

'Living the high life in Glasgow. We ran a florist's. I was Mum's "niece". Suited us both fine. See, I couldn't get a job because I don't have a National Insurance number. I couldn't ever work in childcare, not with all the checks they do. Mum got a loan to buy the shop, and then when the divorce settlement came through she paid it off. When she died she left everything to her "niece". I sold up. Met Moir.'

'Rob Mark Two.'

'You know that thing on Midsummer's Eve, when people used to leave a candle burning so dead souls could find their way home? I did that every year. Every fucking year since he died – like something out of a Gothic novel... Wuthering Heights or something... Hoping Rob would come back. Back through the veil.'

'Oh God, Suzanne –'

'But he's never coming back. I know that. I know Moir isn't Rob. I know he isn't.'

'No.' Helen took a breath. 'He's *ten times worse*. Do you really think he cares about you? Why are you doing this? Okay so I lied about remembering Rob attacking me –'

'You *took our lives*. And now I want mine back.'

'How did I? Just because I told a lie about what happened? I really thought Rob had attacked me. I thought he'd killed you. What else was I supposed to do?'

Suzanne reached out for something on the bedside table. The knife.

She picked it up, and stood, and came across the room to the chair. She put the point of it to Helen's throat.

'You always were a great liar.'

Every time she breathed out, the point of the knife pricked her skin. 'Suzanne!'

'But I think I'd like you to tell the truth now.'

'But I really *don't remember*!'

The knife was suddenly in front of her eyes, the point pressed between her eyebrows. Sharp pain. Blood trickling down her nose.

And she did remember.

Another knife.

Coming to consciousness to find the flat cold hardness of metal against her cheek. Rob on top of her. His hand pushing up her top, grabbing at her breasts –

She must have passed out again. Next thing: Rob still on top of her, but the knife gone. Rob using both hands on the fastening of her jeans. Grabbing at him, pushing at him – putting up her arms to ward off the blows. Putting her hands over her face, lying still – and Rob, back at the zip of her jeans – yanking the jeans down her thighs.

Scrabbling her hand on the ground, searching for something – a rock, a branch – and feeling the cold metal of the knife under her fingers.

Slashing up with it, at his face – Rob cursing her, and then Suzanne descending, a dervish, but with her fury directed not at Rob but at Helen, kicking her in the mouth, in the breasts, as Rob grabbed at her again – and Helen slashing at them both, stabbing at them, and Rob overbalancing, falling towards her, and it was easy to push the knife up into his chest.

'I killed him.'

68

'Well done.' Suzanne pressed harder with the knife. Blood dripped off Helen's nose and onto her cheek.

'I didn't mean to! He was attacking me! It was *his knife*!'

'So that makes it all right.'

Another trickle of blood ran down the side of her nose and into the corner of her mouth. She could taste her own blood.

'*You* attacked me! Not just Rob – *you*!'

And so that was why Suzanne had had to disappear: because she'd been afraid that forensics would show she had attacked Helen; and that Helen remembered it, and would do everything she could to put the blame for Rob's death on Suzanne.

Helen shook her head. 'How could you?'

'You were going for him with a fucking knife!'

'I was trying to get him off me! He was trying to *rape me*!'

'Oh, like you weren't up for it.'

'*What*?'

'I read all your letters to him, remember? And copied out all his to you.'

'But I thought I was writing to Hector!'

'At first you did. But by then you knew it was Rob. By then it was just a game, wasn't it? Tables well and truly turned. You *fucking bitch* Helen!'

'No!'

'And he knew that *you* knew. I thought you were the mug, when all the time the joke was on me. It never even occurred to me, until that night, until I found the two of you... But I should've twigged, shouldn't I? You and Rob always were obsessed with each other. Even when we were kids.'

'What are you talking about? Yes, Rob was "obsessed" with hurting me – torturing me –'

'And didn't you just love it.'

'Of course I didn't! *God!*'

'Sick. The whole thing was sick.'

'On his side, yes! But – you're twisting everything! I never liked Rob! For God's sake, he's the last person – I *hated* him. I really *hated* him *so much.* I tried not to, for your sake, but I *hated* him.'

'Love and hate. Two sides of the same coin. That's what they say, isn't it?'

'That's rubbish.'

Suzanne removed the knife from her forehead and stepped back one, two paces. 'It must have been the ultimate rush, sticking a knife in him.'

Helen shook her head.

Suzanne walked to the window.

'I didn't *mean* to –'

She whipped round, her pixie face contorted. 'Don't try and tell me you thought he was really going to hurt you. You knew he wasn't. You knew *I* wasn't. Don't try and tell me it was self defence.'

'Of course it was!'

'You wanted him dead.'

'No!'

'You wanted *me* dead!'

'How could you think that? *Suzanne...*'

She put a hand to the collar of her shirt and pulled it down. 'You were going for my throat, but I managed to twist away.'

Along her collarbone was a long white scar.

'No.'

'So I'm lying now, am I?'

'If I did that – it must have been by accident – I was fighting both of you –'

'Oh yes, poor little Helen. Poor little innocent Helen.'

'I would never have hurt you, not deliberately.'

'Because you *loved* me so much?'

'I *did* love you.'

Suzanne said nothing.

Helen gulped: 'If *you'd* loved *me* you'd never have written those letters in the first place. You knew how I felt about Hector.'

'That was just a stupid fantasy.'

'It was real to me. And you knew that.'

Suzanne's face changed. 'Anyone else would've seen through those letters straight off.'

'I'm not *anyone else*.'

Suzanne blinked.

'And neither are you.' Her lips were wobbling so much she could hardly get them to make the proper shapes of the words: 'You can't want this. You can't want – what he's done. You can't have wanted him to kill Damian.'

Nothing. Then: 'Damian.'

'*For no reason*. Slung in the boot like a sack of potatoes.'

Suzanne shook her head, sharply.

'You always said he was going to be something special. Well, he was. He was just the sweetest, brightest, most incredible boy. And now he's dead. Moir killed him for no reason. How could he have been any threat? He could *hardly walk*. Did you know he's – he was disabled?'

A slight nod.

'Moir found that very amusing.' She took a breath. 'It's Moir, isn't it? All this. It's not you. You don't want this. If you did, you wouldn't have waited for him to come along –'

Silence.

Then: 'It wasn't Moir I was waiting for.' And when Helen didn't say anything: 'I'd it all planned out years ago. Found out where you were living in London; what you were doing. This guy I knew got me a gun – a Smith & Wesson from the war, like you might have found it at the back of a cabinet in the museum and thought *Hmm... Suicide...* And bullets for it of course. I was all set. Had a room booked in a hotel – near your flat but not too near. A train ticket. Told Mum I was going to Blackpool with a pal.'

Helen couldn't swallow. Couldn't speak.

'But Mum must have suspected something was up. After breakfast the day of my little trip, while I was in the loo she looked in my bag. Found the gun, and the script of your "confession". And it was surreal – she didn't go mental, she was all calm and collected, asking me if I was going to kill you. I turned on the waterworks, making out I'd never really have gone through with it... And she patted my back and said everything would be all right but if I ever did do anything like that she'd go straight to the police and tell them everything. I don't think she'd ever really believed my version of what happened that night. What chance did I have of convincing the police, if my own mother didn't believe me? So I had to content myself with messing with you. Banging on the door of your flat at night. Stuff like that.'

'You had to wait until she was dead.'

'She had diabetes. Poorly controlled. It was only a matter of time. In the event, rather longer than I'd expected. The marvels of modern medicine, eh?' But her mouth had twisted in the way it used to when she was trying to make out she didn't care about something.

'I'm sorry.'

'What?'

'About Auntie Ina.'

Footsteps came lightly up the stairs, and then Moir was back in the room, rubbing his hands. 'Having a nice chat? "I want *you* dead more than you want *me* dead." Ah, family squabbles.'

'You don't know anything about us,' said Helen.

He cocked his head.

'Suzanne doesn't want me dead. She's not a psychopath.'

'It's matter of expediency, actually, rather than psychosis. Any confession you might be persuaded to produce you'd retract, wouldn't you, as soon as you were in a position to do so? And there would be Su's little dream of returning from the dead – well, dead.'

'You've *killed Damian*?' said Suzanne.

Her stomach clenched.

Damian.

Hector, standing at the door of the kirk in his funeral suit, perfectly composed as he thanked people for coming; as he read a slick little summation of his brother's life; as he entertained the mourners after the service.

What do they put in your milk?

Hector, standing in an empty garden; a thrush singing.

Moir reached out and took the knife from Suzanne. 'We'll dump him back at the Mains on our way. Crazy bitch here whacked him before she topped herself.' He touched the red line on his cheek.

'Are you sure he's dead?' said Suzanne.

'He's giving a potentially Oscar-winning performance if he's not.'

'But have you checked for a pulse?'

Maybe he wasn't dead! Even though his eyes had been open like that – maybe he was just in shock or something. She stared at Suzanne's back, willing her to turn round so she could silently beg: *If he's still alive, please save him.*

Maybe Damian was light enough for Suzanne to be able to move him. Or she wouldn't have to – she could drive off with him! She could just drive away.

Moir shrugged, and tossed Suzanne something that jangled. Car keys. 'Check him.'

She left the room without looking at Helen again. Moir sat on the bed, head slightly on one side. 'How are you feeling now?'

'Great.'

'You don't *look* great.'

'Neither do you.'

He smirked. 'No? You used to think differently. You especially used to like my hair.' Coquettishly, he put a finger up to the hair at his temple and twisted it round.

She looked down at her hands, clasped together to stop them shaking.

Slow footsteps on the stair. The door opened.

Moir said, 'So?'

Suzanne's face in the doorway was stiff. 'There's no pulse.'

He smiled at Helen. 'Don't be sad. You'll see him again soon... Or will you?' He stood, and walked towards her, waving the knife like it was some sort of treat. 'Reckon you'll see him in heaven?'

'We should wait. Till it's dark.'

'Uh-uh. They'll be starting a search soon. We have to do it now.'

And she didn't care about Damian, she didn't care about Hector, she only cared about herself, about the knife and what he was going to do with it.

'Please don't,' she said. 'Please. *Suzanne... Please.*'

'Pleease,' said Moir.

Suzanne had turned away.

'*Don't let him!*'

'That little room with the boxes in it,' said Moir. 'Go and open the window.'

Suzanne left the room.

And Helen shut her eyes.

So this was how her life ended.

What would there be, on the other side? Would there be anything?

He didn't touch her with the knife. He moved behind the chair, and she felt the twine around her body tighten and then go slack. But now he had an arm round her, strong and hard. He supported her to her feet.

He squeezed her close to his side. 'Okay?'

She threw herself away from him, her feet, still tied together, going from under her, and she'd have fallen if he hadn't held her up, half-lifting, half-dragging her to the door.

But the twine around her ankles had shifted, just a little: slackened enough that she'd be able to shuffle one foot past the other if she got the chance to make a break for it.

'Have you peed your pants? Helen, Helen. Where's your dignity?'

'What would you know about dignity?' She could only move her arms from the elbows. Useless.

Across the landing to the little box bedroom where Suzanne used to sleep when she stayed over. There was a single bed in it still, with a bare mattress, and against the other wall a stack of boxes. Nothing she could grab.

They were going to push her out of the window.

She was going to smash down on the concrete, where she and Suzanne used to draw hopscotch squares with yellow chalk. Onto her head? Her face? Would she feel it?

Suzanne was standing by the window. 'We should untie her feet and take those wrappings off her.'

'We can do that later.'

'But they can tell, can't they, forensics people, how someone fell? From their injuries? They might be able to tell that her feet were tied when she fell, and her arms.'

'Crazy suicides probably fall in all sorts of weird ways. Our problem's going to be *this*.' He pointed a finger at Helen's forehead. 'Bad girl, Su.'

Suzanne shrugged. 'We could leave the knife up here – like she did it herself.'

'Looks like we'll have to. Okay. Get the window open.'

'It's painted shut.'

Moir pushed Helen onto the bed. She fell awkwardly, her head cracking on the headboard. He went to the window. The lower part shot up under his hands, leaving a gaping space through which pine-scented air flooded the little room.

'Painted shut?'

'Must just have been stiff.'

'Oh?'

'Well it wouldn't open before.'

'Uh huh.'

'She doesn't know anything about my new life. She doesn't know anything about you. We don't need to kill her. I don't want to be Suzanne Clack again. God knows why I thought I did –' She stopped. 'So we can just forget it.'

'Kid down there's dead, remember?' He put a gloved hand to Suzanne's cheek. 'And you think that face isn't going to end up on every front page? You think it's not getting top billing on the News? On Crimewatch? Murder victim who's upper class, disabled, sixteen years old, and looks like that? You think the boys in blue aren't going to be put under just a little bit of pressure to catch the nasty murderer, if we don't supply them with one?'

Suzanne looked from him to the open window.

'I don't think having second thoughts...' He trailed his hand down her cheek, her neck, her arm. 'At this stage...' He pulled her to him. 'Is an option, Su.'

Suzanne's hand whipped into his face and he howled.

But he didn't let her go. As she screamed, as Helen screamed, he lifted her, his strong arms under her knees, and in one swift move-ment he had her up and over the sill, dragging her frantic hands from his shoulders, throwing her out and over.

69

Even over her own screaming, over Suzanne's, she heard the impact – impacts, one after the other, as if more than just one person had fallen.

'High enough, eh?' Moir turned back to Helen, one hand to his left eye.

Helen's stomach clenched and its contents shot out of her mouth over the mattress and the floor. She coughed, and retched again, and squirmed herself to the edge of the bed. She screamed:

'Help! Please help us!'

He shut the window.

She screamed until her throat was raw, until he came over to the bed and grabbed her by the hair and pushed her head down on the mattress. She couldn't breathe. Nothing mattered but getting air into her nose, her lungs – getting her nose and mouth up off the mattress. Not Suzanne, not Damian, not Hector. Nothing else. But he was on top of her, pressing down on the back of her head. She bucked her body, she wriggled, she thrashed her head to the side, she pushed up against him – and finally he released her.

Air tore into her lungs, and she gulped it, greedy for it, and when he smiled at her – oh God, she hated herself. She hated herself for giving him a little smile in return. For being grateful for the air she was breathing.

For knowing she would do anything to live.

The eyelids of his left eye were already swelling above and below, reducing the eye itself to an angry red slit. He touched it, and then reached out and touched her cheek with his gloved finger, like he'd done Suzanne's.

She made herself not flinch away. She made herself smile.

'More convincing this way, isn't it? Damian gets in the middle of the struggle between the two of you – is tragically, accidentally killed. You top her and then yourself.' He brought his face close to hers, his breath hot on her cheek.

She pulled her head back. 'They'll be able to tell that Damian – that he wasn't... Here.'

'That he wasn't killed here? True. The first fight happened at the Mains. Suzanne runs up here – you follow, push her from the window – or does she fall? Then back you go to the Mains, load Damian into the boot, drive back up here to get Suzanne's body – But then it hits you. What you've done.' He grimaced, and touched his eye again, and looked at the window.

He got off the bed and left the room, and she heard his steps crossing the landing; a tap running in the bathroom.

She had to be quick.

She wriggled off the bed and upright, pushing her knees against the mattress to balance herself. Then she started to shuffle, as quickly and silently as she could, one foot past the other to the door. It wasn't properly shut. She heeled it open and then she was out on the landing, straining to hear – there were sounds from the bathroom, but the tap wasn't running any more. He would hear her on the stairs. Unless –

She leant back against the wall and slid down it onto her bum. Now she could wheech herself along the floor, using her feet in front and hands behind. At the stairs she dropped her feet over the edge and pushed herself up onto them, lowered her bum down to the next step, and again, getting into a silent rhythm, down to the half-turn, sliding over it, onto the last flight of steps and then she was on her feet, shuffling through the kitchen to the back door, turning to let her hands get at the doorknob, manoeuvring to turn it.

To pull it.

The door didn't move.

Locked. Of course it was. And so would the front door be. Moir must have a set of keys; maybe they'd got Uncle Jim's from the Mains at some point, and had them copied.

She'd have to get out of a window.

She shuffled across the kitchen, trying to stop her breath rasping in her throat. Trying to hear what he was doing upstairs.

What would she do even if she did manage to get out of a window? She couldn't run. He would find her.

She had to cut off the twine. The bandage.

A knife.

The cutlery drawer used to be the one by the Aga. There used to be a big sharp knife in there at the back.

Stupid. That knife wouldn't be there any more.

She backed up to the drawer and eased it open; turned to look inside.

Tea towels.

The next one down had a box of matches, string, a roll of binliners –

Hands grasped her shoulders from behind and she screamed. A hand came over her mouth and she bit it.

'Shh,' said Hector. 'Shh. It's all right.'

70

He turned her to look at him. 'Where's Damian?'

She couldn't say it.

'Moir – he's upstairs,' she choked out instead. 'Suzanne – he pushed her – from the window –'

'She's dead,' he said. 'Where's Damian?'

He was perfectly calm, perfectly normal, as if he was just mildly curious about his brother's whereabouts. But he had tightened his grip on her arms, excruciatingly, sending pain shooting down to her elbows.

She pressed back against the worktop.

'Where is he?'

She shook her head.

'Helen.'

Her arms jerked under his hands. 'In the car. In the boot.'

He let her go, and she swayed, and would have fallen if she hadn't been hanging on to the worktop.

He was gone.

She shuffled after him, across the wide expanse of the kitchen; into the gloom of the hall, in time to see Hector yank open the front door and a shape move out from the shadow of the stair.

She screamed.

The shape and Hector merged.

They fell together into the wall. Bounced off it. Spun round against the banisters.

Something clattered to the flagstones and skittered away from them.

The knife.

Helen shuffled forwards. Someone, not her, yelled out, and they crashed again into the banisters. The whole staircase shook.

She fell painfully to her knees, to her bottom. Hector had Moir pushed up against the stairs but Moir was twisting an arm free to punch at Hector. Her hands, scrabbling behind her, had located the knife, and then she had it tight in her right hand, but with feet and hands tied she couldn't get up.

A crack, like a branch snapping.

Hector stepped back and turned away. Moir flopped to the floor, his head lolling sideways, and lay still.

Hector had gone.

She let go the knife. Wriggled away from Moir to the wall; got her feet under her and propped herself on the wall; forced herself upright.

Moir didn't move.

She shuffled away and out of the wide open front door – out into the light, to the strip of concrete that ran between the house and the grass.

To Suzanne.

There was blood. Suzanne lay with her arms flung above her head, one leg caught under her, the other pointing outwards in its high-heeled boot. She looked like she was dancing. But there was blood, in a pool at her head.

'Suzanne.' She dropped sideways, onto her hip, but then she had to turn her back to reach with her hands. To touch the silky stuff of the shirt. The softness of Suzanne's upper arm. She squeezed it. 'It's all right.' She couldn't do anything else but hold on to her but that was okay. You weren't meant to move people in case they had a spinal injury.

'An ambulance is on its way,' she said.

Hector would have called an ambulance. Soon there would be doctors to look after her. And Damian. Maybe Damian too. Maybe Damian would be all right.

She moved her thumb on Suzanne's arm. 'You're going to be fine.'

71

How strange life was.

Sitting on Craig Dearg, and looking down at Pitfourie, at the sun on the Lang Park, and Suzanne dead and buried and lying in the kirkyard.

With Dad.

With Grannie and Grandpa.

She and Suzanne had always called them Grannie and Grandpa, although they'd died before the two of them were born. 'And here's Grannie,' Dad would say, pointing to the familiar, comfortably rounded figure in a photograph. It had been a way, she supposed, of acknowledging a love that would have been. That maybe was, somewhere.

She couldn't see the Parks from here, tucked into the lee of the hill. But she could see the yard at the Mains, and a Pitfourie Estate Land Rover pulling into it. Hector?

She stood, and started back down the hill, her boots finding their own way to the path that snaked through the heather and the blaeberries. This was the time of year, harvest time, when she and Suzanne would be sent up the hill with baskets to pick blaeberries, for the jellies and tarts Mum and Auntie Ina would make. Suzanne would nick the berries from Helen's basket when she wasn't looking. 'I've got the most,' she'd crow when they got back.

How could it be, that *that* Suzanne was the same person who'd put the point of a knife to Helen's face? How could Suzanne have thought those things about her?

But then, at the box bedroom window –

She'd tried to stop him, hadn't she? In those last moments of life, she must have known she'd been wrong about what Helen had done.

Or maybe it just hadn't mattered.

If you loved someone, it didn't matter what they'd done.

72

She'd managed in the end to twist herself so she could touch Suzanne and see her at the same time. She'd kept moving her thumb, round and round, on the silky material of the red shirt. Then she'd leant over and put her fingers, very gently, on the short black hair on the back of her head. 'They'll look after you. Soon you'll be in hospital.'

Someone said, distantly: 'Don't touch it.' Hector.

She took her hand away. Of course. The blood might be coming from her head – although she couldn't see a wound. But maybe the hurt place was at the front. She was lying face down, so Helen couldn't see. There was a lot of blood, though, which must have come from somewhere.

'All right,' said Hector. 'It's all right.' He seemed to be a long way away. 'Just lie still.'

'She *is* lying still.'

Another distant voice said something, and she heard her own name: '… Helen?'

Damian. It was *Damian's* voice.

She bent her head close to Suzanne's. 'He's all right. Damian's *all right*.'

There was a lot of blood. Her face must be in the blood. Maybe she couldn't breathe. You were meant to put people in the recovery position and check they were breathing, but how could she do that with her hands tied?

'Hector,' she said. And more loudly: 'Please can you come and help her!'

And then Hector was dropping down beside them, and surreally his torso was bare, like he was one of those action heroes Suzanne used to love, and he put an arm round Helen's shoulders and said, 'She's dead. We can't help her. I have to look after Damian. I'm sorry. Let me cut this.' There was a little penknife in his hand.

He cut the twine and the bandages at her wrists and ankles.

'Helen. She's gone.' His hands were on her upper arms as she reached for Suzanne.

Then he was pulling her away, along the concrete strip that led round the house, speaking over the rasping in her lungs, telling her that an ambulance was on its way, and she was twisting in his arms to look back at Suzanne.

'Is – Damian –'

'He's okay.'

'I thought he was dead... His eyes were – open – and –'

He was easing her towards the gate through to the yard. 'It's quite common for people who are unconscious to have their eyes open. That's why they have to tape eyes shut during operations... At any rate, he soon came round sufficiently to send me a text message. Teenagers' proficiency with texting finally comes in useful.'

As they reached the gate she wriggled free; pushed his hand away.

Ran back.

And now she was taking Suzanne's hand, and begging him: '*Please.*'

He pulled her away, roughly this time, and grabbed hold of Suzanne, and Helen grabbed him and wailed: 'Don't!' because he was being too rough, he was hauling her, turning her over, his voice as rough as his hands as he told her:

'She's *dead. See?*'

She could see.

She could see what had happened to the top of Suzanne's head. She could see what had happened to her face.

'Helen –'

'Yes,' she said.

'I have to –'

'Yes.'

The sound of his footsteps on the concrete, walking away. Suddenly speeding up, and his voice saying, mildly, 'Where do you think you're going?' And Damian, in a thin gasp: 'You know how – in films – they're never really dead –'

'And if he wasn't, what exactly did you expect to be able to do about it?'

As if it was funny. As if nothing much had happened, but what *had* happened was quite funny. Did he not realise? Of course he must, he had told her, he had said: *She's dead.* Did he not care, then? Did he not even think it was anything bad?

Or had she made a mistake?

She looked at Suzanne.

'Scream my head off?' said Damian's voice. 'Possibly literally.' A breathy laugh. 'Is Helen okay?'

'She's fine.'

'Suzanne – It's Suzanne? She's dead?'

'Yes.'

Her hand reached out, to the mess on Suzanne's face, but it wasn't possible to wipe that away and her face be all right underneath because that *was* her face. That was the inside of her nose. White bits of bone stuck together with red flesh.

'You're getting sick on you,' said Damian. 'I'm all sick.'

'I think I'll survive.'

When Hector had pulled Suzanne over, one arm had flopped out to the side. If Helen turned, she could sit so she could only see that arm and her little hand, perfect. Tiny pink nails, like a new baby's, or a dollie's. Cut very short. Suzanne never grew her nails, or painted them, because she didn't want to draw attention to her hands. *My monkey hands.*

Damian said, shakily: 'Some got on your shirt.' And: 'Are you sure he didn't cut you or anything, because sometimes you don't feel it and then –'

'I'm completely fine.'

She took the little hand and held it tight.

An ambulance was wailing somewhere, getting closer.

This hand in hers: on their first day at school, having to be told by Miss Fraser to let go; crossing the burn in spate, shrieking, rain dancing on the water, water inside their wellies; on a moonlit expedition to the kirkyard, hysterical giggles and screams, and getting as far as the gate but then too scared to go in, and all the dark road home still to go.

As the ambulance's siren was abruptly cut off, Damian's voice, suddenly clear: 'They're not going to arrest you.'

She held Suzanne's hand.

More voices, and Hector saying, 'I'm just going to get Helen,' and then, right above her: 'Helen.'

She didn't look up.

He touched her back. 'The ambulance is here. They'll take you to hospital; get you checked out.'

'I don't need to go to hospital.'

'You can't do anything for her now.'

'I know that.'

'You can't stay here.'

She looked up at him. 'If I told you you had to leave Damian, would you?'

'I *have* left him! For once, Helen, can you just – *get a grip* on reality?'

She let go Suzanne and rocked to her feet and drew back her arm and hit him, as hard as she could, with her open hand. Across his face. He didn't try to turn away, or deflect the blow, or avoid it.

'*Go then*! Go to your precious Damian!' She was shaking so much she had to sit down again. She didn't look at him. She grabbed Suzanne's hand back.

Voices, from round the house. The wind, soughing in the branches of the trees at the end of the garden. Something banging. His steps on the concrete, going away.

The policeman put his hand over hers and kept it there until she let go Suzanne's. He helped her stand up and walk round the house and across the yard. There were a lot of men in black police uniforms. Radios crackling. Then she was sitting in a hot car with the door open, and someone put a bottle of water in her hand and asked her name.

'Helen Clack.'

When a policewoman came and sat next to her, and started to say something, she said, 'What's going to happen to her?'

'We'll take good care of her, don't you worry about that. Is she – a relative?'

'She's my cousin. Her name's Suzanne.'

Then the policewoman got out of the car and in her place was a man she knew.

'Helen? Are you all right?' DCI Stewart.

She nodded. 'I don't want to go to hospital. I'm not hurt.'

'Well, that's your decision, but –'

'I have to tell Uncle Jim!' She started to get out of the car but he took her arm.

'First, I'd like you to tell *me* what happened. If you can. The full statement can wait, but if you could just tell me briefly what happened?'

Underneath the concern, the sympathy, why was there an eagerness in his voice? An excitement, almost, as if what she was going to tell Uncle Jim was wonderful, a wonderful treat, and DCI Stewart wanted it for himself?

'And will you believe me this time?' she said.

His gaze dropped away from hers, and he said, 'Yes. I'm sorry about that. I'm sorry we... *I* was so dismissive...'

'Moir,' she said. 'He was at the Mains.'

'Right. And –'

'Then he took us here.'

'By "us", you mean...'

'Damian and me. Is Damian all right?'

'As far as I know, there was a concussion, but he wasn't out for long and they don't think it's serious. When Moir –'

'Hector went with him in the ambulance?'

A little smile, quickly repressed. 'Yes.'

They're not going to arrest you.

'Hector saved my life. Moir killed Suzanne and was going to kill me. He would have done, if Hector hadn't –' She touched the raw place on her forehead.

'If Hector hadn't what?'

'Moir attacked him. With a knife.'

'And what did Hector do?'

'They fought. Moir – They were fighting, and then Moir – fell.'

'The medics say it looks as if his neck's been broken.'

'He's dead?'

'Oh, he's dead all right.'

Complete silence for one, two beats.

'So,' he said. 'You're saying Hector Forbes broke his neck?'

'Moir had a *knife*. He *attacked Hector*. He *killed Suzanne*.'

'Right. Yes. Suzanne.'

'She had it all twisted. She thought me and Rob – she thought

there was something between us. I don't know why –'
'So Suzanne killed Rob?'
What did it matter? 'No. I did.'

He didn't arrest her. He took her to the Mains and said someone could wait with her if she liked, until her uncle got back, but she didn't want that. She wanted to be alone, to rehearse what she'd say, what words of comfort she'd use, but when she saw the Volvo coming down the track and up into the yard, and Uncle Jim and the man who must be Dod get out, all she could do was stand there with the tears running down her face. And all she could say, eventually, into the fusty tweed of his jacket, was: 'Suzanne's dead.'

And it was he who comforted her.

She tried to tell him. When she couldn't say any more he made her go to bed, and she slept. She must have slept for hours. The light was going when she found him again in the kitchen, and he poured her an inch of whisky. She gulped the burning liquid into her stomach.

'Eh me.'

She was able, then, to tell him, as they sat opposite each other at the table, Fly and Ben at their feet. He heard it all without any outward display of emotion, except that when she told him about Suzanne falling he closed his eyes.

'She wouldn't have felt anything. Her head – she hit her head.'

He nodded.

'She was trying to stop him putting *me* out of the window.' She took a long breath.

Uncle Jim nodded; swirled the whisky in his glass. 'And Rob Beattie. Was it Suzanne killed him?'

'No.' And as the tears came again, she told him what she remembered. 'I didn't mean to do it. I didn't mean to – the knife – I didn't mean to hurt either of them. I didn't even remember doing it, until –'

He was patting her arm and bringing her toilet paper to wipe her face with, and telling her it wasn't her wyte; none of it was her wyte. And she wasn't to go telling folk that it was.

A lot later:

'Auntie Ina – she never told you Suzanne was alive?'

'Never a word. But that's not to say I didna wonder.' His eyes went to the window; to the view of the Back Park, the ripe barley pink and yellow and gold in the evening light, and the rooks rising over the trees along the dyke.

It was very late when they came: DCI Stewart and a policewoman.

They sat at the kitchen table while she gave them her statement about the day's events. When she'd finished, DCI Stewart pushed a palm across his stubbly cheek. 'Right. Thank you for this. I'm sorry to have had to make you go over it again.'

'It was self-defence, what Hector did. It was reasonable force – isn't that what you call it? You're not going to arrest him, are you? You're not going to charge him with anything?'

Bleakly: 'That's not my decision, but I shouldn't imagine so.'

Under the table, Fly sighed.

DCI Stewart leant back, and the kitchen chair creaked under him. 'And now. Helen. Let's have the truth about Robin Beattie, eh?'

'Robin Beattie.' She was so tired.

'We know you didn't kill him. There's no way it's possible. You had zero opportunity to remove and hide his body. You were unconscious in a hospital bed, for God's sake. I can attest to that myself.'

'Hel'nie?' snorted Uncle Jim. 'How could it have been *Hel'nie*?'

'That's what I'm saying.' DCI Stewart's voice was very gentle.

'I stabbed him, and then Suzanne – Suzanne was taking him to hospital, but then he died on the way –'

'And so she decided to conceal the body? Why would she do that?'

'She thought everyone would think *she* killed him.'

He sighed. 'We've found the "confession" they made you write… How they expected that to convince anyone, I don't know. Helen, if you've got some confused notion of protecting Suzanne –'

'Aye, she's been that confused,' said Uncle Jim. 'Been calling me "Dad", the poor quinie.'

DCI Stewart was looking straight at her. 'Would you rather wait till morning to do this?'

'No.' She looked at Uncle Jim.

The policewoman leant across the table. She had a nice face. 'Helen? What really happened?'

You always were a great liar.

She made her voice small. 'It wasn't Suzanne's fault.'

'What wasn't?'

'I thought it was Rob who attacked me – but I was wrong. It turns out I was wrong. It wasn't Rob.'

DCI Stewart frowned. 'It was Suzanne?'

'No.' She had to make this convincing. 'I suppose you'll say she was an accessory, because she helped him, afterwards – an accessory after the fact, or whatever you call it – but you don't understand what it was like for her, with Moir. How he controlled her.'

'Wait a second. *Moir?*'

The lie came easily: 'She met him when she was doing her childcare course. In Glasgow. All those years ago. I didn't know – she only told me just before she died. He wasn't calling himself Moir Sandison then. But it was him. It was Moir who attacked me. It was Moir who killed Rob.'

73

Hector came to see her the next day.

'How is he? Damian?' She stood at the door, holding onto it.

'Milking it for all he's worth.' He looked the same as ever: like he'd just come off a hill, in open-necked shirt and lightweight khaki trousers. He pushed a hand through his hair. 'Helen, can I come in?'

She stood back to let him into the hall. 'Uncle Jim's in the kitchen.'

'And is your mother –'

'They should be arriving early afternoon. Mum and Lionel.'

Uncle Jim stood when she brought Hector into the room.

Hector said, without any preamble: 'I'm so sorry about Suzanne.'

Uncle Jim nodded.

'If I'd got there sooner –'

'Na na,' he said. And to Helen's surprise he came round the table and grasped Hector's arm. 'She's gone, and there's an end to't. Hel'nie's back safe, and she wouldna be, but for you. Sit you down.'

Helen put the kettle on, and while it boiled took a chair across the table from Hector.

Uncle Jim said, 'Hae a lookie at this, now.' It was the leaflet, the one about the sheltered housing. 'This is the latest. They're for putting me in this place for doddery aald folk that canna wipe their ain arse.' It was no surprise that he didn't want to talk about Suzanne. And if they weren't going to talk about Suzanne they had to talk about something. But there was something terrible about it, that they even could.

'Mm,' said Hector. 'Although I don't think arse-wiping is one of the services provided.'

'I'll get that gate yet. *And May the Lord be Thankit.*' Uncle Jim chuckled.

Hector smiled. 'My father used to trot that out as commentary on any example of...' He shrugged. 'Ludicrously misplaced pride.'

Uncle Jim nodded, his gaze on the table, but as if he was looking through it. 'She was a grand buddie, Jessie.'

'Dad had all sorts of stories,' said Hector, 'about Jessie Mitchell, and Altmore.'

'Holes in the roof and more cardboard than glass at the windows. Outside toilet and paraffin lights. But it was a rare place to us bairns. Spying on poor aald Jessie, playing at commandos. Once Alec made it to the kitchen and was lifting a bannock from a platie for proof when Jessie came at him – dinged his hand with the griddle pan, for all he was the Laird's loon. Before the arthritis got bad she'd a fair turn of speed.' He chuckled. 'Coorse little buggers. That bannock was maybe all her dinner.'

A little silence.

'Why *And May the Lord be Thankit*?' she asked, as if she cared. 'Was she very religious?'

Hector shook his head. 'I don't think praising the Lord had much to do with it. She certainly sent the minister away with a flea in his ear. Wouldn't accept help from anyone. Not from relatives, not from the Council, not from the Estate. She wouldn't allow repairs to be done on the place because she thought that would put the rent up. She was convinced there was a general conspiracy to get her out of Altmore and into a home. And maybe there was. I think it was after an incursion by Estate workers that the gate appeared across the track end. She must have spent all her savings on it: a beautifully made black gate, with a lock on it, and the name of the farm in wrought iron capitals: "ALTMORE". And under it, "And May the Lord be Thankit". As if Altmore was such an earthly paradise that God must have had a hand in it.'

Jim chuckled again. 'A rare aald buddie, Jessie.'

He stayed fifteen minutes. When she showed him to the door, he said, 'Do you have time – could you come for a walk with me?'

Such an invitation, only a few days ago, would have had her heart pumping. Now she just nodded, and called to Uncle Jim that she was going out.

'You haven't been bothered by anyone?' he said as they headed down the yard.

'No.' There'd been an Estate Land Rover at the track end since it happened, to keep away the ghouls and the Press. Chris sitting there, or Mick or Chimp, was evidently an effective enough deterrent.

But he went ahead of her to the track.

Hector, walking away from her.

In the kitchen at the Parks.

He'd left her in a house with a psychopath, with her hands and her feet tied. She hadn't tried to rationalise it. She wasn't going to kid herself that he'd heard Moir in the hall and gone to tackle him. He hadn't. He'd been at the front door when Moir had jumped him.

He'd left her to go to someone he loved.

They climbed the gate at the other side of the track and headed up the burn, their feet swishing through the long grass of the Low Park.

'I'm sorry I hit you.'

'Don't be.' And as if he could see into her mind: 'Helen – I – God. I left you in there.'

'It doesn't matter.'

'Of course it does.'

'You had to go to Damian.'

He stopped, and so she had to as well. She had to look at him.

'It was unforgivable. Even more so in the light of what you did. You could have got away, at the Mains, but you didn't. Damian told me: you could have just run. But you didn't.'

'I did.'

'But you came back. There aren't many people would have done that. I don't know how to thank you. And how to – apologise –'

'There's no need. Really.' She looked down at the clear water rippling across the stones, all colours of brown and yellow. 'I've been thinking about the text message Damian sent you. It doesn't make sense. Why wouldn't he just call you? Or the police?'

It was a little while before he answered. 'His generation seem to text by default. And maybe he thought Moir might hear him.'

'Can he remember sending it?'

'No. But his memory of what happened is pretty patchy.'

'What did it say?'

'That Moir had got the two of you at the Parks.'

'I've been thinking – maybe Suzanne sent it.'

'*Suzanne*?'

'He doesn't remember her being there?'

'I assume not – he didn't mention her.'

'Moir told her to go and check on him – to make sure he was dead – and she came back and said that he was. When obviously he wasn't. She could have got his phone and sent you a text message.'

'Why would she do that?'

She took a breath. 'Because she wanted it to stop. She tried to stop him, and that's when – he threw her – from the window.'

'You're putting a very positive gloss on her actions.'

'No. I'm telling you what happened.'

'Is it really likely that Suzanne would summon me? When did Suzanne ever do anything that wasn't in her own interests?'

'She died because she was trying to stop Moir killing me.'

'Or had she realised that they were unlikely to get away with it?'

'She never wanted him to kill me. She only wanted –' She only wanted the truth. But she couldn't tell Hector that. She needed this, whatever it was. Friendship. Pity.

Did Hector know about the "confession"? With his contacts in the local police force, he surely must?

She made her voice flat. 'She only wanted me to write this bizarre confession about how I'd killed Rob, and you and me and Norrie conspired to hide his body.'

He nodded. 'I assume it was Suzanne who killed him?'

'No. No, I think – I think that was Moir too.' She couldn't look at him as she told the same story she'd given the police.

'Christ,' was all he said.

'I suppose they'll be opening an inquiry now, into Rob's death – they'll have to look into everything all over again.'

'Fish says a report's already gone to the Procurator Fiscal, who'll order an investigation, concurrent with the one into Moir and Suzanne's deaths.'

'But – they've accepted that what you did was self defence?'

'I think so. Thanks in large part to your statement.'

'I only told the truth. You didn't do anything wrong. You didn't mean to kill him.'

He sat down on a fallen willow, and she sat next to him. She ran her fingers over the bark of the tree; the exact same colour as the stone of the table grave, long ago, in the kirkyard. A knobbly gravestone, and rubbery gym shoes, and an empty plastic lunchbox. And Hector.

Always Hector.

'I'm sorry,' she said. 'To have got you involved in all this in the first place.'

'I think I involved myself a long time ago.'

She wanted to touch him, to reassure him. But she couldn't do that. He was looking off down the burn. As she followed his gaze, he said quietly, 'Water vole.'

They watched it, a fat, dark, purposeful rectangle darting this way and that in the water, keeping close to the left-hand bank. Eventually it wriggled up out of the water and disappeared in the long grass.

For a long time neither of them spoke. Then she heard herself say:

'Are you and Fiona…'

'There is no me and Fiona.'

'But if things had been different –'

'Well, and if they were… who's to say we'd be any happier?' He suddenly smiled at her, and looked back down the burn to where the vole had been, as if that was the issue satisfactorily dealt with.

It was one of his most appealing qualities – this impression that he was completely at peace with himself; completely content. But how could he be content that the woman he loved, and who loved him, was trapped in a life with another man? She went through the motions of her marriage for the sake of that other man and her children, and he went from one superficial relationship to the next, and she came to dinner and he made her a malted drink, and when they had to exchange chaste social kisses at the door they could hardly bear to touch each other.

'So,' he said. 'What're your plans?'

'I don't know. I suppose I'll go back to Edinburgh – look for another curatorship.'

'Why don't you stay on here while you're looking? We can fix you up with broadband at the Mains.' He picked a piece of bark off the willow. 'Or the Parks. If you wanted to stay there.'

How could he suggest that? After all that had happened, how could he think she'd want to stay at the Parks?

They started back down the burn, and he talked of practicalities – of what to do about Suzanne's life in Glasgow; her property and belongings, and the money she'd inherited from Ina.

From the long grass at their feet a pheasant erupted, birring up and away and making Helen's heart thump.

'I think I'd like to go there. To see where she lived.'

He nodded. 'I'll come with you.'

'Oh – no. You don't have to do that.'

'I'd like to.'

They'd carried on walking, and Helen had found her eyes drawn, every few steps, to the Parks, still and quiet across the fields. And into her head had come an image of an old woman, setting a pail down on the cobbled yard at Altmore, and stretching her back, and looking up at Craig Dearg. Jessie Mitchell and her ridiculous pride.

But maybe it hadn't been about pride. Maybe those words on Jessie's gate hadn't been about that at all. Maybe they'd just been an acknowledgement that home, no matter what, is home. That life is life.

She'd let her gaze rest on the Parks, and its so-familiar huddle of buildings, and the laburnum tree, and breathed into her lungs the pine-scented air running cool off the hill.

And May the Lord be Thankit.

74

Hector was here, she supposed, to talk about the Parks. He'd said he'd come over sometime today, that he'd call her, but they'd had to take the phone out of the wall at the Mains, and she'd been out all afternoon without her mobile.

She quickened her pace, down through the plantation, out onto the drove road, into the air that hung here under the edge of the forest, smelling of the morning's rain and pine resin and the field, the stirks and their sharn and the sweet grass.

The late afternoon sun striped the track with light and shade. From one of the dark stripes someone moved into the sun – Damian, loping down the track away from her, stretching up a hand to high-five the beech leaves over his head.

And out of nowhere a rush of anger went through her. He'd nearly died at the hands of a psychopath. In the kirkyard was the body of the girl who'd loved him more than his own mother ever had – who'd probably saved both their lives. And here he was. Full of the joys.

'Well,' she called. 'You seem to have made a miraculous recovery.'

He swung round; called back 'Hello,' as if nothing in the world could be as wonderful as this, as being on the drove road under Craig Dearg and meeting Helen Clack on it. He came back up the track towards her at a limping jog.

His hair had been cropped in a crewcut, and there was a shaved patch with a line of stitches in it, but apart from that she could see no ill effects of his ordeal – although perhaps the hair cut had been sufficiently traumatic.

'I'm sorry I wasn't there yesterday. Hector wouldn't let me.'

The funeral. Press and sightseers all along the road; police hustling the mourners into the kirkyard. The police had put out a series of statements to the effect that Robin Beattie's remains had been identified, and two people 'possibly connected to his disappearance' – Suzanne Clack and a man known as Moir Sandison or James Johnstone – had died in circumstances that were 'the subject of ongoing inquiries'.

Suzanne and Rob and Moir's faces were all over the papers; the TV news.

A minister had been seconded from another parish to take the service. He'd kept going on about the mercy of God, seeming to have decided to say as little as possible about Suzanne herself, as if he'd already decided she'd done something terrible. But Mum and Lionel had been on one side of her, and Uncle Jim on the other; Hector in the pew behind, with Fiona and Steve, and Fish, and Norrie and his brother Craig and their wives.

Damian wasn't smiling any more.

Oh God. How could she grudge him it, his youth, his joy in a beautiful summer's day?

'I should think not,' she said. And: 'I like the new look.'

The grin was back. 'Anna says I look like a cross between Frankenstein's monster and a ned.'

His gorgeousness, as he must be very well aware, was undiminished; emphasised, even, by the crewcut's severity.

'All you need is a bolt through your neck.'

'Ha, yes! But what about you? Hector said you just had some cuts and bruises, but cuts and bruises can be a bugger.'

She lifted a hand to her forehead, to the little scab that had formed there. It itched, like a spot she'd been picking at. 'No, there's just this – just a pin-prick really. How are you feeling? Should you be up here on your own?'

'Famous last words, but I feel perfectly okay, thanks.' He bent to pull a fistful of long grass to hold out to the stirks lined up along the dyke. A shaggy brown head pushed forward, and with surprising delicacy a thick pale tongue accepted the offering.

They carried on down the track. There was no need, she found, to moderate her pace for him.

He said, 'I wanted to say – I wanted to thank you, for what you did. For coming back.'

She stopped. 'How could I not?' And now she was gulping tears. 'You didn't hide. You couldn't –'

He shook his head, and looked beyond her, as if hoping to find someone who could deal with the hysterical female. But finding no one, he took her arm, and made her sit down on the mossy bank under one of the beech trees.

She blinked; swallowed. 'How much do you remember? Do you remember seeing Suzanne?'

He examined the ground before sitting down beside her. 'No. I don't remember much.'

'Suzanne didn't mean – she only wanted her life back.'

In the deep shade, after the sun, it was hard to see the expression in his eyes. 'Which she thought she'd get if she could extract a false confession before your "suicide", so that she could be "cleared"?' He picked up a twig and stabbed its end into the moss.

'She didn't want me to die. That was Moir. She just wanted the... confession.'

'Surely they must have realised it would never stand up, whether they killed you or not?' His tone was light, conversational, but she wished she could see his eyes.

She shrugged. 'The police certainly seem to have dismissed it out of hand. Well, naturally. I mean, Hector and Norrie colluding with me to dispose of Rob...'

He stabbed another twig into the moss next to the first one. 'Yep, the idea of Hector involved in any sort of skulduggery is just so ludicrous.'

'You can't actually *believe* – that *Hector* had anything to do with it?'

'He would hardly have exhumed the body if he had. And he does have an alibi. Of a sort.'

'And if he hadn't had an "alibi of a sort" – if he hadn't exhumed the body – you're saying you could believe Hector capable of – what?'

He stood. 'Who knows what anyone's capable of, given the right – or the wrong – circumstances? Are you okay?'

She got to her feet. 'I don't know how you can think that Hector –'

She started to go past him, but he touched her arm. 'Of course I don't really think he had anything to do with what happened to Rob Beattie.'

Had she imagined the emphasis on *he*?

'Where is Hector?'

'Levelling the ground for the flagstones. Where the concrete used to be.'

They found him swinging a pick in the shallow trench at the front door, a spade and spirit level propped against the wall nearby, the long rectangle of ground marked out with pegs and green string. The knees of his trousers were earthy.

'Here she is,' said Damian, stepping into the trench.

Hector set down the pick and came towards them, wiping his hands together. 'Thought I'd make a start.'

'Thank you. This all looks – very professional.'

'It's the spirit level,' said Damian. 'Prominently displayed, makes anyone look half competent.'

'Yes; you'll note that it's suspiciously clean.' Hector looked at his brother. 'Why don't you go inside and get a drink, and sit down? If that's all right with you, Helen?'

'Of course.'

'I'm fine,' said Damian.

'Humour me then.' Hector caught the boy against his side, and Damian protested: 'Okay, okay,' but he didn't pull away. He submitted to having a hand passed over his shorn head in a brisk caress, and said, 'Shall I get us all drinks?'

'No. Just go and sit down. We'll be in in a minute.'

When Damian had disappeared into the house, Helen said, 'Is he all right?'

'Pretty much.' She expected him to leave it at that, but then he added: 'Gets a bit tired still. Sleeping a lot. Nodded off into a plate of shepherd's pie the other night. But they say there should be no permanent effects – of the concussion, at any rate. I'm not so sure about the long-term consequences of inhaling Mrs MacIver's mince.'

They walked away from the house, over the grass to the gooseberry and currant bushes against the back wall. He talked about his ideas for splitting the land between the Parks and the Mains, as it used to be; about Andrew Begg, two years out of agricultural college and desperate for a farm. His proposal was that Uncle Jim and Helen should take the Parks, and Andrew Begg and his wife and baby move into the Mains.

'I think it could work. He's full of ideas and energy, but short on experience – Jim could keep him right, and he could help out at the Parks when needed. I'm sure you could come to a mutually satisfactory arrangement – in fact, aren't you related to the Beggs?'

'I think Andrew Begg and I share great-great-grandparents or something. The last time I saw him must have been Diane's wedding – years ago. I seem to remember him lying on the floor screaming and drumming his heels.'

Hector laughed. 'Well, he's improved a bit since then.'

'But would we ever get Uncle Jim out of the Mains?'

'That's the beauty of it – he'd still be able to take a proprietorial interest in the place.'

'Oh God, that poor couple.'

'Obviously he'd drive them demented.' He plucked a gooseberry from the bush. The sleeves of his shirt were rolled up above the elbows. There was a smear of earth down one muscular forearm. 'Maybe it's a rotten idea. Maybe you don't want to live here at all.'

'I do want to.' How could she ever have thought otherwise? All the years she'd been away – they had been years, years and years, of nothing. Of marking time. As if she'd imposed a sentence on herself, a withdrawal of the things she needed most: this place, these people. Her own home, and her ain folk.

And in some way she didn't understand, the horror of Suzanne's return, of her death, had ended it. Her sentence. Her exile.

Hector was grinning at her, chewing the gooseberry.

Home.

'Would you consider selling,' she said, 'rather than renting? Selling us the Parks?'

He raised his eyebrows. 'If you like.'

'We'd have to have an independent valuation done – we'd have to pay you the full market value.' With her money from the bank, and what Uncle Jim had saved, and Suzanne's money, which would come to him now, there'd be enough. 'If Uncle Jim wants to do it.'

'You talk to Jim, and we can go from there. There are various agri-environmental options, under the Scottish Rural Development Programme, that might be worth looking into. It would make sense to cut back on the agricultural side, free you up for your consultancy stuff – if you're still thinking of pursuing that?'

She nodded. 'I started on my backlog of emails this morning. There's one from a colleague in Switzerland, asking if I'd be interested in collaborating in this project he's setting up – a kind of pan-European database.'

'Aha. In demand already.' And as they started back towards the house: 'You haven't heard anything more from the police about Sandison? About who he actually was?'

'They're going to analyse his DNA, see if there's a match in the police database. But...' She shrugged. 'What does it matter? I don't care who he was.'

The trees behind them were casting dappled shadows on the grass, reaching towards the house, towards the trench in front of it.

'There were marks,' he said, 'on Suzanne's body. Bruises. Burns. According to the post mortem.'

Oh God.

'I shouldn't have told you.'

'It's all right. It's not like it's any great surprise.' She took a breath. 'I know it's a cliché, about children needing boundaries, but I think Suzanne... she was desperate for someone to give her boundaries, and that's what they did. Rob. Moir.'

They were standing on the edge of the trench. Poking out of the dark soil was the end of an old clay pipe, smoked by some Victorian farmer or labourer, and broken, and thrown away. It looked like a tiny bone.

He said, 'Seems rather an extreme reaction to being spoilt as a child.'

'Suzanne was nothing if not extreme.' She turned to look at him. 'In the tabloids – I suppose, legally, they can't say anything yet about what happened, so they're dredging up all this nonsense about her – they're almost making it sound like *she* was a psychopath too. Like she was – damaged. Not right.'

He held her gaze. And as she turned away, he said, 'Helen. I know how you felt about her. We don't choose the people we love. But sometimes they just aren't worth the heartache. Your uncle knows that. You're going to have to accept it too.'

'No,' she said. 'I'll never accept that.'

When they'd gone, when she'd rinsed the three glasses at the sink, she climbed the stairs, pulling herself up by the banisters like an old wifie. Suzanne, climbing these stairs for the last time – what had been in her mind? Had she just sent a message to Hector? Had she been frantic about Damian? Had she decided to save Helen too, if she could?

Or had her thoughts been quite different?

At the top of the stairs she crossed the landing to the box bedroom.

The bed had gone. Just a bare room with a white-painted floor. She walked to the window and put her hand on the frame.

Suzanne had been trying to buy time, when she'd told Moir the window was painted shut. To buy time, until Hector could get here. And then, when that didn't work, she'd said: *I don't want to kill her.* Hadn't she?

But in the other room: *You wanted me dead.*

She closed her eyes. How could Suzanne have believed that? All those years; every time she touched the scar at her neck, every time a memory came –

'I didn't,' she said aloud.

I didn't want you dead. I didn't want to hurt you.

It had been instinctive. It had been self defence.

Had it?

Of course! She'd been fighting for her *life.*

Had she?

When she'd lashed out at Suzanne – *had* she been defending herself? Had she only been trying to stop them hurting her? Had she not meant Suzanne any harm?

Or had something inside her finally broken free, a wild raging, a terrible and wonderful violence?

She walked back out onto the landing and across it to her old room.

This too had been stripped of furnishings – no sign of the chair she'd been tied to, or the bed, or anything at all. Just a bare room. The press cupboard in the wall in the corner where she'd kept her school textbooks. The little cast-iron fireplace. The hook on the back of the door where a cream polyester dress once hung.

She crossed to the window, and put both her hands on the sill, and let her eyes rest on the familiar view down the track to the Mains. Just the same: the byre end, the laburnum tree with a chaffinch in it, the stony track. The verges a riot of straggly growth, brambles arching over the dyke. Three teuchits in the Low Park. A crow on a gatepost. A glimpse of the burn, silver light dancing. And if she stayed here long enough, would she see them, the ghosts of two little girls, running hand in hand to the bridge?

Author's Note

Phew! Thank you for reading all the way to the end! I hope you enjoyed Helen's story and getting to know Pitfourie and the people who live there. I'm now working on the second book in the series, *Bad Company*, in which undercover cop Claire Castleford comes to work at the House of Pitfourie as cook/housekeeper – an assignment fraught with difficulties and potential dangers, not least because Claire's cooking skills are limited to ready meals and toast.

Bad Company should be available by the end of the year. In the meantime, if you would like to know what happened when Helen, Hector and Damian took a trip to Glasgow, you can download a free (long!) short story, *What They Found*, here:

https://dl.bookfunnel.com/rwgtgdf4lf

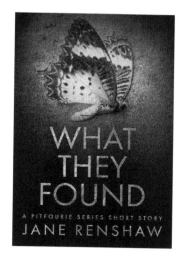

Needless to say, I am very grateful to anyone who takes the time to leave a review on Amazon for *The Sweetest Poison*. If you would like to contact me, please do so via my website (www.janerenshaw. co.uk). I would love to hear from you.

Acknowledgements

Where to start?! This book has been through many incarnations, each of which benefitted from encouragement, advice and input from many people – family, friends, authors and agents.

But first and foremost it was my mother Grace who introduced me to the wonderful world of the imagination – through the many books she read so tirelessly to my sister Anne and me and above all through the stories she invented, usually to our own exacting specifications, in which we could be anyone, go anywhere, do anything!

Later my sister and I 'collaborated' in creating our own imaginary worlds, often built of Lego, and would spend happy hours immersed in them. I found a similar pleasure much later in writing, which started when some of us in the Edinburgh office of Blackwell Science decided it would be laughably easy to write a Mills & Boon romance novel, make our fortunes, and spend our working days henceforth lounging around in hammocks in the South of France. I was the only one of us to get past the first few pages, but my loving crafted romance *Forget Me Not* bombed at Mills & Boon. Too late – I was hooked on writing. So, thanks to Annie Wilson and Rachel Leslie for that!

Since I started writing *The Sweetest Poison* quite a few years ago, everyone in my life has had to put up with me going on and on about 'my novel'. For humouring and encouraging me, thank you in particular Maria Davie, Annie Wilson, Helen Ure, Maureen Riach, Adam Campbell, Helen Holt, Jocelyn Foster, Ally Bellany, Euan and Jackie Smith, Abi Grist and of course my family – Mum for never doubting it would all work out, Dad for keeping his doubts (mainly) to himself, Auntie Witty, 'charming' Uncle Gordon and Auntie Cissie for their intelligent interest, Uncle Donald for all those incisive interrogations, cousins Morag, Ann, Barbara and Catherine, and of course little Rosie, for their unending and often unfounded enthusiasm, and sister Anne for bravely and repeatedly asking, 'And how's the writing going?'

Thank you too to author Anita Burgh and all those on the creative writing course at Castle of Park for your generous advice and entertaining company.

More than one agent has devoted their time, energy, expertise and insights to this book. In particular, I must thank Judith Murray for steering me in the right direction and being so encouraging about my writing generally.

Finally, *The Sweetest Poison* would never have happened without the wild imaginations, unfailing creative energy, humour, kindness, invaluable critical input and wonderful support generally of Lesley McLaren and Lucy Lawrie, my amazing writing friends with whom I've found a new kind of Lego to play with. Lucy is the author of very witty, warm, page-turny women's fiction (*Tiny Acts of Love* and *The Last Day I Saw Her* have been published to critical acclaim and she has a new one, provisionally titled *All Your Missing Pieces*, coming out soon...), and Lesley's engaging, original, exciting crime novels (yet to be published) have been shortlisted for prestigious awards such as the CWA Debut Dagger.

And of course I thank *you* for reading my book and joining me in the imaginary world of Pitfourie.

Printed in Great Britain
by Amazon

73042889R00262